WHAT COMES BEFORE

HEIRS AND DESCENDANTS

BOOK THREE

DANIEL KEMP

My Truth Your Lies

The third book in the Heirs and Descendants Series
By Daniel Kemp

A Story Told In Two Parts

PART ONE
What Comes Before

PREVIOUS WORK BY THIS AUTHOR

The Heirs and Descendants Series:

The Desolate Garden

Percy Crow

The Lies and Consequences Series:

What Happened In Vienna, Jack?

Once I Was a Soldier

The Widow's Son

A Covenant Of Spies

Novellas:

The Story That Had No Beginning

Why? A Complicated Love

Self-Published under the Name of Danny Kemp:

A Shudder from Heaven

Falling Greenhouses and Digestive Biscuits

And for children:

Teddy and Tilly's Travel Series

Despite the fact that nothing complicates the truth as much as a lie, if the truth is as obvious as it is inescapable, then the fabrication of its banality could be viewed as an act of benevolence.

Daniel Kemp

CHAPTER ONE

THE MEETING

Had I not accepted the invitation to Viscount Winston Bottomly's annual shoot, then the outcome to my immediate life would now be very different; but, having accepted the invitation, I must accept the monumental changes it made to my eventual being.

The winter rains and wet spring had left my estate here in Yorkshire without the quantity of red grouse needed to be able to host a shoot of any notable significance. The absence of quality birds of any number left me, fool that I am, in an unusual condition, frantically seeking out a safe haven where I could hang my hat amongst familiar company whilst enjoying the annual shindig of a 'Glorious Twelve' shoot.

There you have it, the rest is history. However, I have normally found history to have been written by the victors, of which I'm not sure I can be counted as one. I shall have to leave you to be the judge on that score.

* * *

I arrived during lunch on the Friday having left my London club, where I had stayed overnight, at around nine-thirty that morning. Given the chance, I would have preferred to have remained with the lady I had spent the previous two evenings with, but the expected arrival of her husband sometime during the day had curtailed that bliss. No matter. Boodles, my London club, was an acceptable if celibate alternative.

I have the same marital status as the lady in question, although in my case divorce has recently been mentioned. I have two sons. The youngest, Breno, almost four, was the result of the same number of years of marriage to Serena Abenazo, a Portuguese multi-millionaire fashion designer with her clothes label—Zabreno. My other son is named Luca. He came as the result of a brief, but passionate relationship with a woman who, unbeknown to me until after the event, was, or rather is, my aunt.

Yes, like the rest of my life, it's a complicated situation, perhaps one having little direct bearing on the proceedings in this story, yet contributing nevertheless. Suffice it to say that the mother of my son was the daughter of my great-grandfather's illegitimate offspring, Paulo Tovarisch Korovin, a Russian master espionage operator. Here, I would hasten to explain that my affair with Luca's mother, Katherine Friedal, took place more than five years before my marriage to Breno's mother. In the most part of the early years of my marriage I was faithful. My later behaviour took me many miles away from being loyal.

Nowadays, I see Luca infrequently; that's partially because of Katherine's father's death in March of last year and partially through the distance that now separates me from her and our son. They settled into Paulo's home in Switzerland a month before he died, to help supervise his care and allow Luca to have what Paulo never had with his own father, Maudlin, my great-grandfather. I visited Paulo as many times as possible, particularly after he moved there from London, but his liking for the fresh, clean air of Switzerland did not suit my disposition as much as his.

We played chess and walked a bit, chatted about times I knew nothing of and drank a few glasses of fine whisky. Notwithstanding all of that, Paulo's greatest enjoyment was to pay tribute to his grandson's development—'Little Luca's musical education is progressing smoothly,' he would say in his once authoritative voice, progressively becoming croakier and weaker more quickly than I had imagined, holding on to the strength he had to award his praise as though nothing else was to be expected from him.

Looking back on his days in his mountains of Switzerland, it was not the fresh air I objected to, it was watching this once great man wither so quickly away. I had sat beside my own mother's bed, holding her hand as she cried her tears of regret, before death finally took her from the pain of life she had suffered. I had seen others of my close family die without the need of any further education on the subject of death.

There are more lessons that cannot be taught in any school or place of academic learning; they must be learned under the cold stare of life, and the acceptance of death is one of them. One of those lessons came after seeing every patriarchal figure of my family, my great-grandfather, grandfather and my father, each laid out in the chapel on the Harrogate Estate. I had to reconcile my weakness, in not being able to bring back the buoyancy of the life that surrounded them and me.

The vigour, or buoyancy, I refer to, was what I first felt as lost forever when I identified the two members of my family who were murdered fairly recently. Having identified the bodies of Elliot, my father, then Edward, my youngest brother, I had to accept what the wickedness of death can do to the living and I lived inside a life where death was ever next to me.

* * *

With his mother's guidance, and his grandfather's persistence, Luca gave piano entrance recitals at two musical academies in Switzerland and one in Russia. He played so well that he was accepted in all three, making the choice complicated. After each of the placements was discussed in great detail and given careful examination by his mother and me, it was decided that the Conservatoire de Musique de Genève would be the ideal place for him as well as his mother. I do plan to visit them both soon, it's just that I haven't yet found the time, which brings me to probably my second favourite subject of all time: me.

Allow me to introduce myself, then, and like many before, you can form an opinion on what I can tell you and you can imagine. However, do save some prejudice that you may initially have until the end of this tale, when I'm sure you will have more reason for the dislike you have by now formed. I am no good around my number one favourite subject: women. As I've openly stated, I'm unfaithful and I expect I always will be until I die. My father was precisely the same even when my mother was on her deathbed, but please don't think I'm blaming him for my faults, because I'm not. It would seem that adultery is inseparable from the Paterson name.

My name is Harry Paterson. I'm fifty-one, but I feel as young as I ever did. I'm the latest to succeed to the titles of Earl of Harrogate, as well as the newly appointed Sheriff of the County of Yorkshire. I am a Justice of the Peace, serving as a lay magistrate as well as representing a rather large pharmaceutical company that pays me an astronomical amount of money simply to use my name near the top of their letterheads describing me as an advisor. I'm known as H.P. to my friends, or, to the more confidential acquaintances, namely, in the main, women, as simply H.

Until recently, my life has been spent between Harrogate Hall, surrounded by the vast Yorkshire estate I inherited on my father's death, or the larger Abenazo estate in Portugal, now exclusively owned by my wife, Serena, to which my visits are no longer welcome. My hope is perhaps I may be allowed to go there sometime in the future if all's well between the two of us. There is the London house still in the Paterson name in Chester Square, around the corner from the once main family residence in Eaton Square, where my old friend George Northcliffe and his wife Sophie now reside.

But what must be counted as my more permanent residence nowadays would include the homes of a variety of married and single ladies, whose bedrooms are used to a greater extent than any lavish sitting room by this travelling rogue, as it is to them I turn when in need of tender care and comfort.

* * *

The Paterson linage goes back as far 1342 and to Elizabeth of Lancaster, daughter of King Edward III. Her husband had a mistress to whom the Patersons are directly related. So, albeit from the wrong side of the bed, we have royal blood coursing through our blue veins. I am the eldest son of two sisters, with now just the one brother.

If I were asked to sum myself up in one word, it would have to be *debauchee*. I have served time in the Life Guards, the senior regiment of the British Army, where I experienced the conflict in Bosnia as well as in Afghanistan. After my time in the army, I joined the secret intelligence services, always my predetermined destiny, but not before I fully qualified as a chemical analyst whilst still studying at university.

But do not worry yourselves too much, as, notwithstanding any profound parts of my active existence, most of the time I play with life more than contributing anything worthwhile to it. Just maybe the situation changed ever so slightly because of the intervening weather in Yorkshire, over which even I had no control.

Having confessed to preferring the indulgent to the conscientious, there was the occasion to which I made a cursory mention in passing, where the proficiency of my analytical training in chemical analysis was used to trace the generic clues to a sadistic killer and child abuser. I passed that test, and helped to save the reputation of this country.

As that operation closed, so Paulo Tovarisch emerged from the leaden arm of the Russian KGB with an untouched memory of 'working' Soviet assets, which he exchanged as part of the guarantee of his welcome into the realm of Great Britain.

He also made his peace with the American CIA, using another collection of Russian agents who had infiltrated their NSA-instigated communications, both inside the continent of North America as well as other parts of the world. There was one name in particular Paulo was able to give to the CIA that was immeasurable in its benefits to their home security, for which I was awarded a certificate of commendation from John O. Brennan, the then head of the CIA. The award would have gone to Paulo, but for politically obvious reasons he could not be recognised.

Tovarisch Sergeyovitch Korovin, to give Paulo his full Russian title, and I, either with Serena, or George Northcliffe, who was his legitimate son, met many times in London since his relocation there, and to my financial cost I learned how masterful he was at the game of chess which he re-educated me to play.

It was his consistency at the game that led me to believe his life was spent in the same manner of considered thought—a mirrored reflection of his days spent as an agent in the field, or as the department head of so much inside the then KGB. The working side and the relaxation side of Paulo were constructed in exactly the same manner.

That similarity was the main reason why it was a slow process for both him and George to come together as father and son, but I'm uncertain that transformation would have occurred if the days they had together had been any longer.

As for myself, the time I had with him was consumed by the examinations we conducted on the various members of the Paterson family, of which his lust for knowledge was in lots of ways unnerving, if his furtive past was not taken into consideration. I believe he had many regrets about the lack of a meaningful family life he'd allowed himself to share since his father, my great-grandfather Maudlin Paterson, passed away. It was, in my humble opinion, the harrowing uniqueness of this man that stood in front of any show of sorrow, or the smallest amount of remorse. It was this same nature that prevented his closeness to his son George. His moral code dictated that closeness to anyone, at any age, was a weakness waiting to be exposed and used.

He'd had an abstract relationship with his father, Maudlin Paterson, who never visited Russia yet nevertheless managed to smuggle his mother away to live in England, leaving the young Paulo with the vision of an aura of invincibility around the Paterson name, but with Maudlin's passing it left Paulo nobody to worship, as those of us left alive were mere mortals in his eyes.

Because of him and his defection I had, it

seemed, served my purpose to this great country of ours, at least until Luca's mother, Katherine, caused the then head of a department of the American CIA to miss a heartbeat in their need of me to solve a puzzle that turned into a huge embarrassment to the highest family in this land. Despite serving the interests of two great nations, I failed miserably to serve the sanctity of the holy vows I had taken in my marriage to Serena.

I had only just managed to complete five months of wedded life before I first wandered from our bed to another's. When she was made aware of my act of infidelity by the private detective she'd hired to keep an eye on my antics, she acted with exceptional civility and refinement. Without rancour or bitterness, she moved from Harrogate Hall to the Chester Square house, and after a few weeks in London she returned to Portugal where Breno was born.

When I made promises to behave, she returned to our London address where I moved in, and for a short while we found a renewed happiness with one another, but alas it didn't last. To a large extent, the beautiful county of Yorkshire curbed my womanising, but in London there was no such scarcity of numbers. I was not equipped to resist any of the hedonistic opportunities the Dionysian capital city offered, in the plenty.

Usually, Serena and I were polite and composed in discussions of divorce but, like others in the same difficult circumstances, sometimes voices were raised in protestations of innocence on my part and indignation on hers. Breno was the constraint applied to arguments when he was not with his nanny. As soon as our angry discussion woke him, our dissatisfaction with each other was put aside for another time. Unfortunately, those times were becoming increasingly numerous. No matter how long the unhappy words were not exchanged, our union would never have worked in the way that falling in love is meant to be. We were a pair of self-motivated individuals who had fallen into separate ways of life.

Neither of us were settled marriage stock. I don't believe the self-driven can be good marrying stock. But neither of us were harmed by the experience. No damage seemed to be done and as far as both of us are concerned, no harm will arise in Breno's life, who, with his mother, now resides almost permanently on the vast, sprawling Abenazo estate in Portugal, along with her personal trainer, chief designer, hairdresser, makeup and nail specialists and a constantly changing array of fashion models. It was the fashion models who held my attention.

* * *

If your estimation of me so far is that I'm a frivolous, shallow, carefree individual, lucky to be wealthy but utterly worthless to the rest of society, then I will not disagree with most of it, but apart from the car I drive, you would never guess that I'm wealthy.

I have a habit that some find annoying, of dressing rather shabbily. Today is no different. I'm probably too confident in myself to care much about the outward impression I give to others. Now you have me. Shabby, rich and couldn't give a flying monkey's fart about the rest of the world. With that in mind, I will begin to tell you the story of a good friend of mine and the life-changing relationship he and I had with a young lady we had good reason to believe was named Miss Samantha Burns.

CHAPTER TWO

BATH

The drive to Bath was pleasant, swift and without any real incident, if my colourful swearing at a particularly idiotic car driver wasn't counted. The entire journey was enjoyed with the roof open and the sun beating warmly down on my uncovered head. You see, months before this day I had received an invitation to stay and participate in the annual grouse shoot from an old army and university friend of mine, which, due to unforeseen circumstances at my end, I was delighted to accept. In fact, on the surface I thought it to be rather fortuitous. But, I'm guessing you as well as I know only too well what trouble can be found in thoughts.

* * *

I had enjoyed a great late July, early August, spent almost entirely away from Harrogate Hall, the ancestral home at the heart of the family estate in 'God's own county' of Yorkshire, without the work involved in the running of that mini empire. It may have been only two weeks or so, but nevertheless it felt as if it was an eternity away from the paperwork which normally would have me weighed down under in its mediocrity. Instead, I had been true to my puerile characteristics and shared various homes with various women in variously shaped and sized beds. My body and mind needed a break from them as well as from London, and until this week the estate manager had managed admirably without me, so I decided to prolong my absence by two or three more days.

I was not being capricious in regards to the estate. There, I had presided over its administration for as many years as Elliot had lived in London in his management of the family bank, some fifteen to twenty years it seems. No, I was far from whimsical with the estate. If you are looking for labels of one kind or another to pin on me, then perhaps mine could be similar to a wine on the verge of being declared a vintage through age, but not quite ready to be 'laid down', as in the culture of wine.

* * *

Viscount Winston Philip Bottomly, or simply Bots to me, was junior in the echelons of nobility to my station as an earl, but far surpassed me in both flair and style. The least pretentious word that could be used to describe him would be 'flamboyant', and the most would have to be, 'exuberant'.

He was all of that and more, in manner, dress and speech.

When in the army, I always outranked him, being first a Captain to his Lieutenant, but the cut of his bespoke uniform was worn with that special degree of sophistication that only those who pay constant attention to the minutest personal detail seem to carry off in a nonchalant way. Even in those far-flung learned days of Cambridge, I was more functional to his aesthetically pleasing on the eye.

As I parked the Rolls, I caught sight of him, above and to my left, standing tall and upright in a military fashion at the top of the grey, granite, broad steps leading to the front entrance of his family home, Devonish House, the name chiselled into the arch beneath which he stood. He was clad in a red and brown striped suit, a pink shirt with an orange cravat and not a hair on his head was out of place.

"Well, well, if it's not the man-cub himself; Harry Paterson in the flesh and tatters! Nothing changes, does it, old boy? Which on this festive occasion I'm so pleased to see and delighted to remark upon. The world would not be the same place without your disreputable self, Harry, old man. By the look of things I'd say you've driven straight from the wilds of our northern provinces without a stop for a brush and tidy-up. Am I right? Is that about the score?"

Bots was not normally one to wait for an answer when in a stream of his satirical condemnation and today was no different, as he gripped the scrolled wrought-iron railing and began the descent.

"So impatient were you that you just couldn't wait to get here, eh! Is that the excuse this time, old bean?"

Stepping to one side of the railings, he adopted the military stance of standing to attention before continuing,

"You look as bedraggled as ever, Major Paterson, sir." He feigned a salute which resembled more of a stylish swish of the hand than anything else I'm able to interpret. I simply waited for the mocking to end. It wasn't soon.

"Someone on your staff still playing reveille at four in the morning, are they, Major? No batman about? Are they all on manoeuvres?"

This brought a brief interlude from his infantile questioning for him to imitate the scornful smile I wore and take a deep breath before persisting with his sardonic exuberance.

"By the by, ever heard of Savile Row, old chap? It's in London."

He began again to descend the double curved stairway to the fine-graded gravel parking area at the side of his family home, continuing to speak as he did so.

"Sell clothes there, you know, for the cultured, loaded gents like yourself. I can vouch for the quality of the tailors one finds who frequent the area. They really are quite good at their trade. Mind you, they do cost a few shillings. How's the money-printing business in that family bank of the Patersons in Westminster, called Annie's? The old family industry still churning out the cash, is it?"

Another pause for a short while, with him gauging my demeanour, then, knowing that he had neither disturbed nor irritated me, he continued in his chiding, perhaps waiting to provoke an equally affable observation. I was simply 'soaking it up', as we used to say of a reprimand in the army. He had not finished with my 'ticking-off'.

"I'm outstandingly pleased that you have decided to honour us with your undoubted expertise this weekend, dear one. Show the rest of us what's what when it comes to handling a shotgun without a modicum of modesty on your part, Harry. I positively insist on that."

Just as I imagined the long-established welcome had come to an end, he found even more to admonish me with. "I do so hope you've brought a dinner jacket, old boy, else it's dinner served in the scullery for you at supper time."

The descent from his lofty position now complete, he gave me the usual once-over, starting with a very disapproving glance at my brown leather, scuffed, slip-on shoes, followed by the heavily creased blue linen jacket I wore with the mismatched, sombre black trousers. Trying to ignore him, which was difficult other than a cursory smile accompanied by the raising of the eyebrows in his direction, I removed my weekend bags from the rear seat of the open-topped car. Then, from the boot, the two-hundred-year-old, elegantly carved gun case. Priorities, you see; I cared about the resplendent pair of James Purdey guns, but not the workaday clothes. Finally, I replied to his goading.

"I do believe Joseph threw a jacket in a bag somewhere for me, Bots, but if he forgot, I'll ask someone to pull the seam of one of yours apart and let some extra width into it. You must have plenty to spare with the amount of weekend parties you throw. I seem to receive invitations to one or another for every weekend in the whole year. But to the point, if Joseph has been remiss, hopefully your man could find a clean one and not one splattered with food stains coming from all your rabbiting on about gibberish. I know for a fact your nanny told you not to speak when your mouth is full," I declared, whilst shaking his proffered hand.

"How did the saying go in the academy, Bots? Ah, yes, I recall—once a subaltern, then always a sub-altern. An age-old tradition of the Guards, was it not? Who's here then?" I enquired, as I thrust both of my bags into his empty hands and without further ado made my way up the steps and through the open English oak double doors carrying the gun-case.

It was a sumptuous buffet luncheon laid across several white-lace-covered tables placed parallel to the four walls, with enough room behind them to be able to walk on both sides. I was in an ornately deco-rated, baroque-styled dining room. Surprisingly, this was my first visit to Devonish House and, from the little I'd seen until now, it struck me as a place that lacked substance, and needed the warmth furniture and paintings can add. In the wide, substantial hall for example, were two rather fine Regency side tables with black and white marble tops, but only one or-nate ormolu lamp. Apart from the tables there was no other furniture, and only three family portraits. I didn't take much time to decide I'd not feel comfort-able staying for any longer period of time than the weekend.

Bots had left my bags with one of his footmen, with another taking the Purdeys. They then escorted me through a spacious, cold, white-painted, minimalistic hallway from where a wide red-carpeted flight of stairs rose to what I guessed would be the bedrooms. On the walls of the hall and stairway were a few surreal paintings. I wasn't sure about them all, but one, a Salvador Dali—*Swans Reflecting Elephants* on canvas—was a copy. I knew who owned the original. I said nothing of this to Winston, however I found it odd that an old family such as his would hang copies of famous paintings. Despite my confusion over the Dali copy on the wall, I was far from confused with the practicality of a buffet lunch, which, in the circumstances of a varied arrival, was the only viable arrangement.

Positioned in the centre of this pragmatism was the quixotic scene of a grand piano, seated at which was a very pretty, dark-haired young girl in a bright, colourful floral dress, playing Alessandro Scarlatti's, *Già il sole dal Gange*. None of the feeding herd were paying much attention to her. I, too, had other things on my mind, one of which was my ravenous hunger.

* * *

Easily forsaking the various salads of unappealing decorative lettuce and the like, I made straight for the heart of the matter; the meat. I was about to help myself to some cold, minted new potatoes, in different coloured glass bowls beside the rib of beef, when I saw her. She was on her own, just past where the shining cutlery was neatly folded in table napkins. She was about to pour herself a glass of champagne.

I did try to look away and apply some sort of self-control, but I had none, even allowing for the common sense approach of *she must be here with someone*. But no! My fascination and surprise overcame the intrinsic deficiency in me. As much as I enjoy beef and potatoes, attractive women would always take precedence, with mysterious ones having an even higher priority. The cold beef was already cold so it could certainly wait.

Having made several decisions, such as that since I set foot inside this house it seemed as though one more would not make much difference, I decided I would not hang around for any formal introduction.

Those who hesitate in the pursuit of beauty will be trampled on, Harry.

This was an epigram favoured by my late great-grandfather who knew a thing or two about attractive women. As I've already explained, the respect for and love of women seemed to run in the family of Patersons.

One of the remarks passed on to the local police when they attended the scene of my murdered father in the Eaton Square house that George and Sophie now occupy, was that Elliot was alone. The actual words were *'he had no company'*.

By that benign remark, George, Elliot's butler-cum-personal assistant at the time, implied that my father was not entertaining a woman.

Unfortunately, the duties of a butler-stroke-personal assistant did not end with my father's death. Amongst the many things he had to deal with was to inform the investigating police of the address of my father's latest flame, as not unnaturally she was a suspect, having a key!

I loudly disapproved of his philandering whilst married to my mother, but I never carried that disapproval into my own life with Serena. I have never suffered from a lack of audacity, either, 'impudent' being a word often used whenever my name was brought up, as well as being a purist, by some who knew me far too well.

* * *

"Good afternoon to you. It would be an honour if you were to allow me to do that. Please. I'm Harry Paterson," I said as I drew alongside my quarry, taking the bottle from her fine, delicate hand and briefly placing my own hand on hers. Her tanned skin was cool, soft and smooth to my touch. There was no ring on the hand where a wedding or engagement ring would usually be. Not put off, I continued.

"You seem so familiar, but I'm sure we couldn't have met otherwise I would never have forgotten your name. It's as if you've graced every magazine cover, every newspaper page and every fashion event I've ever looked at or been to." As well as speaking, I was fashioning the most beguiling smile I could manage.

Continuing, I said, "Please tell me our meeting is not the beginning of a Grecian love tragedy with you being the incarnation of the Goddess Aphrodite and me a mere slave." The glass was full and we were looking directly into each other's eyes. I never stopped my mode of attack. I changed the smile to a frown—

"If you are her, then I must take my chance of seeing you smile, as you're far too beautiful to pass by without at least saying hello and offering my services in any manner you may find satisfying."

I'm ashamed to admit I mustered up the most lecherous, seductive look that was possible before delivering my normal final, flirtatious line.

"Allow me to say just how exquisite you look wearing that stunning dress. You caught my eye the moment you walked in. The colours and the cut, are staggeringly beautiful. Almost as perfectly gorgeous as yourself, but..."

I was not allowed to finish my hackneyed invitation, as the centre of my attention cut me short, taking a firm hold of my arm.

"No doubt you are impatient to add that you think I would look so much better without the dress on, aren't you, Harry?"

Her twinkling blue, vibrant eyes held a magnetism that matched the rest of the attraction I imagined she had over all men. They were now sparkling within the wide, condescending, coquettish smile that filled her face. She was tall, elegant and extremely feminine in every way imaginable.

"Ah, you have me. Yes, that is exactly what I was about to say. There I was, believing myself to be original. I must assume it has been said to you before, and if so, am I about to have my impish face gently tickled by a make-believe slap of annoyance?" I asked, trying my best to be as playfully appealing as I could.

As I was wondering who could have possibly used that 'pick-up' line of mine, her left hand moved, but she was not concerned with admonishing me. Instead, she swept a lock of luscious, unpolished, copper-coloured hair away from her high forehead to nestle behind an ear, thereby exposing the full curvature and line of the delicately defined, shapely face with perfectly formed, artistically high cheekbones, that those who paint can only dream of.

"Not said to me, no." The provocative smile remained as if it was painted onto her face as she continued, "But I'm afraid Winston warned me of your imminent arrival. As a forewarning, he told me some tales of your—what shall I call it?" A lengthy pause whilst she sipped the champagne, her eyes locked on mine, before delivering her assessment.

"Promiscuity," she announced, concentrating her gaze on me more intensely as her eyes narrowed, adding a titillating infliction to her voice.

"He was far from complimentary. I'm only too sorry to say that he didn't stop there. He compared you, somewhat disparagingly I thought, to a rabbit caught in some imaginary headlights whenever you're near what he called an attractive woman.

"I think he was trying to defend you when he said you couldn't help yourself. However, speaking for myself, I do appreciate your flattery in respect of how I'm dressed. It's normally difficult to find the right balance between being sexually attractive, and the more stringent style of what could be referred to as a conventional woman at home."

She was using her right hand to twirl the glass backwards and forwards, whilst balancing it in the palm of her left. 'A woman at home,' she'd said— what did she mean by that? Bots had been right, of course, in his concise summary of me, but her un-doubted beauty was not the only attraction in this case.

"Are you at home?" I asked, somewhat confused.

"Not yet, no, I'm not. So there's no point in you asking to inspect the bedrooms—another thing Winston said you may ask to see, that's if I was at home, of course."

"'Infamy, infamy! They all have it in for me'," I laughed. "Got that line from a *Carry On* film. Way before your time, though. I didn't know I'd told Bots I would use that line. Anyway, I'm not sure that's one of mine. Nor am I sure I caught the name. Yours, I mean, not the film actor who spoke those 'infamy' words." Was there more than one Winston here, I wondered?

"I'm Samantha Burns, but I'm called Tammy for short. Before you ask, it's a complicated story about the alias, and I'm not entirely sure how it came about but I think it started when I was very young, having a fondness for cats.

"Somehow or other 'Tabby', for a cat, became adulterated into Tammy for me. Another reason could have been my name being shortened to Sammy by any one of a number of nannies who, with a speech defect, confused it as Tammy.

"It doesn't matter as I liked it, so I kept it. I do recognise you from somewhere though, Harry Paterson, just can't place from where at the moment. It might come to me later."

* * *

From somewhere within the lilt of her voice came a French accent.

Perhaps it had been forgotten, or perhaps it was deliberately disguised; whatever was the answer, it was there and it was enchanting. Her petite nose curled slightly at the tip, allowing her thick, sculptured lips to form a wry grin as she kept peering deep into my eyes as if they would give me away. Or tell her where she had seen me.

Her deep, sun-induced tan was natural, not the blotched, painted version acquired from a bottle that looks so false. I guessed she was aged around late twenties, perhaps early thirties, certainly statuesque and extremely sexy. My knowledge of her had returned, leaving me knowing exactly where I had seen her before, but I kept quiet for the moment.

* * *

"Tammy, mmm! What a thoroughly delicious and evocative name. Almost edible, I'd say. You suit it so well. You're sleek, feline and, as I've found out, obviously dangerous. Perhaps there's a law against all that somewhere. Inside my wicked head, your pseudonym conjures up the silky vision of a prowling lioness stalking its prey." I was topping up her glass with more champagne at this stage.

"Perhaps you're as striking in character as you are in the flesh. Oops, I'm getting ahead of myself again, aren't I? Salacious talk will never do."

I smiled and was pleasantly surprised to see a matching smile returned from this Samantha-cum-Tammy. I sensed a victory, albeit a hollow one.

"But are you one of those who go in for an early kill, or are you more the stalking tiger type, taking time over your prey before you devour them? I'm sorry, my mind was miles away, drifting onto many pleasurable things. I should apologise," I laughed, but didn't wait for a reply as I replaced the bottle of champagne into the bucket.

"How do you know Bots then, Tammy?"

"Bots?" she asked quizzically, with her sea-blue eyes squinting into the sun.

"The Viscount, our host. It's what I call him. Everyone I know does the same," I exclaimed.

"Ah, he has a nickname which I knew nothing about. How lovely and quaint. Is it from his school-days, or his army life?"

She did know him. My imagination went into overdrive and I had to take a second before I could reply.

"Never given any thought to that one. With a sur-name like Bottomly, he sort of got lumbered with it at birth, I guess. He never mentioned it to you at all?" I asked, with a degree of indecision in my voice.

"I really haven't known him that long. Ours has been one of those old-fashioned, whirlwind types of romance. We met at a nightclub in Mayfair a little while ago. No time at all, really. We then announced our engagement at a party given by one of his friends. You may know him, he's here somewhere."

Moving her head side to side, she looked over

my shoulder to rediscover the whereabouts of the person in question. As she leant nearer to me, I caught a drift of her heavenly perfume. I asked its name.

Allure," she told me, adding immediately, with a higher pitch to her sultry voice, as the pianist reached the cords of her chorus,

"That's the man, over there behind you, standing next to that huge seascape painting. The one with a woman in a skin-coloured bikini in the foreground. Bald chap, bit on the tubby side."

The sparkle in her eyes had left when I turned back from seeing Hugh Pickering, a City financier, amongst other things. I nodded, adding,

"Yes, I know Hugh." There was no smile that met my recognition and just a dispassionate recount of a previous meeting.

"He hired the whole ballroom at the Dorchester for his birthday bash a month or six weeks back. That's where Winston and I announced our engagement. Were you there, at the party? Is it possible that's where I know you from, Harry?"

Her manner had changed. Gone was the mischievous look, the sensuous poise and the confidence she was previously enveloped by. A nervousness had descended upon her, for no reason I could fathom. I didn't answer her question, although that was not where I had first seen her, and she had no need to confirm her acceptance of the proposal. I would have expected nothing less, but the alteration to her composure bothered me.

Abandoning my much anticipated lunch in favour of her arm, I guided her away from the sterile distraction of piano music and my rib of beef onto the crowded, buzzing terrace, with the warm August sun beating down upon all who gathered there. What was left of my mind had slowed to a walking pace. It needed a jolt to engage.

"Sneaky old Bots! Never said a word on the phone when he called me with the invitation to come down here for the weekend. Must have a word with the blighter. I'm somewhat embarrassed now. Hitting on a pal's loved one, as it were. I'm terribly sorry about that, Tammy, but I have no intention of withdrawing the deserved accolades."

Mustering up the most tactful response that I could, I attempted to buy some time for my sickened brain. But she would have none of it.

"I won't have you embarrassed, not in the slightest," she replied, with the most charming smile on her face.

"You were a gentleman doing no more than complimenting a lady. I suspect Winston was being over-protective of me with his whisperings about you. Obviously none of it can be true."

With the edginess now vanished from her voice, she gently pulled away from my arm. That gave me the excuse I was looking for.

"Would you please excuse me, Samantha, I really must go and speak to someone I noticed inside as we came out onto the terrace. I'll look forward to the time we can catch up on our conversation. For now, I'll have to make do with unpacking my things, then finding Bots. I shall give him an ear-bashing about keeping such elegance and charm as you hidden from me."

I pushed forward into the middle of the riotous crowd, making room for us both.

"You'll be safe with this lot, believe me," I stated, with my hand on the small of her back. Her cool skin immediately drew me closer. Curbing my enthusiasm for an appealing woman was something I'd never had the need to practise. I was dumbstruck for a while. After what seemed an age, I found the willpower to say something.

"They are noisy, I'll grant you, but harmless as lambs, the lot of them, although probably the men would rather think not."

With a slight bow of my head, I acknowledged the old friends and enemies alike who were in a collective animated conversation about the wrongs of the world, trying no doubt to put them to rights.

"Ladies and gentlemen." I looked as many as I could squarely in the eye. "I must leave you all for the present, but I warn you to be careful with any slanderous words you may accidentally use. I may sue the lot of you," I threatened them, with a smile on my face.

"Say hello to our host's engaging companion, but be wary. There's to be absolutely no laying on of hands, otherwise it's to His Highness she'll run."

Drawing away from her, I made a theatrical bowing and waving movement of an arm as a way of introduction.

"May I present the divine and most beautiful Samantha Burns, known as Tammy to her friends. Look after her, or you may see her tigerish claws. That's a long story and one am I'm sure Tammy will be pleased to tell you all."

I was under no illusion about those who made up the gathering that day on the balcony, gulping down the free champagne as though it was about to be exhausted. I should have explained there were few people I'd met that felt any form of indifference towards me. At that moment in my life, I found people either loved me or hated me.

"Make sure you keep some of the bubbly to refill Samantha's glass for her. Can't have her searching her future residence to find the cellar, now can we?"

As I left the scene, she was still smiling and made light of my flirting, mumbling something about forgiveness can only come from God, before I lost sight of her as she was swallowed up into the mix. I was utterly confused, but I think I managed to hide it. Thankfully, the room with the buffet and pianist had more people in it now than when we had left, and they gave me a chance to get away and collect my thoughts about Viscount Winston Bottomly and the impending marriage she had spoken of.

* * *

Most of what remained of Friday afternoon was spent in my room on the telephone, speaking to as many friends as I could think of who were absent from the gathering downstairs and who might be able to help. There were not many I felt I could trust with what little I knew, without them building it into something far larger than I could be confident it was.

My bags had been unpacked, with day clothes separated from my shooting attire and hung in the dark wooden wardrobe, which was taking up the wall space opposite the single bed under the one window in a clean, modestly furnished but adequate bedroom. The dinner jacket that Joseph, my butler, had remembered, was already pressed, along with a pair of matching trousers, shirt, and waistcoat and readied for that evening at one end of the wardrobe.

I had not sought out Bots after leaving Samantha as I'd implied I would, nor had I spoken to him since our greeting. Had we bumped into one another, I would not have told him what I suspected about his fiancée; it was, after all, only a supposition on my part.

Afterwards, I spent an hour or so of fruitless telephone calls, accompanied by the large glass of whisky I had poured from the bottle of Jura that Bottomly had remembered was my tipple and graciously deposited in the room next to a glass ice bucket in which, to my surprise there was still ice.

When I had finally finished with the names I could remember, and the whisky, the name of which I could never forget, I laid my head on the pillow and drifted into a dreamy sleep on the comfortable bed. I was woken at about six-thirty by a loud knocking on the door. A male voice announced that dinner was to be served at eight.

* * *

Come the time of my obeying the proclamation, Bots was in a corner of a drawing room that was being used for the quenching of thirsts by a predominantly male congregation of thirsty guests. Waiters carrying more champagne flutes were servicing the requirements of the ladies seated around the spacious lounge. By the expression on Winston's face, he was in a purposeful conversation on his mobile phone requiring some hectic gesticulation.

Before I had made way through to him, he had scratched his head twice and made several, what I interpreted as questioning gestures. At least, that's what I thought them to be. Whatever was going on seemed to make him quite agitated, but he managed a friendly nod in my direction when he caught sight of me. Tammy was engrossed in conversation with other guests whilst standing at his side. She, too, noticed my arrival, managing a delectable smile aimed directly at me.

I decided that a thinking man's discretion was my best course of action, rather than diving into the ruck to find a mythical ball, with what were, after all, unfounded accusations on my part.

Doing what I do least best, I mingled, making trite small talk, until the summons to eat was announced. My stomach felt as though it might cave in at any moment through ravenous hunger, which, when put alongside the unresolved mystery surrounding my good friend, did nothing to stifle my interest in one Samantha Burns.

* * *

At dinner, I was thankful to be positioned away from the engaged couple, being seated next to an old family friend, but a few times I caught one or other of the pair looking straight at me, once having to feign a smile back at Bots as he called out how much of a 'cad' he thought I was.

Fortunately, he never elaborated on the remark, nor did she, leaving it for the assembled party to simply giggle smugly, or childishly comment, then quickly forget. I was neither in an explaining frame of mind, nor feeling particularly comfortable amongst the accelerating revelry on show as the night wore on.

As I suspected, the proceedings inevitably descended into the customary bread-throwing affair, as the fine wines took a toll of the gathered collective insanity, and youthful exuberance exceeded intellect.

It may uncomfortably surprise you, the way the rich and famous, alongside those who make the decisions which impact on our everyday lives, quickly deteriorate into fools when surrounded by their own breed, with unlimited wine and without the distraction of having to appear superior, or, perish the thought, wise.

Unfortunately, it was no different that night. With waiters losing their disturbed attempt to gather bread plates and rolls, the silliness lasted until the last of the leftover bread was distributed anywhere other than its original serving plate and it stopped as suddenly as it began. I was aware, however, of how it could start again at any moment.

* * *

"Are you coming to wager money at the roulette table, Harry?" Lady Rosemary Ellison, my companion at dinner asked, as her husband, the Member of Parliament for Windsor East, was at the head of the rest, leading them away towards another room.

She accepted my refusal, as the Foreign Secretary appeared without his partner, taking his arm instead of mine.

In the other rooms there were various card games arranged for the partially sober, to satiate any remaining appetite as a final course of entertainment to participate in after the sumptuous meal. I declined the invitation to take part, preferring to remain where I was, enjoying the port. I am many things, but I am not a gambler, nor am I one inclined to socialise with the heavily intoxicated.

The one thing that Bots and I had as a common leveller, was that neither of us were gamblers. However, the mention of blackjack served to reinforce my concerns about Tammy, whose attention was deflected in the opposite direction to me. Her demeanour left me with the impression that neither she nor Winston, the far from passive object of her attention, would remain away from the bedroom for long.

* * *

With the raucous enjoyment about to overflow from the gambling tables and snooker room back into the dining room, I excused myself from my company and went to indulge in the solitude of the library, choosing the quiet where I could exorcise the demons flying around in my head and hopefully reach a decision.

That possibility was taken from me within minutes of settling down in an agreeable chair, as the door clicked open like the bolt-action on the old standard issue Lee-Enfield British Army rifle. It then slammed shut like the noise from a military Howitzer fired at close range.

My only defence to what then occurred is that I have never been blessed with foresight.

CHAPTER THREE

GAMBLE

"Bless my cotton socks, if it isn't his honour the Earl Harry Paterson of grand old Yorkshire Moors himself. Hopefully you're not an apparition, old fruit, but you are in good spirits. How's life with you then, sport? Still floating the good ship Isle of Jura, are we?"

He nodded at the decanter on the table, beside which I sat with a glass of my favourite golden nectar beside it.

"How the bloody hell are you? Seems a lifetime ago that we last met." He hadn't stopped.

It would appear I had drawn the short straw in the company I kept. My uninvited guest was Gerald Neil, owner of Crocketts, the famous London Mayfair gaming club, with many more attractions inside than gaming tables. Even though he had just arrived, he was showing the effects of some already consumed alcohol. I mentioned it to him.

"You seem to be on the wrong side of drink already, Gerald. I thought you said you had only just arrived."

"I have just got here. I was entertaining at Crocketts with some of the club's high-fliers. Mike drove me. Mike's my driver. I prefer the word 'driver' to 'chauffeur'. I bet you use the word 'chauffeur' for yours, but so what, none of us are the same.

"As far as I'm concerned, I can't afford to forget where my income derives from. Must keep the wheels greased, and all that. Ah, that's funny—wheels greased and driver in the same conversation and nothing to do with nothing. Mind if I join you, Harry?" he asked, rather too loudly for my taste and certainly for the room, as I'm sure I heard it echoing for an appreciable amount of time after it was said.

Gerald was a heavily-built man, tall and menacing, with a deep, resonant voice as it bounced from the shelves laden with books. He had a full head of grey hair, swept high, then backwards. It was always well-groomed, but was now disobedient in the places that bobbed up and down with his steps as he closed the short distance to where I sat.

The euphoric aura surrounding this man did not match his face, which was a rounded, cherubic affair with small, brown, weasel eyes that seldom engaged your own, preferring to dart from one point to another as though he was looking for something untoward to occur at any moment.

All in all, he was an imposing, well-heeled man with a gushing personality which went well with the proprietorship of one of London's oldest and most prestigious gambling clubs. The club was strictly members only, with the collective distinction of having to be mightily prosperous as the principal qualifying factor for membership.

I had seen many minor and some senior members of the royal family frequent his club, although that would not be for wider public knowledge.

Personally, I had never held the man in high regard, but I'd never had any reason to tell him that. The very last thing I wanted that evening was some monotonous address about the intricacies of the roulette table by a very talkative drunkard.

I have, as by now you will have gathered, a multitudinous mixture of habits, but one thing I certainly do not have, is any foible of being ungracious, and gratuitously rude. Give me reason to be so, and I will, and depending on the severity of the rudeness levelled at me, or someone in my close company, will dictate the ferocity of my reply.

But it was not Gerald's impoliteness I resented. It was his actual physical presence in the room. Despite all of that, his innate characteristics had yet to sufficiently rile me.

"Not at all, Gerald. Help yourself," I replied.

"One thing about the Viscount one can rely on is his generosity with supplies. There's enough to be shared. Also, I noticed plenty of glasses in the cabinet. You're in luck on another thing, I've not yet got round to drinking all the Jura. Nuts and bites over there as well, in quaint little bowls with frilly doilies. Have you eaten yet?" I asked, hoping he hadn't and would go to find sustenance.

"I expect there's lashings of food in the kitchen," I counselled, as he was still near me and making no obvious movement towards the slammed door.

"Yes, thank you, I have. I ate at the club before leaving." I was out of luck.

He grabbed a glass from the bow-fronted, polished walnut drinks cabinet, a crystal affair with the Bottomly coat of arms, an impressive pair of golden peacocks, inscribed into it, and then, much to my annoyance, took the decanter and placed it on another side table, nearer to him, beyond my reach. It seemed not only was he staying, he wanted custody of the whisky with the right of ownership alongside its residence.

"Have you met up with the rest of the crowd?" I asked, standing and making a point of retrieving what I considered to be more mine than his. I replaced the decanter on its previously occupied square silver coaster, with as much noise as I thought reasonable without damaging glass or metal, then carried on speaking.

"There's some blackjack and what have you, going on elsewhere that should interest you, old chap." I tried once more, hoping that he would take my point and go.

"Last thing I need is to watch a collection of inebriates throwing money at each other. If it was coming my way, it would be a different matter, of course."

He laughed in a pretentious way, the kind that means, 'I know more of what you're speaking about than you know, nevertheless I'll indulge you a little'. I smiled smugly, not seeking to conceal my irritation.

"In any case, nowadays this library has become a sort of second home for me." He had obviously decided he was in for the long haul, but he had aroused my interest by the 'second home' remark.

Managing to ignore my far from gracious nod of the head, he expanded without considering being asked, making a beeline to one of the shelves lining the entire room.

"My book is here, look. Have a thumb through the thing while you're deliberating on whatever it is that's keeping you in solitude."

Knowing exactly where to find his book, it didn't take him long before he was handing me a two-inch thick, beige-coloured hardback with the title embossed in blue lettering: *From Dulwich To Fastnet Rock And Return,* by Gerald Neil. The cover had the image of a racing yacht sailing quickly through a heavy sea. It didn't take much intelligence on my part to deduce he was a frequent visitor, if not a frequent guest.

"I'm President of the Royal Ocean Racing Club and I'm off down to Cowes on Sunday. I'm blowing the start horn for this year's 'Half Ton Classic' race. It's a week-long regatta race windward and leeward around the Isle of Wight. It comes with a full week of social engagements in the RORC clubhouse."

I felt his eyes boring holes into my face but I didn't look his way, I kept my gaze forward, successfully ignoring him. Even so, it didn't take him long to start again.

"I've taken part in the race itself on six occasions. Twice as crew and then skippered my own yacht on the other four. Came home runner-up twice."

He frowned in disappointment, a sentiment which I must say I felt as well, having tasted defeat a few times myself.

"Never did win the blighter," he added slowly.

He paused and took a drink, as if to wash away the blunting memory.

"I'm only here for tomorrow's drive, then I'm off for the important stuff at Cowes. Unfortunately, I have some business to discuss with His Highness, our friend Winston. Then I'll be gone. I take it you're staying for both days, Paterson?" *Blast*, I thought, *he wants to stay and natter.*

"Yes, I am. We hung on to the last minute at

home, but had to postpone our own shoot, due mainly to the atrocious wet winter we had in Yorkshire. All in all, it reduced the stock far below acceptable culling levels. Unfortunately, my estate manager was hanging on for a better spring and to acquire outside birds, but alas, that plan didn't work. He has put the estate shoot back for at least a week or, more likely, two. We might have to cancel this year's completely. However, he and I are scheduled to speak on Monday to determine if it's at all possible to hold one and if so, when to send out invitations." I didn't offer Gerald a place on the mailing list.

"Knowing how Winston throws such a good bash at everything, I thought I'd spend the weekend down here." I never referred to my friend as 'Bots' to unwelcome acquaintances.

* * *

I use Crocketts on my visits to the devil's lair of London, as it has one of the finest private eating venues in town, far better than Boodles, which I only use for meetings and things I can't get out of. I don't usually take rooms, preferring Chester Square, but I couldn't be bothered to open it up for such a short period of occupation. The times I do use the club are for nights like last night, when it's unexpected and I'm dog-tired.

A great attraction of Gerald's club is the sights to

behold inside the plush and comfortable premises. Not necessarily do I mean the winning and losing aspects of the clientele. The women frequenting the place are normally extremely elegant, beautiful and captivating, worth every penny of the exorbitant annual membership to mingle amongst.

I have, on more than one occasion, met and enjoyed the special company of a few. None of which I shall tell you about here.

By that description, I don't want you to think it was a place frequented by professional escorts or the like. It is not, and nor would Gerald allow it to be so.

However, I am prepared to say that most men, along with some of the women, use the place for what professional escorts would tell you it would be— not unnatural to expect a financial settlement.

It was in Gerald's club where I had first seen Samantha Burns and, I hasten to add, I had seen her there more than once. That was the worry engulfing my every thought since seeing her in the dining room and hearing of my friend's proposal of marriage.

* * *

"You say you have business to speak of with Winston, Gerald? It must be important to drag you all the way from town at this time of night. You didn't drive yourself, surely?" I asked, because of the smell of alcohol on his breath, and I couldn't remember him say he hadn't.

"Do you need hearing aids, Paterson, or are you not paying attention? I think the latter, but never mind. I've already told you I was driven here! I know I'm foolish, but not foolish enough to drive. I have a driver nowadays because stupid me is banned from driving. Got a four-year ban at Horseferry Road Magistrates Court for exactly what you're implying. That was two years ago and, as I've said, I've grown up in certain ways since then."

I thought about his reply for a while, trying to think of some witty rejoinder, but none came immediately to mind and, as it seemed rude to stop him from speaking, I carried on, deliberately avoiding any mention of driving.

"Bit of a wide diversion to the Isle of Wight, coming all the way here though, isn't it? Couldn't you have put the matter of business off to a more opportune time?" I lit another cigarette. I always smoke too much when bored, or trying to be careful what I say when absorbed in a conversation I'd rather not be in.

"No, I couldn't shelve it anymore, I'm afraid. A mite delicate, old chap." He swallowed hard and then, for a moment, turned to face me with his eyes pointed in my direction.

"I'm sorry to say it's a question of money," he announced. "Partially, I guess, due to you and your introduction of him to the club."

He walked around me to refill his glass, this time replacing the decanter to where it was. I was grateful for the gesture, mumbling a weary 'thanks' as he turned away to regain his chair.

"How's that then?" I asked, following suit with the whisky, but adding more to my glass as if to emphasis my co-opted ownership.

"He intends to call on you, Paterson, for the financial assistance he needs. He's left it up to me to first broach the subject. He was embarrassed apparently, or at least that was his excuse. Did it not cross your mind how fortuitous it was for you to be invited at such a late date? His Highness was diligent in finding out how treacherous your weather was. Was he not? He had good reason to be. The follow-up invitation on the phone didn't come about through simple friendly benevolence, or past associated Guards allegiances, you understand. He called you as he's a user of people as well as a loser, your friend Harry. He's an incorrigible and unlucky gambler, is our Winston Bots."

"He is what?" I demanded of him in a raised voice, utterly thrown off balance by his accusation.

Gerald Neil's disrespectful use of the name Bots instead of Bottomly had irritated me intensely, but it was news of financial worries that shook me so dramatically. I rose from the chair with the ease of the predator I'd earlier suggested Samantha Burns might be. His attitude, allegation and lack of good manners had catapulted me into a raging temper, causing me to end up standing directly in front of him with hands forming fists hanging at my sides. The veil covering Bots's involvement with Samantha Burns was beginning to lift and I wasn't liking what was hiding behind it.

"Sit down, Harry. Would you rather I hide the truth from you? That would do none of us any good whatsoever. Least of all him!" As cool as a cucumber, he stated this emphatically, remaining seated, legs crossed.

"It's not my fault our mutual friend cannot keep his hands inside his pockets for long, now is it? I'm sorry about this, but he's mortgaged up to the hilt and then some. I have managed to sell his boat. He asked me to do that, said he didn't have the time, as though he was rushed off his feet doing something productive." He stopped for enough time to sample the whisky, as if it might have deteriorated since his last taste. Unfortunately for me, it hadn't.

"Nice little thing, the boat. But I already have two boats, I certainly don't need a third. A shame, really."

For a moment I thought he was genuinely concerned, but if he was, it was only for the boat being sold. It wasn't long before his succinct recollection of events was repeated.

"But you were set up for this meeting, I'm afraid. The weather was a bonus, of course, and when you said that you were coming, well, he was thinking it would save his day."

The concern was gone, replaced by a huge, supercilious grin following on from the 'save the day' remark that lingered whilst he continued.

"Otherwise, he would have to have thought of another way of—how can I say?—enlisting your help. Winston suggested the 'twelfth' to be a genial time in your calendar and I was not going to miss my appointment at the Royal Squadron. Prince Philip will be there on Sunday, you know. I'm hosting the lunch for him. It's a really big day for me. I understand you and he have met more than once. Anyway, I'm off the subject. Bottomly phoned me as soon as you arrived. He told me about the card games he'd arranged. He added that you would hide yourself away from any of the superficial friendliness those sort of amusements create. You're a creature of habit, old boy. He and I knew where I would find you. To give him his due, he is genuinely worried about asking. He's hoping you could open up the vaults of that bank of yours in town and lend him some cash on favourable terms. That's what he's after. Personally, I don't give a stuff where the money comes from, just as long as I get paid."

"Good grief, man, what on earth are you saying?" I had regained my composure, returning to my chair before posing the one question that possibly changed my life.

"How much does he owe you, for goodness sake?"

* * *

He emptied the contents of his glass whilst looking straight in front, avoiding my gaze. This time, I was determined to hold on to the decanter, offering to re-fill his glass for him rather than him taking it. After that ritual was completed, he waited for me to add some whisky to my own glass before adding his reply.

"I managed to get just shy of nine hundred for his boat. As I said, it was a nice little thing. I was hoping to get more for it than that, but I was told the market is swamped at the moment, added to which his instructions were quite limited."

From what I'd seen at his club, he had a capacity for drink and the fact he had been drinking before he arrived showed strongly in his mumbled speech which, by now, had not changed for the better, but as I was no angel when it came to drinking, all I could do was trust he would stop, and go away soon.

"I almost talked myself into taking the darn thing, but business is business, besides which both of my boats are larger. One of them sleeps eight comfort-ably, plus anywhere between five and eight crew. That one cost me over twelve million two years ago.

"The other one wasn't cheap, either. The smaller one sleeps six and the same number for a fully crewed boat. I've had her for a good number of years." His eyes narrowed as he went into in deep thought.

"I forget how many years now." No matter how deep he thought, he couldn't decide.

"Whenever it was, I think the boat cost me about five million. So neither boat is a tiny four-berth with a teddy bear squeezed in for luck. The smaller boat of mine is at Cowes. That's the one I'll be sailing when I get down there. It makes more sense, you see, to keep two boats.

"The larger one I have moored off an island in the Thracian Sea. The island's called Samothrace. Heard of the place, Paterson? No, not many people have. It's not far from mainland Greece."

He hadn't given me a chance to answer, nevertheless I did not know where it was.

"There's a very efficient marina in Samothrace, very safe and secure. It's managed well by people who know how to look after the big spenders, getting shot of all those around the Mediterranean without a pot to piss in. I have a small, but well cared for, estate on the island. It's in the hills, away from the heat by the sea. Near a village called Alonia.

"Grow my own wine up there, it's good for the vines on the slopes, you know. Bottle and label it, before selling it locally. I've been having talks with a neighbouring land owner, an English chap, to buy him up and expand my winery operation.

"But back to the here and now. I sold Bottomly's

boat for just over what I'd priced it up for. I did what he asked and sold it on the Continent, not here in the British Isles where I think I would have got more for it. He's vain, that was the truth behind it.

"There's no accounting for people's vanity. He didn't want to lose face, you see. Yes, it's all about image with him. Mind you, there's a lot of people I run into like that. I guess you must come across quite a few.

"His boat went to a German from somewhere near Hamburg. Your friend Bottomly's remaining debt is just over eight. Eight hundred and forty-three, to be precise, but that figure is without the interest. I won't set tle that on him now. The total shouldn't have gone beyond five.

"I had a marker down at the club for that amount, but he got himself involved in a poker game with some serious players when I was absent. My chargé d'affaires was too soft on him.

"But I simply raised his debt when I settled what he owed to them. Saving that precious face of his. It could have been more than his pretty face they would have damaged, had I not. Anyhow, I'm not looking for a medal. I want it all settled, out of the way."

His slit-like eyes darted along the bookshelves as though he was looking for a particular book, until he spoke again in a softer voice.

"Overall, I thought he was good for it, you see. He gave me no reason to think differently until he came clean about his debts. It seems as though he's in hock to all and sundry. I don't know if you noticed when you came in, but I understand most of the family's valuables have been sold off." His sombre, disheartening address knew no end.

"Three weeks ago, there was an auction at Christie's of fine art where he had some of the family's portraits auctioned off. I was told he got a fair sum, but nothing came my way to pay towards his debt. That's what tipped the balance for me, Paterson. I'd had enough when I heard that."

"Eight hundred and forty-three pounds? Surely he has that?" I asked, in total disbelief.

"What? Where does that brain of yours live? Is that estate you have in Yorkshire in cloud cuckoo land along with the rest of the aristocracy? Eight hundred and forty-three *thousand*, man. Nearly a million! Are you serious? Before I sold that yacht of his, the financial obligation stood at almost two million. I incurred various expenses for that sale and I'm keeping what I got for the boat to go towards paying those expenses. But for Heaven's sake, Paterson, be real, please. What do you think of me? I wouldn't have gone to all this trouble for a mere eight hundred and forty-three pounds. Can it be I look so poor to you?"

I didn't answer, of course, I was still trying to get my mind around those astronomical numbers. How could anyone owe such a huge sum of money as that?

Ponderously I leaned back into that red, winged, leather armchair, allowing the softness to swallow me up. Maybe it was the comfort I found that caused an overwhelming feeling of claustrophobia to slowly intermingle with the realisation that my belief in a friend's integrity had been wrong. I was bitterly distraught and angry, not sure where to target my anger.

"Is this house part of the security you hold for his debt?" I managed to ask, not at ease with any answer, yet not at ease in silence.

"Not at this time, no, but it damn well might be. He was in the club last weekend with his usual obsequious mob. Most, if not all, I expect are here, soaking up his booze. I call him, and them, *rent a mount mob*. If the battle of Waterloo was being fought this Sunday, poor old Wellington could not count on Bottomly and his *rent a mount mob*, they would be laid out on the floor here."

His drinking had slowed but his unwelcome attempts at being funny had not.

"Bottomly came to me last week and asked if I would lend him two million pounds against a part of his family's landholdings in South Africa. I made a few enquiries and apparently he is worth a mint of money out there, but I told him no. 'Repay what you owe me first,' I said, and he got a bit loud about it. He can be a bit cocky when he's with that noisy crowd of his."

"Did you know he's engaged?" I just spurted it out without thinking.

He laughed quietly then added, as if it was an afterthought, "No, I didn't. Has she got money, perchance? Now, that would be a bonus for all three of us, wouldn't it? That could be why he's marrying her? Or is it she's delusional in believing him to be a wealthy, titled landowner, poor girl? If she does, you had better put her straight, Paterson, before the *I do's* on the big day and the tearful disappointment following on from the nuptials. Now that would be a scene worth viewing."

Who was marrying whom and for what, was one of the things I had been trying to find out by telephoning so many of both Bots' and my friends. I had no knowledge then, nor suspicions, of a financial issue like the one Gerald Neil had laid out before me, but now it formed the major part of my concerns. At first, I'd thought she was after Bots' fortune, only now I had found out there was none. Did she know he was broke when he asked her to marry him? Metaphorically, I was on the ropes with both eyes closed.

"Name of Tammy, short for Samantha apparently, but I never got the surname." I don't know why I lied, but I did not tell him the surname.

"Very attractive woman," I declared, again keeping the secret for some unconscious reason.

Gerald's attention up to this point had alternated between his whisky glass, his fat Cuban cigar, and any point on the wall between the door and the fireplace opposite where some logs were warmly ablaze. Despite it being August, there was a distinct chill in the night air. Perhaps it was the warmth from this fire that was keeping him here. It hadn't looked likely he would leave for some considerable time; however, on the mention of the names of Tammy and Samantha, his neck almost broke as his startled reaction whipped it around to confront me.

"Tammy?" he asked excitedly, standing up abruptly.

"Know of her then, Gerald?"

It was an unnecessary question as it was obvious in the way he'd acted that he did. His answer was breathtaking. He took a noisy slurp of the remaining whisky in his glass, accompanied by a long draw on his cigar whilst composing his reply.

"No, can't say I've heard the name before. Very nice for Winston and, of course, for her. Look, old chap, I'm a bit knackered and I'm sure all this talk about money could be continued some other time. I'm for bed, to catch up on the sleep I must need. Loads of late nights at the club have finally got to me. Goodnight, old bean, I've enjoyed our conversation. My only wish would be that it could have been on some different subject.

"There are some good photographs in that book of mine if nothing else. Quite a few snaps of the Greek island I told you of as well. It became very famous a few years ago, but not for anything I'd done. Some collection of valuable artefacts, I think, coming from an archaeological dig on the farmer's land I'm interested in buying. The one next to my estate.

"As I say, there are some nice photos of the island, as well as my yachts. If you're ever in the market for a boat, let me know, I can normally get a good price for a friend."

Now I'm a friend, am I? Any more whisky and he might propose marriage!

"I never wrote the book, you know. Can't write a letter, me. I just sat in my office, dictating some stuff into a recording machine. Sent the tapes off to an address my publishers gave me and it was written by a ghost-writer who put no bones into the narrative. Shame, but I guess it's like the world all over, lacking soul. Bit of a joke there, Paterson, ghosts and soul, but never mind. Guess I've overstayed my welcome. You will have a chat with His Highness though, won't you? I'm trusting you on that one. I'd hate going down the legal route."

With that, and a farewell look into his empty glass before he diligently placed it on the table, he was gone, leaving his final spoken words dispassionately trapped in the foggy fug of cigar smoke mixed with my cigarettes, drifting between the floor and ceiling.

CHAPTER FOUR

MORNINGS

I was out of bed and showered early the following morning, not simply because of the previous night's events, although they still worried me, but it was a routine for me to check my guns before using them. I am, it's true, a creature of habit, but habits can be good as well as bad.

This particular custom probably derived from my days in the army where the rigorous checking of guns, as well as the rest of the kit, was drilled into your memory by the company sergeant-major, there to remain no matter what rank you finally achieved.

It wasn't only time spent in the military that made me disciplined in my approach to ordinary life. That started at the Methodist Church Preparatory School I attended until the age of thirteen, when it was reinforced at Eton College before university life made it a necessity, especially so when a systematic process was essential for my degree in chemical analysis.

Being methodical has helped me in many ways and it most certainly is of great help in remembering the names of lady friends who would not be amused to be referred to incorrectly. I have drifted away from the subject somewhat, running the risk of deviating onto my favourite theme, so let me return to where we were before my lack of discipline took us from it.

Back home at The Hall, I was fortunate in having a dedicated gun room, where it was a pleasurable ritual every weekend to clean the guns, used or not. There was always something to polish or clean. Here, my gun case was at the foot of the wardrobe, not locked away in a purpose-made cabinet as they would be at home. I ran a wad through both barrels, then, with one final wipe and a quick shine to the stock and forearm, they were put back in their case waiting to be collected by whoever was appointed as my loader.

There were two drives scheduled this Saturday. The first was for eleven o'clock, then another at three-thirty in the afternoon. If there were sufficient numbers of red grouse remaining that needed culling, a drive would be conducted before lunch on Sunday, then, after another of Bots' hearty meals, we would all drift away to wherever we called home.

* * *

All the breakfast plates, tureens, cutlery, and other essential things were beginning to be assembled by the noisy house staff in the cleared-away dining room, but apart from them I seemed to be the only one up and about. Not wishing to pester the industrious workforce, I made my way to the kitchen and poured a cup of tea from the large communal teapot, but even allowing for not having eaten much the night before, there were other things I was in need of before food. One of those things was a clear mind.

The sun was low and bright, with the day offering a warm promise as I set off for a stroll around the outside of the house. I hoped my mood would improve to match the potential of the forthcoming day. There was no sign of any other guests up at this hour, as I passed in a leisurely way along the corridors and then out through the main double doors into the shadow cast by the watery morning sun.

At first, I thought my pensive state of mind was due to the concern I had for my friend Winston and his preposterous relationship with a girl who had literally just walked into his life, but as I ambled over the fresh-smelling, dewy grass, passing webs made by absent spiders strung amongst the clipped yew hedging, I thought that being away from the hustle of London had contributed in a big way. Perhaps it was more than what I'd first thought. Whatever had caused my desolate mood, thankfully it didn't last.

* * *

As I rounded a corner of the building I saw the two of them, Winston and Gerald Neil, on the same terrace where I had left Samantha the previous day. Bots was looking despondent and heavy-hearted, pacing backwards and forwards with his head held skywards, looking into the blue morning sky as if that was where he would find an answer. I presumed he was looking for spiritual inspiration as he seemed to be exchanging few words. He merely shrugged his shoulders and nodded his head to whatever was being said, whilst Gerald was gesticulating in an operatic fashion.

Not unnaturally, I suspected they were talking about the money Gerald had told me Winston owed. Having no wish to interrupt them, but with an overbearing desire to hear what was being said, I dived off to my left and entered the building via an unlocked service door. A full-length, bolted, black, wrought-iron gate was at the top of a short, seven-stepped, winding, concrete stairway leading to the balcony. If I could reach the top without being seen, I would be able to hear it all. I was almost too late. It was Gerald who ended the proceedings, as both their shadows passed across where I was headed. They were walking back towards the main part of the house.

"I don't care how you do it, just get rid of her,

then I'll wipe the slate clean. You have my word on that."

I heard no response from Bots.

Just get rid of her, and I don't care how you do it —in what sense could that mean, I desperately wondered?

* * *

I continued with my walk, not caring what it was that had woken me. Now I was mulling over all the snippets of information, as well as the gossip I had managed to garner from my telephone enquiries. As I walked, I kept quietly repeating Gerald's closing remarks, thinking of different ways they could be interpreted. As if in sympathy with the dark thoughts those few words were beginning to mark on my mind, I found I had walked deeper into the trees, away from the cultivated grass, trying to silence the doubts I held about Samantha Burns and what could be her involvement in all of this.

There was no place to bury the knowledge I had of Bots' debts and Gerald's previously spoken demands to settle the eight-hundred-odd thousand pounds. Was it my fault in not jumping in quicker with an offer to help my friend that had forced Gerald Neil to threaten violence? Or was it my imagination together with the odd occasion to fantasise, working on overdrive? There was one more phone call I could make that just might open the door to the truth.

I did not tell Gerald Neil my family had a connection to the Royal Yacht Squadron at Cowes, on the Isle of Wight, through my father's participation in the legendary Fastnet race, as it would have kept him in the library longer than I wanted. Neither did I wish to be a nuisance when I made this telephone call. I needed to have my speech well-rehearsed before calling and I used the trees as my audience, continuing my walk to nowhere on springy ground, kicking at the odd fallen leaf until I was satisfied my speech would suffice.

I had met the person I was calling quite a few times, knowing of his liking of early mornings. I also knew that time would be at a premium as he, too, would be shooting this weekend. An hour after placing my call to him, I had all the answers I needed. The trouble was, I didn't know how to apply all the answers. I searched my phonebook for someone who might.

* * *

Bots was nowhere to be found, and neither was Tammy by the time I had a semblance of a plan. I had asked three members of staff if they had seen either of them and drawn a blank from each. Returning to my room, I put on some old cords and a pair of even older boots for the shoot, then made my way first to where the breakfast was laid, to look for my host. Not having any change of luck, I grabbed a slice of dry toast from a rack I found at the end of one table then took a quick look at a notice pinned to a door. It read—List Of Loaders For The AM Drive. Saturday Guns. I was naturally interested to find my loader's name, which was Phil, but it wasn't his name that I found the most interesting. Against Winston's name as his loader was Samantha's.

My knowledge of her was obviously sparse, to say the least; even so, I considered my deduction, that she had never been a loader on a game shoot before, to be a pretty solid assumption. I could not think of many more dangerous places to put a novice than here, in an adrenaline-charged event with guns going off all around and the possibility of a mistake never far away.

As a final location to check on the whereabouts of Winston and his intended, I made my way to the indoor swimming pool, thinking I must be wrong and she would have been on a shoot before. It was as I was trying to reconcile that thought that I saw Bots coming in the opposite direction. However, the chance to speak was taken from me.

"Hello, young Harry. Saw you at lunch yesterday

when you looked engaged in other things, of a female context as usual. Off somewhere in a hurry and miles away, you were. I didn't make it to dinner. I'm afraid I overdid the champagne at lunchtime, that was fatal for me. But I never learn." He laughed in a self-deprecating manner.

"And then to my shame I fell asleep," he continued. "I've often remarked on how dangerous it is to drink during the day and there I go, ignoring my own advice. I will admit to scoffing like a pig this morning at breakfast. Lovely it was, too. There you are, even at my age one never grows too old to make a mistake, young man."

He was stuck between crying and laughing when he suddenly stopped speaking and simply gazed into space. It wasn't long before he continued with his memories of yesterday.

"Muriel passed comment on how you looked lost in thought last night. She said you weren't your normal loquacious self. Your withdrawal from the evening card table left her most disappointed. She was counting on you to be her bridge partner, you know. It wasn't all uncultivated chaos at the tables."

He pulled a long face to imitate his wife's disappointment, then began again, this time with a question.

"How's things at home without your father these days? I particularly miss him for the debates in the House. He was many things, was Elliot, but not one of those who only turn up to take the daily monetary allowance. He always seemed to have plenty of things on his hands and so little time to attend to them all.

"Such a terrible thing, his murder, and then all you discovered about his killer. Regrettably, our safeguards were not what they should have been back then, but many transformations were adopted when the inquiry finished, all of them, I might add, with an eye firmly on the future. Still, we should leave all that for a more suitable day," he exclaimed, with a genuine sadness in his voice, before adding, "You would have been pleased with the outcome had you stayed around. Incidentally, I heard about the terrible winter you had up north. I understand there was flooding in the centre of York?"

"Sir Leonard, good to see you. And yes, unfortunately York was hit particularly hard, nonetheless, I'm pleased to report my local was saved. Being high up on the moors helped." I smiled at my attempt at a joke.

"But no matter, we northerners are used to worse things than that. I did speak to your dear wife last night, enquiring after you. As always, she was very diplomatic." I laughed as I shook his soft hand.

During the last years of my father's life, any spare time he had, he preferred to spend in the company of the female first violin of the BBC Philharmonic Orchestra. Sir Leonard probably knew that, but if he didn't, I had no reason to educate him on the finer points of any non-appearance at the House of Lords. When I had a chance to look beyond Sir Leonard, Bots had disappeared and I wondered why, as he must have seen the two of us.

"I must say, young man, you always stand out in a crowd. Here's the rest of us keeping up appearances with all the regalia of plus fours, shooting jackets and what have you, then there's you. Some moth-eaten old leather jerkin and a T-shirt! You could do with a haircut as well, by the look of things. Do you never feel conspicuous by looking so conspicuous? Even slightly?" he asked with a smile, not as a reproach or dismissal, nor expecting an answer.

"Come on, you scruffy young man, let's go bag us a few brace for cook's fricassee tonight. I hear the kitchen here does a rather presentable one."

"Tell me, is it a requisite of becoming Solicitor General to possess a silver tongue, Leonard? You have this amazing ability to capture me every time with your repartee." We both laughed as I took his arm, steering him towards the outside door.

"Is the good Lady Muriel staying in the house for the morning flush, or are the women accompanying us onto the field of carnage and watching from a safe distance?" I asked, with Tammy in mind.

We continued our affable discourse, discussing everything and nothing as we made our way side by side in great humour to the assembly point. I did not think of my lack of breakfast, as the conversation, although not long in time, was pleasing beyond description. Albeit the day may have begun mysteriously with unfinished balcony hazards, the promise I felt on leaving the main house and first stepping into the daylight had distinctly returned in full.

Winston was waiting beyond the yew hedging where the cultivated garden began its meandering path into the woodland. Waiting beside him was the distinctive figure of Samantha, dressed entirely in Burberry country clothes with a cartridge bag slung over one shoulder. Over the other shoulder was a matching Burberry shotgun slip, with a broken gun being carried across that arm. Trust Bots to bring his impeccable style to the arena. I could not mistake my loader, who was waiting with my two mismatched shotgun slips. As much as my vision was consumed by other matters, I noted the absence of Gerald Neil.

* * *

"For those who do not already know of my engagement, may I present my fiancée to you, ladies and gentlemen; Miss Samantha Burns. Miss Burns will be loading for me today," he proclaimed gleefully to a collective cheer of congratulations, then added, with a wide smile plastered on his face, "I would be obliged if the 'gentlemen', if there are many here, kept their envious eyes on the birds in front, not on the delectable one behind me."

This was met with applauding approval from the assembled ladies, and a few light-hearted 'boos' coming from the men. I smiled in her direction and she smiled back. Bots saw us and fixed a fearsome stare at me. I had never experienced his temper aimed in my direction and didn't know how to properly react, I chose diplomacy as my approach, mouthing the words 'we need to speak' when I knew I had diverted his full attention away from her. He gave an imperceptible shake of the head, along with a grimace that anyone else would probably think was indigestion.

As it was obvious that my unease over his situation was not the uppermost thought in my friend's mind I decided my worries were most probably misplaced and now was not the ideal time to spoil the party by making myself look the fool that I was, so, as the long winding column moved out through the tall trees, I took up the rear with Phil walking alongside me.

* * *

Most of those present to shoot I'd seen at lunch or dinner; however, there were two men I did not know, nor had seen before. I was curious, with no obvious way to assuage my curiosity without appearing presumptuous. It was not, after all, mandatory for me to be acquainted with every guest, as often in country house shoots neighbours or close local friends are invited to the event.

That clearly might have been the case, had it not been for the fact that both had American accents that could be plainly heard twenty or so yards away from where we were. Normally, I would have expected either Bots, or someone from his estate office, to have introduced them to the main party, but perhaps, I thought, customs were different in the south of England to those of the north.

After a gentle thirty-minute walk, we reached an old-looking manmade clearing where felled trees, some of which had been blown down by winter gales, had been moved into positions to make excellent covers. The final directions to our 'stands' were given by the estate manager.

I was positioned at the end of a line of twenty-six guns stretching over a distance exceeding a good four hundred yards or more, away to my left. The ground was fairly level and even, no trouble for Phil to find a safe place to stand, preparing my pair of guns. My mood had picked up. I was looking forward in anticipation of a good morning.

As would be usual, the least proficient 'guns' took up the centre of this culling area, as that is where the birds would fly more in a pack. Grouse are very agile in flight, flying low at first before rising quickly, then dropping into a fast, zig-zagging glide. Their flight made them extremely difficult to hit when the group found the open sky. The tall conifers and broad-leafed trees that stood a hundred or so yards in front of our positions would not make it easy to pick the birds out as they soared high into the sun. Any bird not killed outright would be dead as soon as a dog got to it.

* * *

The gun dogs had been in a state of collective excitement since early morning, as if sensing that it was to be their day. Now, most of them were in front of us with the beaters beyond the trees, barking in a frenzied expectation of the day to come. The estate manager, with five or six dog handlers, had the re-trievers behind the guns, awaiting their turn in the proceedings.

I had the right flank, with the sun slightly to my left. Some thirty or so feet away was Bots, with Tammy standing almost alongside, still readying his guns. The thought of them being very close came second to the one where I was worried over her ability to handle the loaded guns, as her hands were visibly shaking.

Standing to the left of Winston was Sir Leonard with his estate loader, and both men were perfectly calm and ready for the approaching excitement.

Leonard turned and waved to his wife who was standing with the other women on a grassy mound, sheltering from the strong morning sun under some of the chestnut trees we'd passed earlier. Phil, a heavily built, tallish chap of thirty-odd years with a weather-beaten face, wearing a tartan cap, stood directly behind me, holding my second gun in his large right hand, broken, but loaded, the barrels pointed towards the ground with its safety on. My other gun, also loaded, he'd passed to me, and that too was broken, but this one was lying across my arm.

Now was my first real chance to speak, but Bots took the initiative away from me as we met halfway between our allotted places.

* * *

"Harry, I'm sorry that you had to hear about my affairs from that bore of a man, Gerald Neil. It was taken out of my hands, but all's okay now, I can assure you. I won't be calling on our friendship to settle loans, neither will I be embarrassing myself further. I'm somewhat ashamed by it all. I'll be going abroad soon. Too much has taken place in my life since Father died, and in truth I find the responsibilities of one's family's heritage has become a tiresome load for me to carry."

He looked crestfallen, completely detached from the moment. It was not something I expected to see when several guns were about to be fired all at once. Concentration was needed, certainly not any sort of distraction. I tried my best to reassure him.

"Nothing to worry about with me, Bots. The important thing is you and Samantha are okay." I looked straight into his eyes, trying to discover what was on his mind in this instance.

"She has handled shotguns before?" I asked, desperate to know. I never had a satisfactory reply, as in the distance I heard the shrill of the start whistle as it was blown and the shouts of the beaters now joined that of the barking dogs.

"We'll have a talk later," he said as he turned away, making his way back to Samantha who was smiling as she gave a little wave in my direction.

"Ear protectors on now, ladies and gentlemen, please. They're off!" the estate manager announced in a rousing manner, demanding attention.

On the whole, everything was fine when the first flush broke cover, but, as so often happens on these occasions, the dogs and beaters had disturbed the centre of the flock leaving the outside edges almost untroubled, meaning the flush was concentrated more over the centre of the firing line. On the edges where Leonard, Bots, and I stood, there were not many birds at which to fire. Over where we stood, behind those fallen trees with their roots exposed, there was very little activity, but there were a few targets to shoot at.

It was split seconds later when everything went so tragically wrong. I am still unable to be precise with the details of the incident, nor am I able to differentiate from when my shot left my gun, to when I heard a noise, even though time seemed to stand still. One thing I'm absolutely certain of is that close by, I heard a short scream that was as sharp as a Gurkha's kukri knife, then, almost simultaneously, something hit the back of my neck with a wallop similar to a softish tennis ball striking one's head at speed.

My eyes had not moved from the sky, searching for grouse in my area. There were grouse to fire at but, from the time whatever it was hit me, I hadn't fired. Instinctively, I realised something was wrong. I lowered my gun, breaking it open as I did so. That's when I saw the blood together with something I couldn't recognise on my left arm.

Everything next to occur went, as they say, 'in slow motion'. I turned towards where Bots should have been standing. At once, I had to lower my eyes, as he was kneeling on the ground cradling the misshapen remains of a skull in his hands. There wasn't much of it to hold.

A gory red lump of distorted bone and sinew with bloodied unidentifiable matter that were overhanging his knee, once belonged to the beautiful Samantha Burns.

Lying on the well-trodden ground where I stood, was what had hit me; a part of her lower jawbone with bits of teeth still attached. As I've already said, everything seemed to move slowly; however, one part of my brain clicked into gear ahead of anyone else near me.

Winston's unbroken gun was abandoned on the grass between himself and me. I have been around guns all my life, appreciating their integral danger when loaded. I picked the thing up to make it safe. After putting the safety catch back on the gun, I broke it open to remove the unfired cartridge. I held the palm of my hand over the end of the barrels in order to catch the ejected spent cartridge case. I was shocked as I did so, as two empty cases were ejected.

It was at that stage I fully understood the conse-quences to Gerald Neil's earlier remark of, 'get rid of her'.

I should make one thing perfectly clear—when I heard those words spoken I did not suspect my friend would murder the girl. Never did that thought cross my mind.

When it came to game shooting, Winston was like me; a traditionalist, preferring a Purdey side by side gun to the modern 'over and under' variety. All such traditional guns have two hammers with two triggers. It's the triggers that make the gun fundamentally different, and in some ways, safer. A modern over and under shotgun has one trigger, therefore it does not require any withdrawal or movement of the trigger finger.

Any person handling the gun, especially someone inexperienced such as Samantha, if my suspicions were correct, might be liable to pull one trigger accidentally; however, to pull both triggers requires a tiny, nevertheless a deliberate physical movement of withdrawing the finger from the first trigger of the gun, moving it around the trigger guard, then inserting it onto the second trigger. The action of removing the finger from one trigger, then inserting it onto the second trigger, could not be done if firing the first barrel had killed her. The only conclusion to draw was that Winston Bottomly had deliberately fired both barrels into Samantha's face as he'd taken the unbroken, fully loaded gun from her.

With so much noise coming from the centre of our line on the first drive, nobody had either seen or heard the slight difference between taking a gun from the loader and firing the gun precipitously into the loader. However, it is impossible to accidentally pull 'through' both triggers.

It took no time at all for me to realise my friend had murdered his fiancée. The conclusion I came to did not matter to me. A friend is a friend. I had no time to consider the consequences of my actions. I inserted the live cartridge I'd taken from my gun, when making it safe, into the right-hand barrel of Winston's Purdey. My choice made it appear as though only one trigger had been pulled, thereby making it seem as though it could have been a tragic accident due to the naivety of the gun loader—Samantha Burns!

I had acted slightly quicker and out of sight of my loader, Phil. As I was making safe the gun on the ground, he had rushed to aid Winston. Between them, they had placed the remains of Samantha's head on her body. Neither of them had looked in my direction and, as far as I could see, nobody else had.

There were several people now rushing towards the horrendous scene, and there were also loud and unmistakable screams from behind me where the ladies were standing. The downed tree would have shielded me from their view, as would have done the broken tree to the rear of where Samantha and Bottomly had stood.

Sir Leonard was standing over Bots looking down at Samantha's decapitated body. When I had the chance, I thrust Winston's loaded but safe gun upon him. I saw him empty the live round I'd put in the gun and place it in his pocket as I comforted and pulled my friend away from the terrible, distorted body. As I did so, I whispered in his ear, "It's okay, Bots. I know what you've done, and I've covered it."

In an equally quiet voice and without waiting he replied.

"I knew you would, Harry, that's why I put us standing so close to you. I'm sorry, but I was given no choice. It had to be done."

* * *

Both Bots and I were covered in blood, as were the barrels of his gun.

Although I was acting calmly, I most certainly was not calm inside. Let's be clear—I knew my actions were covering a murder and as such I was guilty of a serious crime. The last thing I needed at that moment of time was a police officer asking Winston any awkward questions, as I couldn't be sure of his shaky reactions. I could lie. I had great practice in its art. But as far as I knew, Winston was a different kettle of fish. A period of calming composure from all was required. I acted in a manner I thought fitting.

"I'll take the gun into the house, Leonard. Both Winston and I could do with a clean-up and when we're there I'll get someone to wipe all the blood from the gun."

"That is not a good idea about cleaning the gun, Harry. I'm sure the police will want to examine it first," he stated emphatically, as he kept hold of the weapon.

When I'd had the gun in my hands, I'd taken the opportunity to smudge both triggers with my own finger, thereby erasing any of Bots' prints. I was sure nobody had seen that. Samantha wore gloves, brown leather ones and if she had accidentally fired the shotgun, nothing from Winston's fingers would have remained on either trigger. I believed I had covered everything.

CHAPTER FIVE

(ONE)

Evidence

At the inquest which was held ten days later, a verdict of Accidental Death was returned. There really was nothing else the coroner could do. Winston gave his version of what had happened at the shoot. He told how he had fired both barrels of one gun, hitting one grouse. He held the empty gun in his right hand with the barrels pointing skyward. He had hold of the pistol grip, behind the trigger guard. Then, keeping his eyes forward and skyward, towards the flight of the incoming grouse, he would have stretched out his left hand for the gun Samantha should have loaded. She should have taken the empty gun, pressing the loaded one into Winston's empty left hand. He offered to demonstrate the action to the coroner using two empty guns, but his offer was not necessary. The coroner was familiar with the practice, being accustomed to shooting game.

He went on to tell how the next thing he was aware of was there being no gun. All there was, he said, was the loud sound of a gun being fired from close behind him.

"The gun went off very close to my head. It was difficult to fully appreciate what had occurred as I always wear ear defenders for the duration of the shoot. It was only when I saw Samantha on the ground with most of her head blown away that the scale of what had happened really registered."

The coroner took further evidence from the attending police, as well as from Sir Leonard Miles, the serving government's Solicitor General, and, of course, me.

The police sergeant who attended the scene told how, on receiving the gun from Sir Leonard Miles, he examined it and found an unused cartridge in one barrel. That one piece of evidence conclusively pointed to the incident being a tragic misfortune instead of the act of murder it truly was. At the end of the hour-long inquiry, the coroner judged it to have been another of those accidents where the inexperienced are allowed to handle firearms. A clear case of Accidental Death.

The case made headline news internationally, as do most things involving the English gentry, but there was nothing inopportune to discover by any inquisitive journalist. None had my connections, nor the power to do the research that had been done on my behalf, then make it all add up.

You see, here is the twist in all of this; what I found out when Highgrove called me back earlier that Saturday morning was part of the reason for my actions. My friend there had clearance to material that was far removed from others further down the chain such as me; and he had particular reason to keep abreast of Samantha's life.

* * *

Gerald Neil's first wife of some twenty-seven years had been found dead in her burnt-out car, almost exactly eighteen months before this August date, a short distance from their shared house on the outskirts of Bagshot, in Surrey. The distraught Gerald was questioned about the circumstances, but there was no forensic evidence to suggest it was anything other than a road accident even though no signs of what had caused that accident could be found. Gerald had a cast-iron alibi. He was with a women going by the name of Charlotte Marchand on the night of the accident.

In Charlotte's statement, made to the investigating uniform officers, she said that Gerald had left his matrimonial home, taking up residence with her two days before the events surrounding his wife's demise. Every minute of the forty-eight hours could be accounted for. No flaw could be found in either her, or Gerald's, evidence. Subsequently, the police report stated 'Driver Error' as the cause of the crash, and the case was closed.

The late Mrs Kathleen Neil, Gerald's dead wife, was a cousin of the equerry to Prince Charles. It was he who had rung me back at Devonish House that fateful Saturday morning. He had the authority to demand the man in charge at the General Register Office to search the records of births, deaths and marriages. This he did, finding Charlotte Marchand to be the woman's name until it was legally changed to Samantha Burns, sometime after the death of her father. Burns was having a very secret affair with Gerald Neil when his wife met her unexplained death.

* * *

In a later conversation, after all had been dealt with and the ambulance had removed Samantha's body, Winston told me his fiancée was extorting money from Gerald. That was the topic being spoken of on the terrace that morning. Apparently, she had been doing so for some months leading up to this weekend, hence her visits to his club.

Bots took the phrase, 'get rid of her', as exactly

how he'd dealt with it, but Gerald could have meant just to take her away from him. However, Winston saw her death as his only way of protecting the family's name. I asked him if knew why Gerald Neil was not at the Saturday morning shoot, having arrived with the intention of taking part. It seemed odd to me that if his suggestion of 'get rid of her,' was to be taken in the manner Winston had, he would leave Devonish House without waiting to see it carried through. However, Bots did have an idea why he left.

Gerald had taken a phone call as the two men were ending their fatal conversation on the balcony. He told Winston he had something urgent to attend to at his home and could not stay. Without further explanation, he collected his belongings and Bots saw his car drive away with him in the back shortly after.

I never used Crocketts again—until, that is, something happened and I had no choice. That event took place further on in this story, so unfortunately you must wait to hear the reason why that occurred. What I can tell you now is I never caught sight of Gerald Neil again. I pushed him away from my memory, confining him to a distant point inside my mind where he would have remained undisturbed had nothing of further interest been added to this story of murder, intrigue, mystery and, oh yes, a fair bit of lying, but that was not the case.

Regretfully, this once straightforward tale became so complex that only those with an acute analytical mind would be capable of cracking open the impenetrable subterfuge that was uncovered. I hope you find this account of what happened as enthralling to unravel as I did.

Allow me now to return you to the story.

* * *

The next time I saw Winston, I was in the bar at Claridge's Hotel with two ex-army friends who Winston knew from the Guards in which we had all served. What Winston did not know was that these friends were serving counter-intelligence officers in MI5. Winston was in the company of a young lady with whom he mysteriously appeared uncomfortable.

I asked him if all was okay and he used a kind of code he would em ploy in the army if he was ordered to do something he thought was either disagreeable or awkward; he would use a word that took me some time to find out what it meant. That word was —carbolic.

He used it in the same way people use expletives that are, sadly, becoming more and more in common address today. Apparently, Winston attended a weekly-boarding prep-school where carbolic soap was extensively used as a means to wash away the bad elements in life—as the head teacher declared each day at school assembly. As tradition dictated, Bots moved on to Eton College after finishing with his prep, where he again found carbolic soap, this time used, as Matron said, because it acted as a mild disinfectant for all the cuts and bruises young men stumbled into whilst in her care.

The testimony of two senior adults in young Bots' life as to the value of carbolic left an impression, in such a way that he used that word to drive away what others would swear at. Unlike profanity, his word caused no offence. It only lifted a few eyebrows in puzzlement, which added to Winston's pleasure.

* * *

On this occasion in Claridge's, it meant that the lady on Winston's arm had seen her husband's sister in the ladies' cloakroom and she was bound to tell her brother, as they were very close. Winston could feel the indignation the husband would feel before their unavoidable meeting. I tried to calm him the best way I could and I thought, by the time the pair left, I had succeeded, but the story did not end there. Some people might say the story only started in Claridge's.

As Bots disappeared with his pretty lady and his forthcoming trouble, I finished my drink and made to depart, and as I did so one of the two previously mentioned friends sitting with me casually asked how long I had known Viscount Bottomly, as I'd introduced Bots. I replied how our two families had been in business in one kind or another for hundreds of years, but I had known Winston as a friend for as long as I had lived.

He started to tell me of a person using Winston's word, 'carbolic', being red-flagged at MI5's headquarters, and now they had a face to fit the word. They advised me to contact their boss, at Millbank, to help their inquiries. The conversation turned to the shoot held at the Bottomly estate.

As I listened to their understanding of the tragedy, I felt embarrassed at being unable to tell the truth. As I told the censored version, one of them began to write Sir Leonard Miles's name in a small notebook he carried, indicating Leonard would be interviewed, which did nothing to help my embarrassment.

As I understood things, an active cell of Russian dissidents, here in London, had been infiltrated by MI5. It was from their asset in that group that the information about an Englishman known as The Count who was prone to use the word 'carbolic' came. He was overheard speaking in Russian on an open telephone line to someone with an authentic Russian accent. Now there was no need to point their fingers at anyone else other than Bots!

Despite hearing the allegations, I felt no moral or legal impulse to declare exactly what had happened on the twelfth of August, thereby ruining a life that in my view did not deserve such a punishment. However, by being aware of the specifics of how Gerald Neil and the then Charlotte Marchand conspired to murder Kathleen Neil did not give me the right to hide the crime of murder.

The reason for my evasion of the truth was based entirely on my previously mentioned friendship. I knew I could not escape damnation in this sordid matter from a Higher Being than any here on earth. I shall try to come to terms with the whole severity before I'm called to give my life testament.

At one time, I had believed the matter of Samantha Burns could have ended, but alas, with officers from MI5 counter-intelligence involved, I knew it was not. I could not, however, at that time appreciate how much more would be discovered before all could be successfully concluded.

CHAPTER FIVE

(TWO)

Affliction

Sometime after Claridge's, I was in the throes of travelling home to Harrogate when fate stepped in, as it so often does. It was Sir Leonard Miles who contacted me by telephone on my arrival at the Chester Square address. I was there alone.

By this time, Serena had chosen to live permanently in Portugal and carry on with her request for a divorce. It was, I guessed, an inevitability, but even so I was saddened by her decision. She was being extremely civil about the whole thing as there was to be no valuation placed on any property that was held in our individual names, nor were bank accounts and other assets to be halved or appraised with an equal division in mind.

All she asked for was to have a say in what happened to our London home, and whilst it was still our property, access to it whenever she had need of somewhere to stay in London. I, of course, agreed, having recognised and admitted to my faults.

Sir Leonard's call was an invitation to discuss a fault of another nature the following day at his grand offices just off Whitehall where the pictorial representation of a once mighty colonial empire was emblazoned on each wall that greeted me. I waited to be called into the luxurious 'visitors' suite, before a very attractive young lady escorted me up a grand, elegant marble staircase to the first floor, then along the deep-pile, blue-carpeted, sunlit corridor to where my host stood in front of two towering, majestic, walnut-veneered, gold-leaf embossed doors.

"It's kind of you to come at such short notice, Harry. Your acceptance of the invitation has been acknowledged in much wider circles than just you and me, but perhaps I can elaborate a bit later on that, if there's time," he asserted tantalisingly.

He gestured me to enter, which I did and sat back in one of the two, long, soft, grey sofas that were arranged on opposite sides of a rectangular red and white marble coffee table where two wide, glass, kaleidoscope-coloured dishes were packed with assorted sweet pastries and placed equidistant on a cotton runner with the letters H.O. embroidered at each end. As I was placing my walking stick to lean against one of the cushions of the sofa, he began to enlarge on the reasons behind his summons. It was then my life began to change, yet again.

"The thing is, Harry, I was approached by one of my bosses, the Home Secretary's number one, about our mutual friend Viscount Bottomly. The Director General at Millbank notified the Home Office of some undeniable photographic evidence of Bottomly in conversation with a very dark permanent member of the Russian embassy delegation, meteorology section. From what we can fathom out, he's the only one in that section." He fashioned a small chuckle, to which I smiled.

"I expect you are absolutely flabbergasted to know the Russians don't consider our weather warrants more than one expert over here, aren't you?"

He didn't expect an answer to interrupt his smile and I didn't disappoint him on that score. As I sat quietly waiting for him to begin again, he pulled a document box from beside one arm of the sofa on which he sat, then opened it, withdrawing a single sheet of paper on which some times were typed in bold print.

"This Russian chap flew into London from Berlin, arriving in London on the day of the inquest. He was filmed with Bottomly the very next day in a restaurant in central London. Bottomly was waiting for him. Here, see, Harry?" Sir Leonard turned the page around to face me, pointing at a photograph of

Winston with another person in a restaurant I did not recognise.

"A few hours after the two parted, the Russian, named Valery Agapov, caught a plane out of England for Washington, D.C. On Sunday afternoon of the following week, Bottomly took a plane to the same destination. Would you know where in America might he be heading?"

"He told me he was to visit an aged aunt he has in Hagerstown, in Maryland. I'm afraid that's all I know, apart from her name being Alice, Leonard."

"That's okay, old chap. I'm sure it will help. There's another concern we have that you may be able to help us with. It's about his deceased girlfriend. In particular her connection to a city banker, a Hugh Pickering, with whom, as I understand things, you're on the board of a couple of private City of London banks?"

Although there was no mistaking the inflection to Sir Leonard's voice, it felt as though he was not only making an inquiry into the world of City banking. It was in the change of tone where I felt accused of a crime against moral criteria, or worse.

Since the change to the Patersons' family responsibility to Annie's, the private bank in Westminster my family were in charge of for centuries, I found myself on the board of directors of four private City banks as well as two boards of international banks. On two of those private boards of Directors, Pickering and I served together. However, I had not come across his name initially through any banking source. He was pointed out to me at a meeting at the IOD, the Institute of Directors, many years back, and in the time since then, we must have spoken no more than two dozen words to each other. Even allowing for that, Leonard's questioning made me feel uneasy in a way I could not explain.

"I sit on two boards where he also serves, Leonard, but that does not mean we speak, in fact we rarely do. The sort of meetings I'm involved with usually happen on a biannual basis and are purely business-orientated. Like many of the other directors, I'm not present at each and every one. Bankers in the main seldom speak of anything other than about money, then, if they speak to one another again, it's about more money.

"Generally, we are not known as great conversationalists at these meetings. I don't make notes, it is considered discourteous, but from memory I doubt I've exchanged more than two dozen words with Pickering.

Nor do I remember seeing him at any meeting I've attended this year." I felt an abnormal need to explain and separate myself from him.

Leonard sensed my mood. "No, Harry, please. Nobody is accusing you of anything. Quite the reverse, actually. Several people are looking for your help." He seemed a little bit flustered before he composed himself as he changed tack.

"As I was on the train this morning, on the way into town, I was thinking about the grouse shoot at Bottomly's place. An horrendous thing for all to see. I'm only too pleased Muriel was out of sight of the explicit bloodied details. I can't seem to shake away the pitch of the screams coming from where the ladies were gathered. I know Muriel was distraught when I told her who died, but that's not what you're here for. Well it is, but it's not." He was wearing a warm, friendly smile which made me worry more.

"We are distinctly aware of how deep your loyalty goes, old boy, and we're wondering if we can count on you in another affair concerning our friend the Viscount? Your action on the day of the shoot at Devonish House is to be commended, young man. To save a friend when in difficulty is the highest form of loyalty one can ask." I gave Leonard a quizzical look, but it wasn't necessary.

"Yes, of course I know you placed an unused cartridge in a barrel of Bottomly's gun. I'm also aware your act covered up Bottomly's murder of the girl. Our problem is probably the same as yours; we can't understand why he killed her."

Now I was concerned. Why say I probably had the same problem they had? Did he, and whoever else he was talking about, think I knew why Bots murdered her, thinking it was connected to this Russian weather forecaster? Worrying indeed!

At this point, I thought it safe to assume he was unaware of Winston telling me about Samantha blackmailing Gerald Neil and then Gerald's request to rid her from his life in return for wiping away the debt. Which left me with the conundrum of how to tell him, or whether in fact I should. I chose to keep my powder dry on that one for the time being. I also decided to find out what he, along with the department of MI5 he was representing, knew before I told them.

"I'm not at all sure what it is you're accusing me of, Leonard, so I cannot admit nor deny anything. All I would ask is that you don't go spreading any allegations around, please. I'd hate that to happen and spoil our friendship."

"No, I wouldn't think of it. But I have told someone who may be of help to us if the need of help ever arose. As you're well aware, I'm as much implicated in this cover-up business as you are, old boy. But less of that for now. Tell me about the secrets surrounding banking in the City and what you know of Hugh Pickering. He's become quite a mysterious figure for those who deal with mysteries."

I shared all I knew of Pickering with him willingly, concerned, however, by his reference to him being implicated, but again I decided not to mention anything about the grouse shoot. I concentrated on the City of London with its myriad of private and international banks along with the financial institutions, all of which were awash with money, a lot of which, in the exact sense of the word, could not be reliably accounted for.

It would not be true to say all the money deposited in London banks could be traced to legitimate business organisations, but any question regarding how the money was come by before it was deposited was an altogether different problem. Such a problem a board of internal directors would be extremely wary of asking and would normally not ask, unless an external financial inquiry of some magnitude demanded verification.

There was gossip amongst the banking groups I was connected with, as well as within the walls of the City Of London Club, where I was also a member, about how the interrelationship between the private bank, owned by Hugh Pickering, and a 'hedge fund,' managed by a splinter-foundation, came about. The gossip came down on this fund being not only managed through a major American internationally renowned bank, with offices in Canary Wharf, but through American government representatives in the Central Intelligence Agency.

The rumours went on to say that on more than one occasion, money from this 'hedge fund' had rescued the financial state of affairs at Pickering's, the unoriginal name of Hugh's private investment bank. I did not mention the allegations to Leonard, simply letting the conversation run its course.

As the Solicitor General speculated on the reasons for Winston's actions, I was left listening and gazing upon the assorted portraits that hung on the walls of his spacious, opulent rooms and wondered how the minds of Clive of India, or Wolfe of Canada fame, would have legitimised committing murder in the name of the Empire. As he finished his weighty analysis of Winston's actions, he returned to his place on the sofa with two glasses of whisky in his hands. One full to the brim with ice; mine.

* * *

It turned out I wasn't entirely wrong about Samantha Burns, but then again, neither was I anywhere near the mark in all the assumptions I'd drawn. One of the points on which I was right was that she did indeed have French blood, coming from her mother. When her mother was in her prime, she was a well-known French singer achieving a considerably high degree of success, but when age caught up to her and the songwriters found the younger performers to be more lucrative, she confined her performances to live audiences in a world-famous night club in Paris, with only a few more records released before she suddenly died.

She had married Samantha's father, Mr Christopher Burns, in May 1989, Samantha being born the following year, which made my estimation of her age, late twenties, spot on. For the first eleven years of her life, she lived in a substantial house on the edge of Parc Georges-Valbon in an area known as Saint Denis in Paris.

It was from there, throughout the early years, that her father would take the Metro into the centre of the city to take up his position as Head of Security at the British Embassy. Four days after Samantha's twelfth birthday, her mother, Maddie, suffered a life-ending heart attack. Christopher no longer had a desire to stay in Paris, surrounded by the memories of his loving wife. He decided to return to England.

He resigned from the English civil service in May 2002 and started in business on his own. He formed a company known as Burns Security, supplying private protection to those who could afford the expensive fees he generally charged. All his employees were either hand-picked from those he had known working in other embassy positions, or came with first-class recommendations.

Rather than occupy a seat in the plush offices he rented in Hanover Square in central London, he preferred keeping his hands in, as it were, working at the coal face. He accepted a lucrative protection contract in Kuwait safeguarding an oil-rich Kuwaiti.

As a consequence of his decision to move to Kuwait, Samantha was left to live with Alice and Edward Burns, her paternal grandparents, in Egham, Surrey. Whilst there, she attended the local grammar school after sitting an entrance exam instead of any nationwide examination. Her early academic years were rewarding, with her advancing from her grammar school to Surrey University, from where her progression continued ever upwards until she was accepted into New Hall, a women-only college in Cambridge University, to study for a degree in Sociology. Notwithstanding her success, all was not well. Abruptly, her life ceased to continue in an elegant, climbing curve.

* * *

At the age of twenty, her world descended into a turmoil from which she may never have recovered, when her father died whilst protecting his Kuwaiti employer, Sabah Al Salim.

The searches I subsequently made not only confirmed what Leonard told me, but enlarged further on this attempt on Sabah Al Salim's life, the one Christopher prevented. The attempt was mounted by two Iraqis with an Iranian, taking place in a suburb of Kuwait City. According to reports I read, the three men were each armed with Tondar submachine guns, which were manufactured in Iran principally for their military personnel.

Christopher shot dead both Iraqis as they approached the vehicle, which was stationary at a red traffic light. The weapons were being discharged towards the Range Rover where, in fact, several hit. The Iraqi man was already at the scene, seated on a motorcycle parked parallel to the car on the kerb. He managed a short burst of automatic fire into the Range Rover, hitting the driver in the upper arm and Samantha's father in the head, killing him instantly, but not before a shot from Christopher's hand gun had shattered the would-be assassin's shoulder. He was arrested at the scene before he could make good his escape, only to die in mysterious, unexplained circumstances whilst in police custody.

Sabah Al Salim had been saved by Christopher Burns' fast reflexes, but be that as it may, the reasons for the assassination attempt were not mentioned, nor was there any speculation in any report I was able to read. Finding nothing more from my research, nor from Sir Leonard, I was left with no more than mere supposition.

I vaguely knew Sabah Al Salim, having met him on a few occasions when I was in the company of his half-brother, Shaikh Al-Sabah. Shaikh and I shared a love of horses, and the faster they ran, the more we enjoyed them. From the few conversations I'd had with the older Sabah Al Salim, I would say although he enjoyed horse racing, he did not share my and Shaikh's love of horses. I never wagered money on the outcome of a horse race. I was raised with a respect for honest work, for the value of an honest wage, and for the elevated position in life the Paterson name had reached. Neither money nor heritage was for a Paterson to waste.

However, I do enjoy the competitiveness of a wager. I confess my guilt of wagering the cost of a dinner in an expensive restaurant with Shaikh on more than one occasion and, as I understood things, I had enjoyed more dinners bought for me by him than I can remember buying for him.

My attachment to horses was well known throughout the circle of associates I moved in, also the fact that I was not a gambling man when it came to money, but as far as I knew Sir Leonard was indifferent to the leisurely pursuit of horse-riding and the light-heartedness of the speculation of the outcome of a race between two horses. I considered it prudent not to mention horse breeding or horse racing until the question of how I knew Sabah arose.

* * *

From what little was available to me, I made the judgement that it was an act of benevolent compassion which compelled Sabah Al Salim to send his private jet to collect Samantha from England, to enable her to take up residence alongside her grandparents in the expansive Kuwaiti complex he called home.

He did not solicit the publicity this attracted, but nonetheless it did.

The publicity that arose was too much for an otherwise quiet girl, forcing her to tell her benefactor how sorry she was for not being able to manage the interviews and fuss. Again, I was speculating that he understood and with that understanding he helped her to change her name from Burns to Marchand, her dead mother's name.

The family house was sold, allowing Samantha Burns, now as Charlotte Marchand, when it suited best, or Burns when it didn't, to move into the spacious luxury apartment owned, under an elaborate shrouding of a nom de guerre, by Sabah Al Salim, and live in an apartment at the Grosvenor House Hotel, a stone's throw away from Gerald Neil's Clocketts club.

* * *

There was no one alive, nor was there any document to disclose when she and Neil became lovers, as that was something which, according to Sir Leonard, was still being investigated, but she joined the French equivalent of our civil service two years before she died.

At the age of twenty-seven, Samantha Burns began her employment in the human resources administration section in the French Embassy here in

London. I cannot say how the interviewers on the French Board conducted their selection affairs, but I'm confident in saying that had it been a British board of selection, then the familiarity she shared with Sabah Al Salim and, as a repercussion, the Kuwaiti Government, that would have influenced the final decision. In the eyes of the English, the French are many things, ranging from obnoxious to magnificent, but one thing they're not is idiotic when it comes to intelligence gathering. In that, they have been one of the best.

I discovered later that one of the reasons Samantha Burns was recruited so easily was precisely because of her connection to Sabah Al Salim. It was suspected by the British secret intelligence service that he was a French asset. That unsubstantiated suspicion influenced the handling of the Samantha Burns case all the way through. Although her career may have been a relatively short one, it was not solely confined to assisting the French. I learned through another source that she had been used by the Ministry of Defence military intelligence, better known as MI5.

CHAPTER SIX

JEREMY FURLEY

"I didn't know this personally, but our sister service, MI5, had a longstanding arrangement with Gerald Neil to gather what intelligence he could from those who frequented his gaming club. It was gossip mainly, I expect, but I'm reliably told that on occasions, certain operations were deemed to be necessary using one or two of the girls who were employed at his club. He had an agreement with an outside agency who supplied the majority of the woman who worked at his premises, but, as I'm sure you understand, not all of them were paid solely to make the place look inviting."

Jerry Furley had been looking beyond one of the windows of his office that overlooked the Thames onto the Houses of Parliament, but after his reflections on Crocketts he turned his chair and looked directly at me, staring in a quizzical manner, as if searching for a reaction. I had none.

"Samantha Burns, for example, Harry, was not from any agency. As far as I can see, she was a girl badly used by so many grubby hands in this sordid business of ours." Again he stared, making me feel uncomfortable.

* * *

The head of the British Secret Intelligence Service, more commonly known as C of MI6, leant back in his maroon leather, reclining desk chair, swivelling it away from me towards the middle of the three windows overlooking the reflecting expanse of the busy river, with sun-drenched pleasure boats drifting besides commercial tugs, vying for their best positions. He rose from his chair, taking the few paces it took to reach the tallest of the windows. When he deemed himself close enough, he turned to face me again and continued.

"We are not sure what came first. Whether Neil introduced her to his club, or her French handler told her to use it, but one of them did and I'm backing the Frenchman. My reasons will come clearer as we go on. Drink, Harry?" he asked, to which I readily agreed. Then, as I sipped my whisky, he continued with his dissection.

"My argument relies on her being told to use

Crocketts when she was promoted from the French Human Resources to personal assistant to a Mr Page Boucher, a fifty-year-old French career spy with a roving eye for a beautiful woman.

Boucher's use of Crocketts coincided with Burns being introduced to the club by Gerald Neil. So, using the line of thought we are known to employ on this floor, we are of the opinion Gerald Neil took the Euro money as well as the proper stuff from us.

Over recent years, I've found this service to be less of pure patriotic spirit than the love of money. It doesn't seem to matter where that money comes from."

He slowly shook his head, mumbling a stifled 'hmm' as though something was disappointing him. He then asked, "Another?", looking at the glass in my hand.

* * *

Jerry Furley, or, to be precise, Jeremy Isaac Furley, had occupied the top chair of the legendary 'C' at the Vauxhall headquarters of the United Kingdom's secret intelligence service for a little over five years and, from what I'd heard filter down, it sounded to me as though he was exactly the same meticulous and careful man I had worked with in Odessa, Ukraine, a major seaport on the Black Sea, when Serena and I were still clinging onto our marriage, with her brand name at the very pinnacle of the fashion business. Her Milan show, a couple of years previously, was the opening to the higher end of the markets she and her cattle-loving, ex-navy, head designer Tanta had worked so hard to achieve.

In spite of her success, or maybe because of it, my fascination dwelt not on her fashion label per se, it was more with the models she engaged to wear the clothes, then later, being without any of her designer clothes.

I lost count of the different girls I shared enjoyable acquaintance with at the fashion displays around the world, but my memory of Odessa is not clouded by them, even though it was there that the word 'divorce' was first mentioned in Serena's screams of irate indignation on discovering one of my indiscretions.

In Ukraine, it was my responsibility to 'hold hands' with a former Soviet Union Vice-Admiral who had a wife who was stricken by Western fashion. My job was to persuade him that the embarrassment he had recently suffered when his superiors refused his written request to accompany his wife to London to enable her to 'shop', could be the blessing in disguise we had previously referred to.

I had met the Vice-Admiral twice over the last year, both times in Russia, to speak of his defection to the West. Incentives and rewards had been finalised, all we wanted was the opportunity. Serena's fashion show was exactly what was needed.

He had conveyed his superior's refusal to his wife's request when attending a staff conference dinner with her in Moscow. It had helped the situation. His wife's disappointment did not impact that night. She and he behaved impeccably. However, being in Odessa when a fashion show was in town presented them both with the chance of not only shopping an exclusive array of clothing, but presented the possibility of never having to face any kind of embarrassment ever again.

By the time of the Odessa show, I'd made friends with many, if not all, of the top figures inside the premier fashion houses of Europe, so it wasn't any trouble for me to get Maria Kovaleva, the wife of Vice Admiral Kovaleva, a preview of that year's dresses and accessories with a hefty discount on the lines catching her eye.

Through the normal commotion of the event finishing, I managed to get Maria Kovaleva onto Serena's personal jet aircraft carrying the identity papers of a German makeup artist, and again, by first using the false papers one of Jerry's departments provided, we smuggled Viktar Kovaleva out of Ukraine, obscured from sight behind the false backing inside one of the lorries carrying Serena's equipment and clothes en route to Bucharest. In the capital of Romania, we were met by Jerry with a couple of heavies from the appropriate internal department.

There had been a few rough edges to be

smoothed away, but generally everything worked well. I was subsequently told that the Vice Admiral provided some top drawer intelligence of great value to us and other NATO members. His wife was already planning a trip to the next Milan show. Back in those days, as now, I was never told any real details.

Although most parts of the subject matter of Jerry's briefing had changed, when it came to the details there was no change.

"Wherever Boucher was stationed, he showed a distinct weakness for beautiful women and that applied here in London when he clapped his eyes on Burns. As you can guess, we were not slow in using that debility of his. Threats to disclose any one of the photographs we had collected of his infidelity to his wife and children, concentrated his wayward mind onto what we, here in GB, wanted from him. Of course, it's from him that I get this perspective.

"We have an operative inside the French government communications Ministère in Paris who notified us of a communication with a folder attached, which contains a file in which the names of several 'illegals' who are engaged by South African intelligence operating in the Middle East appear. Over the years, we've tried to keep an eye on what was happening in Southern Africa, what with the Cubans having a presence in the area and of course, there's the Russians crawling all over the continent.

"To a large extent we've been triumphant. Yes,

good word to use in the circumstances. I do consider us to be at war in some places in the world where interests overlap. However, incursions by the South Africa Secret Service, or, as it is known today, the State Security Agency, SSA, away from home into the Middle East where we have a direct interest in Iraq, Iran and Saudi Arabia, is constantly monitored by GCHQ, as well as the new IOMS system that was instigated after one of your last operations for this agency.

"Until now, we've had no hard intelligence on any of their agents. Our operative was keen for us to know of this file, which is attached to an ordinary email containing the working code names of eight of the SSA illegals, alongside three of their operational handlers' names. One of the latter, we have good reason to believe, is Winston Bottomly. We have to get our hands on it, Harry, and not just in order to spite the French.

"We had our own agents in place in those Middle East countries and could not afford to allow the French to go bungling around with the possibility of exposing operatives or current operations mounted by this country.

"My information is that initially, when in cybernetic form, the information in the encrypted file was unobtainable to our man, but with it being attached to an email it was a different matter entirely. The email we were interested in was due to pass through the French Consular General, then be forwarded on to the French Ambassador. We are told the file contains enough information on how post-quantum cryptography is about to become obsolete."

I must have looked suitably dumbfounded, as the topic of conversation altered course from something abstract becoming obsolete to my seldom in use, tangible brain.

"Yes, Harry, it's called post-quantum cryptography. And yes, the technical people had me baffled as I listened. What it means, in simple terms, is that all sensitive material nowadays that's encrypted on computer files, which we thought was safely guarded from attack, is not safe. Or, actually, in the very near future, it won't be safe.

"I gathered from the aforementioned IOMS unit all the encryption we use, at the moment, has a single algorithm keyword pass, whereas if all's been, or will be compromised, everything will be reclassified as moribund. Imagine that, if you can. Frightening! Everything new will have symmetric key algorithms with several keyword passes, which is far more time-consuming as well as expensive to install. It all makes life in general very difficult, not only for international hackers, but for us as well.

"When we were told the file was being sent on an ordinary email to the Consular, not only were we suspicious of that arrangement, asking ourselves why that was, but we couldn't believe our luck—if it were true!

* * *

There were many questions to be asked and answered before we could make a move. Why, for example, was it going through London? That question couldn't be safely answered until we were able to see inside the thing. The only thing we were able to do was work on what we had been given from inside the French communication hub."

He paused to light his pipe, a straight stem and brown bowl with a black mouthpiece which had rested in a circular ashtray placed above the red blotter on his desk. The ashtray was a simple, plain glass affair, the sort you'd find on any café or on a bar table. Which is exactly where Jerry had found it, in a bar of sorts.

It was a filthy-dirty place where Jerry and I were drinking on the night we learned of an American Admiral taking over all the military authority on behalf of NATO from a French General, when we were all in Bosnia. We were told the change had been made in order to enforce the Dayton Peace Accords.

At last, intelligence reports that we were responsible for would not go through French hands, where we suspected there was a leak to the Bosnian army control. When we left the bar, somehow that glass ashtray had found its way into Jerry's army issue greatcoat. In its own way, it was exactly the same un-prepossessing image Furley portrayed outside of these offices.

Perhaps my persona was also a façade as I was on my fifth, or even my sixth, attempt to give up smoking, but my resolve was too weak. On seeing him lighting the pipe, I removed a cigarette from the packet of Dunhill International I carried, and lit it.

This was the first meeting I'd ever taken cigarettes to. Either I was expecting a long appointment, or confidence in my willpower was already disappearing before I arrived. Maybe it was a bit of both of those things but, as I drew deeply on the cigarette, I knew the satisfaction it gave me was not something I wanted to be without.

As I replaced my lighter in a pocket, he continue with his outline of the situation.

"We believed the contents of the file would have logistical positions itemised in the draft. Apparently, the thing's called a one-way compression function." He sighed just as a big puff of smoke settled above his head.

"Whatever they're called, they would have procedures that were presently in motion as well as forthcoming assignments. We believe there would be the locations of important, permanent resources.

"Present speculation is, it's the son of the French ambassador whose name we think is included in the

index somewhere in this email. We have long suspected his home in Tehran is being used as a safe-
house. If it's true, it could be the reason for it to pass
through London, presumably for the ambassador to
rubber-stamp it. But of course, coming back to what
I've said, unless we have eyes on the contents, there's
no way we could give substance to this hypothesis.

"We instructed Boucher to get it for us. It was to
be a one-time burn, Harry. Something this big meant
using all our persuasive powers we had on him. It ne-
cessitated the return of every bit of incriminating evidence we held. But no matter. It had to be done and
we left him to decide the best way forward.

"Boucher prepped Samantha Burns, who was
ideally placed for this undertaking. On the
Wednesday before the shoot you attended, Burns
downloaded the file from her French Consulate computer. She left it on the system but stopped its immediate delivery to the embassy. First, she made a
physical diversion.

"Page Boucher arrived in England, via Eurostar
from Paris, on the Monday of the same week and took
up temporary residence with an old flame of his at an
apartment block at 199 Knightsbridge, roughly
halfway between the consulate and the embassy.
Using one pretext or another, he made sure all the
equipment necessary for what she had to do was in
position for her at that apartment.

"The folder was opened, then the contents were

downloaded onto a flash drive. When she completed the task, the email was rerouted, allowing it to travel on to the embassy. There was no mention anywhere of the extra ten to fifteen minutes the email had taken, so we assumed our interference had gone undetected. Even so, it left us with a problem, or more precisely, at least two problems."

I interrupted him, as I thought I knew exactly where he was going with his explanation.

"That would be Boucher with his old flame and possibly the owners of the apartment as well. From an operational point of view, they couldn't be allowed to pass on whatever knowledge, albeit the slightest, they had of that file, or the fact that British intelligence had stuck their nose into French business matters, could they?"

"Exactement—as the Frenchies would say, and probably pronounce better than I. Yes, an unfortunate truth in this business is that people get in the way, but it became more earnest when Burns-stroke-Marchand took matters into her own hands. It now becomes guesswork of course, even so it's conjecture based not only on many years' experience, but with the experience of many others in the analysts' department."

He leant across his desk, pressing a button on the telephone console as he did so.

"Would you be so kind, Janet, please? A pot of your finest tea would be splendid at this moment in time. Do you take sugar, Harry? I'm sorry but I've forgotten."

I answered, 'No' to his question, not believing his memory stretched back the enormity of years it would need to the last time we shared a pot of tea, or over the hours preceding this meeting when he'd read my file. So the rumours I'd heard of his supernatural powers of memory did not extend as far as I was led to believe. It would seem he was either human after all, or he was disguising his powers of memory in an attempt to trap me, which I dismissed as fanciful.

Whilst the two of us were discussing the principal cause of death inside our industry, cups of tea accompanied with digestive biscuits, all served on Royal Crown Derby crockery, were delivered to the low, wide, modern coffee table standing between two soft, red velvet armchairs onto which I was invited to sit and listen further to how I was to be used. Although the tea was warm and welcoming, the continuing briefing was neither of those two things. Luckily, there was more whisky to follow.

The feeling I had when Furley ended his analysis of Winston Bottomly was poles apart from what my understanding of him was before I'd arrived. I listened with the same attitude one would adopt when a person who is fractionally known to you decides to disparage the character of a close and dear friend.

No matter how much his scornful dialogue made me glare angrily in his direction, he went further in vilifying Winston's reputation and integrity. His vaulted position precluded any physical retaliation on my part, which was totally out of the question— unless, of course, I had become attracted to some sort of recreational stay in a quiet, damp hole in the ground for the rest of my life.

According to Furley, Bots was spying for a foreign power, albeit a friendly one, his country of birth; South Africa. There, he'd served in differing positions inside the South African Secret Service (SASS) all the time since I had known him, including the years we served together in the Guards.

Jerry's evaluation had taken some appreciable time, so much so that he was on his second pipe and me my umpteenth cigarette by the time my part in the saga was enlarged upon.

I was being asked to spy on a spy, on that much I was clear. What I wasn't clear on was, from where did my invitation come? Jerry had committed the resources from his department of MI6, but the only connection I was to have to MI5 was through the government's Solicitor General.

I presumed I had upset someone. Further assumptions amounted to waiting patiently for a written invitation to mend fences.

* * *

As the contents of the meeting changed, with a conglomeration of muzzy detail being laid out before me by the calm, seated, magisterial Furley, it added a heavy weight to the weakened esteem in which I held Viscount Bottomly. The already dented belief I had of my friend's integrity after Gerald Neil's condemning of him, now seemed fractured beyond repair, but that wasn't all. Jerry Furley had shaken the confidence I had in my own ability to make pragmatic decisions.

CHAPTER SEVEN

MURDER

Before he continued, he apologised for repeating some of his previous observations, the main one being how his department, and beyond, knew Bottomly had murdered Samantha Burns and I was involved in trying to cover it up. He went on to say that my good name, along with the Solicitor General's, was too important to be merely dragged through the press, and morning television. I wasn't sure whether he was being hypocritical or facetious when he said any scandal would not be good *for the general public's perception of Lords and Knights of the realm.*

After that devotion towards me, I was equally miffed when he said I had an unequalled qualification for a specific role. However, he took about thirty minutes or so of waffle before he moved the conversation on to new ground. That came after I asked if the woman in the apartment at 199 Knightsbridge had a name.

The memory I previously mentioned was once again found to be lacking as he needed to thumb through a thin blue file lying to his left on the table. The woman's name was Deborah Simmons, but apart from that and the photographs we had, it was all we knew of her. Later on, the police were able to supply some more information which didn't amount to much. All in all, she remained a bit of a mystery.

MI6 had photographs of Boucher with this woman on the bed of a hotel in Paris taken as late as July, which they had used to persuade him to cooperate. Furley added the dubious note used in the sense of praising his department, but which I found disturbing. He said—*we like to keep in touch with our agents.* He'd asked why I wanted to know the lady's name, and although at the time it was just curiosity moving my lips, it was now something I wished I hadn't.

Despite being judicious not being a strength one would readily say I possessed, I was sensible on a few occasions.

"No reason, Jerry. Just testing your memory, as it were, and to see if I knew the lady."

"Well, did you?" he replied.

"No, I didn't. All the same, you've managed to answer what could have been an embarrassing situation by the use of the past tense."

He made no response to my undisguised accusation. When this meeting began, I'm sure I would have found it difficult to hold back on any feelings of disgust that I might have developed. Be that as it may, I withheld the real reason for my question. I knew Sabah Al Salim owned a property in that relatively new apartment block. I needed to ask the number.

"Out of interest, what was the number of her apartment? Only I did know a titled lady who, when I last saw her, was thinking of buying an apartment there as one had come onto the market. Lady Daphne Constance was her name. Her husband was big in cameras. She was toying with the idea of using a false name to purchase it. Not only so her husband would not know, but also to avoid taxes.

"I thought it was a silly idea, the tax avoidance, not the husband thing, that I thought to be a good idea. I would like to know in case the apartment comes vacant and she does buy it. I might find it distracting to know two people had been murdered in it."

"Good grief, man," he said, as he reluctantly thumbed through the file again. "It was number 75."

That was the address my friend Shaikh Al-Sabah messaged to tell me he was staying at the last time I had visited Paulo Tovarisch in his suite of rooms almost opposite. *'I will be at my brother's apartment at number 199 Knightsbridge. Suite number 75. Call, and we'll have dinner somewhere.*

I'm there until the Sunday afternoon of that week-end.' I can recall the telephone conversation as though it was yesterday, as it was the weekend George Northcliffe's father died.

"Was it that address?" Jerry asked, then followed it up when I was deliberately slow in answering with, "Could it be the same woman?"

* * *

My lie had succeeded in establishing a link between Page Boucher and Sabah Al Salim, a detail that Jerry's department did not know. If not them on a personal level, it at least established the link of Sabah Al Salim and the French government. Although I felt a little boost in confidence, I kept the feeling to myself, simply shaking my head to answer his last question, allowing a petulant look to follow his complaint of wasting his time.

"Right then, if I can get on! We understand Burns was extracting money from Gerald Neil over the circumstances surrounding the death of his ex-wife. From people beyond my normal circle of acquaintances, we have been informed you know something about it, so I'll leave it there and deal with the active problems." His knowledge went further than I had given him credit for.

He continued, "Having blackmailed Neil, why did she not blackmail Bottomly? After all, it's not beyond the realms of possibility that one night, in some bed, he told her his *other* vocation in life."

By the calmness of his voice, it appeared as though any agitation he may have felt after my untimely intervention had disappeared; nevertheless, I couldn't think of a reason why he would want me to sign more official secrets papers, having already been cleared to the highest level. What was in that file that required more signed promises not to commit treason? I wondered. What would knowing those names lead me into?

"Apart from the obscure aliases, along with the technical information that would fly over my head, what sort of information might be in that downloaded file, Jerry?" suspiciously I asked.

"Highly classified stuff, that's what's in there, my friend. It's above what would be normal clearance for this type of intelligence. It's for my eyes and at my discretion only who else sees it. If I decided not to show the PM, then not even he would get to see it. Sometimes the responsibility I have with this job scares the shit out of me. You'll pardon my slip-up there, Harry. Not my normal response."

There was no need for him to ask for absolution. I was well known for the use of profanities in the most unusual situations.

"There is an empty office next door, Harry, where you can take your time reading what we have of the file. From the little bits Gerald Neil was able to remember, with some statistics held on the counter-intelligence, C6, desks, a list of possible matches has been compiled. Possibles, only possibles, because someone operating as an *illegal* makes it virtually impossible to be certain that person will match the coded names.

"Those at C6 section, with the people who specialise in this sort of thing at GCHQ, have had a stab at it, but we're still in the dark. I don't expect you to know how the assumed names convert into real ones, but it's worth a go. Take the list home if you want, but I'm afraid you cannot make notes of information contained in the computerised file.

"All of the electronic stuff stays in-house, at this building. When you finish reading, you will be only the third person we can be certain of who has read it; that's you, me and the PM. It's the ones I'm unsure about that's causing all the worry.

"I must tell you by agreeing to go further, i.e. entering the room next door, you commit yourself back on active duty. And, more importantly, you could be with us for an appreciable amount of time. I would be remiss in my duty if I did not ask if you do fully understand? If you do, then say you do. Nodding your acceptance is no good for the recording machines."

"Of course I understand, Jerry."

He turned the palms of both hands towards the ceiling and his head to one side, imitating the actions of a beggar soliciting money, only Furley needed no money, nor was he in need of any applause for his theatrical display, which was quickly forgotten as he carried on with his lecture.

"There are some more defined nondisclosure documents requiring your signature that you won't have seen before. Came into existence a little while after your last piece of work on behalf of the country. The forms are more punitive than locking a traitor in The Tower of London and throwing away the key.

"Those in the seats of power deem it necessary to place emphasis on worldly possessions now as much, if not more, than the loss of one's liberty. If I'm being slightly too obtuse, then an easier version would be that they'll strip you of everything from your home, from your estate, along with all you own, both here and abroad.

"When they've bled you dry and removed all your titles and privileges, they will unceremoniously throw you into one of the prison cells kept exclusively for traitors on St Helena Island, part of the Ascension Island Group. You get the picture, I hope?

"Before having a look inside the folder, there are some areas we should clear away. The first one being Hugh Pickering, someone who ticks more boxes than not. Even so, he has the same trouble as a lot of his kind, they grow into thinking they're indispensable, particularly to us. Sadly, that is far from that mark. He's dead, Harry.

"Ah! That's the first sparkle of attentiveness

shown on that face of yours for quite a while. I'd almost buzzed the medical rooms for a defibrillator. I had seriously forgotten what a display of attentiveness looked like on you. Why is that so, I wonder?" he asked, with a heavy hint of sarcasm.

"Maybe it's because, apart from looking at people's assumed names, I'm still waiting to be told what precisely you expect me to do?"

He hadn't a chance to reply to my question before his office door opened and the same red-haired, pasty-skinned girl who had delivered the tea and biscuits was at his side, this time pushing a slim green folder across the table in my direction.

"I'm afraid you'll have to sign it before you can enter next door. It's the very latest edition. Those in administration love nothing more than the modernisation of official documents. Open and sign, old chap, then you can be filed away under P with all the other Ps."

* * *

So there was no preamble, no slap on the back along with a cheery 'Glad to have you back on board, old chap. The game was dull without you.' No, none of that. The years roll on, until you no longer notice them go by. There was not even a sniff of alcohol from my would-be-leader to toast the future together. I was officially back in the intelligence regime once more, but not due to a debt of honour in saving a family's reputation over any outstanding money. No, oh no, not that!

It was to be simple retribution with revenge following the equitable, cold, hard gospel, according to the chief 'C' of British intelligence who hadn't finished with me. Quite yet!

"Our thoughts of the situation lead us to believe Bottomly recruited Samantha Burns sometime in the not-so-distant past for the exclusive purpose of infiltrating French security. However, the Russian desk, along with the experts on our Middle Eastern desk, believe Sabah Al Salim not only had Burns, he also has his hands deep into Bottomly's pockets. I would imagine that's not something you will find easy to accept?

"The unnerving part for us is we cannot be certain how much intelligence has been siphoned into this Kuwaiti's ears, nor what the Russians have been told either by him, or Bottomly, who incidentally we must treat as hostile. But by doing so we come across an interesting point, Harry, don't we?"

The look that descended upon his face was far more than the unexacting, questioning gaze he'd previously adopted. It was as if he was accusing me of the treason he'd earlier touched upon. For the first time since I entered The Box, I felt nervous.

"What would that be, Jerry? This 'interesting point' of yours?" I asked.

"I understand you and this Sabah Al Salim are friends? That could put you in a compromising position, if it came to a hard ending."

"I'm not entirely sure what you mean by a hard ending, but I'm afraid your intelligence is not entirely correct. I know Sabah, but not as a friend, purely as an acquaintance. As I believe I've said, fairly recently, I know his half-brother, Shaikh Al-Sabah, far better. We share a love of horses, but as I no longer own a large, or any kind of, racing stable, we haven't met for ages.

"Nowadays, sadly, I have only my own horse and the one my estranged wife would ride if ever she visited the estate. If I'm honest, I'm keeping her horse for sentimental reasons. I'm keeping my own, because I can't stand the thought of having to reduce what's left of the stables to rubble.

"I'm being excessively nostalgic about them, I do realise that, but there is a stable manager with a stable lad who both rely on the job. In the real world I have no need of either of them. However, with them in mind, I've got my estate manager to work with an architect, exploring the possibility of building on what's there and turning it into a riding school. We may be able to employ more.

"I would like to aim for all ages, but especially the young. We would have to add on a few buildings for classrooms, offices, changing rooms, along with other facilities of course. I might even be able to offer an educational kind of thing along the lines of the National Curriculum, if we could find local interest. It could come with a whole range of experiences. It's really quite exciting."

"All very commendable, but I have serious concerns over your ties to Sabah Al Salim, no matter how tenuous. At the moment, our operations in the region seem to be quite fluid. All round, it's a situation we need to firm up as soon as we possibly can.

"My own worries extend to the amount of information this Burns woman may have passed on. C6 are working on the principle that in the past she has been quite lucrative, but not entirely detrimental to us. In fact, on revision, it would appear we have benefitted through the information Gerald Neil has supplied his handlers. Hence our knowledge of Sabah Al Salim and most of his runners and activities, especially where it has any bearing on our business.

"Our cooperation with the Americans is determined by certain protocols, none of which have been broken, but we have expressed some concerns recently about ABCUS counter-insurgency measures with high value targets who could be at risk. We must keep our eye on affairs in the region and that's where I might have need of you."

It seemed to me as though he had drifted away onto something miles away from where we were, when for no apparent reason he stopped speaking. I suspected I was the cause. I'd pulled a puzzled face on hearing the abbreviation ABCUS, as I had no idea what the letters meant. He was distracted by, I suspected, the look on my face. Before the stoppage, his eyes had not travelled away from his tidy desktop, but now they were drilling holes into my own eyes, as if I had become the interrogator. I watched with amused interest as his thick eyebrows rose to meet in the centre of his furrowed brow.

"You said Bottomly had helped us with intelligence about the Middle East, only I'm wondering where exactly he has been of help? For instance, did he know of Sabah Al Salim?"

It wasn't as though I mistrusted Furley. He had a job to do and it probably entailed not telling me everything he knew, but even so, I believed the truth lay in what wasn't being told to me. Before I gave my whole self to this would-be operation, I needed more.

"I would like to get something out of the way, Jerry, and hopefully we can be a bit more truthful with one another. You're right when you said I was complicit in the murder of Samantha Burns. What else could I do? I wasn't going to drop a chum in the shit, now was I?

"If you think I'm going after Bottomly to kill him and retrieve the information you're missing, then unless you provide me with an eminently good reason, which until now you haven't, then I'm not. I knew exactly what you meant by that 'hard ending' rubbish when you were speaking of Sabah Al Salim, but again, unless I have the absolute blessing, in writing, from the relevant departments of state, then I'm not killing anyone.

"I may have stumbled into this international plot through an act of loyalty, but I'm not a fool, so please stop treating me as one. Could we make a start with who instigated the downloading of the file? As far as I can see, your department did not.

"It would be nice to believe your agent in Paris told you, then you told Gerald Neil or Boucher, then whoever told Samantha and hey presto—a file. Clean and easy, eh? Not so. I'm hedging my bets between the five principal suspects: Bottomly, Boucher, Al Salim, MI6, then Samantha working on her own. Are there more?"

He laughed, not loudly, nor soft and empty, somewhere in between, with a smile more polite than sincere. I couldn't read all of his face.

"I can't be more definite, I'm sorry. The latest thoughts are centred on Al Salim ordering it done. Our latest consensus is, you were either lucky or, looked at in a different way, unlucky, with the winter weather in Yorkshire forcing your shoot to be called off. Next came the Bottomly shoot, your next convenient choice.

"You landed on my desk because you rang to confirm your participation. I don't personally know the Solicitor General, Sir Leonard Miles. I know of him, of course, and have met him on official business a couple of times, but to know him in the sense of asking him to do what he's done so far in this affair, would strike me as one helluva good friend to have. You and the Viscount are very fortunate, Harry, in more ways than one. Please don't read anything into that remark as there is no hidden meaning, it's just an observation, nothing more."

"Don't flatter me, trying to side-track the conversation. It's answers I'm after. For example, if, as you have said, Winston helped this country with intelligence interpretations, then why would he need the exclusivity of that file? Your analysis suggests he would know the categorisation of the names you're concerned with, so why not share the information with you? Please tell me if I'm missing something there, won't you?"

"My, my, you are the impatient one. Of course Bottomly would have known who the codes referred to, or at least he would have more of an idea than we have. He would have certainly shared the knowledge with us, had it not been for some specific outside events happening in the same timespan in which this affair happened."

He rose from his chair to stand and stretch out his arms as near as possible to ninety degrees away from his shoulders, then pulled them backwards, rotating both arms and shoulder joints. When he finished, he let out a sudden exclamation of satisfaction.

"You will have to slow down, Harry. I'm getting there, old chap, but in my own time, please."

I was expecting him to sit, but he didn't. He stood where he was, turning slightly, just enough to see out of the side windows to the office. At the same time, I could see he was looking at me through a corner of his eye.

"The anti-terrorism desk has worked up a model showing Burns assisting Bottomly to clear his monetary debt by agreeing to Gerald Neil's request to supply him with the French data on the South African operatives working inside foreign sovereign territory. It may be only circumstantial, but we do have evidence that shows that to be the case, Harry."

It's possibly my fault, only this gave Jerry the chance to show just why he was suited to the role of a fastidious administrator; he loved detail.

"Let's recap on where we are. We were first alerted by our asset inside the French Embassy, in Paris. He informed us of a folder attached to an email, inside which was a file containing the coded names of South African illegals operating where we had interests. Right?" His eyes opened wider, inviting an answer from me to his implied question. I nodded dutifully.

"Later that day, he contacted us again to say the email had been digitally encrypted in such a way that it showed evidence of the file having being downloaded onto an external hard drive. The French were looking no further than their courier, one Charlotte Marchand. Which then shone a very bright light on the whole selection process. Marchand, you see, not Burns. Each name was missing, as initially was Boucher. It took a spot of time to trace Page Boucher, who was able to verify the authenticity of the report. That was our sole aim at first—to trace him.

"When he was eventually found, he was in his lover's apartment with his throat slashed, lying next to a women who was also dead. They had been professionally executed, but not before Boucher had been tortured, severely, after being injected with Rohypnol.

"With your qualifications in chemical analysis, you will know what that anaesthetic-inducing drug will do. That all took place on the Thursday evening before your shoot on the Bottomly estate, to where you had yet to travel. As the timeframe was of a sizeable magnitude, we decided to keep away and watch what the French decided to do.

"Later that Thursday evening, just before midnight, Marchand surfaced. Using that surname, she ordered a cab in order to contact Gerald Neil. She offered him the download. Why him? We can only guess it was for Bottomly's debt, but we don't know for sure. Whilst she was with him, she stressed the importance of what it contained. But this office has not had as much as a glimpse at it!

"As I've told you, Gerald Neil did have a peep.

From this point we are working on what he told us. According to him, the file contains the five coded names we are interested in, but that's all he says he remembered. The codes. What he knew of the coded names was passed on to cyber analysis, at the same time being sent on to the code deciphers you've used in the past at the National Cyber Security Centre. I'm told NCSC were completely flummoxed by it. In their view, they are clean and virginal. It would appear the only one who can put names to those codes is Viscount Bottomly.

"This where it gets a bit fruity. The use of something so uncontaminated as these codes appear to be, when used by anything close to being classified as an enemy, is normally viewed as a precursor to a major operation. Not just as penetration or incursion, Harry, something far more septic. If you put that conclusion next to the technical content, already a cause of massive consternation, then you have acute alarm —it's ulcer time for us who worry. We are unable to say if this is terrorist or government instigated, but whoever is behind it all is causing us to lose sleep."

I judged the look on his face to be one of genuine concern as he adjusted the position of his seat before sitting and continuing with his analysis.

"Our interests in the areas where it's believed these illegals could be functioning are critical and utterly indispensable. We cannot be exposed by a 'friendly' nation, or an enemy one. It's the same risk."

"If Gerald Neil had his hands on the file, do tell me again what happened to it, Jerry?" I asked, thinking I knew the answer before I had heard of its disappearance.

"It was returned to Marchand. She allowed Neil to see into it, and that's all. Or more precisely—read page two of a document containing four pages. She then took it back."

I jumped in before he'd quite finished."And Gerald Neil allowed this to happen? Was he over-powered by a woman? Is that the type of man military intelligence use today?" I sniggered in derision.

"If you are to interrupt me, do so at a point where I've concluded my breakdown of the situation, please, and refrain from stupidity. It's tiresome otherwise."

Duly chastised, I assumed the role of a studious schoolboy sitting upright and concentrating as the tutor guided me through what little was known of the activities of the so-called illegals, the name used for South African mercenaries, operating in parts of Africa and the Middle East.

My friend Winston Bottomly was suspected of being heavily involved in both their recruitment and their training, especially how to transmit information or communicate face to face when necessary. In essence, he acted as the control, as well as the handler, for all six. Jerry's MI6 had gone to elaborate lengths to elicit more of the missing information, drawing a dead end with all of them.

CHAPER EIGHT

NEXT DOOR

According to the file I was allowed to see, C8, a section of MI6 devoted solely to the interpretation of reactions shown to particular words, thought it was the mention of a terrorist group named Daesh, along with its acronym of ISIS, that spooked Bottomly into keeping the download of the file he had from Burns. Even though it was circumstantial, it was a reason that could not be discounted.

Another circumstantial involvement was that of Hugh Pickering. The name of his private bank appeared on an appendix where the Central Intelligence Agency was mentioned as controlling two operatives in a group known as Islamic State of Iraq, the Islamic State of Syria, and the Islamic State of the Levant, with highlighted payments going through a London private bank named Pickering's.

There were a few vague references to the Kuwaiti, Sabah Al Salim, here and there, acknowledged by no signature, with nothing concrete linking him to either Samantha's death or any other person connected to the affair. Perhaps it was only my imagination playing tricks, but I could not rid myself of the thought that I was being permitted to see only a proportion of this story.

Despite my previous knowledge of the man and the experience I'd had of working for both intelligence services, I could not remove the suspicion, lodged deep inside my congenitally suspicious mind, of Furley having sanitised what I read.

I catalogued those apprehensions for another day and perhaps another line of inquiry; after all, he who pays the piper calls the shots as it were, and it was Furley's MI6 who wanted to pay me and, presumably, provide the gun.

As I read on, I came across a report from the agent Jerry had inside the Paris Ministry of French communications that made for very compelling reading. It was here where he notified the duty officer at Vauxhall of the email being copied.

The device revealing the tampering of the email had been standard equipment inside every French embassy, as well as intelligence stations along with government and police stations; anywhere in fact where email traffic was a method of constant communication.

Presumably Samantha Burns knew this, as it was common knowledge. Therefore why download the file, unless she had a plan—but what plan ends so disastrously? She certainly hadn't planned to have her head shot off at the weekend. Maybe there was a Samantha Burns and Sabah Al Salim game-plan waiting to play, which was wrecked by a Purdey shotgun? I couldn't see past a brick wall.

* * *

According to information from Boucher, whose assassination was not speculated on, Samantha was deployed directly from the headquarters of the General Directorate for External Security, the French equivalent of our MI6 agency, with them detailing Boucher to take the reins as her control, but with External Security delegating the everyday handling of her field work to be overseen by an unspecified person of the Trade Consular General at the French Embassy in London. No matter what lists I looked at, I could find no further reference to this Trade Consular General, in any of the files on French sections.

If a race of people could be described as enigmatic, then my understanding of the French would be justified. But that cannot explain at all the French disregard of specifics, which is not a characteristic I find can be levelled at 'La France' in general. There were a couple of conclusions I was able to draw. I went for the second. The first was that the department in question was part of Boucher's imagination to disguise Samantha's purpose, while the second was that the name of this non-existent department had been planted in Boucher's mind by a sinister player, as yet on the periphery of this game; Sabah Al Salim.

The French, in Boucher's words, were not playing a friendly game of boules with Samantha Burns, who wore the classification badge of de Procédure Fumigateur, one of two such labelled women and, going by the photographs I was shown, both very beautiful. One enormous omission from Jerry Furley's briefing had been, what was the French objective for employing Samantha?

There was no way I could determine if External Security's interest in Samantha Burns was as Boucher said, but at least that department did exist. Look as I did, there was no sign of a Trade Consular General anywhere! There was another question yet to be answered and that was—why would a world power such as France allow an underqualified person such as Samantha Burns anywhere near highly classified material like this email?

I thought the answer lay in the reason why the department designated as Samantha's control, called the Trade Consular General, did not exist and why employ her in the first place if it was not to strengthen ties to a well-connected Kuwaiti such as Sabah Al Salim? Page Boucher was a known inveterate liar who developed an ability to use deception on a world stage, not just in his marital affairs, only this time keeping the lie about the existence of a Trade Consular General might have cost him his life.

I was about to leave the rest of the screen unread as my eyes were tiring, but my analytical work had taught me how perseverance was the only difference between success and failure. It was as I was giving those tired eyes a tender massage, imagining a softer hand rubbing against my face, that my eyes fell upon what appeared to be the un-coded name of a man the French had working as a technician inside the Iranian Atomic Energy Organisation.

Further along the page was the coded name of an operative the French had managed to conceal inside a Middle Eastern intelligence agency; unfortunately it did not say which agency. The next item contained the membership details of another French illegal. This man was on the staff of a serving minister of the Islamic Governing Party of Iran.

I continued to scroll down the screen, coming to a section under Furley's signature. It was headed:

Summary

The intelligence services were made aware of the existence of a French file containing information on digital conversion, including its expansion into post quantum cryptography. We also knew it would contain the working code names of French illegals in regions of the Middle East where we too would have working operatives.

We were given the impression the French were also in possession of a record of South African illegals operating in various parts of Southern Africa. With the withdrawal of Cuban forces, Russian advisors with Angolan terrorists in tow, we assumed any South African interest would decline, even so the file would be a major trophy for future referrals. We had posted instructions to intelligence assets to be vigilant, acting with due diligence to source this file.

Copies of both documents would obviously be of interest to us as this country has extended political interests in Africa, as well as a duty to safeguard the interests of our allies in NATO.

The feasibility of the above actions became a viable option when I was directly informed by GCHQ of the flash signal traffic emanating from the French Embassy in Knightsbridge ratcheting up tenfold during the late evening of Wednesday the ninth of August, overlapping into the early hours of Thursday morning. I was further told of the top-floor General Directorate staff of the French intelligence service, Paris headquarters, still entering the building at a little after two o'clock on that Thursday morning.

Classifications in the first three IOMS deciphered signals from our Paris agent, indicated the files collected but still missing from the consulate contained material less sensitive than departmental heads of any French Directorate would deal with in normal time, let alone being called in to examine. The head of the French Dispatch department in Paris, posted a password up on the screens setting wheels in motion and hey presto: ping goes all our warning structure. Our composition is geared in such a manner that certain numerical codes will automatically notify senior members of the government along with chief civil servants, as well as heads of particular stations.

* * *

The 'Why' to Samantha's infiltration into French secrets was inked in as 'next' on Jerry's 'active' agenda. To any interested onlooker, it appeared as though Page Boucher had introduced Samantha into Bottomly's life with the same purpose everyone else had: to gain information into closed-off areas of international interest, and it was to that end Boucher was tutoring Burns.

With the benefit of hindsight, perhaps her schooling was too thorough. By this time, I had re-entered Jerry's office with the intention of having a last whisky before a weary journey to Chester Square. I poured two glasses without waiting for an invitation then, without thinking clearly, asked a question.

"Did you know of the coincidence between this Burns woman and Winston Bottomly?"

"I'm not sure I do, no. Is there one?" he replied, distracted by finding nothing in his memory.

"They were both adopted, of sorts." Quizzically, he looked at me before replying, "I knew that of the Marchand woman, of course, but not of Bottomly. There's nothing recorded in his service papers. Surely it would be there if he was."

"He told me when we were on one of those boring post-operational leave duties when everyone's climbing the walls due to being confined to barracks. His adoption came about way back in time, in those days when there was nothing unusual for the landed gentry, in this case the Duke of Bath, to spend years away from England in one of Great Britain's dominions, or would-be conquests.

"In the Duke's case it was India and later, Southern Africa. He spent the first part of his time with the Honourable East India Company, where he made astronomical wealth from diamond and gold mining before finally settling in South Africa, to set up home.

"Back in the eighteenth century, one of the Duke of Bath's daughters had a son born out of wedlock. Apparently, tut, tut, the father was a house footman. Any scandal that could have arisen would have ruined the girl with the gossip. After consideration of all the facts, the Duke was left with no option; he adopted the boy as his own, his wife having failed to give birth to an heir to the family name. And so, down through the passage of time, came the Viscount we have today. The one you're alleging to be an enemy of this country, as well as the murderer I'm supposed to have saved, that you now want dead. You have him, and me, in your vice."

"Where on earth did that come from, Harry? That's the second time you've implied yours and his insecurity. Nobody is suggesting anything like that. What we want is relatively simple; the identity of the operatives South Africa have in the areas where we have an interest. If he had anything on the encryption business, that's a bonus we'd love."

He went for another keep-fit stroll around the expansive office as I suddenly appreciated how having a large office was probably his personal requirement in the design. His stroll didn't last long.

"Another drink or coffee, Harry?"

I opted for the coffee, as I needed as clear a head as possible to decipher all I'd been told. Had I really asked the question of killing Bots before? Perhaps I was losing part of my own memory. Trying hard not to feel sorry for myself, I watched Jerry summon the refreshments from a wooden console matching the imposing ash-veneered desk, but without its magnificent golden marquetry. It wasn't long after going through the repositioning routine of his chair before the coffee arrived. Maybe, I thought, if I had a routine my memory might improve.

"Somewhere along the timeline of this collapse of French security, I was notified by the duty officer on the counter-terrorism floor that our asset inside the French Government offices had discovered the name of his government's operative who had a direct correlation to the cell we have inside Iraq. If there was a leakage of information naming him or, perish the bloody thought, anyone inside our group, it would be catastrophic for the intelligence services of both France and this country.

"This Daesh, ISIS group, we've mentioned, is growing in strength as well as in its authority. If they ever got word of our effectiveness in detecting objectives, then the ensuing mess to our dominance would take decades to overcome. That's if it ever could be completely cleaned up. Incidentally, something I've been meaning to ask. Doesn't Bottomly's father permanently reside in South Africa, nowadays?"

Is he really losing his memory the same as me, I wondered? Not being a strong believer in coincidences I doubted that.

"The father, no, Jerry. He died about three or more years ago, but you're right about the family being there. I'll take another drink now, if it's okay with you. If we're both losing our memory, we might as well drink the ship dry as the wheels come off."

He was laughing as he pressed the same button on the console. The ice arrived as he was pouring the two glasses.

"The Bottomlys sold their possessions in India when that country was granted independence. I guess it went against the grain, so they upped roots and left for South Africa. The present Viscount was a young boy when their holdings were sold off, but by that time he had made great friends with Mountbatten and the equally aged Prince Charles, who was a fairly regular visitor to the Viceroy's residence. According to what Bots told me, the family still have investment property in Hong Kong that they are quite worried about."

"Ah, now I see how you got the information you wanted, from a member of Prince Charles's staff. Are you and he on speaking terms? By that I mean Prince Charles, of course," he added, to avoid confusion, then, without waiting for a reply, he carried on with his interpretation of what had occurred with the French.

"A redacted list of what the French lost was rolled out to us and we readily agreed to the French request of allowing them to clean up their own mess. As this had all happened on our ground, we left it to Special Branch to approach them through diplomatic channels, asking for the name of any person involved in order to alert Border Controls.

"At first, they hedged a bit, but sense prevailed,

and the name was readily given up. But, to our complete and utter wonderment, they wanted to play a waiting game with Miss Burns-stroke-Marchand, allowing her the freedom to roam around London. Be that as it may, young Bottomly did not agree. Why do you think that difference of opinion might have arisen, Harry?"

"Hmm, perhaps he didn't want any name to circulate further than it already had."

"Yes, that's where we're at."

Adopting the now regular, scrutinising facial expression, with his downy, cherry-coloured cheeks lined by the strain the years of responsibility had taken, he stared at me, searching for the answers I did not have. I sat listening to him reciting from his cerebral script, maintaining Samantha had first shown the download to Gerald Neil before it got as far as Winston. The next disclosure came as a shock, but looking back, as I'm now able to do, it shouldn't have.

"Samantha Burns was captured on several of the static cameras entering Pickering's Hampstead home on the Thursday before the shoot. His body was found early on the following Tuesday morning, impaled on the iron railings on the ground floor of a house a short distance away in Primrose Hill. One person who certainly never killed him was Miss Burns. Nevertheless, as I say, she had been a visitor.

"Apparently, there was a delivery from a UPS van, the Monday evening following the weekend shoot, at just after eight to the Hampstead home. The UPS delivery van was not legitimate. UPS have no record of a vehicle with that registration. From then on we are, I'm afraid, literally in the dark.

"All the cameras operating at the front of the house were disabled an hour or so after that time, presumably to make the escape. It was a feeble system, with no reputable end-server other than a recording device that was found on the premises hidden behind some panelling on the landing. It was examined by the Met. Police forensic department, resulting in sweet nothing.

"Needless to say, no photographic evidence was discovered. All was decommissioned. There was an alarm system in both homes, neither of which was operating. At this stage, we do not know if they were armed, or if they had been tampered with before or after the event.

"The police found one neighbour who reported seeing a man in UPS overalls pushing what he called a 'sack trolley' with a large cardboard box on it. It looked heavy, he said. He did say he thought it was suspicious, as the vehicle was parked in the drive next door to his house for a good twenty minutes. Whilst being interviewed he was asked why he never reported it at the time and he said he lived a quiet life and didn't want to get involved.

"The police are working on the assumption he was taken from Hampstead to the house in Primrose

Hill in the back of the fake UPS delivery vehicle, the image of which has been captured by the six traffic cameras placed on the direct route between the two properties. The time it was last recorded was at 9.14 that night. But..." What followed was a heavy sigh, followed by a pause, followed by the reason for the heavy sigh,

"There's no worthwhile photograph of the driver. The distance between the two houses is no more than three miles, that's my estimate talking to you here and now, so don't quote me on it. The time difference is just over an hour, so, roughly a three-mile journey after drugging and lifting a... big man, was he, Harry?" I simply nodded. "Yes, I thought so," he said, then continued.

"There were signs of a heavy weight being dragged through the house. That leaves a good hour unaccounted for at the Hampstead end. His body was not found until 4.20 am. It's a quiet part of London, is Primrose Hill. The police found a burnt-out van, similar to the type used by UPS, on some waste ground underneath the Westway in Shepherds Bush.

"Why Burns went to see Pickering on that Thursday is open to all kinds of speculation, as is why take Pickering to Primrose Hill, but we do have some clues already floating in the cauldron. The day following on from the misappropriation of French property, Gerald Neil told Burns he had a photograph of a Russian playing away from house rules. We know this is the truth because military intelligence told Neil the story.

"That's what it was, Harry, a story concocted by Five. There was no Russian, nor had Gerald taken any photograph. All was fabricated. Burns went to Neil with a copy of the download, willing to trade. Why, is a question we have no answer to, but trade they did. But Neil was too slow. He reported how he went to find his phone to photograph the bloody thing Burns had brought, but couldn't find it. The phone, that is. Burns was jumpy, so he said, she couldn't wait. She ran!

"We're attributing that as the reason Burns went straight from Gerald Neil to Pickering's house in Hampstead to tell him the news. It sounds plausible to us. Pickering, not unnaturally, wanted the name of the Russian, or his companion.

"Conjecture, I know, but she told Pickering of Bottomly's debt to Gerald Neil. He in turn offered to pay off Gerald and free Bottomly if he could get the names in the file and the photo. But, as you now know, there was no Russian in any photograph. It left Neil in the proverbial, unless, of course, he got a copy of the file.

"When we were told of this encryption business, we had to stop the file from finding its way onto any-one's shopping list. It wasn't rocket science to figure Boucher would be involved somewhere along the line. We made an approach to him whilst he was at his home in Paris. By this time in his life he was divorced, but he still had four children to provide for and who would like to think of him as a good, patriotic father, not the man he really was. We worked our magic, persuading him to give us what we wanted in exchange for the photographs we'd collected down the years on his philandering habits and thereby maintain the display he had portrayed to his nearest and dearest.

"We also agreed to keep the French intelligence authorities in the dark about his participation. This is where things spun around a bit. He alleged that the whole affair with Charlotte Marchand, aka Samantha Burns, had been set up years ago by her Kuwaiti benefactor, Sabah Al Salim. Nothing to do with anyone in French intelligence. Al Salim made Boucher the mother-hen of everyday work conditions for Burns with him, Sabah, watching and monitoring all communications, in and out, waiting for one particular email from a hybrid critical IP address attaching an encrypted collection of coded names appearing on an attached file. The secret was not just hidden in a file. It was hidden in the script! That information was not known at first by Boucher; on the other hand it may have been known to Marchand-stroke-Burns.

"Boucher believed someone was pushing Salim's buttons, with him simply providing the money for the operations and legitimising the legend that was essentially Samantha Burns. When we spoke to him, he denied having knowledge of where the file could be. Incidentally, when we left him he was alive. We were working on a remote access link to the computer Burns used in the French embassy in London. Untraceable, state-of-the-art thing through the IOMS project.

"Over time, Boucher was very useful in showing French weaknesses in various HP technologic areas as well as in HC3 areas. Our people were suitably excited, whetting their appetite for the incoming file. When this blessed thing never arrived, the specialists busied themselves looking back over what Boucher had provided. They came to the conclusion that all he'd said about Sabah Al Salim was correct. It was he who sanctioned Burns in this operation. This was later confirmed—unequivocally.

"We had dismantled the Iraqi group when the first signals emanating from Paris were authenticated. We were in the process of withdrawing our man and repositioning his section when the news reached me of your belated acceptance of Bottomly's invitation to the shoot. It was because of your acceptance we exerted a little pressure. I'll be honest with you, Harry, your name had not crossed my desk up to that point, but when it did we went into overdrive. In regards to the French, they were still giving Burns free rein and who better to shadow her than her fiancé.

"Bottomly's proposal of marriage to Burns had

come by way of his own volition, before all this occurred. We had not asked for a favour. It did not come from us, nor from Pickering. What we can't be sure of, is if this Al Salim did not persuade Burns to exert some feminine pressure on Bottomly. You may be the only one, apart from the Viscount, who would know if he would be susceptible to such a move by a woman.

"It looks as though your chum was in love with the girl. Notwithstanding the obvious, we had our doubts, as we are paid to have doubts where two people like them are concerned. We had cause to investigate and again turned up a surprise. Burns had a casual affair with Pickering. This, what could be festering, information was discovered in the most insecure place imaginable; on her work computer, and that is where we are able to confirm Salim's participation. Bear that in mind, my friend, because I'm of the mind, it's important. I knew you would never mention a sum of money to your friend Bottomly. A long way from a thing a gentleman does, isn't it, pass comment on what's owed as a gambling debt?"

CHAPTER NINE

I'M OF THE MIND, IT'S IMPORTANT

It was a few years before Minsk when I had first came across Jerry Furley in an encampment outside Srebrenica, Bosnia, in late June 1995. In those days, he was a Lieutenant Colonel attached to the Royal Netherlands army, in a logistical support tactical unit, part of the United Nations Protection Force, and I was the Guards Captain in charge of the multinational communications hub. To say the least, it was a hectic set of circumstances. To summarise, we were expected to pinpoint local hostilities whilst overseeing the withdrawal of Dutch troops and at the same time denying that an assembly of NATO aircraft were on the ground, waiting for instructions to attack the Bosnian Serb army.

The political will to stop the massacre was nonexistent. Our company headquarters were the same as every other operational HQ, impotent. A ranking soldier is used to indecision from above because the soldier does not understand all the facts, but usually Lieutenant Colonels do have possession of the facts, or at least some of the facts. Not so Jerry, and the frustration showed.

The way he sat back in his leather chair behind the magnificent desk in his superbly appointed office thousands of miles away from any encampment in the mud, sheltering from the rain, waiting for orders, reminded me of those days. And I wondered what could have made him annoyed enough to say: I'm of the mind, it's important. It wasn't long before I found out.

"We had leverage over Pickering, as well as this woman, Burns, when we found out they had been involved in an affair. When we were satisfied this engagement was real, Gerald Neil cornered the Viscount and told him his fiancée had not only conducted a sordid affair with Hugh Pickering, but she had evidence of him, Gerald, consorting with another man: not true.

"He put it to Bottomly that his one and only way out of debt was to murder the love of his life: Miss Burns. We cannot be sure which offer twisted your friend's arm the most, be it Neil's offer above Pickering's, when that materialised, or vice versa, but insert the words 'chivalry' and 'lack of loyalty' into the equation and we probably have a decent enough answer as to whom he sided with. Everything fell into place when you arrived on the scene. One of your strengths is your loyalty, Harry. It's something that's hard to find, nowadays. I knew what would occur on the shoot if, as seemed most likely, Bottomly decided to end the life of Samantha Burns."

Again he sat examining me. Allowing for what he had just said to sink in, I wondered if there was a need? I'm of the mind, it's important. Yes, it was important! It was not a pleasant feeling to know the innermost values you place on life were known to the degree I showed that day. My loyalty at the scene of a murder. After a short period of silence while proving his point, he returned to the conversation.

"Some interesting up-to-the-minute intelligence has come into our possession courtesy of our Paris asset. I'm in no mind to share it with other allies, having given due regard to the geopolitical positions of some.

However, we must keep you abreast of the facts, because of what's being asked of you. This puts you in a privileged position, but unfortunately it's also one that carries a dangerous risk. Let me explain."

* * *

And so he did. According to the intelligence he had, using it to brief me, the French had investigated all of Page Boucher bank accounts, finding some unusual deposits. From these investigations it appeared Sabah

Al Salim had been financing Boucher for several years. Sabah had notified Boucher, who in turn notified Burns when the file that was causing so much ballyhoo was in transit. The intelligence did not cover two main issues: from where Sabah heard of the file's transit, and what was Winston's role in this complex intrigue.

That's where I came in. With Jerry Furley advising, it was the decision of the Joint Intelligence Committee to send me after Bottomly, to, in Furley's words, 'size him up'.

In departmental language, it meant discovering if he had anything from Burns. Did he have the file, or a copy of it? If he did, then see if he wanted to trade with us. They also wanted all he had on the so-called Black Vault illegals operating in Afghanistan, Iraq, and Iran. It was understood, by the JIC, Bottomly had an acquaintance who might have some leverage within Pakistan intelligence, at a high level. That was highlighted in the report. Said to be a nice present for him to share with us.

As an incentive they were willing to trade up to a certain level if he had silver-lined, platinum material. Ask nicely, was my instruction. It was then tempered by, You are to be issued with a service side arm. Carry it at all time. Use at your own discretion.

My journey home had been delayed by a mountain of questions that needed answers, but before I could utter another word Jerry pressed a concealed button under the desk top, ushering in two men I did not know. They sat, one each side of him, in the middle of the long, polished table at the opposite end of his office to his desk. I was ushered to sit facing the three of them. As the two strangers were introduced, they each withdrew laptops and official forms from the bags they deposited beside their chairs.

"These two gentlemen represent the legal side of the intelligence industry, much different from your day. Sadly, nowadays it's digital before being stored away a hundred feet under the Thames where the whisky is bolted up. Apparently there is a special tunnel packed full of empty bottles.

"Everything is done on paper today, Harry, but this is just a preliminary meeting for us to exchange pleasantries, old chap. The legality of future actions, with protocols, together with the rules governing any physical engagements, will be covered by these two gentlemen. In the event of you, or anyone you are in company with, killing any other person, both on UK soil, or on foreign soil, you will be covered.

"You must understand how serious your recent unethical behaviour could appear if made known on a public forum. They are here to make sure no disclosure can be made."

What on earth was he talking about! I had added my signature yet again to the Official Secrets bits and pieces Act. So was I being set up here? My expression must have changed because it drew an unexpected postscript from Furley.

"You cannot surely expect the secret services not to be somewhat circumspect when it comes to dealing directly with you. Of course, what you did a few years back was of great service, but your findings caused quite a few very large waves throughout government circles and establishments, not least this one.

"That memory lingers on. Those in the seats of power fear you, Harry Paterson. They want me to tie your hands up so tight that if, perish the thought, you discover I'm spying for Russia, you can only tell me. I'm lying, of course, but I'm not lying about how much you're feared, Harry. Be cautious, my friend. You do not have many allies, let alone friends in this secret world of ours.

"With your permission, and with the recording devices of these machines switched on, I want to divert our powwow somewhat. Gerald Neil is still AWOL. When he was acquainted with the some of the facts I've explained to you, the precaution of fitting a tracking device to his car without his knowledge was taken. The logic behind it was a concern for his safety. Rightly so, it seems, although procedure could have been applied differently.

"After leaving his home on the night he was apprised of the situation, his chauffeur drove him straight to the club in Mayfair. He stayed until a few minutes past two in the morning. That pattern, with a slight diversion which we know of, was repeated on Thursday, but on Friday he left his club early at around ten-thirty and was driven straight to Bath to confront you over the debt Bottomly had incurred." His engineered studious gaze preceded my questioning stare.

"Is that another one of your bemused looks? Or are you wondering if a government department such as mine perhaps had something to do with Gerald Neil's disappearance? Let me carry on for a while longer before you agonise about those things, unnecessarily, I would add and nor do I require any comment.

"Neil left the Bottomly estate around seven in the morning on the Saturday, driving to his home just outside Bagshot in Surry. It's understood this was not his plan; nor was it what he told you. 'Stay for the Saturday shoot and then leave on the Sunday.' That did not happen. At home, his car never left the drive for the whole of Saturday. We were expecting him to leave for the Isle of Wight by at the latest mid morning Sunday, but we were monitoring the vehicle outside way after the racing had started at Cowes.

"A couple from Military Intelligence were despatched and arrived to find Gerald's driver and housekeeper both dead. Gerald was missing. There were no signs of any struggle near either body, both of whom were shot once in the head and once in the heart by soft-nose shells. As you would expect in the circumstances, the casings of the bullets were not found.

"There was the trace of a recent tyre track imbedded into the grass verge leading to a 'way-out' gate. The police assessed it to be the escaping vehicle, with the killer, or killers, inside, mounting the verge in haste. The local police and officers from this department are developing that lead and at the moment it's believed those tracks were made by a light van, rather than a car. Not much help, is it, but it's all we have. We're hoping you could go over the conversation you and Gerald had on Friday night and come up with some idea why he left the company before the shoot started on the Saturday morning."

"I'm sorry, Jerry, but no, I've no idea. Like you I thought he was off for the sailing at Cowes on the Sunday. He made a big thing of telling me how he had the honour to ring the start bell, but as far as I knew he was with the rest of us for the shoot on the Saturday. I did see him and Bots talking on a balcony early that morning and I overheard him saying the words to the effect of getting Samantha out of Winston's life whichever way he could. With the benefit of hindsight, it didn't sound as if Gerald meant just dump her.

"Obviously something had spooked him. Which brings me round nicely to your veiled threat about the gun Samantha blew her head off with. I can't believe you're threatening me, because if that's the case, you're also threatening the government's present Solicitor General who is complicit in any deception. He testified on oath, there was a 'live' cartridge in an unfired barrel of the gun."

"Yes, you're right, Harry, he did say that, didn't he? And there was one. The thing is, though, the cartridge did not match any of those in the ammunition pouch Miss Burns was carrying. It did, however, carry the same maker's marks as the ones you were using. Indubitably, the answer is simple. It must have been mixed up with those in the boxes that Bottomly gave her. But then, you see, Sir Leonard never examined the shell case.

"We are merely discussing our mutual acquaintance, one Gerald Neil, and the events that happened at Bottomly's estate. If you have finished, may I carry on?"

I simply nodded my acquiescence after hesitating for a moment. The difference in the shell case was something I hadn't thought of and I should have. I hoped he didn't think I was being in any way petulant. I was being nothing but genuinely concerned. I had no difficulty believing in Furley's integrity, but I did have trouble granting the same trust in those yet to appear on the scene. The cartridge case was a blunder I hadn't foreseen. I was brought down to earth by Jerry's next question.

"When you met Gerald Neil in the library, did he ask if Pickering had arrived at Devonish House?"

"No, not that I recall. But Samantha pointed Pickering out to me when I first approached her at the lunch with the champagne flowing. Something about a party he'd held." I smiled at the memory. "Looking back on the day, she acted slightly odd when she pointed him out to me."

"Odd? How odd would you say?"

"Nothing specific that I could put a finger on. Just a change in her demeanour. Before his name cropped up, she was vivacious and charming, but when she pointed him out she became a bit withdrawn, but it didn't last. I had no idea of their previous flirtation, but now I do know, I realise it could have been the reason."

"From an infinitely deniable conversation Bottomly had with Sir Leonard, your ex-army pal was adamant you would replace the missing cartridge solely because of your sense of loyalty. He also thought you would use the fact of the Solicitor General being present to add weight towards the conclusion of it being an accident. He was right, and now we must call on your loyalty to the Crown, Harry. Can we count on it?"

I must be honest here and admit to feeling overwhelmingly patriotic, belittled by such a request yet excited beyond imagination. Of course he could, but I wasn't going to cave in so easily. Besides, I wasn't completely sure I'd heard the whole story up until now.

"Who makes up the 'we' in all of what you have been on about, Jerry? I'm sure it's not your intention to hide them away, but I'd like to know who needs my loyalty the most, and in what way. I've followed you, of sorts, up to the point where Winston does away with Samantha, but it's still unclear why he did that. At first, I believed it was purely for money. I'm doubting that now.

"Nevertheless, I'm finding the reasons you've given me extraordinarily difficult to accept. Are you accusing my friend of being guilty of all three murders: the Burns woman, Pickering, and now Gerald Neil? That's presuming he's dead of course, which would be a pretty good guess. Are you going to extend your accusations to Page Boucher and the woman he was with? Did Bots kill all of them?"

He started to shake his head as I heard the first words of any denial, "No, I'm not," but I gave him no chance to carry on.

"Bottomly is many things but he's no mass murderer, Jerry. You've met him, for goodness' sake. Surely you can't believe Bottomly murdered all those people?"

"Not all, Harry, no, I don't. But that's not to say he's not implicated in them all."

By the slight inclination of his head, he reminded me so much of my Latin tutor at Junior School when I was utterly lost for an answer in his class, leaving him to look upon me as though I needed a kick up the butt, and, although Furley did not expect a scholarly answer, he did expect a reaction. I displayed none.

"I have two questions for you, Harry, before we move on to how I believe your friend is implicated. Both these questions are linked and neither is difficult. Ever heard of the Selous Scouts, or the Rhodesian SAS?"

"I have heard of the Scouts, yes. I read a Wilber Smith novel where they had a mention. The Rhodesian SAS must be disbanded by now, so no, I haven't come across them, not even in a novel. Why do you ask, old chap?"

"Yes, you're right, they were disbanded. Even so, they are relevant. In the mid-Sixties, some of the middle-ranked commanders of the Scouts, with three officers from the Rhodesian SAS, organised their own version of the two services. It relied on the original ethos of the two units, that is, sharing intelligence and working together on counter-intelligence operations.

"It was with this evolved model that the Bottomly family became seriously involved. Of course, that was fifty or sixty years ago. We have been able to bring things up to date by infiltrating one branch of the legitimate South African Special Forces Brigade, called Recces, thereby accumulating a fair amount of intelligence on Viscount Bottomly.

"Even so, we have not narrowed our vision. We have gathered intelligence from Recces that not only helps us with the Hugh Pickering murder, but until this latest intelligence came into our hands, on what we could only assume to be a murder, that of Gerald Neil too. I wonder if you remember someone who was close to Bottomly and yourself to a lesser extent; a certain Liam Gibson?"

Yes, I knew Liam, as did Bottomly, and yes, he could kill someone just for fun if the mood took him. I had seen Liam kill and it was not a pretty sight.

Jerry reopened his portrayal of the situation with a question. "Have you ever paid a visit to Viscount Bottomly at that London house of his. No?"

He'd caught me off guard as my obvious surprise had given me away. I knew nothing of Bots having somewhere in London to call his own. All of a sudden, he had another secret to go with his gambling. It had been impossible to conceal my astonishment, but no amount of imagination would have prepared me for the extortionate price Furley was willing to extract.

"It's very spacious, you know, but wait; you don't know it, do you?

How silly of me."

There was a brash edge to his rhetorical question that dovetailed into the smug expression stapled across his mouth as the next words left him.

"And by the looks of things, it was a costly venture. I'm surprised you didn't know though, as the family have owned it for years, according to his neighbours."

My tormentor was in full flow, having me on the edge of screaming at him to finish. I hoped I was wrong about the direction he was driving the conversation towards, only I knew I wasn't.

"Some of the reports crossing my desk say the decor, along with the fittings in all four of the bathrooms, are a bit on the ostentatious side of good taste, but hey, who am I to question another person's preferences, or the way they live? Mind you, it's in one of my favourite parts of London, only way beyond my pay grade.

"Highgate. Short walk to the shops at Muswell Hill for his morning pint of milk, or short walk to the underground station if he's going to work in town. Overlooks the parkland as well. It's big, Harry. Some might say enormous, but that might imply my distaste, and who am I to judge?"

He swallowed hard as he filled his pipe in a kind of religious fashion that now, as I looked closely, duplicated the same actions he'd used on the three previous occasions. First, he would open his soft, grey leather pouch of tobacco with the flap facing away from his body.

Next came the small pocket knife, red in colour with a white cross on both sides. Only the one blade, but two accessories slotted into one end. Perhaps one was a pair of scissors and the other a hook to pull stones from horses' hooves. I had an identical one in a drawer somewhere in my office back at The Hall in Harrogate.

He used the knife to scrap the bowl of his pipe, then knocked the residue out into the glass 'bar' ashtray before laying the pipe on the open flap of the pouch and filling it from the tobacco it held. Lastly, came the rehearsed draw before the lighting and the first inhalation with its anticipated contentment.

"It's Victorian! Least I think it is. Not my thing, architecture, but I've seen a picture. Beast of a building. Straight out of some gothic horror film. Mind you, they're all a bit big and imposing around there. They were built to house hundreds of servants, back in the day. Five storeys high, all of them. Six if you're counting the basement. Apparently, the poor sod didn't die instantly. Hung around for hours, so I was told.

"Unfortunately, there was nobody close enough to hear if he could answer the questions that were put to him. At the end, they pumped him full of alcohol, added some recreational drugs to his bloodstream to make it look as though he was high when he cut his own wrists. His phone was smashed, but we managed to trace the last person he called; it was Viscount Bottomly. They spoke for almost twenty minutes. There was a plethora of forensics around the house but nothing that pinged up on any screen to cause undue excitement."

He paused, and this time his study of me was as

one person might examine a horse before making a bid to buy it.

"We got one facial recognition from a camera that's a bit hidden away. It was tucked under some decorative edging on one of the shops in a small parade in the village. It gave a clear image; one of Liam Gibson. We were lucky enough to confirm the information from our man inside the Recces unit.

"Gibson boasted about going to talk to, and then kill, two people a friend wanted dead in England. Would you like to add any comment at this stage, Harry? Perhaps, fill me in as regards to Gibson being in London?"

It felt as though I was being interrogated yet again. I was being made to feel very uncomfortable; dirty, in a sense. It was as though he believed I was the culprit and he was trying to catch me out. I most certainly was not the culprit so I was not going to act as one.

"Yes, I know Liam Gibson as you are well aware, Jerry, but I have absolutely no idea why he was in London. If indeed he is, or was. I'm none too clear why you have so much hostility towards Winston Bottomly. As far as I can see, he's done what you wanted. The only thing he hasn't done is give you the name of his agents. Why should he give you that?

"There's no suggestion of South African Intelligence fouling up any of your operations. If that was their aim, they could have done it already. Why are you fretting over who murdered Hugh Pickering? He was nothing to you. Or was he working for you and the CIA?

"If he was working for both, wouldn't his death help MI6 to claim to be made up of humanitarians who are extending the goodwill of international banking worldwide? Could that make them worthy of a vast injection of funds from Whitehall? Or are you suspecting Liam Gibson of being involved in Gerald Neil's disappearance, Jerry?"

"Yes, we are, Harry, and I'm going to let you into a big secret now, one that cannot leave this building."

CHAPTER TEN

C.O.W

We were eating a late lunch in what was called Parliament View restaurant on the rooftop floor of The Box, overlooking the pleasure boats packed with colourful tourists going up and down the river, when the possibility of not returning from the situation I was being coerced to join was broached.

The restaurant was empty apart from the two of us. The accentuated noise of cutlery made the emptiness of the place increase the sensation of being tied to a wooden pole about to be shot, as I was listening to the screams rebounding inside my head. This was no nice, clean James Bond film I was being recruited to join. This was a job where I would not get the lady at the end of it, and I might not even be coming home.

"The current working intelligence came from the

source I told you we have inside a department of the ruling Iranian party. Gibson and our man met in Kuwait, where Gibson was playing the 'look how big I am' card. He tells our man he has to travel to London to get some information from two men a friend of his wants questioning, and then killed. Our man said Gibson was being very scary.

"By the time all that intel reached us, Gerald Neil's torture was impossible to stop. Pickering was dead and Neil missing. Torture, yes, Harry, not a word I would generally use, but that's what it was. I will have to get to that later, though. Bottomly wanted his friend Gibson for his talents in torture.

"They teach all that in Special Forces training, as you well know. And you and I know of places where Gibson used some of that training, don't we? It would seem the people we are dealing with are of a different nature than you and me, my friend. I trust all the legalities, including next of kin, were settled."

I nodded, adding a quiet 'yes, all's been signed, Jerry', whilst munching on some fancy rabbit food and wishing it had never rained last winter back home in Yorkshire. Silently, I pledged to replace my estate manager with a giant umbrella. By the time I had finalised my mental rearrangement of the employment side to The Hall, I had finished the salad and was waiting for my steak and chips. Jerry was speaking.

"The set-up we have inside Iran is something we

cannot allow to be discovered. It is never mentioned in front of the Americans or other allies. It gives the UK government a first-hand brief on Iranian nuclear ambitions and, to speak plainly, their plans give me an intense bout of cold shivers. But at the moment that's all they are—ambitions, and I'm still here to shiver.

"'The principal target would be Israel, of course. There are no neat specifics, just the whole country. Anywhere with population and not necessarily military. To negate the threat they pose, we and our counterparts in NATO, are putting together an operation against the Daesh, ISIS group I've told you of, but there is a snag. And this is where you and Bottomly come in.

"There is a group inside South Africa who still hold a huge grudge against the Union of Great Britain, dating back to the second Boer War. They are threatening the stability inside Iran and the surrounding countries, including Saudi Arabia. As you may know, we are playing second fiddle to the CIA in what's called arrangements, but we are holding our own cards in what I call the game."

I noisily placed the cutlery on my plate when hearing his interpretation and ownership of the favoured word 'arrangements', suspecting there would be an American involvement somewhere. But the ending revelation of our separatism from our so called cousins, in his 'game' concerned me owing to the proximity of the Suez Canal and the history we shared with Israel over that part of the world. Before he could continue expanding on any partnership I might be freely walking into, he stood, as I heard some heavy, flat footsteps approaching across the blue-patterned carpet of the restaurant.

* * *

"Hello there, Paterson. It's been a long time since the two of us have run into each other."

I had first met Charles Oswald Wallace, the tall, bulky figure now seated opposite me and smiling like the Cheshire Cat, not in Alice's Wonderland but in Eton College, having the distinct pleasure of not having much to do with him other than on the rugby pitch, where I captained the school first team from the back row of the scrum and, because of his size, he played in the second row directly in front of me. Our paths were to cross again at Cambridge, where I continued to play that game, having the great honour to represent the university, whilst he preferred to use his size in other ways.

He was thought to be earmarked for some kind of government position due to his family's history in a variety of eminent parliamentary or civil service positions. It was my opinion that nepotism in his case would be more influential than actual ability. Be that as it may, if what I'd heard at a university union dinner some year back was true, the upward climb he needed to succeed had been delayed by his dalliance with a Member of Parliament that had exasperated his father, the head of the civil service, to such an extent that the person telling me suggested it was impossible for the civil service mandarins to forgive him. The Member of Parliament was, of all things, in open favour of a reform to the civil service.

Most casual correlations can be forgiven in time, but the union between a red-blooded, right-wing family and a reforming MP, on the final chapter of Keir Hardie's From Serfdom to Socialism, would take a mammoth amount of understanding and forgiveness in the upper echelons of this country's real power.

His graduation from the bed of the shadow Minister for Culture and Arts to his seat as the Permanent Private Secretary to the high Office of the Prime Minister, might have taken longer than his father and his father before him, filling top tier roles for the Crown in one capacity or another with admirable solidity and aplomb; nevertheless, that's where he now planted his backside. I wished he'd removed himself, returning to his position of a Machiavellian Wallace as quickly as possible, but it crossed my mind he was here to sign my death warrant.

* * *

He had parked himself in the chair vacated by Jerry Furley, who was at the bar pouring three drinks. I wondered if protocol demanded that Furley go through Wallace to ask the Prime Minister for permission to eliminate Boucher, a foreign national, and his lady friend on home ground, or could he authorise it himself without informing MI5?

Wallace was a bully when we were at Eton, having fun intimidating and crushing those below him. At six foot five inches tall, there were few taller.

I had come across him only once since leaving Cambridge, when he held the position of the permanent secretary at the Foreign and Commonwealth office. It was when I was engaged in business to unravel a mystery I'd rather had not been brought to my notice. Nevertheless, it had, and he had moved up several grades to now become the most powerful man in government circles. In essence, he was the most powerful person in political circles without having the inconvenience of being a politician and having to seek re-election every so often.

The first thing that entered my mind when I looked at him, was that from somewhere, I'd heard he was indisposed to travel from his offices in Whitehall. Perhaps the thought of blood had brought him out. That thought was further cemented into my mind when Wallace waved a dismissive hand at the two waiting-staff members standing by the serving table, who immediately left.

If I was not to be strung up, did his arrival mean it was more likely I would be strung along by those known to be the masters of deception? I was about to find out as he started to speak.

"Allow me first to reiterate what you were told at your first meeting with the government's Solicitor General. We are indeed indebted to you for answering the national call, Paterson. It was a wonderful thing you did for Viscount Bottomly on that shoot of his and now, perhaps with your help, we can go one step further," he announced.

Did the whole of Westminster know what happened at the Bottomly shoot? I was wondering this as Furley returned to the table with three glasses of whisky, which I was pleasantly pleased to see, as my glass had rested empty on its coaster for at least ten minutes. When at rest, my mind would hold a kaleidoscope of mixed images and thoughts that would entice me to rationalise them into a chronological order. At the beginning of that semblance of order, was the thought of whether it was in the basement of this building where they shot people?

I had never confronted thoughts of inadequacy before coming here to meet with Jerry Furley, to which the appearance of Wallace, with his reference to the shoot, added more incapability to any manner of rational thought. Would I go mad trying to guess how many more were basking in the sunlight or slithering through the shadows of Whitehall aware of my guilt? Would the path to sanity go past or over Samantha's grave? How many more glasses of whisky would it take to anaesthetise the bullet?

Furley raided another table in the empty restaurant to steal a chair, placing it between Wallace and myself, moving the glass ashtray that contained his pipe across the table and closer to him. I thought he looked accustomed to doing things like that, putting Wallace first and himself second. I lit a cigarette, more in defiance of any regulations Wallace might invoke than the need for nicotine.

I recalled how Wallace was an ungracious pupil at those shared places of education, with this impolite lack of acknowledging the head of MI6 on entry helping to reinforce my view. Basic politeness was also absent from his tongue when Jerry asked if he had eaten lunch: 'Would you care for something to eat, Charles, before we have the place to ourselves?' To which Wallace's one-word reply of, *no*, in a curt, blunt, and severely discourteous manner, served to ignite the missing spark of defiance I had finally found, lifting me from my state of lethargy.

As my refilled glass was returned to the table, I added a loud, unmistakable 'thank you' which, in my book, is never misplaced when appreciating a kind gesture, but not so Wallace. With a disrespecting wave of his right arm, he dismissed Furley from the room before he'd a chance to sit in the chair he had only just appropriated.

I had never seen a man so demoralised as the head of MI6 appeared to be, with the contemptuous words, 'we can manage without you, Furley', hanging in the room, serving to seriously stoke the fuel of my newfound energy.

Despite this confession, I have one more; I'm afraid to admit I did not hit him. But I made absolutely sure he expected it!

* * *

At Eton College, Wallace was known by the acronym of COW, made up, of course, by the initials of his name, but as understandable as it may have been, it was not liked by any inch of Charles Oswald Wallace. Whether or not it was the name-calling throughout his youth that drove him to become a bully or not, I'm not qualified to say; even so, it was as a bully that I first came across him.

Early one sunny winter's morning, I was in the town of Eton, not far from the Burning Bush public house, when I came across Wallace and three mindless idiots who were picking on a younger Etonian for some reason I had no wish to ask. I knocked Wallace down and knocked out one of his helpers who came to his aid.

The cold, or missing the soft parts of their faces, had seriously hurt the knuckles of both my fists, so looking on as the other two decided they would rather keep their puny faces as God had made them and not have them altered by one of my damaged fists was a relief to me. Their retreat saved me from breaking bones in my hands.

Whilst Wallace was on the ground, I told him if I ever found him in similar circumstances doing what he was doing to this younger and much smaller pupil, I would give him an unhealthy beating before dragging him before a 'beak', the name we gave to a form teacher, or, failing that, all the way to the headmaster, where he could expect to be expelled. I never heard of acts of bullying by COW again.

When the boy who I'd knocked out came to, he told how COW had paid him and his two mates to come with him, adding 'weight' to the physical intimidation. The boy I was talking to had not been told the full story of the 'crime' the younger boy had committed against COW, other than it involved those three initials.

Rationale dictated that no matter how much the episode had left a nasty taste in my mouth, it could not be allowed to become the fundamental premise on how I judged him. But I never grew fond of the word 'rationale', nor did I employ it often, certainly not when came to relationships.

* * *

He had risen from the table as my 'thank you' was echoing in the empty room and was now holding the door with a look of panic in his wide eyes as I closed the distance between the two of us. He was thinking, of course, that I was about to carry out my threat. Common sense might have commended me to apologise to this unsteady figure because of the exalted position he held in government, the ear of the Prime Minister no less, but I didn't.

"Oh, Charles, what a big girl you are. I didn't even raise a finger and you're tripping over your feet to get away."

I was still a table's length away, having a chance to study him for the first time since I left academia. From searching my memory, I thought he always carried a heavy frame, whereas now, as he was shaking, he was a fraction of the size I recalled. He had grey, thinning hair swept away from a lined forehead, below which was a pair of sturdy, blue-framed, thick-lensed glasses. From the distance I was at, I could see his eyes were a dull, lifeless brown with broad pink lines across the sclera. The outline of his face looked drawn, with fleshy jowls hanging almost below his feeble, pointed chin. His overall appearance made me feel guilty. I seriously wondered if the man was terminally ill!

* * *

My university years were relatively problem-free in regards to Wallace and his activities; however, I heard a few tales of his twisted attributes that spread a smear across my memory. Having run into him a couple of times outside of those school years, I pitied anyone he formed a dislike towards.

It had crossed my mind to wonder whether anyone really knew Charles Oswald Wallace, as it was not only the bullying that I had knowledge of, it was also known to a few including myself that his middle name of Oswald was chosen by his parents as a symbol of respect to Oswald Moseley, the leader of Fascism in the UK during WWII.

I heard from Bottomly of parties thrown by the Wallace family where the reenactment of some of the worse activities of the Nazi party were participated in. Now, as I thought of it, all the updates of Wallace had come from Winston.

In spite of the fact that Wallace must know about Bottomly telling me, it was not mentioned, and if I was wrong about him knowing, then I had no reason to say anything about it at this stage.

The fact that the choice of Oswald was not his to make, coupled with his adolescent-inspired abnormality of being a tormentor, had seemingly disappeared; my dislike of him had been chiselled into my chest and would not be altered by time. My mind was a million miles from the inviting amber liquid in the ice-filled glass I had abandoned. It was focusing squarely on a small, timid lad in Eton regalia trying to plead for his safety with a much larger built, older, fellow Etonian with others intent on violence. The image sickened me then, as it still did. From what I'd seen of him, he had not changed.

"Sorry, chum," I said, when I was in front of him and his eyes were lowered to the floor. "I must have missed your courteous greeting when you interrupted the conversation Jerry and I were having. Or maybe I was asleep when you entered the room."

I indicated Jerry Furley, carrying on speaking with as much ridicule in my voice as I could muster.

"The man there is named Jeremy Furley. He is the head of this country's intelligence service. The same service helping to keep you safe in your bed from terrorists. Nobody warrants your impoliteness. I have been raised to expect the normal, civil niceties that make this country of ours warrant the title of Great, before the common Britain, not just the UK, the initials some like to belittle us with.

"I am a guest of the government's head of external intelligence and, what's more, I happen to be an hereditary Earl, as well as the Sheriff of the county of Yorkshire. I have, of course, a permanent seat in the House of Lords. I have a right to a great deal more respect than you have shown me and my host. I shall not discuss any business to do with my good friend the Viscount Winston Bottomly with you, nor will I shake the hand of a deafening fool."

Jerry was looking on, somewhere between hoping I didn't hit Wallace, forcing him to intervene, and hoping I did not say anything to regret.

"If Jerry here is obliged to have dealings with your office, then I am genuinely sorry for him, because I most certainly will not. Good day to you both. Thank you for your hospitality, Jerry, it was most welcome. We will have to discuss whatever it was you were going to tell me another time. I should be at my Chester Square home until sometime tomorrow afternoon, when I plan to drive back to Harrogate. If I'm not at Chester Square, I'm sure you'll find my mobile number somewhere in my file. I would be glad to work with you, Jerry, it would be an honour. Under no circumstances will I work with this clown."

To give the man his due, he profusely apologised for being so rude, citing work as his excuse. He begged me to stay, which I refused. I had no need to lie. I cited a bona fide prearranged appointment.

CHAPTER ELEVEN

DOORWAYS

My watch showed I'd been inside air-conditioned passages within the MI6 building for over five hours, but if asked, I would have said it had been more like ten days. Talking, or discussing, outcomes had never ranked highly on my list of favourite pastimes, particularly if it had not solved anything, as was the case here. At least I had not met my executioner.

Nobody could describe the walk under the River Thames as being scenic. The tunnel is not uninteresting, though it must have been so for the person watching the television monitors as I never saw anyone else walking through it. I had been told the tunnel ran diagonally under the river until roughly between Vauxhall Bridge and Lambeth Bridge, when it then followed a straight line underneath Millbank, passing the House of Lords, then Westminster Palace into Whitehall.

It was a more-or-less straight line walk for roughly a mile and half or so, along a tunnel I had walked many times in each direction before today's stroll. That was in a time when there was not one of the nine colourful prints of subjects ranging from a view across Lake Windermere, to a scene depicting unrest painted on an abstract background with human shapes holding placards of various sizes asking for—Justice For All.

They made an inspiring addition to the uninspiring grey concrete surface with the usual communication, lighting and other electrical cables, fixed in regulation spacing until some of them entered grey metal boxes bearing large warnings of death by electrocution if tampered with. It had crossed my mind once to force one open to look inside, but I didn't do it; now I laughed at the memory, but wondered why I hadn't.

Was I sensible in not punching COW? I was sure I would have punched him in the same year as I thought to look inside the mysterious grey boxes. As I walked on, I wondered if the angry side of me was slumbering in some dark corner, waiting to be aroused.

I was used to being on my own back home at The Hall. Sometimes, I would see Joseph first thing in the morning and then nobody until dinner, which I could be eating on my own unless I was out somewhere, or entertaining. That situation could last for days on end; however, never before had I found myself doing what I was doing now. I was quietly speaking aloud, in time to my footsteps which were slightly echoing on the red-linoleum-covered surface.

For reasons I have no way of explaining, I was reciting over and over the only two lines of poetry I could remember. They were from Percy Shelley's sonnet, Ozymandias, which was supposedly a metaphor, portraying the gigantic, crumbling statue of a king to the dwindling state of politics: My name is Ozymandias, king of kings. Look on my works, ye mighty, and despair!

No doubt a psychiatrist would say I had only re-membered those two lines because I was self-ab-sorbed. A person in that position would have lots of letters after their name so would probably be right. I'll leave you to decide that one.

As I estimated my journey as nearing Lambeth Bridge, I came to the short branch of a narrower tunnel leading off to my left, with a sign bearing the capital letters of SIS on it. I carried on walking in a straight direction, passing as I did a plethora of shorter, narrower tunnels, some more like corridors but all with uniformed armed protection details be-hind what I thought to be registration desks, shielded by glass from floor to ceiling. All seemed to have clip-boards and writing pads on the desktop.

The foot traffic was increasing. When I'd started out, I was alone, but now one other person had emerged from the tunnel going towards the MI5 building, and I could see another walking in the same direction as I, with two other people walking towards the two of us. All of them seemed to be gazing at the official-looking papers they held. I walked on in silence for another five minutes, before I came to the first heavy door that opened onto another that did not differ in weight nor size.

Beyond this last door was the registration desk with an armed Ministry of Defence four-man protection detail; here, I deposited my 'Visitor' badge, providing a signature on the hand-held clipboard at the same time, before being waved through the checkpoint. I was out of the air-conditioning but not away from the cameras or security. I found myself reminiscing as I walked along the final corridor leading to number 15 Craig's Court, off Great Scotland Yard; strangely, I was thinking of the days my father spent at our then London home in Eaton Square with George Northcliffe as his personal assistant, now married but continuing to live at the same address. Memories are strange at times.

* * *

It had been decided Sir Leonard Miles was to be my link to Section 9, at The Box—my operational control, with the myriad of corridors and tunnels leading off from Number 15 Craig's Court, the characterless building in the cul-de-sac near the hubbub of Trafalgar Square being my entrance and exit from the various government offices I needed to visit.

Craig's Court was a well-chosen spot, as here was the hub of all the secret underground network that criss-crossed the river from government offices to the offices of the civil service, those hidden faces staying together when governments are changed at the ballot box. There are tunnels that I've travelled leading to private offices inside St James's Palace and tunnels again I've travelled leading to government car pools, with its garage exit from the buildings in the Foreign and Commonwealth complex. There were miles of tunnels under London, most of which could be entered from Craig's Court.

As if by magic, I had walked through the final glass revolving door and I was now standing in front of the security station. It was as if I had been separated from my mind, as I had no recollection of how I'd arrived.

"Slap my thighs and tickle my arse! If it's not the Major, Lord Paterson himself." These words were spoken by a tower of a man stationed behind a laminated glass, bullet-protective screen, standing nearer seven foot than six and spreading wider than most doors fitted to most homes. It was Colour Sergeant William Mullet, who had exchanged one striking army uniform for the dark-blue, bland and lacklustre attire worn by the Ministry of Defence Constabulary. His greeting was remarkably similar to Winston Bottomly's when I arrived at his estate.

The Colour Sergeant and I spoke of a few inconsequential matters and for a while I was back in the regiment, performing my duties without thinking. My refuge was ended by the ring of my mobile phone. I apologised for the bad timing of the call, leaving the Colour Sergeant to his duties, as I returned to mine.

I recognised the number, calling it back when in the process of hailing a cab. It was from a lady I knew. The lady in question invited me to dinner that evening at her apartment in Mayfair. She was lonely, with her husband away in Brussels for three days attending a European Science get-together of some description. Of course I accepted the invitation. It would be rank bad behaviour to leave a beautiful lady alone to cope with a boring evening watching TV. Would it not have been?

It was good to know how my tactile world had remained untouched by my absence. The sombre inclination I'd previously suffered from was immediately lifted as I caught myself sporting a supercilious smile from the shadowed glass partition that separated me from the driver of the cab. I was, at last, back in 'the land of the living'.

* * *

I requested the taxi driver to set me down in Eccleston Street rather than have him turn into the square, as I wanted to make a private telephone call. However, my search for an answer to what could be a problem was not forthcoming, and the range of enquiries I needed to make were seriously restricted by its sensitivity. The issue that caused me to worry was that just before I had hailed the cab, I had seen a woman, standing at a bus stop in Whitehall, whom I was sure I'd seen when I had arrived. On my arrival, I'm sure she was walking towards Trafalgar Square.

It could, of course, be an innocent occurrence. Perhaps she had business in Whitehall and had concluded whatever it was by the time I had concluded mine. Or, I could have made a mistake. Equally, she could represent a foreign government interested in what I was doing. My phone call to Jerry Furley produced no authentication of its purity nor any of its guilt. I agreed to 'keep my eyes open' as he advised.

Another agreement I entered into came when I was a few minutes from my address. It came from Sir Leonard Miles. He offered an afternoon meeting at White's Club in Pall Mall the following day. White's is regarded by some as the most exclusive gentlemen's club in London. Most of the males in the royal family are members, but the expectancy of a meeting, where one might bump into a royal or two, did not hold me back from enjoying the dinner I shared that evening, served behind locked doors on the inside of a luxurious penthouse apartment overlooking the moored yachts in Chelsea Harbour. And, I'm only too glad to admit, it most certainly did not stop the satisfying after-dinner pursuits my tantalising Italian lady friend and I participated in.

* * *

As I think I've already confessed, I'm not one to hurry, nor am I one to waste opportunities that arise when the capricious wheel of life's circle of opportunity is in the ascendency. I took advantage of the absence of my friend's husband in Brussels for all of the following morning and some part of the afternoon after our previous shared night, and if I was wearing an unusually smug face when I arrived at White's, it wasn't because I'd won a monetary wager with any of the present members known to like a 'speculation' or two!

CHAPTER TWELVE

BODIES

Sir Leonard was waiting for me inside the door at his club, signing the register before we were escorted to the table in the bow window on the ground floor, the one looking out onto St James's Street. It was considered to be the most distinguished position within this centuries-old institution and one only bestowed on its most highly regarded members within this exclusive gentleman's club.

Never before had it crossed my mind why Boodles was our choice of club and not here, but, for one of those 'I don't know how it happened' moments, it troubled me and, more particularly, it troubled the social side of my psyche.

As we walked the short distance to the table, he could not stop himself from apologising for being unaware I had unpleasant history with Charles Oswald

Wallace. He suggested he acted as an emissary between the civil service and myself. I told him I couldn't see the point, as the only agreement I was under was to work with MI6.

In that case, he said, he would act as the buffer between Section 9 and the government, leaving Wallace at the end of the chain, which in his opinion would be more beneficial as he could keep my name completely secret. He then started to reiterate why that was.

"We need you to go abroad, Harry. To persuade Winston to tell you things that, as a friend, he might say to you, but not to us. If that works, then any information you're able to prise from him will come to me after first going to Jerry Furley. I can filter anything contentious out before sending it off to Charles Wallace. How does that seem?"

"That sounds okay, Leonard, but I don't care where Wallace is in any chain you construct. He's immaterial. I can't see any contentious issues, as you put it, arising, nor I can see any reason why you're involved," I said facetiously.

"I hope you don't treat everything so flippantly, young man. It's not very wise, you know." Having reprimanded me and being satisfied I would change my ways, he continued.

"We would like some information on the Russian he has been seen to keep company with. That would be a good place to start," he said sternly, his voice betraying how his confidence in me changing was not so certain after all. "I'm completely serious about this, young man. Winston was supplying MI5 with a little information on the Russians whilst he was taking their money."

I realised the importance Bots was to play in this puzzle by listening to Furley; presumably Leonard had spoken to him, otherwise how would he know about Wallace and myself? He was speaking again.

"I attended a meeting in the COBRA office, months back, convened by Wallace, where Furley was invited to attend as an outside observer representing the SIS. The other parties attending included the chairman of the Joint Intelligence Committee, the head of Military Intelligence, along with the Assistant Commissioner with Special Branch responsibilities. The Director of GCHQ also attended via a video link. The briefing was about Bottomly and the Russians.

"We were told how various military intelligence departments, including Cyber Crime, Technology, with Operations and Overseas, had all used information from Bottomly in the same way as they used information from Gerald Neil. In an operational sense, both men were considered as double agents. With Winston, the intelligence going from MI5 to him was first-class stuff we had from a source inside Kenyan government circles.

"This Kenyan source was getting material from

someone inside the Lithuanian embassy on Russian military movement in Kaliningrad. Apparently, Bottomly loved whatever came his way out of Kenya. A unit he was able to put together stopped a weapons shipment coming from Kaliningrad via Egypt down the eastern edge of Africa, heading for Namibia. He is a clever operator, so be careful.

"The unit he put together comprised mainly of pirates from Somalia who boarded the ship off Mozambique. They made the Captain turn his ship around until he was just outside Mombasa. When his ship was in the pilot channels for the port, the pirates broke away, turned tail with their bounty stored in their holds. So, as long as we kept Bottomly in the loop with the Kenyan source, all was well until the Samantha Burns thing.

"Sometime earlier in the year, at one of our usual get-togethers, Bottomly told me he'd invited you to the annual grouse shoot, but as of then, he'd had no reply. I think that was the week before the eleventh. I tried to reach you at your place in Yorkshire. I wanted to twist your arm. Your man Joseph, told me you were —inadcessus. The exact word he used, not mine. Is Latin often used at Harrogate Hall, Harry?"

He had not asked with an expectation of an answer, but had he wanted an answer, it would have been, *yes, occasionally it is.* Joseph was an extremely erudite person. He is much loved in the Spyglass, the local pub, because of his general knowledge. The

Spyglass and Kettle won the Pub Cup Competition every year because of his expertise on quiz nights. As I expected, Leonard carried on without waiting for an answer.

"He must be well past retirement age, that man Joseph of yours. Would you know how many years he's been employed by the Patersons, young man?" Although he asked, he was not faintly interested in any answer, merely wasting time, I thought; but why, I wondered?

Joseph was not only my butler but I counted him as a dear friend. He had served as butler at the family home in Harrogate for my father before he'd been murdered. When my father was alive, he seldom visited Harrogate Hall, preferring to live away from his wife, my dying mother, indulging his fantasies in the fleshpots of London, taking many lovers. His last being the violinist I think I've already told you about.

During the investigation after my father's murder, I discovered George to be my great-grandfather's illegitimate grandson, whose birthright had been successfully hidden from members of the family for some forty years. As I contemplated on how the Patersons were a complicated lot, I realised I was almost as complex as Lord Maudlin, my long departed, sadly missed and tremendously loved great-grandfather.

"Yes, funnily enough I do, Leonard. He has been with us for fifty-two years. We celebrated the anniversary with fifty-two candles on a cake, this April just gone. Fortunately for me, he's not old at sixty-seven and tells me he's as fit now as he has ever been. He's retired, well, semi, but I wouldn't know what to do without him. He no longer lives at The Hall. He and Mrs Franks, whom you've met more than once, is no longer my full-time cook. She visits The Hall but now acts as my housekeeper. She and Joseph married two years ago and have a house on the edge of the estate. I don't know if you met Mrs Squires, the cook, from Eaton Square? No, no matter. But she also has a house, the one next to theirs.

"I don't entertain as much as the family used to. Nowadays, entertainment is mainly to do with county business or farming concerns. Mind you, now I give some thought to it, there seems to be a reception of one kind or another each weekend. I have a greatly reduced staff nowadays. Not many are 'live-in'. Most are part-time, as well. There isn't the need for so many. I have my valet, of course, couldn't do without him. There's the kitchen and house staff who live-in, but then after them, not many at all."

"Would any of them miss you if you spent time away on Her Majesty's business, Harry?" he asked, his soft blue eyes as wide as two old shilling pieces.

"Hmm, I'm of the mind they wouldn't. But I most definitely would not admit that publicly." I laughed, but inwardly I wondered if it was true.

"Joseph enjoys the time he has without me being there. He thinks he can organise my diary far better than I can, he's probably right as well. But before I agree to anything, it has to be Jerry Furley who's in charge of the whole thing. I will not stand for being kept in the dark about anything, nor with interference from the civil service." I had a hunch and wanted to float something, seeing where it came down.

"One other thing, Leonard, I want you to tell me what is really going on? For example, I was under the impression that Gerald Neil's entrapment photo was a MI5 illusion, but on the document I was allowed to see I read how Burns handled a real photograph, giving it to Winston. I wonder if that bit of information slipped out by mistake? What did happen, or has the truth been buried too deep to excavate?"

There was a slight hesitation before he replied. "Bottomly's role was quite straightforward. He met Samantha Burns that Wednesday night at Gerald's club and she told him what Gerald had told her. Bottomly passed it on to us and Gerald Neil was summoned. As I said—perfectly straightforward."

"What happened to this Page Boucher, the Frenchman who Samantha Burns was involved with? I know I've been away for a little while but this is more fanciful than fact, old chap." I allowed my disapproval to sink in before adding, "Despite all that, I have one proviso."

"Name it?"

"I want a sweep over Bottomly's contacts inside

the Russian Embassy, along with anyone else whose name is associated with Winston, in order to guarantee that my journey through Craig's Court and subsequently on from there, has not been noted, nor commented on. Then, when the operation is in full swing, I want transcripts between the two of us on two mobile phones I'll supply. They have special encrypted SIM cards inside. They are untraceable and unbreakable when it comes to codes. I have no idea why that's so, but I was told they have cipher points from one phone to the other that don't use the usual transmission aerials."

"I wouldn't want it any other way, Harry, but I think I can put your mind at rest on one of the concerns you have. By using Craig's Court, it would appear to any prying eyes that you are visiting my offices. There's nothing to say you're using the tunnel to Vauxhall, as it's well known we're friends. I can't see how anyone will suspect you are working for either of the intelligence agencies simply by going to Craig's Court.

"A lot of people use the same route as you did and I will be using it in my dealings with Furley. As far as I'm aware, my connection to either of the intelligence services is quite secret. I'm more than comfortable with the press being unaware of the Solicitor General's full role inside the government of the day, but let's try to explain what you're unclear about.

"Obviously, I don't know the full extent of your

briefing in Jerry's office, but I do know he will have touched on the in-line encryption that's having everyone jumping up and down. I confess to you I'm one of those who do not understand all this technological jargon about volumetric spears, let alone multiple-layered analytic engines with static analysis sandboxing. What on earth is that? The point is, Harry, somebody does know and apart from that somebody not being either of us, it's also not some of those in the 'should know' sections.

"If it's only available to an enemy, the hidden method can undermine a controlled system run on a computer. That would include domestic as well as industrial power, affecting hospitals as well as homes. If this fictional, *hopefully* fictional, enemy is about to launch an attack, then if they're using this system it would greatly reduce the capabilities of any military defensive response. At this stage of the affair, nobody is suggesting Viscount Bottomly is masterminding a world takeover, but someone he knows maybe is.

"This Sabah Al Salim is not someone we know a whole lot about, in fact we know very little. We also know very little about the South African illegals operating in the Middle East. We would like you to rectify any potential predicament by finding out all you can about the inadequacies we have in cyber security.

"We are fully aware of the presence of CIA agents operating in Southern Africa paying particular interest to Al-Qaeda and this ISIS, or other like groups. Counter-intelligence has unearthed three active cells who we believe are similar in persuasion to this ISIS group. Apparently, they pose a real threat."

The sheer graveness expressed in his voice testified to the phrase 'a real threat', making it feel uncomfortably close.

"There's a story Furley is aware of about an American serviceman who had been accepted into the command structure of ISIS, subsequently being thrown into a prison cell because he used the word 'Daesh' in public when that word has been declared punishable by beheading," Leonard continued.

"This individual is vital to the West. He was born to an American Air Force father and a Syrian mother. They met at the Shaw Air Force Base where the father was stationed as a pilot and his mother worked as an Identifier inside an integral part of the Tactical Reconnaissance Wing, stationed at the Shaw base.

"The son was trained at the Federal Law Enforcement Training Center, in Georgia, before starting down the road to the Farm, as it is colloquially called. He was cleared all the way up to the 1st Special Forces Command at Fort Bragg, attached to the Special Operations Sustainment units in which he served as an advisor on the Strategic Studies Command Council.

"He was destined to be a big-fish, but went quiet until his name is showing again when he's into a five-year stint at the Defence Intelligence Agency, or

DIA, before something, or someone, tipped him over the side at the age of thirty-two. He changed over to ISIS when he was on a detail monitoring radio signals out of an Iraqi military base at Al-Qa'im. He was one of a pair in a covert placement near the Iraqi border, in Turkey. He slit the throat of his number two when he jumped.

"We have highly sophisticated satellites nowadays, particularly the reading of such from these multiple IOMS units. To my shame, I know nothing about these things, nevertheless I can tell you one of Jerry Furley's Middle East specialists found him eleven days after his defection. He was spotted entering a house near a mosque, in Mosul. A day or two later, his location was verified on the ground.

"The next move he made was in the back of a truck. He travelled about three hundred miles across desert tracks normally only goats roam, to a town in Syria named Ar Raqqah. It's a place that's been bombed almost to oblivion by the Americans and us.

"It was at one time a beautiful, peaceful city nestled on the banks of the Euphrates River. I visited there some forty-odd years ago. That's not important; what is, is he was not alone in the back of the truck. There were two others.

"One was a deputy leader of the ISIS army contingent in Syria, a person named Abu Ala al-Mulard. I'm afraid we have no idea who the second man was. Be that as it may, we do have an image from a satellite camera. In spite of the fact he's looking skyward, his face is too blurred for the facial recognition process. Here, take a look, Harry. He's either saying hello, or expecting to find a drone."

Across the table he passed an A4-size brown envelope he had taken from the black leather, well-used document case he had carried. The envelope was not sealed. I don't know why, but as I looked at it I was overcome with a sense of trepidation. It was the type of feeling one might expect when an anticipated letter carrying important news arrives, and one is hesitant to open it. I pulled the black and white photograph from the envelope, holding it to the light from the sunlit street.

"I was hoping against hope I might be able to establish who he is by asking you, Harry. Please don't disappoint me," he implored.

"I'm sorry, old chap. I don't think I do know him," I replied, whilst slowly shaking my head.

It was the second lie I'd told within five minutes. I was shaking away the cobwebs from my expertise in the art of lying. The first lie was about 'reading' of Gerald Neil's possession of, or lack of, a photograph. I had not read about it. I was guessing. I had wondered what, first Pickering, next Neil, could have seen to have warranted torture? Obviously Pickering had not seen a photo, he wouldn't have died so quickly if he had, but I couldn't be sure either

Samantha or Bots had shown Gerald Neil one. My money was on Neil seeing one.

* * *

I can't remember who it was who told me; more likely than not it was great-grandfather Maudlin, who was the person who gave me most of the valuable advice I have relied on throughout my life. What he had said about the telling of lies, was along the lines of, never tell a lie unless it is either to save a friend's life or, by telling the truth you endanger what the truth of a situation may be. I never understood what the second part of his advice meant, *by telling the truth you endanger what the truth of a situation may be.* I did now!

* * *

The name of the person in the photograph that Leonard wanted was Sabah Al Salim, but I could not trust anyone with that knowledge, even Sir Leonard. If the machinery could not tell them, then I wasn't going to.

"Ah, well. I'm not completely surprised you didn't know, old boy. If the Americans couldn't identify him, then I doubted if you could. Even so, it did seem a bit ironic, him looking up at the sky like that, along with the choice of destination, Ar Raqqah. At one time it was a major ISIS city until they were forced out a couple of years ago by the bombing. At least, that's what we thought.

"Despite the intricacy of the guided weapons being used, they are overlooking a complex which our uniquely equipped IOMS unit identified as the remains of the military command of ISIS. One person still hanging around who they did identify with a strong degree of certainty was Abu Saleh Al-Sabaid, another of these deputy military leaders they have. The British army briefly came across this one in Mali, when ISIS was temporarily in control of the country. He escaped capture by seconds after a unit raided a 'tent city' where it was said he'd been."

I jumped in when I thought Leonard had finished speaking, asking for his permission to take photographs on my phone of this man Abu Saleh Al-Sabaid. I asked for permission to take one of the unidentified image I had secretly identified of Sabah, saying perhaps his name might come to me.

If Sabah was the third man inside the truck with Abu Ala al-Mulard and the American, I wanted the man Leonard did not mention. He was coming out of what had been identified as the ISIS military command post, wearing a Syrian army uniform, perhaps that of a captain, but I wasn't quite sure of the rank. I didn't want to ask Leonard who he was, as again I thought I knew.

There was a big question I wasn't asked. It was why would Sabah spend all the time in the back of a truck with an American who he could have interviewed later in a lot more comfort? This email, the one with an encrypted script hidden inside the body which has the potential of cataclysmic proportions, must have been composed by this highly trained American cryptography officer who was waiting to be beheaded. Did they know that all the time he was alive, there remained the possibly of him writing programmes that could contaminate the whole computing structure from within? In his case, being alive was the crime warranting death.

* * *

As we were finishing a rather nice brandy, reminiscing over his and my father's past adventures, our conversation fell on the general deplorable state of English cricket as shown in the latest Test Match in Manchester, where England were 'hanging on' with a slim hope of rain saving any pride they had left, when he suddenly switched the topic back to the French and a question of mine he had failed to answer.

According to him, it was Page Boucher who played Samantha Burns into Viscount Bottomly's life with the same aim as everyone else. However, as far as anyone in our SIS was concern, they were positive Boucher knew nothing of Samantha's involvement in the death of Gerald Neil's first wife. The French had their financial interests to protect in the Middle East and to that end Boucher schooled Burns expertly.

* * *

Someone was not happy leaving Samantha with Boucher as her control. Leonard knew of that, as well as the responsibility for her being transferred to the Paris headquarters of the French External Intelligence Agency. He was also aware of when she was moved to this impenetrable Trade Consular General. But he had no answer that included any name. It all seemed to be far more complicated than necessary, with a huge, empty end.

He then tried explaining more of the details of the French end of what would be Samantha's role. As of yet, I had heard no word of her ever receiving training in the complicated art of deception and lies; maybe she came to the French ready-trained in those skills, by Sabah Al Salim.

* * *

The External Intelligence Agency were not, using Page Boucher's simile, 'playing a friendly game of boules with this one'. Sir Leonard confirmed Millbank had classified the French action as an 'A' level operation, with all the appropriate protocol assigned.

At our end, the relevant combination of internal

security agencies were appraised of the situation of a French operative being missing and holding classified material. Singular provisos were issued to both Special Branch and Border Control. We then did what Jerry had told me—put our feet up to watch the French giving her a free rein.

The awkward trouble the French were having, shot up to a higher level when the specific name of the French agent they had planted inside the Islamic Governing Party of Iran pinged up as a target on the computer screens of the Development Section, three floors below Furley's desk at the Box.

I learned more of the French when Furley and I met for the second time, on the same floor as the Development Section. Our meeting was held in an office marked Homomorphic Encryption. As I walked towards that door, I noticed the door to the office next to the one we were about to occupy.

It was marked in a similar perplexing manner—Enhancing Technology Cipher Text Office. I may have appeared confused, but not so Jerry, he was in a jovial mood.

"A friend of mine saw you and the Solicitor General having a good old chinwag the other day, sat in the window of White's. Hardly a secure place for you and he to meet, one would have thought, unless of course you were not discussing anything of interest to my office?" He carried on without waiting for an answer.

"The French would not listen to me. My European language skills have never been that good, but I do remember an aphorism of theirs—'Mieux vaut prévenir que guérir'—it's better to prevent than to heal. Alas, as yet I'm waiting for an invitation to overhaul their internal security. I had a good old laugh when they didn't!"

His Denis-Healey-type eyebrows were rising and lowering on his forehead as the filtered office light bounced from his bald head, reflecting on the painting of the Queen that hung directly behind. He was laughing at his own joke and I was trying to remain stony-faced. I was successful. He was not as cheery when he continued.

"You must understand it was a complicated situation for everyone concerned. Your friend Viscount Bottomly, the French security services, and of course the Americans, but where the Middle East is concerned we cannot ignore anyone. Not the Chinese, or the Iranians nowadays. Even so, I normally find that after you separate all the players, it becomes a little clearer.

"That's what you and I have to do, separate everything. By the way, if my memory is correct, that Liam Gibson I mentioned to you the other day was part of an SAS detail in Bosnia. When I asked you about him, I was not in possession of information on some actual operations. He and three others were scattered over the ground doing vital tidying-up work of what was called, at that time, 'leave-behind' stuff. I never got a full description of what all that meant." Coarsely, he cleared his throat as he continued with his reminiscing,

"We were all in the army together, but it wasn't long before you and I made the jump across to intelligence."

We skipped around a few things concerning Gibson and our shared time together in that 'Hot Spot', moving seamlessly to when Bottomly and I arrived in the other main theatre of war existing in our time, Afghanistan, where we found Jeremy Furley had been made up to a full brigadier.

I too had been promoted, in my case to the more humble rank of Major,remaining in Communications, where I grew accustomed to seeing the daily briefing of the press being overseen by one Brigadier J. Furley. In the here and now, not much had changed.

He was the officer in charge and I was his subordinate. The only person who was there then, but not present now at this private tête-à-tête, was Bottomly, who was not missing spiritually, he was the centre of the conversation we had.

The plan Jerry worked up with Section 9, who were never supplied with my real name, was for me to meet with Bots in a place called Clear Spring, just outside of Hagerstown, Maryland, where he was purported to be staying with his American aunt, name of

Alice. When I arrived, I was to persuade him to return to Great Britain and pick up again with his Russian handler.

Counter-intelligence in London had devised an extraordinary scheme whereby a serving Czech army officer, stationed in Olomouc, on the Morava River in the Czech Republic, would be exposed as the German spy he was, in exchange for something big London wanted from the CIA. I asked what I thought was a not unreasonable question—why did the CIA want the UK to expose a German agent when they could probably do it themselves?—and he abruptly finished the meeting with a curt, 'That's all, Paterson. I'm pleased you're with us on all of this. Any questions, don't hesitate to get back to me.'

I have never had a wish to remain where I obviously wasn't wanted, so I thanked him for his hospitality as sarcastically as I gauged appropriate, leaving by the tunnel as far back as the Admiralty in Whitehall, then, as the weather was so hospitable, I carried on walking for the short distance to St James's Street and my own club of Boodles. There I sat for a peaceful hour or so enjoying a glass of my favourite tipple, wondering why it was Jerry had made no mentioned about the main subject of my meeting with Sir Leonard.

Without trying too hard, my quiet deliberations extended to include his omission of the American Sir Leonard described in so many ways without ever naming him. Which led me to the issue of whether the name of the encryption analysis expert would be given to the British Intelligence Service when the Czech Republic's army officer was sold down the river to the Czech Government.

* * *

I was acutely aware that in such trickery played by the grandmasters of deception, nobody, including myself, could be safe. I thought one way I could make myself relatively so would be to have a valuable secret tucked into my back pocket. I thought I had two. The one I had about Sabah Al Salim was pretty good. My knowledge of him being in Syria might well prove useful to someone. I shall not comment on the second, until I can be more certain. There could even be a third yet. That depended on whether or ot I could identify the Syrian 'Captain' behind Sabah in the photo at Ar Raqqah, whom I was sure I knew.

* * *

Let me tell you a short story of me as a thirty-odd-year-old Captain in the Life Guards. I was presented with a great honour, that of being selected for ceremonial duties at Buckingham Palace for a state visit in 2002. It was of the Syrian President, Bashar al-Assad, who was visiting these shores with his charming wife, Asma. Whilst on this duty, I met a Syrian army Captain named Hafez al-Rifaaz. I was ordered to perform another role. This one was extraneous to normal military life. It was to escort Asma, with Captain Hafez, around London, on a detailed private tour.

Whilst we were driven from one landmark to another, I was given the chance to learn more about the lady. For a start, I learned she had been raised in England, graduating from King's College with a Bachelor of Science degree in Computer Science. She also had an interest in chemicals, hers being more of a financial nature than mine.

Apparently, at one time she had worked at J.P. Morgan, the private bankers, who I'd worked with in the past. I also learned her specialised knowledge was in biotechnology and pharmaceutical companies. I was impressed, and not only with her business acumen. It took a significant amount of effort to focus my attention away from such a confident and beautiful woman.

There were four of us on this tour of London I escorted her on, whilst her husband was away on official business. There was a Syrian protection-trained driver with myself in the front of the vehicle, whilst Asma was with Captain Hafez in the rear of the Syrian-supplied embassy car. We did the normal sightseeing tour which the visitors found fascinating, but it wasn't just buildings the two in the back were fascinated by. The attraction to each other was obvious when they were alone.

As I say, she and Hafez had a close relationship, which in my opinion was too close for a country's First Lady and her protection officer, who would often share his hotel room with Asma. On the few occasions I took notice of Hafez, or had reason to speak to him, I found him to be tactless when it came to common politeness and self-absorbed enough not to notice the two teams of two men who had been following us all day. I didn't enlighten him to these four, who were not in the official presidential party I met at RAF Northolt. I made enquiries, which on the second day of the tour were answered. The four I've mentioned were recent additions to the Syrian embassy staff here in London, under the diplomatic guise of special advisors to President Bashar al-Assad.

* * *

I looked at the photographic image again but it didn't help. If this was the same Hafez al-Rifaaz in the photograph, why was he still the same rank and how on earth was he still alive? Surely the President would have had him killed if those four followers had reported what they'd seen to him or to the ambassador.

There was one other thing that I remember quite clearly when it comes to Hafez, and that was his hostility to the West in general, but America and Great

Britain in particular. There was an occasion when we were driven past the American Embassy on our way to somewhere and the jingoistic language he used was extreme and embarrassing to not only me, but the First Lady, who rebuked him, only for him to say something along the lines of— it was the duty of all Moslems to raise a Jihad against these imperialistic monsters such as America and Britain.

At that point she again tried to reprimand him, but to no avail. He started to quote passages from the Koran, then mentioning death to all infidels quite a few times. Asma again apologised to me on his behalf, explaining to him how they were guests in this country.

I reported what was said on my final day inside the car with the Syrian First Lady to my company commander, who told me he would pass it on, but I heard no more of it. If it has been recorded, I wouldn't know where.

* * *

When I had a chance, I asked Joseph to look up the Syrian army in the military book I keep in the library at The Hall. The rank of Hafez al-Rifaaz was my interest.

I have a heavy yearly edition from The International Institute for Military Affairs, that tabulates the commissioned ranks of each and every man, or woman, serving in every branch of the military of every country in the world. It has been an addition to the Paterson library since the 1805 Battle of Austerlitz, when Napoleon defeated the armies of Russia, Austria and an army sent by the Pope, in Rome. Over the years, the editions had grown thicker, even though all commissioned ranks below a Captain were omitted.

Joseph found the man after 'an intensive morning's search', he said. Hafez was alive, but was not the Captain I had thought. He was in fact a Major General. I had mistaken the insignia on his epaulettes. As I had been correct in recognising his blurry image, I concluded my eyes were in fair nick. I ended the conversation from a telephone booth in Boodles, feeling good in being me.

So I had an ace. I knew of a Major General in the ISIS military command. A man who had hated the West, as well as being not the most discreet person around women I'd ever come across. Joseph added another slice of useful information; Bashar Al-Assad is still the President of Syria. I wondered if my knowledge of Major General Hafez al-Rifaaz could be of use in the future?

* * *

I ordered another whisky, signing my account when it arrived, but not quietly. With the club room almost full, and with at least seven people I did not recognise reading newspapers, I created a small fuss when I broached the subject of driving in America with my drinks waiter, who had a broad expression of bewilderment.

"I hate driving in America, don't you?" I said, in a pretentious man ner. "They drive on the wrong side of the road for a start and have little or no courtesy when it comes to thoughtfulness shown to visitors to their shores."

I declared this in an unnecessarily arrogant voice, pinning my hopes on someone in the room reporting back to the relevant MI5 section on how I was complying with SIS wishes. The truth lay in a different direction, as I had no plan to comply with much of what they wanted. You see, I certainly knew Bottomly had an aunt named Alice who lived in Maryland, America, but he was not there.

We had spoken on the telephone late one evening following the inquest. At that time, he was staying with an army friend of ours in Durban, South Africa, but his eventual place of retreat was to be 'up-country in Pretoria,' where his family owned property, a fact I thought was unbeknown to any person other than me and ex-sergeant Liam Gibson, our Durban-based South African ex-army colleague.

Liam Gibson was often referred to as 'Mike,' named after the famous Irish and British Lion's rugby legend Mike Gibson, because of his impressive skill as a centre in the army's rugby team the three of us had represented at one time or another. Jerry Furley's information about Gibson was correct. He had been part of the 22nd Special Air Service Regiment the two of us had dealings with in both Bosnia and Afghanistan. On leaving the British army, Gibson took up a career in what's now called the South African Secret Service, or SASS, for short. I learned he was the director of its Angola desk when I contacted him.

It was becoming apparent that there was more not being told to me than was. Furley would have known the position Gibson held in the SASS, so why not save me the trouble of finding out? Also, I couldn't fathom out why Bots had not met the same end as, presumably, Gerald Neil had, and Hugh Pickering if, as I thought, their death was to do with a missing photograph. Perhaps the answer was that Bottomly had murdered them, but why, if Samantha Burns had given him the photograph? No, that was not the answer.

* * *

My flight was booked for Friday. I needed the extra time the delay allowed to finalise the details of the proposed shoot at home with the estate manager, who was jumping through hoops worrying about the quality of game he could provide. He wanted to cancel, but with only a few days to go he hadn't the heart to tell me. I think he was worried I would blame him for the number of birds not increasing. The blame didn't lie at his door, it was the wet weather. With the business to do with Bottomly, I could not set a date for my return, so I took the worry away from him and cancelled it.

Although that sounded straightforward, it was anything but. It would leave the unpleasant duty of cancelling the invited party of forty-four guests at rather short notice. Mrs Franks needed to be told the house did not require preparation for people staying, nor did we need the normal truckload of provisions to feed them. No additional staff were required, which would please Joseph as he hated change. As I was preparing to return home, I heard more details of Gerald's death.

THE CHAPTER AFTER TWELVE

THE WASHINGTON POST

"What was the business you wanted to talk about before Wallace so rudely barged in our lunch the other day, Jerry? You were a bit mysterious, saying you didn't want it leaving the building at Vauxhall."

Jerry Furley had called me at Chester Square, arranging to meet me at, of all places, Westminster Mortuary, in Horseferry Road. I walked around the corner and caught a black cab, arriving a few minutes before he did.

"The thing I wanted to tell you about was how Gerald Neil died, Harry, but on reflection, then wouldn't have been the optimum moment. Not all the pieces were together, and I mean that literally. Hopefully today is a better day. I've got the chief Home Office pathologist supervising the post-mortem, at the end of which I hope we will be in a better position to ascertain the cause of death, with maybe a few clues as to who did it thrown in."

Jerry's spoken words were my introduction to the post-mortem on what remained of Gerald Neil, a person I have already said I did not like, but I could not wish a death like his upon my worst enemy.

* * *

Gerald Neil's non-appearance at Cowes for the start of the Sunday yacht regatta was first remarked upon by the secretary of the Royal Ocean Racing Club who, on mentioning it to Rear-Admiral Sir Thomas Rice, was told to, '*go find the drunken idiot and get him here before Prince Philip arrives*'. That request could not be implemented, as unbeknown to those at Cowes, or those who searched for him, at that precise time Gerald was, almost certainly, almost dead.

His body parts were discovered in an odd sort of way, by a woman out exercising her pet dog near the Pavilion Café in Highgate Woods, not very far from Viscount Bottomly's property on Muswell Hill Road. Part of his remains were thrust upon the woman rather than found by her, when the dog she was walking, a German Shepherd puppy, brought his severed left hand, depositing it at her feet.

The dog then waited, as he'd been trained to do, for his mistress to play. It would normally involve her throwing a ball, so the dog, named Leo, would chase after it, fetching it back. Playing the canine game of *fetch* was not exactly Patricia's first reaction.

Her first, second, third, indeed fourth reaction was to scream, which the playful dog could not understand. He picked up Gerald's left hand and ran off with it, wagging his tail, looking for another human who might want to play.

Leo's owner, Patricia Compton-Ellis, recovered fairly quickly considering the circumstances, being made of stouter stock than that of a panicking dowager. Watching out for Leo as carefully as she could, she found her mobile phone and called the police. Holding the phone closely to her ear, she went after her dog, unmindful of the place her dog had first discovered the hand. She heard a scream.

Making her way towards the site of the gruesome noise, she saw Leo run across her path, hand still in mouth.

Patricia called his name, shouting loudly, "Leo, stop!" Poor Leo did stop, which meant owner and dog were reunited, connected to each other by a polka-dot, coloured, plastic dog-lead. 'Connection' was not a word Patricia could use when referring to Gerald and his hand.

* * *

The first police presence on the scene was the local patrol car, blaring siren being heard almost a mile away from the dog and his new toy. After the police, as well as the dog owner, had tried to calm the spirited Leo, it was a detective who persuaded Leo to relinquish his ownership by the presentation of a bribe, a custard cream biscuit. "Oh, gosh! That's one of Leo's favourite biscuits," the dog's owner articulated, somewhat excited.

Whereas it took a sufferable amount of time for the forensic team to cover the final site of where Leo had been separated from Gerald's hand, the site where the two first came together was an insufferable distance away, which the dog's owner had no distinct knowledge of, even now when only in a slight state of shock.

Notwithstanding that shortcoming, it wasn't long before scores of uniformed police were methodically searching for his right hand along with the rest of him.

Before very long, his head was discovered under the graceful, leaf-laden trees of Highgate Wood, wrapped inside a black plastic, household rubbish bag. The conclusion the investigating team unanimously agreed upon was that he had been murdered elsewhere.

The search continued into the early evening, until a police constable almost tripped over some ripped open, black plastic wrapping, inside which was found Gerald Neil's naked, violently abused torso. The bundle had been hastily abandoned under a flimsy pile of ancient soil in a shallow ditch.

In a nearby gully, no more than six or seven inches deep, were more black wrappings containing his right hand, both arms, legs and feet. Having recovered all the remaining parts of Gerald Neil from this site, the investigating detectives concluded it was from the same part of Highgate Wood that Leo had found his playful prize. The search was then terminated.

* * *

Gerald's murder and subsequent dismembering had taken place no more than four hundred yards away from the site of his abandonment, but the two were not instantly connected; that did not come about until Gerald's facial photograph was displayed on the front page of all of the national newspapers the following day. The meticulous autopsy, which Jerry and I attended, was held three days later.

I thought it strange the post-mortem was not held closer to Highgate Mortuary, particularly as I was told that at first, that was where Gerald's body parts were sent. I thought Highgate, which was about six miles from the centre of London, was judged to be too far away for the Home Office pathologist to travel to conduct the post-mortem.

My derisive thought was not the case. The distance from the Whitehall seats of government was in fact the reason, but it was not the pathologist who did not fancy the journey; oh no, not him. But you've guessed who, haven't you?

"Good afternoon, Lord Paterson, and you, Mr Furley. The Prime Minister asked me to appraise him later, gentleman." The rhetorical declaration came from Charles Oswald Wallace.

* * *

Wallace seated himself next to Jerry, with me four seats away listening to how the owner of Crocketts had been systematically tortured then shot twice in the unearthed head, a modus operandi all too familiar to the police, who were not only responsible for investigating his murder, but had taken over the investigations into the murder of his housekeeper and chauffeur from Surrey Constabulary.

Hearing the intricate explanation of how Gerald was kept alive enduring the agony as parts of his limbs, then whole limbs, were systematically dismembered before he was killed in an orgy of drugs and blood, was repulsive.

I cannot be sure if the grotesque nature of the post-mortem induced the unfamiliar conciliatory tones from Wallace, apologising for, in his own words —'*my theatrical attitude where I failed in my duties to acknowledge your presence, Paterson. I shall not re-*

peat it' —but I tend to think it must have been. He went on to suggest we forget the past and work together in a more cordial fashion.

Within the vast diversity of mankind I have come across in the life I've lived, I have frequently found the irony of opposites being attracted, or the science in pairings, a useful study. An example of the last would be those that aspire, and those that inspire. A small difference in spelling but a sizeable difference in outcome. At the 'inspire' end of a phraseology spectrum, one could inspire someone else, or indeed oneself, to aspire to reach a pinnacle.

I suspected Charles Oswald Wallace's lofty position in the vocational power spectrum he presently occupied was one that many at the beginning of a career aspired to achieve. However, in the years it had taken him to achieve his orbital position of authority, I doubted his personality had 'inspired' any wishing to attain the end to his pinnacle.

It was the opinion of the experienced pathologist that Gerald Neil survived the questions which someone, most likely Liam Gibson, had put to him for three days, before he was shot to end his torment. Knowing what kind of pressure Gibson would apply, I found it absolutely impossible to comprehend how anyone would survive that long if he knew the answer to anything he was being asked. Had there been an answer, he would have submitted to the pain he was sub-jected to and welcomed death a lot sooner than three days.

I could see Wallace was restless when overhearing Jerry Furley repeating my silent thoughts. He even questioned him as to why he thought the way he did. Not knowing the precise methods Gibson would apply was never going to be a detriment to Jerry's logic, which again seemed to agitate Wallace, maybe more. We left him with his sense of anxiety, both of us returning to our individual places of choice, but not before something else was said by Jerry, away from Wallace.

"There was another reason for holding the post-mortem here and not in Highgate. It wasn't just because of Charles. I wanted to hold it as far away from Highgate as possible and, in that way, do all I could to keep the findings out of public reach. I've given the police Gibson's name as a person of interest, old chap. They've been told to liaise with MI5 when they find him. I understand they have their own agenda, whilst cooperating with us."

Something was going on but I had no idea what it was. But I do know some traits of a liar! When one is a habitual liar, there are certain habits one falls into without fully realising. I call it the 'soft-touch approach'. With this, it is customary to distance oneself from the truth by raising the pitch, or tone, of one's voice in the conversation one finds oneself in.

For this approach to be successful, one must

never use forenames rather than the more conventional surnames, especially early on in the exchange. Furley compounded his mistake by adding an ill-advised, affectionate 'old chap', in order, he hoped, to complete the deception. My task now was to unpick the lie I was being peddled by him with his slippery friend Charles Wallace prominent in the shadowy background.

Despite my feelings towards this man, I needed to know how far he would go to withhold the truth if I was to be of service to Viscount Bottomly who, with the murder of Gerald Neil, was, I assumed, debt free. If the amount owing was as much as Gerald told me in the library on the night of his arrival, murder presented itself as a giant incentive.

As per an arrangement I'd previously made, I heard from Liam Gibson some fifteen minutes after arriving at the Sofitel Hotel from Dulles airport, Washington, D.C. My overnight bag was at my feet, with the hotel room keycard lying on top of the bar next to a large measure of Scotch whisky poured into a tall glass filled to the brim with ice.

"Excuse me, sir, but are you Mr Yorkshire from England?"

Leaning closer to me across the top of the bar, the hotel barman quietly posed his question in the universal conspiratorial voice often used by such people, man or woman, when not wishing to be over-heard. 'Yorkshire' was the name I was called in the many mess halls I'd had the pleasure of attending whilst serving my country as a soldier. I knew the person asking had to be Gibson. I replied that it was me.

"There's a Mr Ireland on the telephone for you. He described you perfectly. Here, you can take the call on this, sir."

'Ireland' was the pseudonym I'd asked Liam to use. The barman placed a yellowing telephone with handset on the bar in front of me, then withdrew to serve another customer's needs.

Gibson had hidden Bottomly in the Marriott hotel in Springfield, Virginia, a short drive away if I'd had time to hire a car, which I had not. Over the phone, Gibson told me to meet him outside an office supply shop called Staples, two blocks away from the hotel where I was. He suggested I should ask the barman for directions to the shop and leave my bag at the front desk, not in my room. Then he gave me the registration number of a blue Toyota Corolla that would be waiting opposite the store.

He mentioned again how it was coloured blue, but doubted I would notice the colour at this time of night. More minor instructions followed, until we ar-rived at the driver's name. It was York, Tommy York from New York, he told me with obvious amusement before replacing the telephone. I was smiling, too, when I requested those directions from the barman.

* * *

Tommy York was, of all things, a cockney from Lambeth in London, who spoke the adulterated English language like an American native. Proudly, he volunteered the fact that his family had been living and working in the country for thirty-two years, since he was eleven. He added as an afterthought, how he had served eighteen of those years in the American Marine Corps. He met Liam Gibson in Iraq during the invasion of 2003.

I didn't bother asking if he had a role in the South African Secret Service, I just thought he would be another of their number. I then started worrying why South Africa figured so frequently in what up until now appeared to be an English affair. Before I became too unsettled by that peculiarity, the front passenger door of the Toyota opened and the car shuddered as Gibson took the seat, ordering York to drive towards Springfield.

"Hi there, skipper, it's been too long," Gibson remarked, as he turned around in the front chair to face me. It was as we were awkwardly shaking hands, whilst driving under the street lights, that I noticed his weary eyes with heavy lines of exhaustion engrained into his face. They had the same dead look about them that I remember so well, along with how he never seemed to blink, just stare with an unwavering focus.

"You were followed by four Russians from their embassy. They were waiting for you at the airport. Tommy and me, with a few others, followed them and you. The four changed to three at the hotel. Two followed you on foot with the third in a car hanging back.

"The fourth Russian went to the hotel where they are staying. You're a popular arrival, skip. They did not see us following them, but they've seen us now. It's no matter. We'll lose them before we get to Major Bottomly."

I could see him smiling in the vanity mirror as he gave me the detailed summary. Perhaps the points of importance were to remind me of his skilfulness in the field, I wasn't sure. Nor was I sure if mentioning the promotion would seem a mite too crass. I decided against it, leaving any comment to when I met the man himself.

"They've been working you very hard, Liam. After what you did in London you must feel like a rest." I wasn't expecting a reply.

"I saw two of what I thought were Russians when I came through customs at the airport. They stood out like a sore thumb. To balance it out, I would be surprised if the barman at the hotel wasn't from the home agency. I did not see you though, Liam. And I looked! Maybe I didn't see you because the cover you're using, as a rough sleeper, is so good." I looked at Tommy York's eyes in the driving mirror; he looked worn out, too.

"If you two don't look out for yourselves, the South Africa bureau will have you both in an early grave. It might have been better if you'd chucked the Viscount on a plane and left me to see him at a place of your choosing."

"I'm adaptable, skip. The cover varies to suit the job. I might get confused with being you if I carry on dressing like that. I'd better smarten up a bit, eh! But, hell, no, we couldn't leave you doing it all." He smiled, as did I.

It might have been an educated guess, but it was still a guess. My instinct was as sharp as ever. I was right about Tommy and I was right about Gibson being in London as the interrogator of Pickering and Neil. To ask him outright what he was after would not be a clever move. I would bide my time before asking that. The answer to any question about who he was working for, was an easier option. The answer to that one was, it must be Winston.

"There was a bonus in it for us over here, as none of us had seen those four faces before, so we've been able to enlarged the photo bank by adding some more mug shots."

"Are you sure they were the only ones following me? Nobody from the FBI?" I asked.

"They were all I could see, skip, but Tommy and his crew will run a few crossing lines as standard on the way out to meet with Mr Bottomly, just in case some of the home team turn up."

* * *

I'm afraid to admit my self-importance gladly agreed to his suggestion, greedily wanting to find someone being assigned by the American intelligence services to follow me, someone so good Gibson did not see them first time around. How could I believe MI6 had not asked the FBI to watch where I went? Maybe they knew already?

* * *

As I remembered, Winston had never been a heavy drinker in our army days, nor had he appeared that way on the occasions when we'd met on leaving the military, but something had made him change. Liam unlocked the door to his room in the Marriott and the heavy stench of alcohol was sucked out into the corridor where I stood. As we entered the room, Bots was sitting at a writing table with double doors to his right-hand side which were wide open. These doors led onto a narrow balcony overlooking what appeared to be a golf course where a few floodlights were still shining.

As I looked in on my friend, I remembered how he was drinking heavily on the Friday evening before that night's dinner, looking as though he'd had a few glasses by the time I saw him. Was his reaction due entirely to dark moods over Samantha's death, or was there another reason?

Despite my suspicions of him being drunk, he'd managed to stand and greet me okay, then sit at his writing table where it looked as though he was composing a list of some kind. At no time had he shown any sign of difficulty, nevertheless there was the distinct odour of alcohol on his breath and oozing through his skin as we shook hands.

To confirm what my nose was telling me, there was a little less than half a full glass of what I guessed was diluted whisky on the table in front of where he'd sat, with two half-bottles of American-labelled whiskey, with their annoying 'e' added before the 'y,' on the shelf, beside where the television stood.

Both bottles had been opened, with one completely empty. If I needed confirmation, it was in the waste bin under the same shelf; six emptied miniature bottles of a variety of alcoholic spirits, discarded on top of a copy of *The Arlington News*.

At first, I believed the suppressed emotion in his narrowed, lifeless eyes could have been sorrow for Samantha Burn's passing, but it wasn't that. Regardless of the booze he must have drunk, he gave a lucid explanation of why he was here, as he repositioned the chair to face into the room and began to tell me a harrowing story of what had happened.

"I've never told anyone other than Mike about what happened, but on the day before I called you from Durban, there was a knock on the door at Bath which my man Harris answered. I was in the library looking for a map I had there. It's not important now what the map was for, but of course I clearly heard the knock.

"After a while, I called out to Harris as he hadn't come into the library to announce whoever it was who'd called. He was a congenial type, was Harris, and I thought maybe he was at the door chatting to someone.

"He always had a smile and something good to say about his fellow man, did Harris. Seldom would he say anything negative, but that was not the man who stood before me that day.

"There had been nobody at the door when he'd answered it, he told me, more in a murmur than in his usual self-assured voice. He added how he was looking around when he saw the small package left on the doorstep with an envelope pinned to the top.

"He said he'd taken the package through to my office and left it on the desktop. I dare say someone like you, who can disregard everything in life, might find this hard to imagine, but I was extremely upset and very jumpy about things after the inquest into the incident involving Samantha.

"I'm sorry to say, my edginess had settled onto Harris as well, so much so that the shakiness in his voice did nothing to improve my own self-confidence. It was just a vicious circle we were both in."

He emptied the remaining whisky in the glass that he held in one swallow, then, rising from his chair, he asked if I wanted to join him in a drink before fetching an open half-bottle from which he refilled his own glass, ignoring me. Gibson showed what an attentive gentleman's gentleman he was, as before I could answer, he had found another glass, unopened a remaining half bottle he'd found and was already pouring.

"No worries, skip, we have a couple of spare bottles when these run out. Do you still pack the glass to the hilt with ice before the Scotch?" he enquired, smiling, as the ice cubes tumbled noisily clicking against each other into the tall, empty glass.

I accepted it from Liam's hand, tasting it as I sat on the chair at the balcony end of the writing table. It wasn't the finest whisky I'd drunk, but it would do. I lit my first cigarette since arriving in America and offered the packet around. It was refused by the two non-smokers as I expected; however, as I'd been surprised so many times recently, I was primed for anything.

Bottomly took up his recount of the parcel that arrived on the Monday.

"I wasn't going to open it, especially when I read

the note Harris said was lying on top of it which accounted for his strange behaviour. The message on the note was short, in block capital letters and bold print; it read: *Something for your loss.*

"That worried me, Harry. I think it might have worried most people, including you. Anyway, I phoned the police and left it where it was. An hour and bit later, the police were able to confirm what it was—it was a bomb, old chap.

"The officer in charge of the army ordnance disposal crew said there were enough explosives inside to have killed me outright, and probably Harris as well. I told the police I had no idea who could have sent it to me, and that was the truth, in part. I had no definite idea, but there were a few I could think of who might want to try,"

I had the chance of a question, when he stopped speaking in preference to sampling his whisky. "Aren't you being a bit melodramatic? Are there really people out there who want to blow you up?" I asked incredulously.

Liam Gibson was pacing the room speaking to Tommy York, courtesy of his mobile phone. "Take another look, Tommy. This time do it in the opposite direction, but slower. Get a picture if you can, but without showing out."

Bots had not noticed Liam speaking into his phone, or, if he had, he didn't comment. Instead, he answered my question.

"For a start, there's the Russian who Gerald was blackmailing. I wanted away from it, for good. Whatever information the Russian was supplying London, I would eventually see it, that's if I wanted to look. I told him I didn't want to know the name, but oh no, he told me.

"Had to, didn't he! Wanted me to know so he could use it as another lever in forcing me to murder Samantha. He said if I didn't kill her, he would tell Hugh Pickering that I had the name. If he did that, Pickering would come after me."

Whilst he was taking a sip from his glass, I should have been able to get my head around what he was saying but I couldn't, it was too confusing.

"Samantha told me all about his past dealings with Pickering and his friends in the CIA. I did not know she and Pickering had been, as Gerald put it, intimate friends, but most of what he said was fabricated. I asked her and I'm satisfied she was honest with me. I'm not a fool. I know everyone wanted to climb into bed with her. I bet you did when you first saw her. No, I don't need an answer, Harry, I know you."

He was drinking whisky as though it was going out of production. I had no wish to keep up with him, refusing his offer to refill my glass at least three times when he was refilling his own.

I chanced a look at Liam, wanting to message him not to bring any more bottles to the table. I thought I might have to physically stop him the next time his glass was empty, but for now he was content with speaking.

"I knew Gerald Neil's prime concern would always be his money and he'd do anything to get it back, but by the time he'd strung it all together in his threats to me, I believed there could have been a lot of truth in what he was saying about Pickering working all sides of the fence with his secret CIA contacts. I am well aware of the type of man Pickering is, as well.

"I'd met him once for lunch at a restaurant just off Fleet Street, near the Goldman Sachs building in central London. It was a year or so ago, so maybe the company has gone by now.

"He was in the company of what he called a couple of investment bankers looking for opportunities. He wanted them to meet me. If they were bankers, then I was an astronaut. Anyway, it seemed to me Pickering was always surrounded by dubious characters whenever he was in Gerald's Crocketts club.

"I wouldn't put anything past characters like him, especially if he thought he would be threatened by my continued existence. I doubt he would be able to kill me, but I'm not so silly as to think he wouldn't know someone who would. What do you think?"

I didn't answer, but I did take his empty glass away from him, giving it to Liam, saying I thought we'd both had enough for the night. I was surprised Winston made no attempt to argue, but I was not surprised he continued speaking.

"By now you probably know I've worked for home security. Gerald Neil had no idea of my connection to MI5. It was because he didn't know, that he told me he'd not told anyone in the Home Office the truth about him knowing the Russian he'd caught on film.

"The truth was, Gerald was simply a gossip who wanted to keep close to Pickering with his friends from across the Atlantic, because they throw money at his tables. He was also on friendly terms with a few high-rolling Russians who used his club. It was all for the money.

"He probably told Pickering, as well as those other Russians, everything about himself. He certainly told me, so why not them? He told me about his Greek island, with his wine-growing estate on it.

"Not forgetting the big, expensive yacht he has moored there. Plus, he told me *his baby*, that's what he calls the obscene size of a boat he has at Cowes, cost some astronomical amount of money. It was so obscene I've forgotten the total, Harry.

"One night he was so full of himself. More so than usual. Ha, ha, I should talk, shouldn't I? I'd get a gold medal at the Olympics for talking at this rate. Where was I? Oh yes! I remember. Gerald Neil. Yes, he was boasting how he'd pulled off a huge coup.

"I remember his words because I thought it was a strange choice of words to use. He said he'd been a wily *old pigeon.* I went along with him, praising him, etc, etc, and open up he did.

"He said he'd taken a fortune from a high-ranking Russian officer to use a back room at the club with a woman he was going to introduce to the place. He said he wasn't completely sure, but thought the Russian came from the London embassy as he seemed to know his way around. The woman, he'd never seen before.

"She came in with him, then left with him after the fun they'd had with the sex and the coke they'd been snorting. He'd got them on film doing lines of the stuff the Russian had brought in with him. He said the Russian took away a couple of bottles of his overpriced champagne, leaving Gerald with an over-sized Russian wad of cash in his back pocket.

"I believed most of what he said, but there was something about...well, about them not knowing it was being filmed, as well as him not knowing who she was. I wasn't sure about either of those. I can't tell you why, Harry. I just had a feeling."

Before he continued, he looked for his glass. Not finding it did not stop him, nor did it stop the heavy sigh he gave before taking another cigarette from my open packet. For a non-smoker, he was doing rather well. I copied him, watching his steady hand light his cigarette first, then mine.

"Gerald said he'd told Samantha the name of the Russian in the photo. To give him his due, he said he thought it was a mistake to tell her. What's more, the stupid fool told Pickering she was the only other one who knew the name.

"Pickering, no matter what he is, is certainly no fool. He knew she would tell me. He called me on the Thursday before the shoot, but he never mentioned it outright. He never normally mentioned anything outright. He was going everywhere with the conversation, bar the subject he really wanted to speak about.

"Eventually, after my ears were worn out listening to him, he got there. Said he had a couple of friends just arrived from across the pond who he would love to invite and show them just what the English gentry get up to in their leisure time. He said we could have a bit of a competition. Bit of a friendly wager sort of thing. Him and I against the two of them in a shoot-out. That was his suggestion. I remember him saying we could hire some cowboy outfits. He knew a place in Shaftesbury Avenue where they'd have them. He got out of his pram then. Asked me if Samantha wore one when she was... I shall not repeat the words he used. I'm sure you can guess."

No matter how I considered myself when it came to drink, this man was most certainly a hardened drinker who, until fairly recently, I'd thought of as almost a teetotaller. Another thing about him was he could most certainly hold his drink. I had caught him looking in the direction of where Liam was a couple of times, presumably for a whisky, but he made no fuss when none was forthcoming. I was content to sit and listen.

"I exchanged a few hostile words with Gerald at that stage, forcing him to apologise when I said Samantha and I were to be engaged. I think I only said it as I was in a fit of temper. I've got no other explanation. Yes, I'm plenty sure I loved her, though marriage... hmm, well no. I wasn't ready for that. No, not that far. That's when he told me the name of the Russian. It was the same man I regularly met to exchange the information I'm given from military intelligence.

"I've never been so jumpy than when Gerald said it was Valery Agapov. He's told me he's the Russian meteorologist at the embassy. Honestly, the hairs on the back of my neck were on edge when Gerald said that name. I did know Agapov had a reputation, but I had no idea he knew, and used Crocketts.

"I called the duty officer at Millbank the following morning. To be honest, I was a bit far gone that night. I didn't want to get anything jumbled up by slurring my voice. Up until now, I think I've been more than just useful to MI5. I've covered operations both home and abroad for them. Some with Liam on our own, some with Liam and parts of his South African lot. It would not suit the British, nor American intelligence, if some of what's been done came out."

* * *

To say I was a bit confused would be an understatement of the facts, not only by the sad but serious look in Winston's eyes, but part of my state of confusion lay with his admission of being drunk the night Gerald Neil shared the Russian's name with him.

Was it a true admission, or a simple lie used to conceal his deceit? If true, it made my not-long-ago admiration for his drinking capacity misplaced! The other part of my confusion lay with how was I supposed to know what he was threatening to do, along with the reason why? However, I did have to take his threat seriously.

As far as I knew, nobody was threatening him, least of all me, but I felt uneasy, particularly with Liam Gibson so near. Liam was, as I said, a killer. That was behind my reasoning to sit facing where he was.

* * *

Gibson was born in Belfast, in Ireland, and told me a story of when he was fourteen, three Catholic boys, somewhat older than him, picked a fight. He said he couldn't be sure they knew he was the only one without a knife.

There were only two Catholics who left the place they had chosen to fight Liam, alive. From that day onwards, he never stopped killing, simply curtailing his energy until the Crown required it, after joining the British army.

He often quoted a motto—*don't worry about the fight the dog's in, worry about the fight in the dog.* He had enough fighting vitality inside himself to supply many dogs.

He did his basic training at the Army Foundation College, the grounds of which are to the north of the Paterson estate in Harrogate. He completed his final ten-week training at Catterick, the centre of all British infantry training. He went on to join the regular Royal Irish Regiment, seeing service in the jungle of Brunei in an infantry battalion alongside some of the best Gurkha fighters around.

It was because of his conduct in Brunei that he was selected for his first tour of duty in a squadron of the Special Air Service, going on to not only serve in their counterparts in South Africa, but to command sections within the regiment. He killed people with as much regret as an ordinary person would have if told they had trodden on an ant. Also some people would have more respect for the ant than Gibson had for life.

* * *

My experience of combat was nowhere near as extensive as Gibson's, but even so, I had operated under a British service licence, of one kind or another, before in Europe, knowing full well the rules of engagement, although my recent exposure to secret intelligence service protocol did not include any end-of-life procedure.

However, my training and natural ability to lie provided me with enough deceitful ways to carry off an authentic Machiavellian grin in order to keep me in the game. I continued to listen as Bots carried on with his assessment of the story.

It was not long before his tale sent my memory racing back to Sir Leonard and our lunch at White's Club in St James's. Our lunch was where I tried to convince him of my misunderstanding of how Bottomly's name became enmeshed with the Russians. Leonard was enlarging on his account of Gerald Neil's MI5 contributions, seeming oblivious to my concerns.

"Gerald's capability of carrying off a two-way trade seems to have gone wrong this time; tragically wrong for Samantha. But it started when he told Pickering what he'd done. That meant he was no longer in charge of his own destiny. Pickering would, without a shadow of a doubt, want everything Gerald had. He would want to be able to give it all to the

CIA, in order to ingratiate himself further, but when it became known Gerald had told Samantha all about it, then the currency he was holding decreased drastically in value.

"Whatever caused Gerald to realise it was not he who controlled the market place, we will never know. Be that as it may, but we do know he suddenly became aware of wanting the girl removed from the negotiations. More than likely he realised he'd made a hash of everything and he would be in need of protection. That's when he opened up to first us, then you."

To my mind, MI5 could not have allowed the trading to continue with Burns in the middle. I was thinking someone told Millbank it was Valery Agapov in this mysterious photo. That someone could have been Gerald Neil, Hugh Pickering, or Bottomly, it wasn't important who told, but his name had not much value. That wasn't so of the woman. It seemed to me her name was either being protected, or her name wasn't known. But was she the important part in the photograph?

I knew I was tired; the last thing I needed was more whisky to drink but Bots seemed to be wanting more. I made an excuse, which wasn't completely a lie.

I said my memory was playing up because I was short of sleep. I'd had some on the plane but not much. I suggested we both got some sleep then saw how we were in a few hours' time. I was going to catch up with Liam before I left, but there was something else. A question that needed an answer.

I asked if he had recognised the woman in the photograph, or had Gerald or Samantha told him who she was?

"Nobody told me who she was, or told Samantha. She said Gerald had shown her, but took it back straight away. She said she'd hardly glanced at it and never held it in her hands. I think I saw Agapov on the Friday before the shoot.

"I'm sure it was before the shoot, but it might have been after. I'm sorry. Whenever it was, I asked him for her name. He clammed up tight. Shook his head a dozen or more times, really slowly, being really deliberate about it. But to reiterate and perhaps draw a close to it, he repeated he didn't know her name. If he did know, there was no way he was giving it away.

"This will sound strange, but nevertheless I'm going to say it. The last time we met, which wasn't long ago, I got the impression he wants to flip. Defect, go over! From somewhere, not from me, but he knows it's you who's ferreting around about something. He mentioned your name. He said he'd heard how you helped a highly prominent Russian get away without causing any fuss. He was laughing, but I'm positive he wasn't being funny when he asked if you get Russians away from Russian grip regularly. I replied I'd ask, and that's when he said if ever he wanted to jump ship, he would like you to be the pilot. That's what made me think he wanted to defect."

I smiled when I said I'd get some cards printed with my phone number and the words, *Russian Defection a Speciality*, printed in calligraphy. I asked again about the photograph. This time asking when he had seen it. I was trying to catch him out.

"I told you I hadn't seen it, Harry, so please, don't ask again or I might think you're coming after me." It didn't work. Or did it?

CHAPTER FOURTEEN

THE CONVERSATION

I started at the place where I've always believed it best to start; at the beginning. Despite that belief, my beginning was a long way into this story from Winston's point of view. I began by telling Liam the story where I first heard Samantha's life was in danger.

"I overheard Gerald Neil say 'get rid of her, Bottomly', or words to that effect. At first, I didn't believe he meant it in a fatal sense. I wasn't sure what I thought, but I do know it wasn't that. I know how strange, let alone unreal, that must sound, having heard what happened on that drive at the shoot. When I believed Gerald's story of how much money Bots owed, it wasn't hard to form a picture of what must have gone on in his mind. That's only if he thought he had no other way to repay the debt, but he hadn't asked me as Gerald Neil said he would.

"I'm finding it very difficult to believe things had got so bad that he could not have come to me sooner to ask for help. Did you know how much trouble he was in, Liam?"

I could hear the shower running in the room adjoining the balcony as I tried my best to unravel the situation as I knew it, but I thought it was not having all the facts that was holding me back.

"I knew nothing of it until after the inquest, skip. All he said was there had been a terrible accident and he needed a fast exit from the UK. I've heard those words 'accident' and 'exit' too many times in the past to mistake the true meaning—*I've got to run*—but I never asked anything further until we met up at King Shaka. The airport in Durban.

"He hasn't really told me much, other than he killed a woman because he had no other choice, but he hasn't elaborated on how it happened. What he did say was that you stepped in to make it appear to be the accident the inquest said had happened. He added you'd been the good friend he knew you were.

"I flew up to Pretoria last week for provisions to stock up his farm. I arranged for extra security for the place when he said he thought his life might be in danger. I really need to know the extent of any threat, and until I do, I can't gauge what we'll require to stock in food and munitions. I have enough of both for a good while if it starts out as a stand-off or siege of any kind, which wouldn't work anyway, but it would be good to know what he expects."

"Are you expecting some form of retribution following what you did in London, Liam, and will that impact on the Major? What was it you were after that needed lumps to be cut out of Gerald Neil?"

"What did you do, Liam?" It was Bots, all showered and smelling better. He appeared genuinely shocked. Gibson, wanting no interrogation from us, stood up, crossed the room without speaking and left, quietly closing the door as he did.

I waited whilst Winston denied any knowledge of Gerald Neil's archaic torture or dismemberment. He said he could not think of anyone who would want that, or why it would be wanted. I'm genuinely sorry to say I didn't believe him.

There was nothing in the way he voiced his denial, or in the words he used, it was simply a feeling on my part. Although I had no answer to the way I felt, I could not see my friend Bottomly authorising the torture of someone.

I was trying hard to be objective to the situation, not allowing past friendship to cloud my judgement. All of a sudden a chill came over me, at the thought that perhaps it was my naivety that was making me ideal for this job?

* * *

I said my farewells and, with Tommy retracing the steps we'd taken, I returned to the Sofitel in the reaffirmed knowledge there was nobody I could trust. It would seem suspicion had become a guileful instinct to sit beside me for the rest of my life, where learning to trust was a far from easy thing for me to do.

Perhaps, whilst searching for an answer to something else, I had learned the answer to the lack of a true, meaningful relationship I had never been able to build. At that moment, I hated myself more than anyone or anything I could imagine and it took the rest of the journey, travelled in silence, to come to terms with the job I was here to do. At the hotel, I thanked Tommy, more in a mechanical mood than anything else. I blamed tiredness, more in hope than knowing it to be the truth.

* * *

I locked the door to my hotel room and made some telephone calls. The first was to enquire about Breno. Serena sounded happy as she told me how he was exceeding all expectations with his academic work, as well as, more importantly, if my ex-wife's eagerness to explain had anything to do with it, his ability when riding a horse.

Equine pursuits were the foremost forms of exercise known to the Abenazo family, of whom Serena and then our son Breno were the final survivors. Her younger brother, of the same name as our son, had died when riding more dangerously than he should have at the vast country home they once owned.

That Breno, Serena's brother, had shown early promise at the ivories of the piano, only for his interest to fade as riding took over. Despite Breno showing no expertise or liking for his lessons at the music school he attended, Serena persisted in her desire for his education in the piano.

My other son, Luca, was excelling at the piano keys in Vienna, gathering comments in writing as well as spoken, giving his mother, Katherine Tovarisch Korovin, great satisfaction in his and her achievements. Although I was unaware of any Paterson being musically gifted, I did know, or at least believe, them all to have been adept on a horse. I promised myself I would ring one of my two sisters, who might know more about our musical history.

As I lay on the bed in my hotel room waiting for sleep to take me away, I thought of Serena's father with whom I had been friends for many years, though sadly I had never known her younger brother, Breno. Even so, from the stories she told I felt very close to him, sharing in the same admiration she felt.

It was not hard to see how Serena wanted to resurrect her brother through our son, but it was a seemingly innocent remark she made about a current news story that made me sit up straight and take notice: had I seen the news coverage of a ship allegedly carrying highly sophisticated weaponry to Lebanon, being seized by the Israelis? It was boarded by them when it had apparently strayed into Israeli waters.

In spite of not seeing anything about it, instinctively I knew I should have. What should have been a relaxing telephone call prior to sleep turned out to be the opposite. No sooner had I closed my phone than it annoyingly rang again. I looked at the displayed time. For the previous call, it might have been a civilised seven o'clock in the morning in Portugal, but here we were an uncivilised five hours behind them.

For some unknown reason, I was marvelling at the phone's technology to automatically change from London, England time to Eastern Standard Time, when I suddenly thought about sleep. I wasn't tired, but equally I wasn't as wide awake as Liam Gibson was, on the other end of the telephone.

"There are two ugly Russians in the bar of your hotel, skip, and one of them asked at the front desk if Mr Harry Paterson was registered. They emerged from a cab which is parked across the road. I checked its registration plate and it's a ringer. It's not a cab at all. It's a number on the registry we have at the embassy. We call them SAVs. A Standard Alert Vehicle, for Russian use. There's one guy built like a gorilla left inside it. I don't know what they feed them on nowadays but they keep coming in the extra, extra large fit.

"Tommy has eyes on the cab, and he's called up a couple of extra guys from the pool to help. I didn't want to alarm anyone by saying I was following you and Tommy here. I'm a bit short on street people though, skip, having left two of my original covers with the Major.

"We don't have to do anything unless you want to, but if you do want to move your accommodation I have a spare side arm with me and I'm in the foyer with a girl, name of Oona. She's one of us. What's more, she's more than a bit useful in any kind of fight."

Before I'd had a real chance to kick the lack of sleep clear from my head, I found myself advising caution inside the hotel and, if possible, a staggered tail of the cab when it left. I considered myself safe behind the name of Yorkshire in the hotel register. It should not trigger any reaction from the two Russians had they looked. For now, I had no reason to believe the name had rung any bells. If the embassy sent anyone with an intelligence background they could join the dots. Nevertheless, as of now, nobody had associated the 'Yorkshire' name with me.

Despite Liam never having enlarged on his statement about Oona's prowess in a fight, he did add something else; apparently she was an expert cryptographer employed inside the South African Security Services who had been assigned to cover all radio signals emanating from the Russian Embassy in Pretoria relating to Major Bottomly, code named Thanatopsis, by those responsible for such things inside the FSB. I'd asked how they knew Winston was in America.

"We think, and this is only a guess, Mr Paterson," it was Oona who offered the answer, "the Russians had the algorithms running measuring blackbody radiation changes when Major Bottomly was leaving the UK. That's their speciality at the moment, using electromagnetic wavelengths measuring solid particles. I could get more technical if you want, sir, but assuming you don't, it must have started from there.

"That assumption is based on the fact that our communication loops started measuring interference when he was in transit in the proximity of the North Pole. We never attempted impinging on the condition, remaining pretty quiet, as I believe Mr Gibson told you. We adopted that stance mainly because we didn't know what to expect.

I have personally been responsible for supervising all the communications from our hub regarding the security placed in and around Mr Bottomly's person, as well as the surrounds of the family estate. That's a highly secure, sensitive area from which I can guarantee no spur from the hub signals are intercepted. I've seen the ratings and the

SASS is a little way in front of any opposition in that sphere."

I tried to appear suitably impressed, but when I asked why she thought the Bottomly estate needed to be a *secure and sensitive area* as she'd put it, she mumbled something that sounded as though I should address the question to Bottomly himself, to which I added a completely unnecessary remark about highly valuable cows wandering around the Veldt hand in hand with the cock and bull from the nursery rhymes she and Liam were peddling. Her lost expression reminded me of a puppy dog when first told by his, or her, owner to obediently sit.

$$* * *$$

It was as I was looking at her that I felt what my late mother would described as someone walking over her grave. It was a chilly draught running through my bones, making me shiver for a second. I was being dragged deeper into this for some reason, but my mind was firmly stuck on Bots's invitation to his grouse shoot having come about by way of an accident caused by nature, so to imagine it all being manipulated was ridiculous... or was it?

CHAPTER FIFTEEN

MAYFAIR

I left the brigade of Guards in June 2003, three months after the beginning of the war in Iraq, and my path and the one Bots travelled along crossed on a few occasions. However, there's one in particular that our conversation in the American hotel room brought swiftly to mind. Not having a wish to count the days on my fingers, I'm guessing it was about five years or so ago that Viscount Bottomly and I met purely by the word that I have been thinking of whilst I slept, and the word would be—luck.

I wouldn't normally be so utterly confident about the timing of a meeting, although journals are kept at The Hall, primarily for recording the dates of dinner parties, guests who attended them, and of course the food served, with diaries being similarly kept in the Estate Office, for the recording of point-to-point races, farming shows, any other horticultural events either held on the estate, or ones we transported stock to and from, plus the regular visits by veterinary surgeons.

I myself did not keep a regular paper list of lovers' names with addresses, nor where we would find our amusement; all of those were kept safely on my phone in my breast pocket, or scrambled into a vacant segment of my memory.

Despite those safeguards, my memory differed in this particular case with Bottomly. By the choice exercised by fate, we *accidentally* bumped into one another at an art gallery in Cork Street, in London's Mayfair, where a friend of mine was exhibiting her paintings in the first two weeks of either September 2014, or 2015.

* * *

Bots was accompanied by a very beautiful young woman named Vivian, to whom I remember remarking on how she shared a great deal of her stunning looks with Vivian Leigh, the actress. I do not feel embarrassed in complimenting one beautiful women when in the company of another, unless, of course, I had not paid sufficient tributes to my own companion, which I had on several occasions before bumping into this Vivian lady.

With the lady on Bottomly's arm, it wasn't so

much the colour of her eyes and hair that compelled me to make the comparison I did, although those attributes were remarkably similar, it was more her sculptured lips and the enigmatic look she had when her chin was tucked inwards towards her neck, forcing her head to tilt forward into a petulant kind of expression that was markedly there when I decided, for the sake of chivalry, that I would allow Bots to take her from me. I distinctly recall how her expression changed to one of arrogance when he purchased a pricey painting that she said she'd fallen in love with.

I made those remarks to the lady in question within earshot of Winston, but any reference to the 'arrogance and petulant looks' I made privately to my own lady friend when her exhibition closed and we were alone.

My observations were made casually, without realising how much of an effect those two words would have on her until we were comfortable at her mews house just off Kensington Square. Once there, she made me award her points for showing both of those inclinations when we were making love.

Before her love of painting had taken her over, she was by profession a writer, which might possibly account for her reciting a quote she had learned whilst at university in America. The quote was from Vernon Howard, the one I knew—*A truly strong person does not need the approval of others any more than a lion needs the approval of sheep.*

Not only was Howard's astute remark perfect for the moment, it made a very memorable evening even more unparalleled, as I recall my partner was peerless at being both arrogant and petulant, with aplomb.

Of course, none of that is relevant other than the following mid-morning, Winston called me whilst I was still at my lady friend's address. It would seem my friend was his art tutor and conveniently he had her number. He had telephoned to reschedule an appointment.

So much for an *accidental* meeting, I thought. On the face of things, that wasn't the only new thing I learned of Winston Bottomly that day. We arranged to meet for lunch at my club; however, it wasn't there we met!

On my arrival at Boodles, Simon, the concierge, handed me a note, which, when unfolded, had a phone number written upon it. It had been handed in by a Mr Gibson, he told me, adding, "He said outside centre number 12, and you would know what that meant, sir." I did, of course, and rang the number from the public telephone box around the corner in Jermyn Street.

It was Bots who answered my call. He changed the rendezvous to the bar at the Mayfair Hotel, a short walk from where I was. He was calm in voice, but not forthcoming when I asked for the reason behind the change of meeting place. Nevertheless, I set off immediately for the hotel and the shock of my life.

After all the running around to appease this newly found need of subterfuge, I was expecting at least the offer of a drink to quench my thirst, but no. Nothing was offered. Thoughtfulness had been forsaken. Worse was to follow. He had inexplicably discovered the requirement to vehemently declare, accompanied by strange, wild gesticulations, that his chastity was intact when it came to my lady friend, his art teacher.

I could only then, and can only now, guess at the reasons that compelled him to make such a proclamation in such a spectacular way, and that guess would be he was not telling the truth. Here was another liar. The surprise in it all was the lady in question and I were not married, as well he knew, so there was absolutely no need for his bashfulness, nor his lie. Make of it what you will, without coming to the same conclusion.

* * *

At the time this puzzled me, leaving no alternative other than to regard everything from that moment on, coupled with all that I could remember of consequence, with more caution applied than normally I would have. And, this hurts me to say, I came to a conclusion: that in future I should treat everything from Bots as a lie, then I wouldn't be disappointed if it turned out to be the truth!

* * *

I had no evidence to suggest he was a compulsive liar, but a man who feels the need to deny an affair with a beautiful, unmarried lady is not a respectable person —not the type I would have had much to do with, in the past. Normally, one would expect men to brag about conquests, even exaggerating some. They do not deny a relationship unless there is a compelling reason.

"I know you work for the intelligence mob, Harry, that's why I engineered that meeting we had. Sir Leonard Miles told me. I'd asked if you were in the secret service. His answer included the fact you'd shot a man in Hamburg. There's no need to look so worried though, he didn't elaborate further.

"He added that you had done something that had mightily pleased the Americans. He did add one re-mark I thought was very strange, though. He said you had upset the home establishment and they didn't approve of you very much. I found that hard to be-lieve. He had a look of disapproval on his face when he told me."

* * *

All of a sudden, the doors to my hitherto confidential life were being easily prised open, along with the beliefs of a friend's virility shot to ribbons. The shock of both left me about to catch a cold from the razor-sharp draught. I tried playing the innocent party, wounded and nearing death for such a claim, but he knew my secret was beyond denial.

"There's no-one else I can ask. I got caught up in something in Iraq after you were posted home. It was all rather stupid, I'm afraid. I was attached to the FCU—it's the Forward Control Unit, if by now you've forgotten all the abbreviations we used. The unit was following the ground assault into the country.

"I thought I would be with my company operating Scimitars on recon missions ahead of the assault teams. It wasn't to be. For the first week, FCU was a mobile control hub, shunting from one post to another catching up to the situation, but by the second, we had a static position where the press corps began to filter into a growing presence.

"I don't rightly recall how or why it came about, but it didn't take long before I was appointed as the coalition press release officer. Soon after, a very lovely French journalist by the name of Colette made herself known. She caught my eye because from day one, she was always the first to arrive and the last to leave the briefings. Incidentally, I'm unsure if it's important but she said she worked for Le Figaro"

Bots had an annoying habit of interrupting a decent story with unnecessary facts with the equally unnecessary figures. This time, unlike so many in the past, I was very grateful he quickly regained his stride "I'll cut a short story even shorter by saying we ended up in bed but I didn't know she was a Russian spy until much, much later, and that's the truth. Not a single word of a lie."

* * *

I believe I have already explained where I stand on the necessity of adding any reflection on the truth of a statement. Having already decided where the truth from Winston was to be filed, I treated what I was listening to with just a tad more interest than I was showing the speck of dust on one of my shoes.

Dumfounded, I asked, "What on earth! How were you expected to know, Winston?"

"Well, in the circumstances it would have helped. Had I known then, it could have saved my future embarrassment. You see, some photographs of us together in bed found their way to the O.I.C. and I was summoned to appear before the Polish Brigadier, Commanding.

"There was no standing order I'd disobeyed, nor had I breached security, so it was a mystery to me why I was ordered to appear. While I was waiting, the most I could imagine to happen would be a rap across the knuckles for acting in some inappropriate manner, but, as I've said, at this stage I had no idea she was a spy. I had better make it clear there was nothing I'd given her that was in any way sensitive. It was exactly what I'd read out as the day's press release."

Was there a need to repeat himself? Were my suspicions getting the better of me, I wondered. And while we were on the matter, I wondered who designated material to be—*sensitive?*

"Inside the O.I.C.'s office there were to be no rapped knuckles, nothing of the sort occurred. I was formally cautioned, then threatened with a court martial, accompanied by a dishonourable discharge with a long stay in the glasshouse thrown in for good measure if I did not comply with any orders I was to be given.

"The charge was consorting with an inappropriate foreign national. There was a civilian seated at the same desk as the Brigadier who was silent throughout the proceedings, keeping his head down, looking as if he was scrutinising some papers spread out on the table in front of himself. He never looked up once, Harry.

"The whole thing took no more than a couple of minutes from when the charge was read out to when I was dismissed to wait in a room beyond where the inquiry was taking place. Whilst I was there, the same civilian from the enquiry approached and informed me of Colette's Russian connection. I wasn't left with much time to assimilate what I'd just heard."

"Did this civilian introduce himself?" I asked, interrupting him, my interest having increased.

"No, he didn't. But if he wasn't important, he certainly acted as though he was. He instructed my escort to leave the room while he spoke to me, then, when he finished, he called them back in and asked them to take me to wait in the Comms outer office. There, I was ordered to stand until I was joined by three other men, all in civilian clothes.

"They showed their identification to the escort, who handcuffed me behind my back then draped a bag over my head. I thought I was going to be taken outside, then shot! Seriously, I was really that frightened. But there was no pole, no firing squad.

"Instead, I was marched along the airstrip until I could hear an aircraft on my right-hand side. I knew there was an American C-17 transport aircraft waiting to take off very near, so that's what we must have disembarked in.

"We touched down roughly six hours later and then I was driven to a place that was an hour's drive away, maybe less. I wore that bag all the time, but I reckon you could make an informed guess at where I was, Harry."

"Perhaps I could, but not without something more in the way of clues. There's not much you're giving away, so far. What about the civilian in the Iraqi base, what did he look like?"

"I would say he was mid-forties, Mediterranean-coloured skin with freckles, that I thought was rather odd. Black hair with an angular face, very pronounced chin. He was shorter than me, maybe five foot ten or round about that."

That was too vague for a man such as Bots with a presence in the South African intelligence gathering service, so I pressed for more.

"Why did you think the freckles were odd, Winston, and how about his voice? Any accent, or anything distinctive about that, or his clothing?"

"Nothing distinctive about the voice, H." He paused for thought. "But it was certainly polished, more smooth than coarse. I'd say an army officer of rank rather than an NCO. I hope that doesn't sound snobbish as it wasn't meant to be. The only freckles I saw were on the back of his hands. That's why I thought it odd. His shirtsleeves were buttoned up to the wrist so I couldn't tell if they were on his arm, but they were certainly not on his face. As far as clothing goes, then I'd say it was expensive, but unobtrusive tailoring."

"No, it wasn't snobbish. If that's how he sounded, then that's how it was. Carry on with your flight, and how it impacted on that time in your life."

"When we landed, we must have been close to the sea because I could taste the salt and smell it when we exited the aircraft. Another thing happened when we got away from the tarmac. I got a glimpse of at least a dozen Viking armoured vehicles, which I believe is the standard transport issue of the Royal Marines. From wherever we were, we went on that hour's journey in what felt like a Land Rover military jeep without any springs. They took the bag off when we arrived and I was right about the Royal Marines and the mode of transport. Their insignia was on the side of the Land Rover.

"When I was permitted to disembark, I was inside a walled garden at a side entrance to a sprawling old English Tudor house. I could smell the freshly mown grass and perfumed roses. Where we had landed, I'd heard several Scottish accents and at least one Geordie one. Wherever it was I was taken, it was a British base."

* * *

I had an idea he'd landed at the Royal Marines barracks at Poole, in Dorset and now, after that road journey, he was at Beaulieu, home to Lord and Lady Montagu, also the starting point for inclusion into all branches of the secret service. As Bots had said—I was indeed conversant with Beaulieu House.

He went on to tell how they had held him there for three days, giving him a rudimentary insight into what was affectionately referred to by the instructors as 'tradecraft'.

The idea planted in his head was to continue the affair with Colette whilst working alongside a person, yet to be introduced, whom they called his Control. An elaborate system was devised to avoid mistakes, whereby he would know he was communicating with the right man. They got as far as instructions to implement on his return to active duty.

Once he was back in Iraq, this Control fellow would make himself known to Bots by saying — *Henry Liddell's eldest daughter was the young girl Lewis Carroll based a book on called Alice's Adventures in Wonderland.* When he said that, Bots was to reply, *Secunda*; then, if this was the right man, he would reply using the Latin for 'third', *Tertia*.

After all that song and dance had been settled, and trying to reassure Winston, they said this Control chap would guide him along and eventually become a friend he could turn to for advice.

That made me smile, but I quickly lost the smile when I learned it would be this man who would judge what material could be passed on to Colette. There were very few facts Bots was told about this Colette. All he was told was she was a Russian asset, with a Russian mother and a South African father.

I wondered and asked if he thought they kept her background secret in case he recognised her family. I'm afraid I was then distracted into telling him about a woman friend I had with the same name. If you will excuse me, I shall repeat it here.

"I once knew a French Colette from Paris. Met her at a polo match over there in France. She was such a beautiful woman. Full of style, grace, and elegance. She had everything the French are renowned for, including, in her case, the additional advantage of being unmarried and filthy rich. She even had that quality that few women have, of arriving late but making it seem as though everyone else arrived early. It made me giggle silently. I never let her know I was amused by her tardiness.

"I can't remember what happened to her. Oh yes, I do alright! She married a horse breeder I had introduced her to and then, to make matters worse, she became a faithful wife. Now that's what I would call real disloyalty on her part. How boring must she be? At least he had his horses to go to when he was bored." I tried to get back on track by asking Winston if he thought he was being used.

"Is it the fact that Colette was using you that's knocked you back so much, or the fact you got found out, because neither can matter now, surely?" I was right and wrong.

"But those things do matter and on an international scale they do. At first, I admit I was a bit put out by her picking me as her *target*, as those three men who did the briefing continually wanted to label me. Yes, I was a bit ashamed at not recognising her as a spy, thinking it was my good looks that had attracted her, but I got over that when I took into account the obvious personal benefit I was experiencing. After all, I'm not a complete fool. It would have been fine if she and this Control fellow, who at last had a name—Jackson—had not mentioned Angola, along with my family's interests in South Africa.

"She wanted to know where the family holdings were, as did Jackson. Except his inquiries were more obtuse than hers. I was happy enough to play along until we got to that point. By the look that's been clouding your face for the last half an hour or so, Harry, I'm reckoning you're working along the lines that I am an utter fool being led up the garden path with a Russian maid doing the leading. I'm not, you know."

"No, you're wrong. I'm just listening to you. Simply concentrating, old man, nothing more, I assure you." I almost said—*honestly*!

"Okay, my mistake. I'll carry on then. Shall I?"

"Of course, but tell me again if you would, who appointed this chap Jackson? If you don't mind me saying, you were a little vague on that point."

"Was I? I didn't mean to be. Sorry about that. Someone called me when I was back in Iraqi. I'm sure he said his name was Jones. But it was a fictional name, H, I'm sure."

He was a bit on the slow side with his reply, but I

couldn't decide if he was thinking on his feet, as it were, or whether he was tired and the drink was still working its way through his body. I fashioned a smile, trying hard not to damage all the bits and pieces jammed into my brain. I gently nodded my head before adding a weary, and insincere, "Carry on, old bean."

"Right then," he announced. "On the first night back in base, when I contrived to meet Colette, there was no surprise on her face at all. I've no idea why, but I wondered if she'd been told I had gone to England, with the appendage of to be careful. There was another thing, it never seemed to me as though she tried to pretend.

"She greeted me in Afrikaans, which she'd never done before, and went on to say '*n Aap in die mou hê*', which translated literally means to have a monkey up your sleeve, or in English, to have a cunning plan up your sleeve. I thought she was accusing me of having a cunning plan whilst she continued to ask about the family's estate. It crossed my mind she was being primed for my benefit. I found myself asking—why me?

"I formed the impression that she and Jackson were working together for one purpose only, to find out if I knew what happened to what F. W. de Klerk called 'the programme'; South Africa's nuclear weapons. She wouldn't be the first one wanting to know. Klerk was on record as saying that by the time the 'programme' ceased, there were six fully completed nuclear missiles, each one ten times more powerful than the bomb the Americans dropped on Hiroshima at the end of World War II. His message did not mention the seventh bomb that was under construction.

"According to the former president, it was the breakup of the USSR, with tensions easing between South Africa and the communist-backed Cuban troops in Angola, which saw the need for nuclear weapons fade away. He said the threats to peace had dramatically changed. In the speech de Klerk gave, it was never mentioned where the South African Defence Force stood on the decision to disarm.

"There were many factions at that time in our history who suspected the ruling government could see what was coming on the political front, leading to what motivated them—a crucial desire to prevent atomic weapons falling into the hands of a black government. My own family's participation in all of that did not end with the de Klerk's speech.

"There's something I've always wanted to admit to you, but I've been too embarrassed. My father was a staunch supporter of racial segregation. In fact, most white South Africans would tell you my family were one of the founders.

"Father had been a secret conduit for funding of the National Party for a great number of years before real apartheid was introduced. He and his influential friends were never going to relinquish power as easily as the disarming of nuclear weapons might lead one to believe.

"In my possession are the records of very important men who contributed huge sums of money to construct a monumental underground network of interconnecting bunkers, running through rocks under land my family own out in the high veldt, hundreds of miles from any built-up areas. From the way this Colette was leading the conversation, I figured the location of this complex was the only thing she really wanted to know."

"Are you sure it was Colette leading and not this inscrutable Jackson behind the questions she was asking, Bots? He being the organ grinder and she being the organ grinder's monkey?"

"Yes, I'm quite sure, Harry. You see, I never met this Jackson chap. Yes, I knew you'd be surprised. We used predetermined drop-off points for our communications. We had a system he'd devised.

"I would wear my sleeves rolled down if I had a message, rather than how I would usually wear them, rolled up to regulation height, just above the elbow. Taking all things into account, it was a reasonably effectual system in which at no time did he ask for the sort of details she was asking for.

"Jackson's interest lay in the British and American military plans for a free and orderly Iraqi before they could make a structured withdrawal. Of that, he wanted to hear the forecasts on withdrawal dates, even if they were far from settled. Again, even if they were only estimates, he wanted the numbers of designated divisions or contingents scheduled to leave for US bases, and from what battalions would they be withdrawn. He asked for the tabulations on the military units that were staying. Another requirement was for a list of the Iraqis who assisted the coalition. I refused that request."

"What did he say when you refused?"

"Nothing. There was nothing he could say."

"Did you think the list of Iraqis working for the coalition would be for reprisals?"

"Yes, I did, and that's why I wasn't going to supply him with one."

"Do you think there is an all-inclusive list, Bots?"

"I'm not sure there's just the one, Harry. I think that could be what he was trying to find out."

"What's worrying me is, if you had concerns over this Colette and Jackson chap, why not report it?"

"I thought I could bluff my way through it and use them both."

* * *

Evidently there was much more to Bottomly than I'd ever imagined there could be. He was, in fact, more of an active intelligence officer than I. By now, 'tradecraft' was second nature to him as, I was forced to assume, was the telling of a lie. But to be any good in this business, one must be able to lie with a straight face, never giving away a single clue that one was not telling the all-important truth. That ability can be tested many times in many ways.

Governments worldwide use ordinary people for acts of espionage. Some are successful in not being discovered. If they have enjoyed the excitement they carry on. But some are not successful and their lies, along with the secrets the lies are there to conceal, are discovered. That discovery can lead to the death of the agents, as well as those the secrets may be defending.

One of the pearls of wisdom my fading memory can recall from my great-grandfather, Maudlin Paterson, was about the retention of secrets. I was about twelve years of age when we were together at my introduction into the annual cricket match held on the grounds at The Hall, when he imparted his truism. He said, *'If you have a secret, bury it deep; so even you don't know where to find it!'*

One of my first thoughts about his advice was, it was idiotic. How could one bury a secret where it couldn't be found? Let alone, how could one find the secret if it was wanted, if it was buried where it couldn't be found? As I grew older, I understood exactly what Maudlin meant.

* * *

Mentally, I was back in my moment of inward examination with it not having passed unnoticed, as his scrutinising gaze paid testament to. Even allowing for the transparency of his fascination, he did not follow it with any probing question, he simply continued in his recollections.

"The only time the protocol changed was when she said Jackson wanted me to contact two cousins of mine who were in the South African Medical Service. All of those quasi-military units, like them and the South African Flying Troop, were pretences for the armed services.

"But this was a weird question. According to Colette, he wanted to know details of my cousins' last posting, including the name of their commanding officer and on what alert footing were their last combatant commands. I knew where they were posted and I knew the officer in command, but I wasn't going tell him any of that."

"Why not?"

"Before their units were disbanded, they were serving where the secret complex is constructed."

"Does Liam know of this hidden complex?"

"Yes, he does. His family were instrumental in it being built."

"Is that where the nukes are hidden, Bots?"

* * *

I had doubted Winston's honesty that far-flung September, yet for the life of me I couldn't think of a reason for him to lie; even so, my incredulity led me to return to Harrogate for some digging of my own in the quiet of that long ago time. It was from my office at The Hall that I made my first contact with an old Special Branch chum of mine. More contact times ensued, with none made simply for pleasure.

CHAPTER SIXTEEN

BLAME

When we left Bots in the Marriott Hotel, he aimed the blame for his lethargy at fatigue rather than the whisky, though whichever of the two he suffered from, the cure was the same—the comfort of a bed for sleep. I had felt the same need. However, not always are our needs met and this was one such occasion, at least for me it was.

I lay on the bed trying my hardest not to think of Iraq and the Russian Colettes of this world, as well as the many different affairs nobody in London had been open about. As much as I was conscious of drifting in and out of that longed-for sleep, the degree of secrecy in London was keeping me awake. Without listing them all on paper, I tried to compart-mentalise the main issues, which wasn't conducive to sleep.

The least straightforward issue concerned Charles Oswald Wallace. Who according to my Special Branch friend, was considerably more important than I first gave him credit to be. As the last advisor to the Prime Minister of Great Britain, Wallace held the pack of inconsistent counselling cards in his hands, allowing the PM to see, or hear, those chosen by Wallace.

If that was a given truth, then it followed to assume that whoever it was from a government department who had murdered Pickering and Neil, had first advised Wallace of that course of action, but a Prime Minister would not sanction that course of action. Would he! More likely, I lay arguing with myself, Wallace did not tell his boss. Where once he was merely a school bully, was he now, perhaps, a vicious murderer of the truth?

Whatever the truth is, it must be out there. Which meant I needed to revise my ideas. I have always believed the maxim of 'keep your friends close but your enemies closer'. I filed him under 'foolish'. Either I should take him out for dinner one night, or pull my own head off?

* * *

Next came the question of the nuclear capability of South Africa which, because it was weaponry, was linked in my mind to the shipment of arms onboard the container ship confiscated by the Israelis. Although I could equate the weapons onboard the ship to the South African military, the Israelis already had a nuclear capability. I'm sure Bots would not sanction the sale of that degree of military sophistication to Israel's enemies, but could someone else?

I was aware of an idea circulating the corridors of The Box a couple of years ago, when a Russian General named Gerasimov recommended a plan to his security council in which he advocated the next war to be fought on more fronts than just one involving the military.

His strategy favoured an environment of permanent, damaging unrest brought about by a series of infringements into social media with misinformation and other ways to weaken the West. This would include interference in national elections, meddling with the banking system with the international structure of currencies, and disturbance of the national infrastructure, of which, by the time of his doctrines, the conception of reliance on fossil fuels, particularly those piped from Russian gas and oil reserves, was being increased in most parts of Europe.

What of Ar Raqqah, with the American encryption expert alongside Sabah Al Salim? How far did their association impact on whatever it was I was supposed to deal with? Who was the mysterious Jackson? Was he in fact a myth? If so, who invented him? Winston?

Was I supposed to find whoever it was who wanted Bottomly dead by sending a bomb through the British post? Was that part of this mission, or would it be something to file under Future Issues? So many puzzles with so few clues.

I had no idea of how long I'd been asleep, nor had I any idea of where I was, but it was the second of those two questions that was first resolved. The answer to the question of how long I'd slept remained unanswered by the person who woke me by his incessant knocking.

"We're going to settle in here for the day, skip. We can't go to the Marriott just yet. There's a couple of Russian problems."

* * *

The time I'd slept was settled on as four and a bit hours. It felt as if it was days, as my head and body seemed too heavy to move. Gibson mentioned a flight to South Africa then on to the Bottomly estate, but I spoke of Aunt Alice of Maryland and of how I needed to show my face. After a short discussion, Auntie Alice was to be my first port of call.

But before that could be organised, Gibson *invited* me to meet Oona. I had no choice, as she was already in my suite monitoring what was going down on the airways between the Russian embassy and whatever their street soldiers were getting up to.

'Whilst not forgetting,' he told me, 'whoever will be logging on from London hoping to find you nestled into your hotel room, skip. Won't you, my dear?" he shouted annoyingly, as my head reverberated around the room.

Oona was speaking softly into a microphone before she turned to speak to me.

"The two Russians have left in the same taxi they arrived in, with the same driver. I've had Tommy, along with three others, in two separate cars, with three more of the same breed on motorbikes, tailing them using a full grid. In other words, you have our royal treatment, Mr Paterson. The Russians made it into the embassy compound while you were chatting to Mr Gibson. There doesn't seem to be anyone else interested in you, sir."

There was a long pause before she ended her summary with the 'sir' bit. I wasn't sure if it was meant in a humorous way or simply sarcastic.

I wanted to ask if she was sure there was nobody from British intelligence, but I thought better of it. Instead, I asked if either of them had ever witnessed Bots drinking as much as he had the previous night. It was Oona who provided the far from expected answer.

"This is the first time I've ever seen Major Bottomly drink, sir, and this is the seventh operation I've been assigned to where he has been the OIC. It's my job to obscure his presence using whatever means are available to me. For this mission, we used diplomatic cover with sufficient radio-wave chaff that would enable the president of this rotten country to be moved anywhere he chose to be moved; or did not choose to be moved.

Whatever the case to be."

* * *

I had enough problems on my plate not to go looking for others involving women, with or without chips of any size on any shoulder. I chose to leave the room in a confused muddle of assessments of Oona, with only one known fact: her right eye was slightly larger than her left. Wisely, I left the forming of opinions for others to decide.

"If London expects you to go and meet Major Bottomly in Maryland, then we'd better get you there, making sure the two FBI agents see you."

"By that remark, I take it I was followed after all, Liam?" I was trying hard not to smile. Then I tried hard not to frown.

"Not followed as such, skip, no. As a general rule, the Bureau would have your details ping up on their screens when you left London, but as you travelled under the name of Yorkshire, a name unknown to them, it wouldn't have pinged up on them. No, you'll meet them at Aunt Alice's place. They have a static watch out there.

"The name you're under would not ping red on the Russians' central screens. The only way that would happen is if someone in London notified them you were coming. I'm sorry to say I think they did, skip. It's only a guess on my part, but I reckon there's someone in London pulling Russian strings. Why else would those goons take up residence outside this hotel but not know the change of name?

"There are no cameras over the front desk, or along the corridor. There are two cameras in this hotel trained on the front door, but by using the kitchen as a way in and out, as we have done, there are no cameras to pass. That's why we chose here when you phoned the Major to say you were coming, but the thing is, how did the Russians know to ask if you were in this hotel after all the precautions we took? While we're on it, I have another question for you."

"Fire away, Liam." He was right. Someone was in touch from London. I had used what I thought was a secure line to speak to Winston in the office next to Furley's at Vauxhall.

"I don't suppose you're going to tell me why you came all this way when a telephone call would have done."

"I came to ask if he would share those names on the file that his fiancée stole for him. London doesn't want anyone treading on our people's toes."

"Don't you have enough to think about, what

with NATO and the Americans wanting to pull out and cuddle-up to the Russians?"

* * *

As much as I didn't want any woman with *chips on shoulders*, I didn't need any discussion with a murderer on the financial state of affairs in America's war coffers. As much as that was true, the same did not hold true for Africa, where my knowledge was distinctly barren.

I wanted to encourage their views and soon I was listening to expert understanding of the governing parties of Angola, Namibia, Botswana and Zimbabwe, with contributions coming from them both keeping the conversation bubbling along for over an hour. All in all, it made me wonder who, from these two with *The Major,* outranked who in the South African intelligence service?

* * *

When not chasing after, or in some cases avoiding, women, my chosen discipline is one of analysing chemical substances. Nowadays, I specialise in the development of chemicals that can be used on farmland where it could be judged as environmentally sustainable. It is a slow, meticulous process leading, one hopes, to a result beyond doubt or uncertainty.

Sadly, the world of international espionage is not like that. Despite there being a considerable difference, there is one thing the two share; the solitary commitment both vocations require.

Intelligence gathering is mostly done in shadowy places by lonely people who value life by what they can take from it. Human life has one commodity this selfish intelligence gatherer is most interested in; education, yet education is wasted on someone who is dead. I've always believed this is where my patience is of the most value and where I thought I had an advantage.

Liam Gibson's judgement of his native South Africa's politics with that of its neighbours did not, unfortunately, widen to include Iran, nor Israel. On the subject of nuclear power he was voiceless, not in the sense of uncommunicative, more in the sense of uninformed, which for no palpable reason I did not believe.

As a straightforward conversation topic, I mentioned the ship carrying arms to Lebanon that was seized by the Israelis. I thought I was neutral in the way I mentioned it, but apparently I was not, as for a split-second I thought I was about to be violently attacked by an SAS-trained killer. His eyes widened, his lips tightened and I saw him clench both fists then straighten his fingers, but his loss of control did not last.

"I don't see why the world condemns the Palestinians so much, yet I don't read bad press aimed at Israel. For example, what you highlighted, skip. All of a sudden the Israelis are heroes. Saved the rest of us from more Arab genocide. With America financing the Israelis, filling their arsenal from floor to ceiling with weapons that would squash any military aggression from the larger nearby powers, let alone the smaller ones."

I wanted to prise more from him by championing the Israelis in their fight for a border free from hostility, one where they could count on peace, but my efforts were to no avail. Although he said he would not countenance violence in the area to procure their dream of a home called Palestine, he most certainly held anti-Semitic views. He did, though, suggest he would be in favour of some form of equivalence. When I pressed him on how that could be achieved, he had no answer other than saying—"That will never be the case if the method of transportation is breached."

* * *

Without disguising the question, I asked Gibson if he either knew Charles Wallace, or had heard his name mentioned. After the direct question, I asked if he thought Wallace may have spoken to the FBI advising them of my visit to Maryland. Without addressing my main issue, his answer covered many points.

"We know there's been no overt cooperation between the FBI and London, because the FBI are not tailing you, skip. We are watching, but not only are the streets quiet, the airways are silent. Nothing between here and the London station. That's where I would expect your Mr Wallace to be monitoring."

I guessed Liam knew of Charles Wallace through Winston, but I judged it best not to press him further. I used my judgement in not changing their lack of knowledge of the operation. Nor did I enlarge on their familiarity with specific roles inside MI6, which meant Bots did not know either, because if he did, then I'm sure, if not Oona, then certainly Liam would know.

The four hours' sleep I'd managed to have was a great advantage, I felt, as I left the hotel by the front door, walking to the car I'd hired in order to follow Gibson's instructions.

"*Go find your way out to Hagerstown, where I expect Major Bottomly should be at some stage, skip. If he's there, or not, I bet his Aunt Alice will be pleasantly surprised to see an Englishman, and an English lord at that.*"

CHAPTER SEVENTEEN

IN THE BASEMENT AT HAGERSTOWN

The trip to Hagerstown to find this mysterious aunt provided more questions than I could have dreamt about before arriving in America. I started to wonder if anyone in London could be aware of his Aunt Alice's potential importance to British Intelligence?

Surely they must, if for no other reason than the CIA would have communicated her existence to some department at The Box, or to counter-terrorism up the road apiece at Lambeth, if only to check their own data. Any information at that level would automatically be sent to the top floor in an 'Eyes-Only' despatch to Jerry Furley. No, someone back home must know.

I was emphatically aware of how London did not trust me near or around the Americans. I wasn't up to date on things American in any sense; even so, as far as I knew, my reputation in the country of America remained on the highest level, so maybe London thought I might be tempted to sign on with them? *Ha, ha*, I cheerfully thought, bringing not only a silent smile but one that fastened itself to my face as I drove from one highway, the 270, onto another, Highway 70, in the pleasant, late afternoon sunshine.

Distancing myself away from needless distraction, I concentrated on my objective; a South African-born woman operating as a full-time espionage agent on foreign soil, whose gathered information was passed on to other agents either before or after it found its way back to the central intelligence service of the SASS. Viscount Bottomly would be one of those recipients.

* * *

I have never liked driving on the opposite side of the road, but the drive from my hotel to Alice's address was without incident and, in a scenic sense, very pleasurable. In a practical sense, I'm sure my face must have been green with shades of envy as I noticed how the side roads seemed to be as wide as motorways in places, not as narrow as they are across the moors back home.

At home in Yorkshire, I had declined the fitting of GPS machines into any motor car I owned. Serena had one in a Mercedes that I had seen her use, but it had not impressed me. I must admit to my dislike being based on hearsay, having heard a story in the Spyglass and Kettle, my local pub, where the driver who was following the GPS instructions ended up at the end of a road with a lake in front of his car. No, I could get lost quite easily on my own, without the aid of a machine. In any case; I'm too set in my ways to change my habits.

Notwithstanding that disclosure, I met Liam's brief, concise guidance on the use of this piece of modern technology in a state of dubious finality, one from which I would not usually change. Despite my hostility towards these machines, what stuck in my mind was how stupid I could be at times. I could not have done without this GPS machine in the Lexus I'd hired.

Apart from some initial difficulty in getting away from the hotel, once I had navigated my way onto the George Washington Memorial Parkway it was, as they say, plain sailing. From then on, the journey went smoothly. I met the only *No Through Road* sign or, more correctly, an emphatic *DEAD END* sign, at the beginning of Alice's road, repeated a hundred yards from her home.

To find her number was far easier than my pessimism had imagined it could be after I'd found the road where she lived, as most of the houses had their number either emblazoned on the wall of the house or, if not there, then on a mail box at the beginning of grassed front areas. There have been many times in London when I've driven past the address I'm looking for because of the lack of numbering. I shouldn't confine that criticism to just London, it's intrinsically countrywide.

The buildings in Alice's road were predominantly contrasting in structural design, but they were mostly all painted the same colour—white. Architecturally, they were, as I say, different, some being three-storeyed, some two, but as far as I could see, the odd one out was bearing Aunt Alice's number. It was a single-storeyed dwelling. It was timber-framed and white-coloured, standing roughly sixty yards before a high railway banking, effectively closing the road.

It was the additional tall telegraph poles on the land beside Alice's home that caught my attention. All along Security Road, the name of her road, the poles were sited in front of the long, grassed forefronts to the houses.

They were on what we would call a pavement and the Americans would call a sidewalk. The expanse between these homes meant that normally, there was one pole opposite each building. Opposite Alice's house there was only one pole, but as I looked into the soft light of this autumnal evening I spotted three more along the length of her buildings.

As I sat inside the rental car, I was yet to discover the purpose of these extra poles. All I could see was the number 903 in black lettering on the white paint of the largest building, with three other structures, not so dissimilar in size, running away and parallel to it.

They were not equidistant, being spread out in no particular pattern. I could make out the telephone wires, from the extra poles, feeding into those three separate properties. In reality, there were four buildings numbered 903 Security Road. *Odd*, I thought.

As I walked towards Alice's home, all four buildings became clearer. They were timber-made, single-storeyed, painted white and in the same decorative condition. At the rear of the main property, where the loose, heavily pitted, grey asphalt driveway finished, were two cars parked neatly side by side on the grassed area.

I thought that strange as well, as further along I could make out three more cars untidily positioned between the sub-buildings. The buildings reminded me of army huts, but the site, a camp with no military order or regimentation.

There were some stark differences between the largest building, which I took to be her home, and the other properties in the road. To begin with, its tumbledown, slightly neglected appearance made it seem somewhat incongruous when set against the other larger, modern dwellings that were capacious in size, with inordinate wooden-built double garages, alongside one or maybe two other outbuildings. Then there were the flags! Homes the length of Security

Road showed their self-esteem in being American, by flying the Stars and Stripes proudly from poles in the front grassed area or attached to the buildings. I passed at least a hundred such tributes. Not so on Alice's site.

When eventually I met with her, I asked about the South Africa flag flying high on her flagpole. I wondered if it was wise to show how different she was to the rest of her neighbours. I could not have been more surprised by her answer.

This large plot of land, with what I called the army huts, belonged to South Africa. A little known fact was that in the American War of Independence, there was a Dutch contingent from South Africa who fought for the Northern states against the slavery practised in the Southern ones.

With money of their own, they purchased the freehold of this plot of land from the Northern victors, who sold it on to them as a way of thanks for their contribution to the victory. In the wording of the freehold it allowed for—*any activity or business the holder of this legal document wishes to pursue, provided such acts do not constitute war, or insurrection.*

* * *

There was a cacophony of noise coming from the other side of a door in the room I was first shown into, but the loudest sound was coming from the woman I had come to meet, speaking on the telephone in the same form of Afrikaans Winston had taught me when we were in Bosnia, without Liam, who was away with his unit.

In modern times, Alice was the culvert through which the South African intelligence service in Durban received all their collated news from North America, before channelling it out to Bottomly and other agents scattered around the world. Alice was not alone in her 'home', nor was she merely a telephonist waiting to pass on information from around the globe.

The phone conversation was ended abruptly just as the door opened and there she stood. She removed her headset, passing it on to the person beside her, a heavily-built American who would be a common sight on the door of any London or New York nightclub. As Alice greeted me and shook my outstretched hand, I silently marked the man who had taken the headset as her personal bodyguard.

"A letter from my nephew arrived earlier this week. It was addressed to my neighbour, so it wouldn't have been read by anyone other than she. It was in code so she wouldn't know what it was about, either. I can't trust my mail not to have been read by some agency before I get it, so written letters get sent to the next door address.

"The woman owes me because of an ongoing

favour I arrange for her. Her son is in jail and we look after his welfare, whilst he's there. To be frank, he depends on it. In the letter, Winston said you would be coming and he owed you a great deal."

My face must have betrayed my thoughts, as before I could interrupt her, she spoke again.

"I'm ahead of you, Mr Paterson. He roughly outlined what you'd done for him in England without going into much detail."

It's time for another confession of mine. There are more things I'm not good at than I am good at. One thing I'm incompetent at is the estimation of a person's age, which is something I should get right but can't. If pressed and forced to give you an opinion, I'd say I was pretty useless at it. That admission must be borne in mind when I say I'd gauged Alice's age to be somewhere between sixty-five and seventy-five, but she could have been a hundred years of age for all I knew.

She was slim to the point of being gaunt. Her hair was the hair of a much younger person, jet-black with not a hint of grey as far as I could see. My guess was she had dyed it yesterday in anticipation of my arrival, or she wore an expensive wig. Her eyes were a shade of grey, with a lighter shade of the same grey for where they should have been white. My appraisal stopped at that point as she began to speak again. Opening up with a question.

"How do I address you, Mr Paterson? Do I say,

Sir? Or would it be better to call by your title, my lord?"

"Neither, I hope. If Alice is fine for you, then Harry is fine for me. So if it's all the same, I'll call you Alice."

"Okay, yes, of course. Harry it is then. And, yes, Alice is fine. It's better than some of names I've heard myself being called." She finished that part of her introduction with a twinkle that sat easily on her heart-shaped face.

When I'd heard her speaking on the telephone, her voice was strong and solid, accustomed to giving out instructions if not orders, but when she was addressing me she sounded slightly apprehensive, as if worried and edgy. Perhaps she was agitated about her nephew and that's what made her seem uneasy.

Bots had warned me about her concern over the recent increase of Cuban mercenaries filtering out of Angola, who were travelling through the Kalahari Basin then merging with a number of known Angolan terrorists outside of Gaborone, in Botswana.

All of that was news to me and I was sure it would be to Section 9 at The Box. This was exactly what London wanted. She was certainly ill at ease when telling me of the military in South Africa contemplating the mobilisation of a special squadron of ex-South African reservists from the Border War, putting them on a standby alert level, before moving nearer to the border. This strategy had been mentioned by Jerry, but now seemed considerably more urgent.

Alice was uninhibited. At one time, she explained this lack of inhibition as a token towards the respect Bots had said he held me in. She was an effusive conversationalist, telling me many short stories; one in particular I remember well. It was of a time Liam Gibson was engaged on lethal business that overlapped British interest and the interests of the SASS. It was the assassination of a high ranking Al-Qaeda official first identified by the image recognition department of MI6.

The man in question was to be travelling through Durban on a visit to see his granddaughter, who was studying medicine at the University of Cape Town. I was not told how the intelligence reached Gibson.

Despite not being told all the details, I learned Bots successfully helped coordinate the ambush at the University highway interchange, before the attack team escaped north into Namibia. A few days later, when the chase died down, they crossed the border back into South Africa to make their own way to safe locations.

The Al-Qaeda terrorist was killed, along with his two fellow travellers, both named members of the same organisation. It wouldn't take much research in

London to find any missing particulars with that degree of information.

* * *

That was not all I learned of Gibson. Apparently, he had been very busy since 'leaving' the SAS. I smiled, passing some banal remark about being loyal when she confirmed the operation she had outlined was completed before he left the British army.

Evidently, he had a source inside a group of commanding officers of a paramilitary internal South African security force known as Klevet. The force was originally made up of white, native South Africans, but now they were outnumbered by more and more former SWAPO guerrillas—a combination of Cubans, Angolans, numbers from Namibia, alongside other blacks who fought against Nelson Mandela's ANC party in the Kwazulu Natal Province.

Over a cigarette and a glass from a bottle that was labelled whisky, but, if she had pressed me on its taste, I would have argued the point, thinking it possibly could be disinfectant, she went on to explain some of the modern history of South Africa.

When her mother country faced an arms embargo because of the apartheid rule of law, it left them to their own devices to acquire modern weapons along with the refurbishment of existing weapon systems. The repair and maintenance of the standing arsenal, when faced by aggressive, militant neighbours, was understandably crucial and inescapable.

Although a covert arms deal was agreed with Israel, through American diplomatic channels, lines of supply were too stretched to maintain a long campaign with their outmoded weapons. Viscount Bottomly was able to provide the name of an alternative supplier.

* * *

"Winston was very protective of you," was her opening remark when her intriguing summary had reached an untimely end. In the same vein she continued, "You would have thought he was your guardian angel, after he'd given you the green light on all our security matters. He never stopped singing your praises, did my nephew. I did some researching of my own on you, of course, but I doubt you would not have expected that."

There was a hint of a giggle in her voice along with, perhaps, a tiny Irish influence I thought I heard.

"I found out you'd worked overseas on more than one occasion for MI6, Harry, which, after getting to know your background, was no surprise. You also did some work for the Military at home. It would be more unexpected if you hadn't, I guess." Yes, there was some Irish in there.

"Let me fully introduce myself and get that chore out of the way. Before the elections in my country of '94, I was employed in our secret intelligence service in Durban mainly, but travelling everywhere. We covered a lot of procedures that were..."

She hesitated for a second or two, thinking of what to say before adding, "The primary purpose of the department I eventually headed up was destabilisation. Destabilisation by terminal means, if it was necessary. I was the overall commander of that unit, going on to command other units along the same lines.

"It was me who issued the order authorising Liam Gibson's command to assassinate Christopher Hani. Don't worry if you haven't heard of him, I'm certain your correlating departments in London will have. In early 1993, as far my departments were concerned, he was considered to be extremely dangerous as the sitting General Secretary of the South African Communist Party. The radical elements of the African National Congress saw him as their candidate to rival Mandela in his campaign to lead a more moderate party."

There wasn't a hint of regret or contrition from this uncompromising, passionate woman. Right, wrong or indifferent, her radical views would die with her. She reached for another cigarette, taking it from a small, metal, green-coloured cigarette box with a thin, gold and black inlaid border. She offered me one from the same box, which I gauged to be modest in comparison to what she could have had. There was no alteration to her face when I turned her offer down, preferring my brand. She continued speaking as I offered to light her cigarette.

"His real name was Martin Thembisile Hani. He was, as I said, the leader of the South African Communist Party, also Chief of Staff of the armed wing of the African National Congress. That's the all-powerful, ever-ruling ANC. You should remember that name with those initials, because his death almost achieved our objective of turning the ANC over. Back in those days, our objective was simple—we wanted to change the history of my country. We came this close to starting the war we so much wanted." She positioned her thumb and forefinger a whisper away from each other as a measurement of closeness.

"We wanted to kill him, then to have his death blamed on those that controlled the political side of the ANC. It wasn't to be! However, it set a precedent. I'm quite sure you would know part of the back story of South African history before you left London, and I guess you read how it was the Whites who exacerbated the situation between the ANC and the IFP, the Inkhata party.

"Well, in part that is true. How so, you might ask? I'll tell you! It was us who supplied the weapons by the lorry-load—to both parties. The more they shot each other, the less we had to kill. Practical common sense."

As I breathed heavily inwards, inhaling from my cigarette, my eyes were drawn upon her. The stare from her cold, grey eyes suggested she was firing 9mm bullets into my heart. Involuntarily, I was slowly moving my left hand across my chest as if the smoke could deflect her aim. Instead of firing off another round, she carried on speaking.

"We also ran weapons to the APLA party, the ones responsible for the massacre in a church named after a Saint—St James's."

She had a heavy, serious frown on her face, made worse by a clump of black hair that had fallen across her eyes. As she swept it away from her face, I wondered again if it was a wig she wore, or was the colour straight out of a bottle of dye, but my fatuous thoughts were quickly forgotten as I saw the start of a wide, angry, red scar that had been hidden before her hair had parted. She didn't mention her wound.

"We gave them the AK-47s, the grenades, even the Claymores they said they wanted to use. Whatever it took to kill each other, we gave them with a smile on everyone's face. But—"

As a regretful sigh left her lips when she ended that passage of South African military history, I wondered if it was because she'd seen me notice her scar and didn't want to explain. Even if I wanted to and I did, I had no chance to ask. She wasn't finished.

"It was not exclusively Whites working inside this expanded military combination I was helping to create. There would have been no point in keeping it as a Whites-Only organisation. All that would do is reintroduce an anti-apartheid up-swell in our country, as well as in others. Equally, it would serve no purpose for Whites to be killing Blacks. We had been doing that for years and nobody took any notice.

"No, we had to step away from that. Find another way. *Ons wil mense hê wat vir hulself kan dink, nie robotte nie!*" In Afrikaans again, some of which I understood. I repeated its meaning back—'wanting people who could think for themselves. You were not looking for robots.' She smiled as she complimented me before continuing in English.

"There have been enough robots in the parts of Africa that have never benefitted from having a stable government, torturing and maiming each other for centuries. We didn't start it.

"If you study history, which I do, it wasn't us Whites who invented that *necktie* thing to kill one another. It was Blacks who put the rubber tyres over another Black's neck then doused them in petrol. Do you know they even made them swallow some petrol before applying the match?

"Another imaginative way of killing off their own race they developed was by literally tearing their enemies apart by attaching ropes to their legs and arms and the other end of the ropes to four trucks driving off in four different directions until they were torn apart.

"The Blacks Liam Gibson trained, then employed, were even more barbaric. They didn't need any instructions in how to kill. They were naturals at it. We just watched and waited for the 'mayhem' to begin, and begin it certainly did. Did you know that one leader of APLA was actually called Mayhem? Aptly in his case, as he loved causing it."

* * *

She was smiling and revelling in the madhouse of not only death, but the mutilation that's never spoken openly of. I looked and felt totally disgusted at what I heard, having no choice but to listen and feel part of it. I found it impossible to believe the British government, the opposition, along with all of those on intelligence analysis desks at GCHQ, did not know the details of this.

It was my duty to follow the instructions Sir Leonard Miles and Jerry Furley had entrusted me with. It appeared as though the privacy of using Craig's Court, then the tunnels to reach Vauxhall, for the meetings with MI6 had worked. As far as the thinking of Alice and Winston went, I was here to help a friend first, then British intelligence a long way second, if at all. The collaboration I might receive from that situation could be enormous.

It crossed my mind how it would be useful if Bots knew very little of what Alice did as I reached across her table and poured a large glass from the bottle marked Whisky, dreaming for a moment of my son Luca. Whilst Luca was in my dream, I was lying beside Katherine, his mother. It was Alice who was speaking, but it was Katherine who I was listening to.

'*We will live in Yorkshire for spring and autumn. We will spend the whole summer on your yacht in the Mediterranean, where we will hire a tutor for Luca. For winter it must be Russia. St Petersburg to start with, then further east to follow the snow, but away from Moscow. Maybe the cold might be too much for you. Perhaps your soft skin would prefer the Caribbean, Harry?*' It was Alice who pulled me away from my dream.

"Something you won't know, Harry, is Winston's full Afrikaner name. The name he was given on his birth was: Winston, Henry, Louw, and then the family name. The name Louw comes from his father's closest friend who was second in command to Eugène Ney Terre'Blanche of the Afrikaner Resistance Movement, the Afrikaner Weerstandsbeweging, or the AWB. We are all the same animal.

"Winston was born in England, not at the estate in South Africa. Why was that, you ask? It was because his father had the foresight to see nothing but trouble when apartheid would end. The Bottomly family were joined at the hip to certain people in lofty positions in English society. It was those people, in the governing circles of Westminster, who advised Winston's father regarding the birth.

"After gaining sufficient educational qualifications whilst rubbing shoulders with the *right* people at the *right* schools, they enlisted him in the British army. Then, when he was old enough, he could take up a seat in the House of Lords with, one would hope, a sound military background.

"His father predicted trouble when others only praised the counter-insurgency raids into Angola during the Border War, followed by bloody reprisals on SWAPO forces over the Angolan border. Blood was everywhere.

"The council of the AWB reacted firmly to the riots of the early Nineties, with some of us advising a harder response that wasn't followed. Even so, the Bottomly family name was tarnished when the death count was published.

With Winston in the Balkans on military service on behalf of the Queen, thereby beyond call for military duty in South Africa, his branch of the Bottomly name remained without blemish. I believe a couple of questions were asked in England, but the government left it alone and it settled down relatively quickly.

"Did you not find it strange that the British Army Officer Selection Board raised no objections to Winston's enrolment into the Life Guards, the senior regiment in the British Army, when his father and friends were slaughtering native Blacks in places outside their own country's borders? There were no objections because they were told not to object. There is much for you to learn about Winston, Harry, much more than I can teach you. But from wherever you hear it, some of it you will not like."

* * *

I was expecting something apocalyptic to land on me and to some extent that's what happened. It was based around her assumption that when apartheid was ended, it was stage-managed by the AWB, manipulating the situation from the shadows in a similar way a *kingmaker* of olden days would act. The leaders of the ANC were chosen, to some extent, by leading members of this lethal AWB, or Afrikaner Weerstandsbeweging.

According to Alice, several prerequisites to the overthrowing of the legitimate government by the AWB were now in place. And to take it further in a mythical sense, the White Horse of the Apocalypse was due to arrive with trumpet blaring, anytime soon.

Thankfully, Alice judged it was time to refill my glass from the whisky bottle that, although foreign to my taste before arriving in America, was growing on me. My daydream, although fading, still allowed me to see Katherine holding Luca as they rode away on the back of a horse with Breno on his own mount following them. There was no sign of Serena in the diminishing light inside my fantasy.

* * *

I asked if Bots had ever mentioned his time in Iraq, in particular a woman named Colette with a man named Jackson. Regrettably, the answer was no. She had not heard him mention either name.

Alice emptied her glass whilst I was being more circumspect, conscious of the lack of control I was able to exert over the fast disappearing contents of the bottle. As she was about to remove it from the table I reached for it, smiling whilst I asked that it be allowed to remain.

She returned my smile, but did not do as I'd requested, removing the bottle to a side cupboard. It was probably for the best, as I'd forgotten I had to drive. Rather than leaving the whisky, she continued on the subject of imminent takeover by her White supremacists.

So her story went, it was Winston who was handling the agenda. He met with a former commander of the disbanded South African Defence Force, a General Albert du Preez, in London in the week preceding the grouse shoot.

The discussion was centred around five tribal leaders who were said to be trekking down from Lusaka in Zambia, from Harare in Zimbabwe, from

Maputo in Mozambique, from Lubango in Angola and from Makkhalo in Botswana. The five intended to meet up in Gaborone, in Botswana. The same Gaborone Alice was speaking on the telephone about, when I arrived.

"At this Gaborone meeting, the General spoke of a massacre of the sitting ANC government in Pretoria, along with every ANC card-holding activist in South Africa. Using the General's words— 'all the hand-picked sycophants'. The tribal leaders were sick of the ANC creaming off from the aid given by the West intended for distribution in their countries.

"At the moment, they all complained, no aid of any kind was getting past South African borders. When the last ruling ANC government is finally dethroned, the new government will be more inclusive. At least, on the surface that will be true. But fundamentally, it will be a resurgent AWB party running the country, without the corruption that's become so ubiquitous amongst the previous Blacks of the ANC. The ANC, with all the hangers-on, will be utterly obliterated."

With that pragmatic announcement floating in the smoke-filled air, she told another story London would be drooling over, when I had time to report back. It would appear that some time last year, a person previously trained in covert operations who had been on regular communications with Alice, infiltrated a large splinter group of the Cuban-led militia in Angola.

She told me her source thought the leadership of the group believed the nuclear weapons the de Klerk government announced to the world as being decommissioned, were not decommissioned at all. They believed two out of the six armed missiles were kept by the South African military.

They also believed members of the AWB had knowledge of this arrangement, actively taking part in the concealment of those weapons and regularly participating in the arming and, because they were designed to be mobile, the deployment of the missiles.

The leader of this group of Cuban militia spoke openly to Alice's source of an unnamed person inside the AWB knowing how to replicate, or repair if necessary, the aiming system built in to deliver these missiles onto their targets. For the moment, this information stayed within this Cuban-led splinter group, but there was talk of conferring with their Russian *advisors*, or the *Spetsnaz,* attached to their column.

* * *

It seemed to be a considered opinion only one strategy would be adopted. That would be to find the missiles, steal all the components needed for the nuclear strikes, then threaten an attack on two South African cities. The suspected site of concealment was said to be somewhere along the western edge of the Bottomly estate in a vast, remote region known as Hartebeest Vlakte. It's an area, she told me, where, if you never knew precisely where to look, you would be looking until the day you died and all your children were dead.

I was puzzled by her revelations. She sounded too confident not to have knowledge of these weapons. I confronted her with the clear-cut question of, "Are they right in assuming you have them?" She neither confirmed nor denied, saying that as long as they believed the military had access to them, then that should be enough to be an adequate disincentive. It would either drive them away, which it hasn't, or entice them forward in an attempt to steal them, which seems to have been the case here.

She went on to openly admit how her department of South African intelligence leaked a routine dispatch issued from a communication hub, in one of those outbuildings I'd noticed on the way in, to reach the Russian group of *'advisors'*. The dispatch was formulated in such a way that it appeared to be the ending of an impulsive communiqué requesting an engineer's final remodelling report on a fleet of three transporters.

It gave legitimate model numbers, along with the serial numbers of the trio of vehicles built to the specifications essential to convey missiles of a kind the *advisors* could not mistake. It was utter provocation, but not in Alice's eyes.

Next was what she called a slight problem. Only a small problem. It was the storage of the weapon-grade uranium that was a problem.

Weapons-grade uranium was extracted from the six nuclear weapons South Africa held in its arsenal. Some of that uranium, she had the numbers stored safely away, was used to produce isotopes for the home medical profession, and a small quantity was exported to fill medical commitments. Nothing more was moved.

Originally, South Africa had eight bombs, not six as mentioned. For various reasons, over the years of the de Klerk government, there was close contact with the Israeli government, primarily to assist in the development of a nuclear power grid. The grid was completed, but there was more to the commercial agreement than just a power grid. Alice said she was staying on script by not telling me about that agreement. Regretfully, she told me Winston outranked her, so if he wanted to expand on it he could, but she couldn't. For no reason I could see, she had become slightly irritable. It was because of what she then told me.

"One nuclear device, assembled by South African engineers, was tested in the Indian Ocean as far back as September 1979. Israeli military were in sole command of the installation and detonating process. Apart from the engineers needed to help put the thing together, South Africa had only three other representatives present. Not one of those three were members of the ANC party."

The last sentence was spoken with a heavy tone of disgust in her otherwise monotone voice. The same modulation remained for a short period of time when she returned to her testimony. I was left under no illusion that the sitting Black South African government was a treasured administration for Alice to send love letters to, but by one short statement, with emphasis on the government's abbreviation, she had exposed her unshakeable hatred that could not be confused by anyone.

When her voice returned to normal, on accepting the offer of coffee from an attractive, young, dark-haired, white-skinned, woman who had come from the direction of the hallway, she picked up where she had left her narrative, telling me how, on the day of the detonation of the bomb, a double flash of light was detected by a passing satellite. It was universally declared to be the nuclear explosion it was.

However, after a very short period of time it was downgraded, by disputing the accuracy of the ageing satellite. It was announced to the world by the American press secretary of the time, Jody Powell, that the earlier detected explosion was not an explosion at all. The satellite only just managed to register a flash, he said, adding how it was past its sell-by date. In fact, it was due to be destroyed on re-entry. In other words, it was a *simple mistake, ladies and gentlemen of the press, and nothing more.*

* * *

The reason the world was not told the full truth was because six months earlier, the President of America had negotiated a peace treaty between Egypt and Israel after much twisting of arms on both sides. If President Carter admitted the reported double flash was indeed a nuclear bomb blast, it would leave every Arab nation convinced it was Israel exposing part of its immense arsenal by flexing its muscles.

If Israel was recognised as a nuclear power, it would blow the peace treaty out of the water and return the Middle East to the usual dangerous, unstable position it occupied.

As far as South Africa was concerned, the detonation of the Indian Ocean bomb left seven weapons. There were the six the South African government admitted having produced and a seventh under construction. Not yet serviceable, but not far off. That seventh was the one that was kept, as was the weapon-grade uranium needed to commission the weapon. Only Bots could tell me if that bomb was ever finished.

She then asked me not to tell Winston what she

was about to say. She said South Africa had a weapon more lethal than a nuclear bomb. It was what remained of the chemical and biological programme that were being developed when the Truth and Reconciliation Commission was held in 1995.

She suggested I read a transcript of the report, saying there was just one small chapter exclusively devoted to a spurious government's chemical and biological warfare programme conducted during the late 1980s and early 1990s.

According to Alice, at the time of the report's discovery it had been altered by some government memos to show the development process to be solely for defensive purposes. Had the document not been modified in the way it was, then the present government would, without any doubt, have held prominent members of AWB, Afrikaner Weerstandsbeweging, to account. That would have been exactly what the ANC wanted—a trial for the world's television crews. If, as seemed likely, the concealment of the programme came out, it could lead to a public execution.

She gave a solid example of what had once happened at the top secret plant where development of these chemical weapons, alongside weapons more of a biological nature, were taking place. An administration worker came across stocks of packeted, authentic cigarettes adulterated by the addition of anthrax spores. In another part of the plant, Paraoxon, a highly toxic chemical for humans to ingest, was found. Paraoxon had been used as an assassination weapon in the apartheid-era South African chemical weapons programme.

In a fit of laughter, she suggested it could be used to contaminate alcoholic drinks, including my own favourite tipple. I played along and copied her laughter, while inwardly I was grimacing at the time I would need to code a communiqué to send to London. She had not finished.

There were reports of the AWB producing an infertility toxin along with a cholera serum, that were to be released into the water supply of some Black townships. All of this was said have been cleared away as a result of a secret project, code named Project Coast, leaving South Africa clean.

Alice wanted to tell me another story. Again, she suggested it would be better if Bots did not know. I played the 'timid friend,' telling her I was uncomfortable keeping secrets from him, but as she and I had become such good friends, then I could not betray our friendship by telling him anything of what she had told me, or wanted to share with me. I was here for her, I said, adding she could tell me anything and I would do what she asked.

"I'll leave it up to you, Harry. I trust you." I don't

know why, but that small revelation sent a shudder down my spine.

"Sometime in the 1960s, I think it was '65, three German scientists arrived in Johannesburg from Argentina. I was fourteen at the time and we lived in Melville, a suburb of Jo'burg, not far from the university where these scientists were headed. I remember my father telling me there was a large German community already living on the other side of the city, who had settled in our country when apartheid was an enactment by the National Party in 1948. They were, of course, Nazis, escaping Europe after World War II, and their fascist beliefs were served well by the then racial discrimination practised in the apartheid system.

"When I was twenty-five, I was promoted to Secretary-General under Balthazar Johannes 'B. J.' Vorster, the Prime Minister of South Africa. I stayed as his personal secretary when he became the President a few years later. It was he who sentenced Mandela to life in prison and it was he who oversaw the Soweto riots. He was instrumental in establishing the border between South Africa, Namibia, Botswana and what was then Rhodesia, when the terrorists started moving in. Unfortunately, he was involved in a political scandal, stepping away from office in 1979.

"When I was working for him, he initiated a programme that was called 'Total Onslaught'—a reformed system of racial stratification. A regular visitor to the President's office was a German whose name is immaterial. It's what he was responsible for that's not. Vorster had made me sign a document very similar to your own Official Secrets Act before I could work with him and he trusted me implicitly after I had signed it. It was me who took notes whenever Vorster and the German met. I was there when our President signed the bank draft enabling this German to construct the site to store over three hundred tons of weaponised Sarin gas.

"Vorster told me it was those three Germans who developed the technology needed in the overall augmentation. After the sites were constructed, I was given the task of itemising all the biological laboratories where Sarin gas was stored, as well as listing other sites with other stocks of nerve agents, quantities thereof, and lastly, test results of potency which I would find recorded under the coded names given to each of the German scientists.

"If you're wondering if toxins were used in the Border War where South African units were fighting Namibians, Angolans, Cubans, Soviet Union 'advisors' along with any other mercenary drawn from almost every other African country, then I can give you the location where you would find hard evidence to confirm and support the claim that we did.

"Sarin had been classified as a weapon of 'Final Resort', so it needed to be put securely out of sight. Following the Soweto uprising in June 1976, a suggestion was put to the full defence committee, chaired by B. J. Vorster and where I was assigned, to use Sarin in the water supply to the township of Soweto. Nothing happened then, but that was then. Times change, don't they, Harry?" A stare of evil proportion greeted my look in her direction as the question that was aimed at me died on her lips. There was no need to supply an answer.

"Part of the job I was entrusted to do was to select protected locations where a mixed stock of the toxins could be housed. The four selected locations have remained secret. I will write the locations down for you, but you must counsel caution at the sites. All have systems of concealed explosive devices set to detonate if the locations are breached without operating a sophisticated unlocking sequence I designed with the help of my German lover. Before you leave, I will write down the codes for you to have them safely unlocked."

* * *

I sat looking at this elderly lady, wondering about all the atrocities she must have witnessed through the years of White dominance over a native Black population outnumbering them by about ninety percent. What, I wondered, were the atrocities committed against the Whites in retaliation? Finally, after a period of silence when we both sat with lighted cigarettes, drinking more coffee, I asked her again why she was telling me all of this, and why without Winston's knowledge?

The answers to both questions were the same, she said. It involved her age. She'd had enough of watching death by now. Evidently, Winston had not. Her enlarged answer was she'd had enough of not only death, but wickedness as well.

She wanted it all to end. She said she'd leave me to decide why Winston wanted more, because she said I knew him better than she did. I laughed, telling her what I've told you—how, although once I might have had an idea what made Bots tick, now I had no idea whatsoever. In certain ways he was a stranger to me, I told her. It was her turn to laugh, which led her to tell me one last story. It went like this...

"By 1988, I was head of Section Eight, a part of National Intelligence Interpretation Branch (NIIB). Essentially, it was another destabilising department, first operating inside Namibia to cause copious amounts of unrest and instability as was humanly possible. We recruited Blacks to join Namibian military forces and then disrupt the organisation from the inside. We knew some would just take the money we offered without doing anything, but not all of them. Some would do what we wanted so they could return, wanting more money.

"My section was called the State Security Council, where I was present when the leader of the council authorised the army to use three of the artillery shells that were already armed with Sarin gas. Those shells were to be used against the heavily fortified defences at a place called Chetequera. One of our paid agents informed us that behind these defences was a large detachment of Cuban guerrillas fighting for the People's Liberation Army of Namibia.

"From a military point of view, it was a strategically important position, but from a political aspect it was inside Angola and a long way from our own borders. Some members of the Council were worried that if a protracted battle took place, we could not substantiate our presence nor could we adequately re-supply those lines. A contingency plan was devised.

"The three toxic shells were included in an artillery barrage that consisted of seventy-six shells from four mobile artillery pieces. In total, it lasted for over half an hour, by which time the guns were withdrawn. The prevailing wind was blowing towards the enemy. No shell was marked as carrying Sarin, so nobody manning the self-propelled guns knew of its use.

"The army officer in charge of this barrage was a lieutenant named Albert du Preez. He is the same du Preez Winston met in London last month, only by now he's been promoted to the rank of General.

"There were no survivors from the defending 241 Cuban mercenaries, and there were no casualties amongst the South African Defence Force that withdrew to a secure location inside Namibia. All participating personnel were sworn to secrecy, signing a document to that effect. Later that same day, and without anyone knowing, a unit of our own special services, with a team of engineering specialists, buried those bodies where nothing will ever be found of them after, first, they were burnt; then a concoction of chemicals was poured over the site."

* * *

She told me Winston was not implicated in those actions, either before, during, or after. He was not contaminated in the same way as she was. She was equally worried by the fact that his name was included in her section simply through association to his late father. "But Winston is a soldier," she said, adding— "He's no analyst, like me."

Alice wasn't finished there. According to her, his frailties make him a liability under certain circumstances. When it comes to money he's an utter fool, and when it comes to women he's an out-and-out bigger fool than anyone could imagine. "You must know that for yourself, Harry! I'm sure you don't need me to fill in any details."

* * *

This time I did not laugh, nor did I smile. I clenched my teeth and hoped my eyes showed the respect I felt for this lady. I've mixed with a great many people of her age and some that have been older, particularly within my own family, some of whom lived well past their hundredth birthday. And although at first I thought she still had quite a way to go before passing that ageing milestone, from the way she rose from her chair, I thought I was wrong.

"I must go and deal with a small problem we have, Harry, I'm sorry, but I haven't forgotten those details I said I'll give you. Someone will fetch them for me. I have whole teams of specialists, in one speciality or another, either together in the same building, or working in parts of the other buildings. In spite of having all those people, it would seem as though it's only me who can deal with certain procedures from a part of this building that is best kept dark to the majority of the rest.

"It's no good handling secrets if those secrets can be found. Every preventative measure that's possible to be taken, in order to conceal what South African officials declare as highly confidential, are taken here, you can be sure of that. We even have underground probes that can detect the movement of soil around any building. But listen, Harry, we keep to being a low-value site for any full-blown FBI interest. After all, South Africa poses no threat to another nation, least of all the United States. Right?"

* * *

I didn't quite understand why she told me South Africa didn't want to start a war with America, even so I was sure London would be pleased to hear it. I thought what she meant was it's safer to be quiet and unnoticed than to be boisterous and seen by all. The last thing she said to me, as I finished my final sip of coffee at the same time as stubbing out my umpteenth, far too many, cigarette, is stencilled into my memory:

"If we were to breach the Test Ban Treaty, or openly expose our enemies to the biological weapons we hold, the economic sanctions imposed on us by the rest of the world, would see millions of Blacks die of starvation, whilst many Whites would survive. Why? Because the eventual need would have dictated they should have already put in place 'survival' precautions.

"But if we developed a method that allowed the reproduction of selected heritable characteristics from a chosen White population to multiply, then allowing, by neglect, the Black population to naturally fade away, then in certain circles we would be praised as the new Messiahs; in others, the new Nazis.

"Yes, what I'm talking about is genetics. Or what certain people prefer to call—the reproduction of a particular strain from the present White population increasing under laboratory conditions. Our research

moves on from traditional genetics into the assistance necessary for any strain not selected to diminish. That action, if successful, would leave the chosen characteristics of the selected strain of life to prosper and finally populate the entire planet."

Was my operation about the recovery of exposed names of British operatives, or was it about hidden nuclear weapons? From nowhere, I now had South African research into genetics manufactured by fanatics to worry London about. It was quickly becoming far too confusing for a simple mind like mine to deal with. I needed a deceitful approach to all this.

CHAPTER EIGHTEEN

TRIGGERS

Liam collected me from the Sofitel and together, we drove towards Dulles airport to meet Bots, who was awake, washed, shaved and looking more like the Bottomly I thought I knew. His accommodation had changed. He was now in the Spring Hill Suites Hotel, waiting in the lounge with a good-looking Oona who was dressed in a blue, off-the shoulder blouse and tight-fitting black jeans. It didn't look to me as though she was in work clothes, unless her work was of a different nature than I'd been told! As I looked around, I caught sight of her staring at me. I had to pinch myself to make sure she was indeed real and the alteration she'd gone through was corporeal, not spectral.

I wasn't dreaming, but I was indulging in fantasy which was quickly pushed to one side on seeing Liam who, having arranged for my passport to be here, was waiting at the desk with my luggage due to arrive at any minute.

Through some spiritual qualities of benevolence I wasn't aware of possessing, I had booked an executive suite for myself, along with an adjoining double room for Liam to share with Winston. For good measure, I'd also booked a single room for Oona. No doubt my expense account would be playing havoc in the accounts office in Whitehall when the costs on my business card arrived.

I had not protested when Liam suggested I stayed on in America for an extra few days after returning from Alice in Hagerstown. I'd agreed on the spot to his proposal. I had no deadline to adhere to, and as Jerry Furley had said—'stay until you are reasonably satisfied you have everything', which was an open-ended remark if ever I heard one. Furley's 'everything' could have referred to knowledge of British intelligence being at least compromised, or perhaps threatened by a South African operative, asset, or illegal.

When Sir Leonard Miles had said something quite similar regarding staying and getting information from Bottomly, he had specifically referred to the names on the file Samantha had stolen, saying he wanted either the memory stick itself, or a copy of the file made from Winston's memory.

Although there was a similarity to what the two

of them had said, there was also a distinct difference, and I wondered why that was. Could it be Jerry already knew the names?

The intelligence I had shared with London until now, included a mention of a new ground-based air-defence system for the UK known as Sky Sabre, alongside an anti-air modular missile he'd said his Russian source had told him about, but would not divulge where he heard it. In Winston's words, he'd been very juvenile in his protestations. I never delved deeper, leaving the experience in Bots' memory and Jerry Furley's imagination.

Even allowing for the miles we were apart, the concerns I had over Charles Oswald Wallace had not lessened, which made the decision not to share information with Sir Leonard Miles easier to make. There was something Winston said of his Russian friend that for the moment I was keeping to myself.

It was in a cryptic sentence that ended with —*emissaries having more information can be found where the pastures are closed in the north.*

To a logical mind the phrase had no sense, it was absurd. However, over time an ever-increasing portion of my mind tended to operate in illogical places where, in a corner of my confused brain, I could make sense of it, but the conclusion my mind had arrived at just could not be right. Could it?

* * *

As I poured the first of many glasses of Scotch whisky from a bottle with no 'e' from the well-stocked bar in the suite of the Spring Hill Suites Hotel, lighting the first of far too many cigarettes I would in all probability smoke, the news that reached my tired ears was not what my starved self-esteem wanted. Although the news from Oona, via Tommy, was no different this time around, the fact that nobody was following the journey we had made from the Sofitel was nothing short of tragic. What made the matter worse was nobody else shared my gloom, in fact they were happy with the state of affairs.

On the car journey from Alice's, I'd time to consider one of her statements of knowing how close Hugh Pickering was to the CIA and how friendly Winston had become with him. Perhaps, Bottomly's meeting with a Russian was inconsequential compared with his closeness to the CIA, as maybe the main reason for this operation was staring me in the face if only I could lift the mist from my stupefied eyes.

In the past, I'd had a good relationship with the CIA, but that did not cloud my perception of them. I was fully aware of how they had acquired a shoddy reputation of attempting to influence the politics of countries on what was termed *The Red List*, as they labelled any country deemed to be opposed to American ideals.

South Africa, with its current left-wing-leaning

government alongside a Marxist inner core, must be right up there on any policy-changing list that the American in charge of foreign policy might have tucked away in a file somewhere. As far as I knew, nothing had changed the fundamentals within the government, or with its policies, since the elections of 1994.

So I was wondering why would America want to get involved now? What had changed, or, as Alice would have it, what was going to force a change in American policy? I know it was a stretch of the imagination, but if the AWB could manipulate the situation to where the majority of the Black population was in serious threat, either through privation or civil unrest bordering wholesale killing, then maybe that would be the time for an American intervention. If for nothing else than to stop the Russians from getting too much of a foothold in Southern Africa.

If misinformation such as Alice was peddling could make the present American belief into fact that Russia was the controlling force behind the ANC, then yes, the CIA could back intervention. Would the UK hitch a ride on the back of that? Thankfully, I didn't have to answer that one.

* * *

Bots and I were alone in the lounge area of my suite, with the television broadcasting news of yet another natural disaster, this time outside Guatemala City. But my drinking partner was not showing interest in that. He had started our second round of conversations with a newly acquired cynicism. He was berating the South African Ministry of Defence for inviting Russian and Chinese naval vessels to Cape Town. His criticism did not stop with that department. He included every department, as well as the president himself.

The navies from the two most powerful communist countries had come to take part in exercises which included vessels of the home-fleet. It was an atrocious attack by Bottomly who, with glass in hand, paced the length of the room clenching his free fist, waving it in threatening gestures. I was wondering what he would recommend if he was in a battle management command centre? I would not have been surprised if it extended to the launch of a nuclear missile into the waters around the Cape of Good Hope. This was one more version of the Bottomly I knew in the Guards.

"I would love to know the name of the person who authorised the naval display. I bet whoever it was received a huge bribe." He laughed in mocking derision before explaining what had occurred.

"I think it was in September 2016. The Russian fleet was headed by the *Admiral Kuznetsov*, which was the flagship of the Russian navy in those days. With that monster came three of the Sovremenny class destroyers, as well as four of the new Udaloy class. Just to show off, they also brought two of their huge landing platform support ships.

The Chinese sent two of the same type destroyers, but with probably a different technical fashioning, plus four frigates. They were led by one of their relatively new Yuan class submarines. They are the ones to watch, Harry, the Chinese. I'm telling you!

"I remember the day of the flotilla very clearly, as the following month the aircraft carrier, the *Admiral Kuznetsov*, was severely damaged when the floating dock it was in for a refit, sank. As it sank, one of the massive cranes damaged the flight deck. Apparently, the ship is still unserviceable, but somehow I doubt anyone thought of gathering intelligence on any of the ships. Why should they? South Africa is on their side.

"You see, the country of so many great liberal-minded politicians such as Colin Eglin, Andries Pretorius, Jan Smuts, with many more I cannot name, are heading along the road to become no more than a communist satellite country. It's got to be stopped.

"On the surface, this looks as though it's a comprehensive umbrella government, but it's bogus. It's being eaten away from the centre outwards. The fault lies with the people holding the real power, not the idiots at the all-smiling front with the Western-styled rhetoric. I believe it is the duty of all free-thinking White South Africans to not only take power back, but replace it with something new.

"After having spoken to Alice, you'll know all about me being a member of Afrikaner Weerstandsbeweging, AWB. I would hope she filled you in on all the principal, historical points of South Africa and how the AWB fits into it, as well as how in lots of places, it led the history?

"When I joined the AWB, the oath I was required to take was in the form of a promise to restore South Africa to what it was before the '94 election, when apartheid was officially abolished. That was the pledge I made. It's not the AWB's objective to reintroduce segregation, but we're not ruling anything out and that extends to all sectors, including your own."

* * *

When he had finished speaking I didn't know what to expect, I even suspected the offer of a new job would not be off the table, but it was not a job offer he had in mind. His concern centred on wider issues than just employment for me.

"The antagonism and bitterness the diehard of the AWB felt towards Great Britain and the people, stemming as far back as the end of the Second African War, has been overtaken by the abhorrence we have for this progressive Marxist government with its pseudo cohorts evolving here in South Africa. Our established right-wing views are moving towards inviting Great Britain back to our shores. No, please, let me explain."

I had wanted to interrupt, but he waved my protest away, so, with nothing else to do, I sat back and listened to his attempt to persuade me into some form of cooperation. But, I was wrong. Once again, I was mistaken about him.

* * *

"I've heard some people say Great Britain's role as a globe-trotting military force is over, but that's not for me. It may be a long time ago now, but what your country did when retaking the Falklands from Argentina was truly world-beating stuff. There could only be two, or possibly, three other nations capable of doing what you did."

He waited for a reaction from me and he got it—a big, imposing smile of pride. He did not comment.

"But the intelligence I've seen, or heard, coming out of those two or three other nations, have all said that if they had the same mission Great Britain embarked on, they would have marked it down as impossible at the beginning. Argentina was the continental power of South America, having every conceivable advantage.

"Shore-based aircraft a few flying hours away to

target the troops landing on the island, or, alternatively, the ships carrying the troops before they had a chance of unloading. Having a navy with port facilities a day away, gave the Argentinians one enormous logistical advantage over the British, in being able to re-supply their own troops on the islands, far quicker than anything you could do from Ascension Island.

"The British troops had to carry everything on their backs under skies with no air superiority, having to battle through the Argentine navy and air force in order to make an amphibious landing. And then, if that wasn't enough to deal with, the troops had to fight a campaign against a prepared, well dug-in opponent, outnumbering them by at least two to one.

"Just to make the forthcoming bun-fight even more pleasurable than it was going to be, the operational window was calculated for mid-July, after which the weather would close in and any landing would be rendered as completely inoperable.

"But for now there's a different subject I wanted to speak about. My Russian source told me of a meeting where a couple of the senior members of the ANC met with two representatives of the Communist Party of the Russian Federation, or CPRF for short. Evidently it was a meeting for important people only.

"From the Russian side came Ivan Ivanovich Melnikov with Yury Vyacheslavovich Afonin. Both are Deputy Secretaries of the CPRF. The two of them are members of the Russian State Duma. With two Russian stenographers, they met with Elias Sekgobelo Magashule, known to his friends in the party as 'Ace.'

"He is an important mouth to feed as the Secretary General of the African National Congress. He came with his chum, Jacob Mzampate, one of the founding members of the National Executive Committee of the ANC. They too had people to write the notes.

"Unfortunately, I wasn't told of this meeting until it was too late for me to act, otherwise I would have tried to have it wired for you, but as I say, I did not know. Luckily, not all is lost. One of the two people taking notes for the Africans is on our payroll. Back in London you'd call him an *illegal.*

"He didn't know where it was to be held until an hour before, so he was unable to call me. It was one of the precautions the ANC took. When at last we could speak, he told me the first point of interest on the ANC's agenda was the fast-growing Chinese economy. Elias 'Ace' Magashule wanted to know how the Chinese had achieved such high rates of growth, without the same happening inside the Russian economy.

"It won't be long, Harry, before South Africa will wake up to a version of the State Anthem of the Russian Federation playing on the popular Ukhozi radio station. Next, the Hammer and Sickle will be squeezed into a corner of the Rainbow Nation flag. It will be either that brand of religion or one coming from further east.

"Coming down to a more personal level, you and I saw America's foreign political policies in both Iraq and Afghanistan, then before either of those wars came around, we saw it in the Bosnia and Herzegovina conflict. We both have direct experience of how their notion to how to convince Serbs, Shiites, or even the Taliban to change their way of life, was nothing more than ridiculous.

"I've only seen one policy of theirs, and that's to throw money at it, then sit back waiting until those that are still alive can sign exclusive loan agreements tying their country into buying American produce in order to rebuild. There's always money at the bottom of that shell-hole.

"When the AWB replace this government, we will endeavour to retain the stability that Great Britain's monarch gives to every sovereign state within the Commonwealth of Nations. We wish to build our economy into a position of geopolitical strength. One from which we could become an active part of a wider community embracing the same ideals as all inside the aforementioned Commonwealth.

"From the time of South Africa being declared 'a sovereign independent state' in 1934, and apartheid being adopted by the National Party of South Africa in 1948, responsibility of government was taken seriously.

With the policy of apartheid came trouble. Often the trouble was fanned by an overreaction in the press, both national and international.

"The White settlers were blamed for things beyond their control. Unfortunately, the death toll amongst those settlers was..." He stopped speaking, then looked at me for a reply. I had no answer for him.

"We tried our best to live alongside them but we couldn't. No matter what Alice will have told you, not all trouble was started by the AWB. One thing is for sure, there was never the extent of Black on Black violence before apartheid was abolished.

"It seems to me every native South African, no matter what colour, was treated more fairly in the apartheid years than they are now. We are at a point where the communists want to stir up trouble again. We will not allow anything along those lines to happen."

I was angry and forced an opportunity to speak.

"What's the idea then, Bots? Alice implied the AWB had held on to a couple of nuclear warheads. They have been hidden away somewhere out of sight from passing satellites, with the odd radioisotope or lump of plutonium sitting on a shelf in someone's underground garage, like one of yours. Is the AWB's intention to explode a 'tactical bomb' to show just how powerful you lot are? Or maybe you think the threat to explode one would be enough?" I was just warming up. I had more.

"How about spraying some of the anthrax you have over the township at Soweto, or any settlement at Umlazi? If that doesn't work, you could utilise the odd phial of Sarin gas you have locked away waiting to be used. I don't know a great deal about your country, Bots, but from what I do know, I doubt you'd win many friends for your takeover if that's the ultimate ambition. Don't be a complete imbecile, Winston."

"I'm not, Harry. Look at the facts. After all these years of Black rule, the Blacks are still forced to live in shit-holes. The ordinary Black worker has gained nothing to add to his pocket. The ANC blame the Whites for leaving the country in the mess we are in now, but it's been almost twenty-five years since Mandela walked free, announcing South Africa had become the Rainbow Nation.

"Even he joined the South African Communist party. It's been almost thirty years since there was a major war outbreak between the ANC movement and the Zulu Inkatha movement. Scratch the surface away from what divides the two sides and look at the considerable hatred that's still there. Black tribal hatred is centuries old. It will never change.

"The propaganda leading up to the '94 election was a load of balls. It was then, and it still is. The talk about Russia being corrupt is true, but ridiculous

when you look at the corruption here, in this continent. I am sickened there's no politician in the West
brave enough to say the grossly overweight government ministers of African countries are all that shape
because of raiding the aid budget.

"They are all fat as pigs wallowing in the shit
they create. It doesn't stop with them. After their
faces have been in the feeding trough there's their
family to nourish. Then there's their tribe. The bigger
the tribe, the more likely they will win the next war
between two of them. They prosper on stolen aid,
bribes from pharmaceutical companies and the
weapon manufacturers.

"The financial aid Great Britain, with other
Western countries, sends to Africa for starving children, for clean water, for shelter, for everything else,
doesn't get to the children. It doesn't reach the poor.
First, it goes to the officials who run the charities.
They keep some of the aid for themselves and their
families.

"The culture they adopt of *playing-it-up* means
those Africans at the very top get the most and, surprise, surprise, some of those at the very top have
huge, colossal families. Some of them number up to a
hundred or more. All those mouths need to be fed
and their enormous bodies need to be clothed.

"I believe your wife's designer label is on the
dresses of the elite women who love to wear fashion
labels. If Serena designed clothes for men, the hus-

bands would be clothed in suits from her. They buy from the Italian houses now. Some wear their clothes inside out so the 'mob' can see the labels! You can't make this stuff up, Harry.

"Since 1994, the ANC have created more than thirty-odd government office posts where none existed before the election. They have also generated around an extra five hundred internal service positions to fill and I bet you can't guess who those jobs went to. Corruption is an ANC way of life. It's a culture they multiply within.

"If you can remember, or if indeed you read of it, think back to the times when the Black police force fired on striking Black platinum mine workers. They killed thirty-four and injured about a hundred more. Then the time the police fired on striking gold miners, killing hundreds that day.

"How about the corruption charges? The ANC youth leader charged with laundering millions of dollars through his family's business. How about the President? President Zuma? How many trials for corruption did it take before he went? He still got away with the twenty million dollar upgrade to his private home.

"It doesn't stop there. What about the bribes paid out to, then received back from, the football ruling body FIFA to secure the 2010 World Cup? Oh yes! They played it that way—*playing-it-up*. Paying FIFA just short of ten million dollars for the privilege of holding it, then getting back roughly half the amount to line their own pockets with. Then the deception they employed to allow Sudanese President Omar al-Bashir to stay in South Africa, despite there being an international warrant out for his arrest for genocide and war-crimes. I wonder how many dollars that cost him?"

* * *

Abruptly, he stopped speaking, leaving me for a moment feeling as though I could touch the anger as his eyes narrowed to almost closed and his mouth clenched even tighter, pulling his teeth towards the edge of his upper lip which turned white in the process.

I had never seen Winston so incensed or outraged about anything before, as he always struck me as being able to maintain a composed and calm appearance. He had successfully concealed this incandescent characteristic.

It crossed my mind it was perhaps due to my smoking, as although the doors were open onto the balcony, the air above us was revolving with no urgency to leave and join the cooler outside air. I glanced opposite at the fast draining bottle of whisky we were sharing, making a mental note not to ask Liam to come rushing to our rescue with a replacement.

With no tangible reason, my thoughts went to Oona and what she could be doing in her single bedroom, or perhaps she was alone in the ground floor lounge, or outside the hotel chatting with Tommy's crew and checking for 'hoods', as she'd so eloquently put it. Perhaps she was in the single room but not alone. Where would my mind wander next?

I didn't have long to wait to find out. My altered focus was undressing her. I had the first button of her off-the-shoulder blue blouse in my fingers as I greedily looked at the curves of her small breasts. "Stop!" I shouted, loud enough for Liam to come rushing in. I looked the fool that I was, but my plea of lack of meaningful sleep mixed with the volume of alcohol consumed without food, was accepted by both parties as they returned to their previous activities: Liam to his computer and short-wave radio to Tommy, and Winston to his prejudiced briefing.

"The ANC supporters took over farms from the White families who had husbanded the land down through generations, looking after the Blacks who worked there a darn sight better than the treatment dished out to them after they were 'liberated'.

"The police did nothing to stop this. What made things worse was, if any Whites retaliated by shooting at those Blacks who were attacking their farm, they were arrested and don't think about what would happen if any of the ANC foot soldiers died. If that was the case, the Whites involved were dispatched to Pollsmoor prison where they were sub-jected to unspeakable violence from Black inmates.

"White farmers, the Boers of yesteryear, took the only option open to them; they moved out. Some of the more determined sent their wife and children away to family, took their rifle and joined forces with the others in the AWB.

"I'm not one of the mindless thugs of the far-flung right that could be found in the original Afrikaner Weerstandsbeweging. I can't answer for everyone's motive, but I genuinely want to improve the living standards of the lowest in our country and if, after that improvement, the rich get richer, then so be it. That is the law of commerce. Everyone should be able to improve their lifestyle. All I ask is for you to look at what happens next. Friends should look after friends, don't you think, Harry?"

Fortunately, that was another question I had no need of answering.

CHAPTER NINETEEN

WHAT'S INTELLIGENCE?

"Alice is part of the very foundations of South Africa's intelligence establishment. I think she's been there forever, it's her life. As you yourself will know, there can be a high degree of extravagance by some involved with intelligence gathering. Secrets, even lies, can all come out the same sometimes, can't they? I would say she's one who can certainly be extravagant with the truth. But it doesn't matter if we have nukes or not.

"What we do have are the materials and expertise to put one together. We've done it in the past. You know how it goes, Harry; the Biblical one begets two, two begets three, and so on and so forth, until all of an international sudden, blink of an eyelid, there we are, classified as a nuclear power with a seat in another kind of security council. How about one made up of: South Africa, India, Israel, Pakistan, North Korea, Japan and perhaps Iraq and Iran,? Now there's an eclectic collection.

With no prompting coming from me, he addressed the file for the first time since I'd seen him.

"Going back to the *State of Capture* report implicating President Zuma in so many corrupt business dealings, one of them involved Eskom, the company that built our nuclear power station. One name listed in the file attached to the French email Samantha got hold of, was a Chinese woman who works for Eskom, whose husband holds a position as an unclassified assistant to the Chinese ambassador at their Embassy here in America.

"From the same file, Harry, we got the names of two Russians said to have *interests* in our nuclear capability. One was an electrical engineer working for Lesedi Nuclear Services, the company that maintain our one nuclear power station, with the other one inside the South African Department of Energy.

"We could do nothing about the three people at this moment in time, but when we form the government, then it will be a different matter.

"When the Russians made a diplomatic approach to the ANC asking if South Africa had the capability to construct nuclear weapons, it was met with a flat denial of proficiency. What else could they do? The Russian foreign secretary was told we have no nuclear potential.

"Notwithstanding the ANC's rebuttal of the Russian's accusations of deception, in the AWB it's our belief both Russia and China continue to investigate how far we have travelled towards nuclear effectiveness. They don't believe we have relinquished all thoughts of acquiring that degree of armament. We got all the confirmation we needed from two other sources, our *illegals* as you prefer to call them.

"This Islamic State, Daesh as the world has come to know them, had a source well placed in the Russian Foreign Intelligence Service and I was told this source had overheard a series of conversations relating to the one nuclear weapon that the ANC could not account for when apartheid ended.

"No matter what they said, the Russians did not believe them. I have no answer to why, after twenty-five years of silence, nuclear weapons had suddenly become important, but they had.

"Perhaps the information carrying the most weight came straight from a meeting between the South African Minister of Defence and the Defence Minister of the Iranian government. An unlikely pairing you might say.

"They met in Khartoum at the Heads of African Government meeting held there last year. We had an AWB agent attached to the South African party that travelled with the Defence Ministry. He managed to take photographs and get an audio recording of a meeting he had with a Russian contractor who offered an inducement of $500,000 for the contract to construct the delivery system, along with the supply of detailed site plans for the underground silos. I can show you all of that. The monetary side of the undertaking went into billions of dollars from which other 'inducements' were not only promised, but easily achievable with that amount of money floating around.

"The Chinese were more subtle. They approached the South African-born scientist working for the Iranian government, who has affiliations to our intelligence service. When that approach was made, I had no idea how our service had been penetrated, but I did discover how it was done. The Chinese went through an esoteric online site our man used to find his *'night-time'* female companionship. One night, whilst he was staying in a hotel in Khartoum, the woman who visited his room was a Chinese asset.

"It had previously been judged he was too important to be left alone with so many temptations to steer clear of. That was because he had a 'home service' history of deviant pleasures. It was therefore our policy to monitor his online presence on his devices at home and when away on government business, following up on anything when we deemed it necessary.

"Our precautions were needed, but on this occasion they were not enough. Our man met a messy end at the hands of his female companion. Alice would have to brief you on the details involved, but without her clarity you have to make do with me." There was a slight chuckle to his voice, as there was no disguising the fact he was enjoying himself.

"I was not directly involved in this case so I have to rely on the written reports that were submitted. In essence, we made an anonymous phone call to the police telling them of his murder, adding it was a woman visitor to his room who had killed him. We told the Sudan police where to find the cameras and tape machines Oona's unit had concealed in his room. It didn't take the police long to discover what phone numbers he'd called, but of course by then the girl was long gone."

* * *

He could not, or at least did not want to, go into any of the lurid details of injuries inflicted on the scientist. All he said was the evidence persuaded them to believe the Chinese escort had instructions to painfully interrogate him for knowledge of South African's working policy on expansion of any nuclear competence. They also concluded the Chinese wanted to know how far the Iranians were in developing a bomb themselves.

There was a short break to refill glasses and to light cigarettes. Liam had acquired another bottle of whisky from room service along with, much to my delight, my brand of cigarettes which were terribly hard to find. I broke the pause by asking the questions that were playing on my mind.

"Whilst on the subject of painful interrogation, as we were, why did Gibson torture both Hugh Pickering then Gerald Neil? What was it you asked him to find, Bots?"

"No, I never asked him to find anything, Harry. Did you ask him what he was after?" he replied, with what appeared to be a huge amount of sincere indignation.

"I did ask, but he wouldn't say. I just guessed it was you asking him to find out something," I replied without much conviction, swiftly moving the subject on.

"Have you ever met that Kuwaiti chap, Sabah Al Salim, or his half-brother Shaikh Al Sabah?"

"No, again. I've never met Al Salim. I've heard of him though. Not a nice fellow, or at least that's what I've heard. Gossip, no more than that. I did meet his half-brother Shaikh once when you and I bumped into one another at an art exhibition in St James's. You should have that memory of yours checked, old man.

"That's not a good thing to lose in your business, but wow, that was a good few years ago, now I come to think of it. That Shaikh chap was there with a woman on each arm. Funny though, he didn't stay long after you introduced me and the girl I was with.

I can vividly remember thinking it was something about me that made him leave so unexpectedly. You and he seemed quite chummy."

"I hope you will forgive me, Harry, but I had one of the departments back home look into him. I also had a look myself through any files I could access. We didn't find anything too upsetting, but what we did find I'm sure you're aware of, old man."

* * *

There was something MI6 had enquired into that Winston might have found upsetting had I told him, but I didn't, I kept it to myself. It was about the Chinese female assassin he was telling me about. She did not return to China, or in fact leave the Sudan. After killing the scientist, she went back to her apartment overlooking the Nile River, on the outskirts of Khartoum.

On the evening of the next day, prior to going out for a dinner date when the very last thing on her mind would be the Sudanese police knocking down her front door was exactly what happened.

The normal protocol in the Sudan is to hold foreign nationals who are prisoners locally, to await transportation to a dedicated holding station. Then, if the wheels turned efficiently, a court appearance, which could take quite some time. No matter how good the equipment was that Oona's unit placed inside the scientist's room, there was only one way for Winston to be unquestionably sure their *illegal* had never told the escort girl any secrets and that was to *ask* her.

That was precisely the conclusion Section 9 at MI6 reached. Her mutilated dead body was found in the transit accommodation, near the shopping centre at Salha, ten kilometres or so from the police station, the place she was held, to await investigations.

* * *

If a passport belonging to a Sean Laing, an Irish national, could have been be found, inside it would show the customs stamp from the Khartoum International Airport for entry into Sudan on the same day as the Chinese escort was taken to the police holding centre, where, subsequently, she was murdered. But alas, no such passport was ever found. However, that name was on a boarding card of an Air France airliner that landed at Khartoum in the early hours of the same morning. Sean Laing was one of four pseudonyms known to MI6 to be currently used by Liam Gibson.

* * *

Winston was rambling on a little; perhaps it was the whisky, perhaps it was lack of sleep. I couldn't make out some of what he was saying, but most I could. He was talking about the water supply to a township near Pretoria called Rustenberg being polluted by the discharge from a nearby platinum mine. He said it had taken a long time to be investigated, but when eventually it was, a rare-earth mineral named zircon was found to be contaminating the nearby water supply. The Black mining operators had no idea how to stop it.

I knew from my experience the alloy zirconium was not only extremely valuable, it was an integral part of any nuclear fusion power production or, come to that, a nuclear weapon. It was used in both. I wasn't sure if Bots knew that, but I couldn't believe he was trying to mislead me. I managed to move the subject away from one form of nuclear weapon to another—the copy of the French email, attachments and all.

He confirmed there were the coded names of six 'illegals' known only to the South African security service. He didn't want to tell me the names, but he did confirm some and he did divulge the positions they held. One was inside the group said to be representing the Islamic State, or Daesh as it was better known. Two were officials inside the Iraqi government. Another one had direct access to the defence minister of the Iranian government.

A hugely important one was the name of a scientist working in the Iranian nuclear programme, who was now dead. But the position of the sixth and final 'illegal' operative he did not divulge. He would tell me sometime in the future; *when the time was right,* he said.

Now we were on the subject of names, I asked if he would tell me any more about the mysterious Colette of Iraq. I asked him if he thought Colette was her real name. He said she had told him it was her working name, but she wouldn't tell him her real name. I asked if he knew any more about her, or about Iraq.

As his recollection was unfolding, I wasn't sure if it was the drink clouding his mind or if he had deliberately, or by accident, forgotten about the man London detailed as his briefing officer. That man, named Jackson, might know Colette's real name, as he might know who was on the enquiry board at Poole when Winston was flown back from duty in the desert. I reminded myself to ask Sir Leonard Miles if he knew who Jackson was.

For no reason apparent to me, Bottomly became very melancholy. I decided to let him be, not pressing him about the unexplained or unseen Jackson. I sat content to listen to what he had to say.

"I'm really sorry about Samantha, Harry. As I've already told you, I genuinely did love her." He shook his head as he carried on.

"Even allowing for the love I felt, when she told me she'd stolen a restricted French file because some billionaire Kuwaiti had told her to do so, I forgot about love. I first asked her why she had not told me before going ahead? Did I not count for something? I asked her.

"Then, after I questioned her a bit more, she told me all the names of the people she'd told about that bloody email. I told her, in no uncertain terms—'*it was classified intelligence. You haven't got the right to show it around. It could cost people's lives.*'

"It was then I had to tell her how I worked for South Africa intelligence. After that, I was left with no choice. Everyone who was not authorised to read it, or had seen inside it, had to be eliminated. The instigator of all this trouble, this Sabah Al Salim, the man you mentioned, is still alive. That wasn't my decision. As I've told you, if left to me, he would die very slowly, very painfully. In my mind it was he who sentenced Samantha to death."

He'd said *if left to me,* which implied there was someone above him who was making the decisions. What about that stop-off at 199, Knightsbridge? Did Winston know of that?

"Why did she make a copy of the email? Do you think she didn't know why Al Salim wanted the file, or was there a reason he'd discussed with her?"

"She told me he hadn't given her any reason. But he didn't want the whole thing, just to copy it." He sounded drained.

"I was told the email was copied at an address in

Knightsbridge and it was you who told her to take it there." I added that last bit in an attempt to wake him from the dark place he was in.

"Whoever told you that is lying, Harry!"

In a deep, throaty, gravelly voice he shouted the accusation, his close-set eyes squinting at me. The colour of his face had changed. Now he was more a deeper shade of red, rather than his normal pale pinkish-white.

"I've told you when I first knew about an email so many times, I'm beginning to think I'm being interrogated. Okay, I'll play along with you. I saw it on the Thursday evening when I met Samantha in her apartment at the Grosvenor House. I know nothing about instigating a copy of it."

He was less agitated now, but not completely at ease. His voice had softened to the calmer one I knew, but the furrows on his forehead were still deeply engraved. His facial colouring had lost that look of warning, leaving his nostrils less flared and his eyes less accusing. I'm not sure why but I accepted his denial. I had no evidence to rely upon for that decision, I only had my intuition and instinct.

"I'm inclined to believe you, Bots, but I find it hard to understand how you never knew her apartment in the Grosvenor House was paid for by this Sabah Al Salim."

"Well, that's what I'm telling you, Harry. I did not know. She told me she had sold the family home when her parents died and there was also some money left to her. I never looked further into it. I had no reason to distrust her.

"I expect you would have looked into it all, but I didn't. As far as I knew, her father had owned an English security company and her mother had been a famous French singer. That's the story I heard. It left me to assume that's how she could afford the suite of rooms at the Grosvenor House."

"She never told you anything about stopping at those apartments, in Knightsbridge?"

"No, she did not tell me that. If she'd told me, then everyone who had been at the address would have to be eliminated."

* * *

Ordinarily there could have been three possibilities: one, to believe him about not knowing the email was copied; two, that his Intelligence Service were to blame for not briefing him properly; or three, he was lying. I said at the beginning there could be three possibilities, well, that was not entirely true. The last possibility could not be the truth, as I had good reason to believe Page Boucher and his lover had been killed by London operatives.

"I have to ask you again about Gerald Neil's torture, Winston. I know you owed him a considerable amount of money. Was that the reason he was killed?"

"I never ordered his death, nor any torture. As I understand things, nobody from the AWB touched Gerald, but I do know we looked for him. I expect London told you he was Samantha's case officer." He looked at me as if expecting a reply. I preferred to stay silent. He spoke again.

"I was told Gerald's death was down to Al Salim."

"Who told you that?" quietly I asked.

"Liam did. He explained to me how Gerald had friends all over the place who he could have told what he'd seen inside the email. As far as I know, we urgently needed the names of who exactly he may have told, but, as I said, we did not get that far."

"What about Pickering, how does he fit into the plans you have to replace the government of South Africa?"

"He doesn't, but it's complicated with him. You know how we have an agreement with the Israeli government to assist us in certain matters in exchange for the name, as well as the use of 'the scientist' we had in Iran? They have other stipulations, of course, but to summarise their demands, it amounts to a direct attack on Iran's nuclear programme. That could now become more urgent.

"The Israelis don't believe the Iranians about the programme all being for domestic purposes alone. I've spoken to an agent from Mossad and even if it was the truth, it would make no difference to the government of Israel. The only thing holding them back is they want to be absolutely sure the Iranian radar defence system is switched off before they go in and bomb the hell out of the laboratories at a place named Shahrud.

"As I understand things, the mission to temporarily turn off the radar is under consideration by a small specialist unit of the AWB, but before it's a green light, we need some information only the CIA can supply. I wanted whatever I could get out of Pickering in order to twist the arms of his two CIA friends to get that missing information."

"Was he part of Liam's work?"

"I can't be sure it was Liam himself but it certainly fell under his unit's remit. It was common knowledge how the CIA had Pickering in their pocket." He fell silent again, presumably thinking of Samantha and happier times.

Whilst we shared the silence, my thoughts fell upon the ingenuity of Sabah Al Salim, in being clever enough to hide Samantha's real antecedents and invent the legend she told everybody, including Winston. It was as if she actually believed it.

* * *

My old school chum, the one I had been in contact with before coming to America, also knew Charles Oswald Wallace. My friend was a Major General when he retired from the British army, having given forty-four years in total to the safety of the British public in one way or another.

The last twelve of those years were served on secondment to the counter-terrorism network either with Special Branch or the UK Border Force, both through the Home Office. I had worked with him a good many years ago, when I was grateful for his remarkable powers of memory and, of course, his loyal dedication to secrecy when the job had finished.

We had met at The Hall in Harrogate. He had driven himself with his dog, a Golden Retriever named Buster, named after, so I was informed, Buster Edwards, a member of the Great Train Robbers, seated in the rear of his car.

As my friend opened his driver's door to get out, Buster jumped from the rear to the front and ran out across the drive, onto the surrounding grass frontage as far as the lake. The dog seemed happy when he urinated on the attractive, mauve flowering irises growing at the side, but poor old Major General Sir Rupert Draycott was anything but amused.

His apologies only just gave way when accepting the refreshments Joseph had laid on for us, which we took in the cool of the summer house, as I managed to appease his worries, but he could not appease mine.

After I gave him all the information I could, we parted company with my promise of getting in touch once again when I was in America. He agreed to an equivalent arrangement, but when he delivered on his end of the deal it required an entire reassessment of the situation on my part.

CHAPTER TWENTY

MARIANA

Oona was with Liam in a separate part of the suite where there was an enormous, wall-mounted television. It was switched on and tuned into a CNN news broadcast telling of a forest fire on the outskirts of Cape Town, South Africa. I sat in one of the soft reclining chairs, one of those that wrap themselves around you as soon you sit, and I wondered why I hadn't got them at home. At first, all I could think of was the hefty luxury this chair afforded me. I made a mental note to change the old leather chairs in the reception rooms of The Hall to soft chairs like these.

I think my mind needed the distraction because slowly, I was able to turn my attention towards news broadcasts, but not the current one; ones of years past.

If Bottomly and his pals in this far right-wing

group the AWB were waiting for a catalyst to trigger an uprising, then what happened in the month of August 2012, when the South African Police Service were paid, by members of the AWB, to open fire on a crowd of striking mineworkers at Marikana, in the North West Province of South Africa, must surely have provided it.

The police killed thirty-four mineworkers that day, leaving seventy-eight others seriously injured. As if that assault had not been enough, approximately two hundred and fifty of the striking miners were ordered to be arrested!

This was the time they had planned for the uprising to topple the ANC and install a White governing party. Was it not? I asked of nobody. In a fictional sense, they could have ridden in as mounted knights, disarmed the SAPS and said to the people, *'There, see, it's us who will disband this corrupt force and replace it with one of our nurturing. On your behalf, we will overthrow this unscrupulous government, replacing it with one putting your welfare at the top of the list for implementing.'*

It would be then the public relations people could start to work their magic and before you knew it—apartheid to be reintroduced under a White ruling government with a different name for it. But no, it didn't happen. So why not? Winston had no answer. He implied there was a rift in the upper ranks of the AWB, but he did not go into specifics.

* * *

The AWB, working in league with the security arm of the South African government, had paid the South African Police Service to open fire that day. It was they who supplied the weapons, as well as supplying all the ammunition needed to execute that atrocity. When the time arrived for the inevitable government-inspired inquiry to take a look inside the South African Police Service armoury, the inventory of weapons, with the suitable ammunition, tallied exactly to what should have been there.

Therefore, the investigators concluded in their report to the national and international press agencies, there was no outside interference into what had taken place... *Here check our numbers. It's all accounted for.*

It was yet another example of the inter-union rivalry at more and more mines. The government duly declared their resolve to stand firm against the unions' demands of limiting the number of migrant workers entering the country looking for work.

They quoted the Rainbow Nation tag, applying it to the situation, even inviting an enfeebled Nelson Mandela to add his support to the illicit migrants. I strongly put it to Winston, there still remained the opportunity the AWB, with others, had orchestrated. Lamely, he admitted they missed their chance.

"Next time," he said, "things will be different."

* * *

It was not the television as such that had held my attention for this length of time as the news cameras spanned the intense, roaring firestorm. It was the cynic inside me thinking the film crew and news channel were waiting for the lion, or other big wild animal, to run from the inferno in fear for its life. Was the same fate awaiting me? The figurative run in the face of danger? Should I quit America and run for home? Bots was speaking again, as he entered the room from the lounge.

When the environmental disaster with the water supply at the town of Rustenberg was made public, he said, it would provide an opportunity like no other before. The largest deposits of Iridium in the world are near Rustenberg and if you had not heard of this mineral before, then the AWB spokesman had a press release explaining it all.

Rustenberg would become known throughout the world, as would the fact of Iridium being essential for anything nuclear.

The determination I had come across so far inside the narrow part of the AWB I had met, was most certainly ready to take action; what I didn't know was the strength of numbers in the AWB and the heavy equipment it might have ready to oust the Black government. It would be useful to meet London's agent inside this Recces, the Special Forces Brigade, if only to get their perspective on the regular military's support for such an upheaval.

I knew of none, but perhaps London would know of a Western nation willing to stand shoulder to shoulder with the AWB, covered as it was with an extreme right-wing banner in its war against the left-wing Marxism of the ANC; I doubted either would appeal to backers.

* * *

The picture on the screen had changed from the carnage north of the Cape to a debate in the Supreme Court of Justice building in Washington D.C. With the change, so went my logic. Playfully, I christened Liam and Oona with the pseudonym of 'L&O', then, feeling brilliantly elated by my newly discovered ingenuity, I telephoned Serena, not Katherine, but I haven't a reason for my change of allegiance nor why I telephoned. As I waited for her phone to respond, I told L&O I was off to my bedroom to find some sleep.

* * *

I thoroughly enjoyed the twenty-minute telephone call speaking to Serena and, just as importantly, to Breno, who was coming to the end of his school's late summer break at the family home in the Algarve, just outside the town of Lagos.

I tried to find rest from the crazy thoughts going around on the flightpath I was trying to control inside my head. My subconscious was trying to help me by recalling a moment I'd shared with Alice. Owing to the fact my mind was wide awake, it was a bad choice.

"Has Winston ever mentioned the name Pickering to you, Alice? A Hugh Pickering."

"Not that I can remember, no, but I don't speak to Winston very often. When I liaise with colleagues it's mostly conducted through Liam. Yes, he would be my main source of information outside of South Africa, as well as being the man I would turn to for most things."

"I know I've asked before, but why do you think Winston preferred you to tell me all that you have, rather than tell me himself? I realise I should ask him that question, but I'm finding it all so odd that he's not here and you are."

"Honestly? Don't you find everything he's done recently odd? Like murdering the woman he says he'd fallen in love with?"

"He told you he loved her?"

"Yes, he did, and he wasn't even a bit shy about it. I think he actually loved telling me. "

"Did he ever tell you he had a house in London? He never told me and I thought I knew him so well."

"The family have a huge house in a place called Muswell Hill Road, Highgate. I went there as a child.

I haven't many memories of the place but I do re-member how I used to walk to the flyover at High-gate, then on to Highgate cemetery to see Karl Marx's grave. Highgate flyover and the grave were great tourist spots. I was told, by someone who knew these things, how people used to commit suicide by throwing themselves off that flyover. Weird!

"Anyway it was Winston's great-great-grandpa who first made the money, but his great-grandfather made more of it. He just couldn't help himself. Everywhere he went. I guess that was probably a slight overstatement, the making money everywhere he went, but when I was old enough and knew how to research things, I looked him up and wow, did I have a shock. He was one seriously rich billionaire back in those days. I was so young, I was almost em-barrassed.

"He opened his own private bank in London, sometime in the eighteenth century, I think it was. He sold it when he consolidated all his holdings and settled permanently in South Africa. He established another private bank in Durban. Winston told me how your family has a bank, but not in the City of London. Yours is in Westminster, called Annie's if I'm not mistaken. He told me your bank was estab-lished for European Royalty and the like."

"It was, yes. And you have the name right, but the bank is no longer owned by one family. A few years ago, I decided we needed to change our activities. But tell me, Alice, when did your relative sell the bank he had in London? Roughly, would be okay."

"If an estimation would do, then I'd say round about the beginning of the first Anglo-Boer War. That would make it about 1899. What I do know for sure is that he had a large financial undertaking along the Rand—that's the Witwatersrand, or the White Water Ridge, the ridge where most of South Africa's gold deposits were found. It's where Johannesburg was eventually built.

"The Bottomly family had investments in that area ever since gold was discovered. The story I was told was he wanted to hire enough men to be able to secure all the land he owned in and around the Kimberley diamond mines, as well as along the Witwatersrand, where his gold was being excavated. He needed more money to hire the kind of men who would normally want to dig for gold. Those who knew how to handle a gun well and would kill if necessary.

"Today, we would probably say by having financial interests in London, his lines of supply and communication were stretched too far. He must have thought the same, so he sold the bank and strengthened the positions where he was making the most money. He made the first family home in a place near the Crocodile River.

"It's at the foot of the Magaliesberg Mountains. It really is as beautiful as it sounds. By the time I was born he'd sold it and moved to where the family have their main farm holdings now.

"If you ever go to South Africa, which I'm sure you will, make sure you take a trip out to Magaliesberg. Go do some climbing in the mountains, see what it must have been like before men took a hand in its construction and interfered with what God made."

"Did you ever hear what happened to the private bank he sold, Alice? Because this chap Pickering I mentioned earlier, owns a City bank named after himself—Pickering's. Ever heard Winston mention that name, perhaps with the initials of the CIA? Only I think they're connected.

"I have a copy of a Risk Assessment Spreadsheet of Pickering's Bank for the final six months accounting of 2007. It's not important how I got hold of it, but Pickering's bank had a hefty injection of six billion dollars in November of that year. The money didn't come in one go. No, Pickering's is a small bank with small vaults, too small for that amount of dollar bills. It would have taken a few journeys, probably held elsewhere until needed.

"No matter, there's no indication where the money came from. As I recall, Pickering was very uncooperative when asked by the Bank Regulators of the time, who had an infinite amount of considerations to attend to round about then.

"All in all, the injection of money was very fortuitous considering what happened to a number of banks the following year. Six billion dollars is too large an amount of money to conceal if one looks carefully for its origin. I put some of my people on it when the transaction was uncovered.

"The documents they found said it came from a communications company with only two outlets, one of which is here in America. The company is named the Pegasus Mercantile Company. Ever heard of it, Alice?"

It was at this stage she raised her arm with her elbow to the floor, palm facing me, as though she was a traffic cop signalling vehicles to stop. I took it as a sign to stop speaking. I did as I thought I was being instructed. I was right.

"That was the company he sold the bank to, I'm sure of it. If I remember my Greek mythology correctly, Pegasus was a winged horse that, along with his brother, whose name I've forgotten, was released from the head of Medusa when it was cut off by Perseus. I know! Part of the really useful information a young child learns at school. This Pegasus company doesn't just deal with communications though, Harry. But I bet you already know that," she finished, with a stern look on her face.

I told her I didn't know, and for once it was the truth that I told. It didn't feel any different than if I had told a lie. Maybe the time I've spent stealing other people's secrets, or telling lies in order to hide those secrets, had allowed lies and truth to merge into the same thing. But if that was true for me, then at least for Alice it was not the truth.

The impression I had was of her speaking to me as if I was a relative. The thought was reinforced when she filled in some of the large blank pieces of my jigsaw.

* * *

"The Pegasus Mercantile Company is the operational arm of the Special Activities Division, activated by an executive order signed by Harry S. Truman, one week after WWII ended in Europe, in May 1945. It is part of the centralised CIA except it is assigned a slightly different function. Code-named SAD, it was utilised for covert paramilitary operations gathering intelligence in hostile areas where it was vital the American name could not be dredged up.

"If, after all precautions were taken, the name of America was brought up, then any and all actions involving SAD operational officers would be strenuously denied. Any CIA agent so revealed, would be expected to take his or her own life to avoid capture. Yes, all that is true, Harry."

* * *

When she'd finished speaking, she'd looked at me very oddly. The only way I can adequately describe the strangeness of it is to say it felt as though her stare held not only more suspicion, but a sense of premonition than I had not seen there before. Lying here on the bed and trying to remember as best I could, was to say it seemed as though she wanted to tell me something more about Pegasus but there was some part of her intuition stopping her. After what seemed an age, she began again, only this time the subject had changed and it was some of Winston's exploits she felt under an obligation to defend.

"If the only thing on my nephew's mind was survival, young man, then he would have traded the knowledge he has on the location of the various stored munitions I've told you about. But he hasn't said a word, has he?" I shook my head in reply as she continued.

"I don't know it all, but I do know they have a state-of-the-art battlefield command-and-control network, backed up by a missile defence system using British Army Spike missiles and something from America that arrived via Israel. A lot of that, plus smaller ground weaponry, came through the Israelis. The AWB sourced some really sophisticated radar equipment from the American Defence Department, but of course that's deniable if it's an Arab country asking how we got it. The Americans have lots of double standards."

I thought I detected an insult balancing on her lips, but if so, it was cut short, presumably before adding expletives considered unnecessary in the context of our meeting. When she had collected herself with all thoughts of insults vanished, the time to continue had arrived.

"Anyway, there's enough weaponry to start another two wars against Angola with the Cuban specialists still there. Set the knowledge of that against the debt he had and you can see where Winston's loyalties are. No, he wouldn't trade what he knows. I guess he thought gambling club owners weren't to be trusted with that sort of information. Instead, he went along with the murder."

I had one final question for the lady I decided I just could not afford not to ask.

"Have you ever heard the Russian name of Valery Agapov before? The name wouldn't necessarily be mentioned by Winston, it could have been in some other context unconnected to him."

"Yes, I have heard it. Winston said the name once. It was a long time ago, when he was very sad about something he wouldn't talk about. There was no girlfriend on his mind, nor any murder he wanted to tell me about. What kind of turmoil goes on in an impenetrable mind such as his, do you think?"

I had no answer for her. I couldn't fathom my own mind, let alone one belonging to Bottomly. It was a choice I had never been forced to make. It could explain his sudden excessive liking for, and being unaffected by, drink. My respect for him notched up a gear. Nevertheless, my increased respect did not remove him from suspicion regarding who had authorised Pickering's and Neil's murders.

As if to prove a point to myself, I decided I didn't care. It was not my brief to find their killer. Again, I faced the question about what was my brief, my purpose? With so much confusion, it wasn't surprising I'd forgotten what I'd come to America for. Aunt Alice had proved useful. Even so, it was as I'd known from the beginning; it was Bottomly who held the answers. Maybe one of those answers could be found in the conundrum, issued by Winston's Russian friend —*emissaries having more information can be found where the pastures are closed in the north.*

CHAPTER TWENTY-ONE

DECISIONS

Bots was in the suite pouring coffee from a breakfast trolley, no doubt the same trolley that had woken me when it was wheeled in. He was dressed in the same clothes he wore last night so my question of where did he sleep seemed superfluous to the occasion, but I asked it anyway, before I had properly switched on.

I also asked if he'd seen Liam and Oona that morning, to which he nonchalantly replied they had left to catch a flight to Johannesburg and then they would be going home. Perhaps it was a touch of jealousy in his voice that made him seem edgy, or maybe he wanted them gone for a reason I had yet to discover.

I was grateful for the sleep I'd had and so, it seemed, was Bots. I had not noticed his lack of luggage, nor the fact that L&O had none when we'd arrived here. I mentioned it now and was told it was all under diplomatic protection at the airport ready for his, and their, flight to South Africa.

Now would be an ideal opportunity to try to understand his attachment to the AWB and ask this hovering overhead question of the photograph that he said he hadn't seen, but I thought he had!

I had struggled with three or four different scenarios before I had found sleep, playing with the openings I'd need to get the most response from Winston; nevertheless, I could not find anything that hit the right spot. One half of my mind was not in tune with the other half and I could not join them together.

As I had no tactics for *asking* my photo question rather than *demanding* an answer, my banal but polite inquiry of why he hadn't left with his two colleagues laid open the path to the aggressive return to the uncertainty of—*why? Did you want me to go?* which was thrown back at me.

Where I was cut off from having any decipherable dialect, Bots was happily talkative whilst sipping coffee and smoking a cigarette. I copied him, hoping it might help to calm my newly acquired nerves.

After exchanging the polite niceties people do when seeing each other for the first time of the day, it was of departure that he wished to speak; his and mine.

He planned to leave that day and go to a part of

his family's estate outside the small town of Upington, in the North Cape of South Africa. The location
was chosen, so he told me, not only because it was an
area of outstanding beauty, but because it was
studded with hidden underground chambers that one
could fly over or even walk over without seeing any
entrance.

In some of these, he boasted, the central part of
London could be hidden. I had no reason to disbe-
lieve him, but my facial expression must have given
the effect of incredulity because he extended an invitation to accompany him to South Africa on the private jet which was due to leave with only him on
board.

I promised to go, but not today, or even tomorrow
come to that. I said I was committed today, but I'd go
the following week on the Tuesday if I could, citing
my estate manager as my excuse. I told Bots I had a
friend in New York who wanted to meet me and collect something from. That wasn't the real reason, but
I did have a person to meet who it would be unwise
to tell Winston about.

I was still struggling to find a starting point for a
conversation. Knowing where to begin without
sounding as if I was indeed an interrogator. Whilst I
was still thinking, Winston was giving me a verbal
tour of Upington and a considerable articulated view
of the vast area owned by his family. I was bored,
which I guess is as good a reason as any to interrupt

someone who is speaking. In I went, with all guns firing. With hindsight, which isn't always an ally, I believe my strategy played out to my advantage.

"London wanted me to find all I could about your Russian friend, Bots. I suppose getting a weather forecast from a meteorologist might count as a reason, but not this time." I was hoping my voice carried enough conviction without sounding tyrannical.

"At last I get a decent excuse from you for being here! Of course we all knew why you'd come, but it's nice of you to tell me, at long last. So was it Sir Leonard Miles who wanted to know, or was he obeying orders?"

"Would it matter who it was? The outcome would clearly be the same, I would come with the same questions. Each one to do with your Russian friend."

It appeared as though he made no connection between me and MI6 at the Box. With that firmly in the centre of my mind, any thoughts about being followed were immediately smashed to pieces, which left the secret world intact. I could use Leonard without any mention of Section 9, or Jerry at Vauxhall. The spell of pessimism, laced with the uncertainty I was experiencing, vanished in a split second, but I didn't want to project any alteration to my temperament. I was presented with an opportunity straightaway.

"Are you sure the copy of that email Samantha

stole was not at the top of the shopping list Sir
Leonard gave you, Harry? Because if not, I'm a kan-
garoo walking up and over the Sydney Harbour
bridge, over and over again until I fall off." By now I
was immune to his sarcasm, awash with success.

"You're right, I can't see any kangaroos nor any
bridges for you to climb, so, yes, the copy was men
tioned. However, between you and your aunt, most, I
would imagine, has already been covered.

"When you decided you could not disclose the
identity of the last name on that file, you forgot about
previously mentioning a man named Jackson, who
was working the Russian agent, Colette.

"London will only need to look back and find
who Jackson was, and then we'll have the real identity of your last illegal, Colette. No, it's your good
friend the Russian weather forecaster London
wanted me to ask about."

Without asking, he moved from Colette to Gerald
Neil, saying how he and the Russian first met in Gerald's club some four or five months before the shoot.
He then dropped a bombshell on me. He said it was
the Russian, Valery Agapov, who was in the photograph, but he wasn't going to tell his friend for what
he called 'obvious reasons'. I asked him what were
those reasons and he just smiled without adding any

comment. So the Russian left the meeting with no idea he was the subject of Gerald Neil's interest.

* * *

"Was that correct?" I asked, to which he answered, "Yes, he did." If that was true, it gave this Agapov a very good reason to *ask* Gerald, *several times*, where the photographs were!

Apart from sordid blackmail, I thought there was something else going on with this photograph but I didn't know where to look. Maybe it would be better if I returned to London to ask Valery Agapov. I silently thought it was getting harder and harder to accept anything Bots said without first thinking it to be a lie. With that in mind, finally, I got around to ask the question. Was there a copy of the email in his possession?

He flushed when he replied he hadn't got it. *"No, Harry. I haven't got it."* Those were his precise words.

"Whose phone was it on, Bots? Was it on Gerald's phone or was it on Samantha's?"

He'd earlier said he thought Samantha had stolen the photograph from Gerald Neil. Could it be she emailed a copy from Gerald's phone to her own, or had she stolen his phone, I wondered?

"It was on her phone, but before you ask, I haven't got it, nor do I know where it is."

* * *

In the back of my mind I had the report from my friend, the retired Major General, Sir Rupert Draycott, which was consistent with what I had just heard. He had not discovered the whereabouts of Samantha's phone. Given all of that, the verbal account from Winston was minus one highly potent part and that was his forgetfulness concerning Valery Agapov's political position. Obviously Bots knew he was not a weather forecaster, but what he was, was nothing obvious.

Rupert had discovered Agapov to have been a high-flying graduate of what was called the Soviet Red Banner Institute, where he had been a great friend of the all-powerful, all-tyrannical President of Russia, Vladimir Vladimirovich Putin. It would seem the connection my investigator had uncovered was not worthy of a mention, or perhaps Bots judged me unworthy to know.

Rupert had found more. He had evidence to connect Agapov to a part of the Russian Foreign Service known as Directorate Q, an elite, supposedly self-governing component of the highly secretive Director of the Foreign Intelligence Service, the highest level of eminence inside the entire secret Russian Intelligence service.

* * *

My journey home to the UK began by moving from the Spring Hill Suites Hotel to the Waldorf Astoria, New York. This next hotel, the last, was nearer to JFK Airport, my departure point. The time it took to travel from one hotel to the other I used for hilarious reflection on how from one moment, I could believe I was an ace amongst spies for the way I used both truth and lies, to the next where the truth was; I was a long way away from being a competent, let alone ace, intelligence agent.

When I left the Waldorf Astoria for home, my fair hair had been coloured a chestnut brown by a friend of Oona, who was of a thoroughly healthier disposition than the radio operator I met in Winston's hotel room.

Thankfully, my newly acquired hairstylist had a different approach to a relationship with men. In an operational sense, I was grateful for the change of hair colouring so professionally applied. Even so, I was more thankful for the change of female presence, especially during my final night devoid of the company Bots, Liam, and Oona had provided. But, as the old adage goes, all good things must come to an end, and so it was with my stay in America, as well as with my hairstylist.

However, that stay was not completely over. Whilst I was at the Spring Hill Suites Hotel, I had spoken to my Special Branch friend, Rupert Draycott, after first being certain Oona, Liam and finally

Winston had left for South Africa. I didn't want any of them to be hanging around when I met with Rupert, who arrived with all the information I'd requested. Some of it made for poor reading.

He'd used a roll call of ex-colleagues, friends, and in one case a man he had cause to arrest, who had served a lengthy custodial sentence, in order to uncover the real story behind the man who I knew as Sabah Al Salim, from Kuwait.

It had not been an easy task, as there was no such person listed on any birth document that could be found. His 'half-brother' Shaikh Al-Sabah, was indeed a Kuwaiti, his father being a well-respected oil exporter.

The two half-brothers shared the same mother but their fathers were very different. Sabah's father was an extremely important Iranian. A man who preferred anonymity rather than being acclaimed. He was a director inside the much-hated SAVAK, the secret intelligence service when Iran was under the rule of the Shah. It had been the country's most detested and feared dictatorial institution where death and torture were its everyday practice.

In spite of the bloody revenge, the followers of the white-robed Ayatollah Khomeini inflicted on members of SAVAK during the Iranian revolution in 1979, Sabah's father, along with a few others from that loathed institution, was retained and tasked with forming a new intelligence service to serve the new republic.

Over the years that followed, Sabah Al Salim, with unobtrusive help from his father, managed to carve a significant niche for himself inside this new, exclusive secret institution named the Ministry of Intelligence and National Security of Iran, known by the letters SAVAMA.

Protected by his own, as well as the position held by his father, Sabah's way of life prospered exceptionally well under this new espionage network, where his professional concentration was aimed first at the European Union and in particular the commercial and monetary ties between France and Germany.

I left the part of Rupert's meticulous report dealing with the fragility of the European economy for later reading; instead, I concentrated on how Sabah cultivated his union with the sex-orientated Page Boucher, training him to operate as his personal covert agent. In this capacity, Boucher was able to supply vast quantities of material more usually handled by the French consulate in London. He preferred the consulate to the embassy, so my reading led me to believe, because the philandering Boucher would be able to obtain the details of plenty of younger females who applied at the consulate for visas and passports.

There was an awkward caveat Rupert presented, and it was one that did not rest easily with me. It concerned Winston and his knowledge of Sabah. It was a close association. It was another thing Bottomly had conveniently forgotten when I'd asked him if he knew Sabah.

This was what I referred to earlier when I said Bots had preferred not to tell me about an association he had; it was because the connection the two had is crucial to this story, but it wasn't until sometime after I had read Rupert's report that the full extent of the shared relationship could be discovered and that disclosure saw the opening of a real can of worms.

* * *

The story Sabah Al Salim told of being a Kuwaiti was not the only untruth he told of himself. Although Sabah was not Samantha's benefactor's real name, it was irrelevant to what Rupert had to say. What was not irrelevant was that Sabah was still alive and, so the report said, living just over the border of Kuwait in the Iraqi City of Basrah. There had to be a certain amount of ambivalence in his report which must be accepted in matters such as this.

From what Rupert could substantiate, he was living in Kuwait City when Samantha's father died, successfully saving him from an assassination attempt from a skilled kill-team. Over a relatively short period of time, Sabah had managed to turn Samantha into an espionage agent who passed all her entrance examinations, until accepted with open arms inside the French Consulate in London. When her employment position was made permanent, it was the fulfilment of a promise Sabah had made to his 'friends'. Those were the 'friends' he'd made inside the Iranian SAVAMA Service.

His real friends, those lifelong friends who had benefitted the most by his association with Page Boucher, were the Mukhabarat, a term applied to the Syrian Military Intelligence Division which is reckoned to be one of the most notorious and possibly the most important state security system in the whole of the Middle East.

Rupert had even managed to narrow down Sabah Al Salim's connection to the National Intelligence Service of Iran. He reported to Directorate Four, a department reputed to be responsible for the deaths of thousands of Sunni Kurds in the Fars Province of South West Iran, in early 2010. He covered his involvement with professional skill and assurance.

* * *

Samantha's elevation through the nefarious world of espionage came about by infiltrating many and various places; foreign and domestic government ministries, unions, embassies, opposition groups, as well as the Ba'ath Party, with its plethora of relatives of

Saddam Hussein who filled most of the highest positions.

There was a separate file on a particular relationship she had; an intense affair with one such relative, a Sheikh Talib Habbad. Samantha lived with Habbad, a well-liked cousin of Saddam, for two months before he was assassinated with the killer never being found.

The implication Rupert drew in his report left me wondering if Sabah had something to do with it. There was no doubt he had that much influence.

Rupert found evidence to suggest Bottomly had knowledge of this situation. Samantha sent Bottomly an email early on in their relationship, in which she said she knew a cousin of the late Saddam Hussein, the same Sheikh Talib Habbad, who was assassinated. From then on, Rupert used a great deal of supposition, albeit based on experience of similar conditions.

Page Boucher received the majority of his information from the Iraqi embassy in Paris. Some came from another source; one such occasion came from a direct order from Sabah Al Salim, *'Get Samantha to bump into this man, then cultivate the flirtation,'* as he showed Page Boucher a photograph of Bottomly entering Gerald Neil's Crocketts. *'It's going to be your job to ensure she becomes good friends with this man.'*

Why was it important for Sabah Al Salim to

know Viscount Bottomly? That was a question that went unanswered in Rupert's report. One answer could be Sabah wanting to know the risk, if any, that Winston presented anywhere near money. Even so, Sabah's knowledge of Bottomly using Gerald Neil's Mayfair club left me to ponder why Page Boucher's acquaintance was equally important to Sabah?

If Bots was not vigilant, Sabah's identity could be known by every South African intelligence officer. As I continued to think of the involvement Winston had with Sabah, I came to the conclusion I had underestimated him. Alice had said nothing of Sabah. It was clear to me Alice would be one of the very first to know if Bots was not paying careful attention. He was exceeding my estimation of him, once again.

* * *

Jerry Furley's report had opened up some of the dark recesses surrounding Page Boucher. I filled my glass from the Jura single malt whisky bottle that, at a hugely inflated price, the concierge had managed to source for me, lit another Dunhill International from an almost full packet, sat back and began to read, on my ultra-secure phone, what one of the many departments under Jerry's authority had found out.

Page came from an Armenian family, having ancestral roots dating as far back as 75BC and the Kingdom of Armenia. They had extensive property in the city of Adana where, in the years before the Shah of Persia was overthrown by the Ayatollah, the Bouchers had unconditional control over the Adana Chamber of Commerce.

From their seat of power, the family presided over the division of property and land when that part of Turkey was devastated by war. Finally, after re venge for the massacre of Armenians and the blood spilt in the Iranian Revolution, no room was left for the covert work of Boucher. He and his family re-treated en masse via Lebanon to France.

* * *

The enforced move provided Page with a legitimate reason to visit many of the countries inside the state of what was once referred to as Persia—Armenia, Azerbaijan, Iraq, Syria, and all around the Caspian Sea— passing on what unethical information he could gather from old trading partners to the French intelligence branches he covered.

When he revisited those 'Persian' countries with Samantha Burns on his arm, the flow of secrets from the contacts he'd made soon propelled him upwards in the French Intelligence service, eventually arriving at the prestigious Directorate for External Security, from where he *controlled* Samantha Burns.

At first, Samantha's ways of persuading Page to divulge small passages of intelligence proved to be too seductive to refuse. Initially, this link bore only small fruits, as it was designed to do, but over time the information the alliance was able to accumulate increased, giving Samantha means to repay Sabah many times over for his generosity. Sabah, in turn, reimbursed his Iraqi friends to such an extent they began to worry about Samantha's wealthy lifestyle.

* * *

I moved on to the part of Jerry's report which duplicated all Rupert had found when Valery Agapov held a position in the Russian FSB, before he became the President of Directorate Q. At that time, he administered and orchestrated all the information originating from, or relevant to, the countries of the Levant. Several of these places overlapped the interests of Page Boucher's extended French Bureau.

The inevitable meeting of the two men took place as Page was leaving the Damascus home of a married, beautiful Syrian woman whose husband was fortunately away in Lebanon attending a meeting of the Arab Defence League. It was the weakness for women that put Page, together with Sabah Al Salim, into the bulging pockets of the waiting Valery Agapov. It was as a consequence of that weakness that Samantha Burns was included in Valery's expanding list of usable *friends*.

Time moved on, with everyone concerned happily engaged in gathering secrets from those who had them, then sharing them with those who were in need of them. Secrets were traded for money or favours until that axiom of 'nothing lasts forever' raised its ugly head.

It didn't seem like the end when Agapov's Directorate received word of an unusual encrypted transmitted message arriving at the French Consulate in London, which he learned carried an attachment enclosing a series of named illegal agents working in the Middle East.

He also learned the email had been handled by the stunning Samantha Burns, a woman he had met at Crocketts, when he was in the company of Viscount Bottomly. *How odd*, he thought. Valery could not believe his luck.

In a complex fashion designed by Sabah Al Salim, the instructions to murder Samantha came by way of the Russian Embassy in Paris. Those instructions were formulated by Sabah, but not him alone. He had worked with Valery Agapov, who had travelled to Kuwait on a diplomatic passport in the name of Yuri Bogdan. It was in that same name, that Bogdan had constructed a special relationship over many years with an operative of the CIA who had access into the very top-level of the labyrinth surrounding the Pegasus Mercantile Company.

* * *

Before I could leave America for home, Jerry Furley contacted me with what he said was something I would find *interesting*. He'd had a telephone conversation with the Director-General of something called the American Department of National Intelligence, or DNI for short. I hadn't heard of this department, which was no surprise as I'm rather ignorant of government, although in sheer admiration of the number of American agencies dealing with intelligence.

The DNI serves as the assembly point for the intelligence reports coming in from the other services of America, with its Director-General being responsible for presenting an overview of all the intelligence each morning to the President of America.

From the same department, various confidential briefings on intelligence matters related to national security are provided to the Joint Chiefs of Staff of the Department of Defence, the executive of the National Security Council as well as the Homeland Security Council, then, for good measure, the FBI.

Despite the fact of finding what he said to be interesting, it obviously was not why he called. That came next. It was the name of his caller. The current Director-General at the DNI was a man named Howard James Fredrick Mercer II. A man I knew who, after meeting for the first time and hearing his elongated name, I had christened Jimmy. My first meeting with Jimmy was in a coffee shop near my old army barracks in Reading many years back, the exact number I've forgotten, but I have not forgotten why I went there to meet with him.

Our meeting came about because the branch of the CIA he was then in charge of was holding Katherine, Luca's mother, in custody for alleged spying activities. Jimmy wanted me to explain why it was, after months of silence whilst held in different American places of detention, Katherine suddenly made a cryptic remark about Crows, but not necessarily the birds. She'd said '*Just tell Lord Harry; Percy Crow,*' making it crystal clear she was only prepared to speak with me, Harry Paterson.

Eventually, after a long period of probing, I was able to explain to him, as well as others, its perplexing meaning. Then, Katherine and I managed to make sense of a passage of British and Irish history I personally wished I had never cast my eyes over. It would seem as though destiny had decided to throw the two of us together, once more.

The irrational phrase —*emissaries having more information can be found where the pastures are closed in the north*—had returned to rumble around in my brain. I had scraped away at my memory to rerun every part of the operation in Milan I staged with the help of Serena, where Katherine had paid a brief visit into my life. Why now, albeit under the auspices of Jimmy Mercer, had she returned?

* * *

Katherine Tovanisch had been a complication a good many years back and a very gratifying complication at that. We'd had an extremely brief coming together whilst we were in Moscow. It was her father who'd engineered the meeting. Be that as it may, no matter how brief or not it was, it resulted in her becoming the mother to my firstborn son, Luca.

I knew nothing of this birth until Serena had a hastily convened fashion display for a week at the Milan Fashion Show, where Katherine's father, the great Russian spy overlord Paulo Tovarisch Korovin, showed his face, declaring his immediate wish to defect to London. It was he who told me of my son's existence.

By illegitimate birth, Paulo Tovarisch Korovin was my great-grandfather's son. He was the father to Katherine and father to my dearest friend George Northcliffe, making them brother and sister.

As you can appreciate, both of those relationships were complicated and were made more delicate when all three were at the Milan Show, with Serena and myself. Serena could not have been more gracious or shown more sensitivity on hearing of Luca.

In fact, she had found him herself by logical reasoning—in other words, she knew me too well. It was Serena who alerted me to Katherine's participation with this latest obscure puzzle I find myself involved in.

Katherine contacted Serena by telephone, having

tracked her down through her fashion label of Zabreno, aided by a very helpful company reception- ist. It was all very simple, she said, but I was worried by the simplicity. For some unknown reason, Katherine had chosen to go through Serena in order to contact me, whereas, if she was really looking for simple, then the route to go would have been through Joseph at The Hall. Katherine had the telephone number to call The Hall as well as having my mobile number, so why choose Serena? Perhaps I saw con- spiracy everywhere I looked.

This notification of— *emissaries having more in- formation can be found where the pastures are closed in the north*—came from a man Katherine had en- countered as she exited a department store in New York. They had spoken for a short period of time and then, when leaving, the man handed her a piece of paper with this mysterious missive written on it. Katherine read directly from that piece of paper to Serena, who recorded the message, then emailed the voice message on to me. Included was Katherine's personal email address. The message on the piece of paper that she'd read from was:

'*Please tell your friend, the English Lord, we are also aware of the South African AWB membership of his friend, the Viscount Bottomly. We are aware of the whereabouts of the cache of arms they have hidden. The Russian government will oppose the use of those weapons in every and any way.*'

She then added a personal note which Serena sent to my phone but not before adding a terse notation of her own:

'If you and her get back together, I don't want it happening in Chester Square.'

The personal message Katherine sent was no less threatening.

'*Our mutual friend, the sender of the previous message, is the one we heard of when we were all together with my father in Switzerland. Paulo thought the man to be dead. Not so! It appears he has prospered well in Russia and now holds a principal position in the Federal Security Service of the Russian Federation. He asks for a straight exchange.*'

I physically pulled away from reading the message as a nightmarish vision filled my head. Katherine's father had also spoken of an exchange. He wanted to settle down peacefully in London and in exchange, he offered the names of traitors and operatives inside Russia. The nightmare was about the man Katherine mentioned; I'd heard Paulo speak this self-same name. My concentration returned from mental speculation to the actual message Katherine had recorded.

'*His knowledge of what you would refer to as secrets, and how he came by them, including what the French hold on the British Intelligence agents operating inside Afghanistan and Pakistan, is considerable. He is particularly knowledgeable about the*

British illegals relying on British support in Pakistan. I hope you know of them, otherwise it may be an appreciable shock and I don't want you having a heart attack, Lord Harry. There is a person who could become a member of your highest level Security Council. By whichever way, he should not be allowed to ruffle people's feathers. On the other hand, he would be a veritable prize on your sleeve, if you needed another one.'

This message came from the same Russian Paulo thought he'd had killed—Alexi Vasilyev!

* * *

Paulo thought him dead, as did the elite few Americans Paulo had shared his secrets with in order to ensure a completely peaceful life. Nobody had betrayed Paulo and as far as Katherine was concerned, she had played the CIA to perfection in getting me involved to free her from her American incarceration. Her freedom was the stimulus behind Jimmy Mercer's acceptance of her father's relocation to London from his Swiss home.

His stage-managed death in Switzerland had been confirmed as an accident by the local authorities, including the Russian ambassador. Jimmy had kept his word. There was no reference brought to my attention of that 'death'.

There had been one loose end, one unnamed

person who probably knew the truth about the faked accident and how Katherine had manipulated the unravelling situation in Moscow to achieve her father's relocation. But this unnamed man had remained silent throughout Paulo's Knightsbridge sojourn, so why would he now use Paulo's daughter in this way? But wait, perhaps I had it wrong. Was she using his name to intensify my interest?

* * *

Jerry Furley told me something else. About Bottomly having some kind of leverage in the Pakistan intelligence service, or the ISI, the Inter-Services Intelligence, as it's called throughout the world. I thought it to be important so I had asked Rupert to included it in his investigation and see what he could find.

Luckily for me, he was able to shine some light on the influence Bottomly was said to have. According to Rupert, he had a man inside this ISI who, in turn, had an association with an Afghan Mujahideen. He had fought against the army of the Soviet Union from 1980 until 1989, when they withdrew.

His name or rank inside the guerrilla movement are extraneous to this account. What he did is a matter for another day and another investigator. Rupert found evidence of several millions of dollars the Americans were donating to the Mujahideen that were not getting to the intended destination. Surprise, surprise. But it was not only this Afghan, nor the man in the Pakistani Intelligence, who had filtered some of it into their own secret bank accounts. Names of others were given on the understanding that Winston's Pakistani man was left alone!

From this member of the Mujahideen, who spent the vast majority of his time in various 'fluid' command centres, came details of how, when, and where the Soviets repeatedly used their air power to kill civilians. The levelling of villages was done to deny safe haven to fellow Mujahideen, with no regard to the civilians affected. The destroying of vital irrigation ditches, along with the laying of millions of land mines, all found their way to the international press.

What didn't make the newspapers was how American money purchased all the Pakistani-captured Soviet weapons and financed the secret funnelling of them to the Mujahideen. From the Pakistani intelligence service, Bottomly was given details of unit size and chosen routes of withdrawing Soviet army groups, which, according to Rupert, he gave first to MI6. Rupert then speculated, saying Winston passed the same information on to the Russians. He did not try to guess which Russian.

He based his speculation on a couple of things. The first was a negative; there was no news report, or signals he'd been allowed to see, from either GCHQ or the Royal Air Force Menwith Hill base, in Yorkshire, mentioning attacks on the withdrawing Soviet

Union military convoys in Afghanistan. There most certainly would have been had any sizeable convoy been ambushed using the intelligence from Bottomly.

Secondly, he argued, someone of Valery Agapov's rank would not be the Russian equivalent of a 'control officer' for Bottomly, not if Bots was of small interest to the Russians. If, as seems highly likely, Bottomly first contacted the Russians during the occupation of Afghanistan, that would mean Valery Agapov would have had thirty years to secure the position he now holds in the Federal Security Service, or the FSB, whilst dragging Viscount Bottomly along with him!.

If, as seems likely, Bots turned out to be a consistent and reliable source of intelligence for Agapov, then the two of them would have progressed through the natural filtering system hand in hand. I was coming round more and more to the thought of Winston being the puppeteer rather than the puppet. If that was true, it would most certainly open up more possibilities.

I was left to wonder if those possibilities could include this man, Alexi Vasilyev, who was an American double-agent, code-named Vagabond. So named by his CIA handler, Rudi Mercer, Jimmy's father. Rudi Mercer was head of the CIA's European counter-intelligence division when he was running Vagabond. Could it be possible Vasilyev was escaping from members of the CIA, or maybe Russians, who either had exposed him or were on the brink of doing so?

According to the reports I was given at the time, Alexi Vasilyev had met his 'death' in a rather gruesome manner. When Paulo and I had our meeting in Milan, Paulo admitted using friends he had made in the Russian Mafia to assassinate this Vasilyev. He was afraid of what Vasilyev knew of him. Once, when the two of us were in conversation, he admitted his admiration for his nemesis, but respect can end with death.

If it was known Alexi Vasilyev was still alive when Paulo had escaped to London, there would have been no point in leaving a dangerous loose end like him. There was another loose end if all the intelligence I'd gathered was correct, as it pointed towards Katherine being in love with Alexi. If that was true, would she have managed to keep the fact he was alive a secret from her father?

My trip to America had, as I've said, turned up more questions without having obvious answers. Back in London, I wondered if Sir Leonard Miles, or Charles Oswald Wallace, knew Winston's AWB intentions for the nuclear arsenal they had control over? If so, what did they really want me for?

CHAPTER TWENTY-TWO

BROEDERBOND

Rupert had seen all the intelligence data Jerry Furley had on Recces and the branch of the legitimate South African Special Forces Brigade that was still operating. Liam Gibson was indeed a member of the Brigade as Furley had indicated, and the reputation I had attributed to him was correct.

He was not a member of the Recces unit which, according to Rupert, was not strictly concerned with simple reconnaissance, although that was an area of their activity. Other activity included the more combative Search and Destroy.

One officer in command of a part of this South African controlled Recces unit dealing in Search and Destroy, was a Russian, a Sergei Ivanov. Rupert continued along his path of research, discovering Sergei Ivanov being listed as an assistant attaché in the

Russian Embassy in London. He couldn't be in two places at the same time, or could he?

In the diplomatic hierarchy of an embassy, an assistant attaché came last on the list. He was a subordinate to Valery Agapov, who was listed as a Consular Officer, a meteorologist, fourth in the pecking order behind the ambassador, but above most secretaries, some attachés, or assistant attachés.

It was reasonable to believe Sergei Ivanov was part of Agapov's Directorate Q. Immediately after I read this, it crossed my mind that Bottomly and Sergei could have met in London at any time. Could that have been before either Bottomly, or Ivanov, were noticed by the experienced watchers at MI5?

It would seem that South African intelligence gathering had been remiss in discovering Sergei Ivanov's true allegiances. But, as Bottomly knew, which must be blatantly obvious, they must know and were using the knowledge to their own advantage?

* * *

The word, and organisation, Broederbond captivated Rupert's interest the moment he came across it. By the definition he found at the head of the encrypted, secret intelligence service PDF document, the society was: *A secret, exclusively Afrikaner Calvinist male organisation in South*

Africa dedicated to the advancement of Afrikaner interests.

Inside the MI6 file on Broederbond were references to the Bottomly family name alongside the names of three others: Captain Dalton Coeteez, Mr Graeme Devos, and a Brigadier Jan du Plessis. When I mentioned the name Broederbond, which I called a club, to Bots, he was open and candid about it with a forthright explanation. I was left with the impression that he was ashamed of the Bottomlys' participation, but I will clarify that by saying how wrong I'd been about Bottomly up until now.

"Broederbond was a small but highly influential society to begin with. It was formed after the Second Boer War to restore pride to the Afrikaners who had lost the war to the British and lost their self-esteem. In some circles, Broederbond was said to be an extreme, far-right, ultra-fascist organisation. In others, it was seen as the restoration of the Afrikaner soul. Whichever way this syndicate was looked upon, it could not be denied as being responsible for the introduction of apartheid.

"I'm sure I was told about Major General Bottomly, who was my great-great-grandfather's brother. He settled in South Africa before the rest of the tribe of Bottomlys came from India and other ports, to set up home. They chose an extensive area near Upington on the banks of the Orange River. Parts of the Bottomlys' kingdom is situated in the Kalahari

Desert, which is deceptive, as it's not a desert in the true sense of the word. Where we are, there's very good grazing for livestock. You might be surprised but I'm quite at home on the farmlands. I can get lost out there if I never turn a phone on."

I can recognise the signs of wanting to escape, and the wistful look on Bots' face was one of those signs. I thought about asking why he didn't just go? Pack a bag, take a horse and ride into the wide blue yonder to disappear for a time. I think the idea could appeal to me provided I knew where the cigarettes and Jura were kept.

"By the way, I've sold Devonish House, Harry. All the grounds and the whole estate. Hamptons sold it. It didn't take long. It was only on their books for about ten days. They sent a pretty little thing to do the valuation.

She was so young. Made me feel as if I was a hundred! As she was walking round, I wondered if she did the valuation thing in her lunch-break from school. So much for getting old, eh?"

* * *

If the look had disappeared while he was speaking, it had returned now he had stopped. '*On the banks of the Orange River,*' he'd said. Was that where he was thinking of making camp?

"I don't remember much about my South African

family because my branch of it went to the UK when I was fairly young. I was born in the UK for convenience's sake, but I'm sure Alice told you about all that. I can't recall being told when we came back to South Africa, but I think I was about three when they moved to Devonish House to live permanently. We did return to South Africa on occasions and on one of those visits my mother took me to a township outside of Cape Town, to show me what it was like. She said if the Whites had not installed apartheid, then the whole country would be like that township—one giant cesspool.

"I was told it was a man named Graeme Devos who, along with this Major General Bottomly, had the foresight to see what was coming and had they not established the segregation, it was distinctly probable the Whites would have been overrun by Black natives. After all, it was their country, but what had they done to it that made any real significance?

"The same pair, this chap Devos, with the Major General, travelled on the same boat as Cecil Rhodes and you know how important he was to Africa. He saw the potential and worked to benefit both the Whites and the Blacks. The Bottomlys, with Devos, mined diamonds at the 'Big Hole' and gold in the Transvaal. Eventually, they joined Rhodes to become part of the British South Africa Company. Pure enterprise, that man Rhodes.

"Anyway, all three of them became so filthy rich.

As I say, Broeder bond was intended to be an elite society where successful White business men could meet to discuss matters arising through domestic or foreign politics, as well as business opportunities.

Every Prime Minister, as well as State President in South African history, from 1948 to the end of apartheid in '94, had been a member of the Afrikancr Broederbond.

"As the world knows, things didn't work out as my mother anticipated. Those natives she thought of as less than herself and her other White friends, wanted apartheid to end and take power away from the Whites.

After years of negotiations they got what they wanted, and just look at the mess they've made of the country.

"When apartheid ended, the numbers of murders in major cities like Cape Town and Johannesburg were astronomical in number, as were the other atrocities committed on White farm owners and, in lots of cases, the native workers.

"We needed to react in a more positive way than simply train the natives to work alongside the military specialists we had converted into police officers. That's all changed. Countrywide, there is a strong backing towards taking control of South Africa once again, and we support that. Can you imagine it? White supremacy returning to South Africa at last."

We spoke further and according to Bots, the vast majority of the country's secret services would support a future coup. According to him, this was also true of the chief of police in the cities that served as the country's capitals—Pretoria, Cape Town, Bloemfontein, and in the largest city of them all, Johannesburg. I was thinking of how ridiculous the thought of a non-violent overthrowing of the government would be when my mobile phone rang. I had the volume switched off for most of my time in America, as it was showing a 'no service' logo if I didn't. It was only today I had switched the thing on.

It was my butler, Joseph, calling from Harrogate Hall. Serena had been on the telephone, he announced, in his finest, unmistakable formal voice. Whenever Joseph now took a call from Serena, he seemed to have adopted an aura of insulted indifference towards her. This could be heard in this latest of his notifications.

Somewhere, there had to be a code of conduct that, although neither of us had read, nor signed off on, we both equally adhered to. In his eyes, I was an anything but simple inconvenience, who more often than not never stayed long. In my eyes, he was an antique piece of furniture who was simply indispensable.

"Madam telephoned this morning, Sir. She asked

if she could use the London house for a few days. She was vague over the exact length of her stay, but I did asked her the once. *'How long will you be staying, madam?'* To which she replied, *'I have no idea, Joseph.'*

"And then, in quite a stern tone, she added, *'But if there's a queue of Harry's lady friends waiting to occupy his bed, then tell him to call them all and cancel their reservations for ten days at least. Breno will be with me, tell him.'*

"I'm sorry, Sir, but I do think I have the conversation remembered correctly. She also said she was taking young Breno to the all-England Jumping Course at Hickstead, for a three-day junior equestrian event. It's not far from Brighton, I believe. Apparently, the young man is representing Portugal. A great honour for him and you, Sir. The event starts Tuesday next week. He is giving at least one exhibition on the back of a horse every day. She explicitly asked me to tell you all that. But not the 'honour' thing. That was from me.

"Madam also said young Breno was much admired at home in Portugal. She added that most of her staff will be accompanying her to London."

There was a small cough at the end of that last sentence. A cough usually indicated disapproval as Joseph had little time for those who worked in the fashion industry.

"I'm sorry, Sir, I almost forgot. Madam had another part to her message. A type of red-flag warning part, as it were. She said—'*tell his lordship, Tanta is with me, as is Fiona. We will need the whole house as I've also brought my cook, with her kitchen maid, the housekeeper with a chambermaid. He will have to use his club if he's in London. But if not, he will have to make other arrangements for his Chester Square staff*'.

"Madam did ask after your whereabouts, my Lord, to which I replied that you were unobtainable, somewhere in California. She requested I try my hardest to pass on her message as she wished to avoid any embarrassment. Before ending the call, she passed a comment about you being with a film actress, or maybe more than one."

Although I was many miles away from The Hall, my memory did not require much refreshing to imagine Joseph's phlegmatic face changing its composure, as the furrows that were deeply cut across his forehead, deepened even further with each word of his dislike.

* * *

Joseph was of a Presbyterian upbringing and could never visualise the idea of the master of the house having an affair with a film actress! Far below a lord's position. A duchess, yes, maybe someone attached to the arts, but not a film actress.

He was the occasional butler to my late father,

who would use The Hall for civic duties, or for duties in the magistrates' court where he served for a while as a Justice of the Peace. His preference was for the home in London, where he could carry on his illicit affairs, away from his dying wife, my mother. Notwithstanding the fact Joseph and I never did discuss the situation, he did not like my father and in that we could unquestionably agree.

He never held my estranged wife in much esteem whilst we lived together at Harrogate, and now he found it difficult to mention her name. The members of her court were of an interesting composition.

There was the all-dwarfing Tanta, her head designer. He was late of the Royal Navy, where he was at one time the heavyweight boxing champion, before events forced the disclosure of his leaning towards homosexuality. That honesty made many of his commanding officers uncomfortable, hence his early, contrived, retirement. I first met him at The Hall. I hold no opinion, nor prejudicial thoughts, about anyone's colour, nor about the sexuality of anyone.

However, his size was another matter, as was the length of his hair, down to the back of his knees. I worried about bugs in his hair and the kitchen's capacity to deal with what must be his enormous appetite. The thing that also bothered me was that, according to Serena, he'd fallen in love with one of my cows. That did cause me an appreciable amount of anxiety.

CHAPTER TWENTY-THREE

PIANO

I was pleased to have changed my mind about delaying my return from America, for more than just the reason the hairstylist had afforded me. I was not going to squeeze an extra day and night from the fictitious Mr Yorkshire's expense account. This time would be at my own expense. I needed no Liam with a persuasive argument, nor was there Bots with his following army. It was my liking of the Waldorf Hotel which decided my thinking and although I was not breaking any rules applied to me, I was pushing my remit a bit.

I wanted the time on my own, away from the distraction of people with their own worries and concerns. I wanted some of the luxuries I missed by being away from home, so I had some more fussing from my attentive hotel hairdresser, who shaved me and cut my fingernails before supervising the massage I endured.

I don't recall being told I could not have a liaison with an attractive American hairstylist in a premier-rated hotel room in New York, but neither do I recall being told I could. However, the distraction helped me to make a decision that otherwise may have taken a good deal longer.

* * *

'Spontaneity In Distress' was an expression I heard my great-grandfather use when I joined him at the aforementioned annual cricket game between the family Paterson and those that worked at The Hall. He and I made up the last pair of batsmen after the previous combined effort was way below the score needed.

"Be spontaneous, young Harry. Forget the coaching manuals you may have read. Spontaneity In Distress—the ability to think with one's back against the wall, will win us the game. You mark my words," was his discerning advice. Which I took in as much as young man can when faced with much older men trying their best to win a game neither I nor Maudlin would allow them to do.

Somehow or other, we scored almost eighty-odd runs between the two of us, which won the game for The Hall. Great-grandfather Maudlin's expression was part of a combination of things that persuaded me into the reckless action of travelling to London directly from America, and not via Johannesburg as originally planned. Spontaneity was my excuse. Distress was how I would feel after offering my excuses.

The main factor behind my decision, if one can have such a thing as an explanation if being spontaneous, was to see my son displaying his skills in front of the experts, not with only his mother and friends as his arbiters. Another issue was to speak to Winston's Russian friend, Valery Agapov, and discover where he had heard this phrase—*emissaries having more information can be found where the pastures are closed in the north.*

* * *

My time in America had been fruitful in some areas; in others it was ineffectual. Meeting Alice was its highlight, one from which I hoped the intelligence I'd managed to accrue would help Great Britain in the days to come. There was other accumulated intelligence I was able to pass on directly to Section 9 at Vauxhall, deliberately avoiding the Sir Leonard Miles route and most certainly avoiding any connection to Charles Oswald Wallace.

All in all, I assessed my trip as a seven-and-a-half out of ten, with an end-of-term report reading *should have done better* in certain areas. Those areas of betterment centred on Bottomly, with Sabah Al Salim a close second. I thought I had an answer to the 'emissaries and pastures in the north' thing, an answer that, if right, would not suit Jerry Furley or anyone else in MI6 but, as for me—well, it could be said it was a dire complication I should avoid.

If I was to be successful, I would have to have Furley on side to conceal my interest from Wallace and Sir Leonard where, I believed, my biggest worry would come from. For now, as the extra time in the Waldorf had reached the end it was always to face, with the time in the departure lounge also finished, I fell into the arms of sleep inside the first-class cabin as the aircraft levelled out for its flight to London, where the masquerade as Mr Yorkshire could be returned to the box of other identities waiting for another day with another motive for their exercise.

* * *

John, the long-serving family chauffeur, had retired from driving a good many years ago, leaving the once second chauffeur, Peter, as my driver now. On the flight home, I was trying not to reminisce too much about past times, but I was finding the memories of The Old Man, the affectionate term given to my great-grandfather Maudlin Paterson, far too dear to forget.

He lived in a time when the family home in Yorkshire had a full household of staff. The full number, totalling close to forty, would include those living away from the house, perhaps employed in the stables, or gardens, all of whom depended on my family for an income.

Although Eaton Square was a smaller home, it would boast between fifteen to twenty staff members. As I think I've already explained, there are not as many as there were, but I attempt to keep as many people as I can on the estate's payroll. I intend to do that for as long as I can.

I had telephoned Peter from New York, making arrangements for the journey into London and it was he who I saw in the arrivals lounge at the airport. Before leaving London, I'd agreed with the accounts department in the relevant part of the Home Office to reimburse the government the different cost of certain things, first-class airfares being one of those differences.

I planned to stay that night at my club, with Peter being billeted in the staff quarters, then sit back enjoying the drive to the All England Jumping Course at Hickstead, to watch Breno's riding ability. George expressed a wish to accompany me as soon as I mentioned it to him on one of my regular phone calls. Without thought, I readily agreed. I'd asked Joseph to check the schedule of my son's first round; it was at 11:00am.

I told Joseph I would try to video some of the

event on the phone for him and Mrs Franks. In that relaxed frame of mind, I was comfortable in the back of my car leaving the airport to join the afternoon traffic on the M4. I was about to disable my phone, when it rang. It was Jerry Furley. He needed to see me, he said, in what I thought was an excessive tone of annoyance.

* * *

I diverted Peter from St James's Street as our destination, to Vauxhall Cross. My plans did involve meeting Jerry but not until later that night. Now I must get as much detail as I could on Valery Agapov, who I needed to meet, not only to ask about the *emissaries in the north* message, but also why Bottomly was so important to him.

On arrival, I was pleased to find Jerry's choice of subject was the same as mine—Valery Agapov. Even so, the topic, messages and importance was not. Jerry had chosen to begin with Agapov's alias of Yuri Bogdan and the Pegasus Mercantile Company. Ah well, even the wishes of lords must take a back seat in today's life of spies. At least The Pegasus Company had found his desk.

* * *

I was right about Jerry being annoyed. When he called me, he had just come off the phone from speaking to his counterpart at MI5, with whom his relationship was never smooth. As far as I was concerned, all was fine, particularly with Jerry Furley's comprehension of the situation being far more knowledgeable than I had believed it could be.

It was that knowledge he drew on to brief me on how Valery Agapov became involved with not only Winston but Page Boucher, as well as Sabah Al Salim. So much of what I wanted discussed was about to be, after all.

We started with the history that brought France and Russia to encircle the areas along the lines of the religious Levant. I was intrigued from the very beginning. Jerry's knowledge of the area was extensive, but his prime concern was not of a religious nature, it was selfish, albeit in line of duty. His attention was focused on the security of the British Sovereign Base areas of Akrotiri and Dhekelia on the island of Cyprus. I had not realised the island of Cyprus was included in the area of the Levant.

He referred to the bases as SBAs. Great Britain had retained all its military installations on these two Sovereign Base areas of RAF interest and use, after independence was granted to the Crown colony of Cyprus. The bases served as important stations for not only signal intelligence, but providing a vital strategic part, as well as logistical advantage, for the

United Kingdom, as well as NATO's ability for sur-veillance gathering network in the Mediterranean and the Middle East.

Apparently, NATO was not the first port of call for the shared intelligence. A direct link went to the various surveillance networking agencies in America.

The importance of these SBAs to world peace was shown when, in 1974, following on closely to a military coup by the Cypriot National Guard, there was an invasion of the northern part of Cyprus by the Turkish Military. This left an impoverished Great Britain with no other choice than to withdraw from the island, no longer able to commit enough troops to defend it.

Having lost all of their signal intelligence stations in Turkey, following a dispute between Turkey and themselves, America argued strongly that Great Britain should retain the bases. Those plans to close the bases were cancelled when America agreed to contribute to the costs.

I listened as Jerry read from a top-secret docu-ment detailing what was called an *over-the-horizon* radar system that had been installed in both of the SBAs.

The bases had been equipped with the same kind of radar system for years, but this latest one, devel-oped earlier this year, code-named EROS, had the kind of technology, in Jerry's words, that was pushing the limits of imagination. The equipment, together with the increased use of one of the bases for operational night flights of the United States air force's latest Lockheed U-2 spy plane, was providing intelligence that would be priceless to the Russians.

Another point of interest was with the administration of the two bases. Being classified as military bases, they were not regulated as would be the case with ordinary dependent territories. The arrangement was entered into after Cyprus was granted independence, with careful wording so as not to antagonise either Greece or Turkey. The decision meant the administration reports went straight to the Ministry of Defence in London. Neither base had any formal connection with the British High Commission in Nicosia, on the island of Cyprus, or the Foreign and Commonwealth Office in London.

Before any intercepted signal, or command report, reached the intelligence analysis desks on the Middle East section at Jerry Furley's MI6, it had to pass through the hands of the Civil Service, notably the personal private secretary to the Prime Minister— Charles Oswald Wallace.

There was a note added at the foot of the PDF Jerry had given me to read relating to the two bases. After the one word in the centre of the screen, UL-TRA, the remaining report was heavily redacted. I asked Jerry if I could see a 'clean' version.

"You already know why some of it was hidden, but the last bit, about the intended American input, is very sensitive, my friend. Apart from the serving members of the Joint Intelligence Committee, you will be the only one to know. For political reasons that means even the PM is in the dark."

* * *

From the RAF base at Akrotiri, there was an ongoing British military intervention, code name Shader, against the Islamic State of Iraq from which derives the terrorist group known as Daesh. The operation was taking part in areas of Syria, as well as what was known as the Levant. It was part of a combined British contribution involving the Army, Royal Navy, and the RAF, but it was in the second part of the file where the really juicy bit was.

There was to be construction at the Dhekelia base for two new aircraft hangers of special requirements as well as an unspecified number of accommodation units.

It went on to add that a similar amount of construction at Akrotiri would begin early in 2023. I was obviously pleased to read of our armed forces being expanded, but it was not for us. It was for the Americans.

I had read somewhere of a replacement reconnaissance aircraft for the Lockheed Martin SR-71 that was already flying, called the Space Blackbird. In the report, I'd seen the hypersonic figures for it were fairly speculative, but what was certain was it having a ceiling of operations at over 90,000 feet, which was, I understood, way beyond the range of most intercept missiles currently in use.

The surprise came at the end of Jerry's file. This Lockheed Martin Space Blackbird hypersonic aircraft, that travels at speeds in excess of Mach-5, was to be stationed at the Dhekelia RAF airbase as soon as the hangers and adequate accommodation units were available. Teams of specialised contractors from the UK, along with the US, were to be assembled.

The report went into another avenue of interest. Some of the complexity of the *over the horizon radar* was, I'm sorry to admit, over my head. Excuse the pun. But amongst the areas I could understand, was the reference to its links to overheard satellites. It seemed that these links had been targeted more and more by Russian and Chinese radar signals. As of yet, the report went on to say, no damage had been done, or disruption caused, or signalling interrupted.

However, since the termination of the SR-71 there had been nothing to protect the vulnerable satellites from attack. If an attack was to happen, it would leave a gaping hole in the West's ability to predict what it can't see.

The predictability of orbit and rate of travel of satellites, are weaknesses hostile countries can use to decommission them in the event of war. I read how satellites played a crucial role for the bases on

Cyprus; however, their vulnerability can only be countered by a hypersonic aircraft capable of intercepting whatever weapon was used for the satellites' discontinuation. I wondered what the Russians and Chinese would come up with to combat the combatant?

Having finished reading, I came to the conclusion the name of the agent who the South African Security Service had placed inside Daesh, ISIS was of vital importance to MI6. Equally important was the name of the Daesh agent inside the Russian Foreign Intelligence Service. Bottomly either knew, or could discover, the name of the first agent; after that, the second agent's name should be easy to find. As I was shutting the file away on the computer screen, Jerry addressed me.

"Every mission flown from Cyprus was signalled to the Russians in advance so they could move 'friendlies' away from the strike areas. The Russians are on our side against these terrorists groups, in fact they want us to expand our operational area further inside Syria, which they would facilitate by an incursion of a special forces strike force. I could do nothing when you informed me of Daesh infiltration of the Russian Foreign Intelligence. Had I acted on what you had sent me, we would have had to shut down our communications to the Russians, which in turn, would have alerted the Daesh agent and, of course, leave our 'friendlies' in the path of our bombs.

"Why was it, do you think, that initially, your friend the Viscount did not want the Samantha file to fall into our hands, but later, in some genial conversation, he tells you where all but one of those six names were?" He paused, but not for long.

"Why not tell us in the beginning South African Intelligence had an agent inside Daesh? We need the name, Harry, and you're the only one who can get it!"

"Oh, I think I already know the cover name, Jerry. How about the name of Jackson? I was hoping you would know his real name. Have you any thoughts you'd like to share on him?"

"I haven't got a clue, old boy. I've never heard of anyone going by the name of Jackson, real or imaginary."

CHAPTER TWENTY-FOUR

MEMORIES

When Sophie married George, she took his surname of Northcliffe, but kept her own of Prosser to go with it. At the time, I expressed my unasked-for opinion that no matter which way the two names of Northcliffe and Prosser were joined by a hyphen, it looked, and probably what's more important, sounded unwieldy. As a compromise, I suggested Sophie used her family name for correspondence as well as pursuing her career as an author with a well-known publishing house. She could then, as she'd expressed a desire so to do, write children's stories under the name of Sophie Northcliffe, perhaps publishing with a lesser-known company, leaving nobody the wiser.

My recommendation appealed to her and even allowing for the passage of time since her compliance, it was with a sense of conquest I ascended the two steps to the opened door of number 16 Eaton Square that warm, sunny Tuesday lunchtime, to be greeted by the colourfully dressed lady of the house herself in the most scholastic mood I had forgotten she possessed.

"If you think you are taking me to lunch dressed like that, Lord Paterson, then you'd better think again. Unless, of course, you intended our lunch to be taken at the sandwich shop, near the coach station."

"I have a jacket and tie in the car, Sophie. It's linen! It creases! I'm told it looks rather trendy when all put together."

"Now you're being silly. Not even Serena could make you look trendy. You'll have to do, I guess," she decided, after one more half-hearted inspection of my attire.

* * *

Sophie was not trendy at all, but I had not invited her to lunch to display her or my fashion sense. I wanted her legendary memory, dated as far back as my meeting with Paulo in Switzerland, when I'd asked him if he knew of a man with the code-name Vagabond. He not only knew of him, he later admitted having this Alexi Vasilyev *murdered*. But I'm sure he never expanded on that to me, when we'd first met at the Hotel Baur Au Luc in Zurich. I wanted to know if I had mentioned anything to George on that trip? If so, had he remembered it, passing the knowledge on to Sophie?

Had Paulo let a name slip from his lips on any of the numerous occasions the Northcliffe-Prossers had visited the plush, serviced apartment next to The Mandarin Oriental Hotel, backing onto Hyde Park, in London's Knightsbridge, where Paulo had parked his chess pieces, drunk only the finest French brandy and imagined he was still an active spy until his final day?

I needed Sophie to conjure up something magical from our lunch meeting, but I wasn't sure she and Paulo got on well. My fingers were crossed on both hands as, slightly behind Sophie and George, I climbed the short stone stairs and entered the hotel.

Once seated, I wasted no time, starting with the name of Mercer. Had Paulo ever spoken of either Jimmy Mercer or Rudi, the father?

"Oh, how wonderful. Am I being debriefed, as you spies call it? Your brother has missed you, Harry. Terribly. I digress, don't I? Never mind, I'm with you now. Yes! Both names were mentioned, and in contemptuous terms at that. By the way, he poured scorn on George for not having taken the Paterson name. Fear not, Harry, I am on the same page as you. I'm playing with you.

"'Why not have another hyphenated name in the family like Northcliffe-Paterson II?' was one of his suggestions I recall. That's when he was speaking of the younger Mercer, the Howard James Fredrick Mercer the Second variety. Paulo said, 'The boy thought he could play chess, but he couldn't. I guess even Harry could defeat him. That's if he hasn't played already and won.'

"I recall him having a wide smile on his face when he said that. All of what I've spoken about took place the first time George and I came to visit him in the apartment next door to this place. He had the gall to ask if it was true that I had a photographic memory as well as being one of the few in the world who had HSAM, short for Hyperthymesia. Or was it some other form of exceptional memory? I told him of the examinations I'd taken when nineteen and then when leaving Oxford. I undertook another examination at Zurich University, where I spent a year on a Computer Science degree course when I was twenty-two. It was that examination which confirmed the matter.

"When your Paulo settled down, he added that Rudi Mercer had told him his son would steal the British Empire from under our noses, that's if the Chinese don't get in first. He said Howard the Second, etc., etc., starting in the Far East, actually in Singapore like the all-conquering Ruffles of old"

"Are you sure he said Ruffles, Sophie?" naively I asked, before I was challenged by a barrage of insults questioning whether my birth was normal, or was I bounced on my head down along the battlements for amusement's sake? She had the impudence to wait for an answer.

George was looking at me as if he was standing on some railway tracks only just noticing a train was inches away from running him over.

"Correct me if I'm wrong but it's not Ruffles, it's Raffles with the hotel, is it not? Isn't 'ruffles' a verb—to leave one's hair or clothes in disarray or disorder?" George was looking at me when he finished.

"Sorry, Harry, I never meant to disrespect you, old chap."

"I think you should stop whilst you're ahead, George. You forget you're older than I am. *Old chap;* I ask you!"

George was laughing and even straight-faced Sophie looked as though a giggle wasn't too far away. But she didn't stay that way for long.

"Yes, you are right, George. The hotel was named after Sir Thomas Stamford Raffles who was said to be the founder of colonial-era Singapore, and yes, one could ruffle another's hair. Our present prime minister has ruffled hair, but I think it's styled that way."

George had lost his look of imminent disaster by the time Sophie had stopped speaking, but I had seen that look before, and it was no struggle to remember where I had seen it. It was on Viscount Bottomly's face, when I'd first mentioned the word Broederbond.

"Got any idea what this could refer to, Sophie?" I passed her a note: *emissaries having more information can be found where the pastures are closed in the north.*

"Oh, yes, I do like cryptic clues. Let me see now," Sophie replied.

* * *

It must be seven or eight years on from when I first discovered my distant relative, one Paulo Tovarisch Korovin, then connecting him to my family name as the illegitimate son of my great-grandfather. At the time of that meeting, Paulo was helping in the discovery of the person responsible for murdering my father, Elliot, as well as my younger brother, Edward.

Both murders had taken place in London, inside a week of one another, whereby my participation in the investigations meant I was being debriefed by a stick insect of a woman, answerable to the Foreign Office, not MI5, which, in itself, I thought strange, although I did nothing about it.

The woman's name was Judith Meadow, with whom, I think it's fair to say, I had a somewhat confrontational and, for my part at least, an emotionally confusing relationship. I believed the cryptic message of—*emissaries having more information can be found where the pastures are closed in the north*—referred to her and if it did, then it had been said for a reason, meaning I must go and see her.

It wouldn't matter if Sophie did not come to the

same conclusion as I had. In all probability she wouldn't, as she did not know where Meadows was, but my levels of self-belief wouldn't mind a boost, and after all—what harm is there in asking?

Although my life has altered down the passage of years I've mentioned—I've married, I'm being divorced, I've even fathered two sons—nothing had really changed me from the person Judith Meadows once referred to as being a *superfluous* person, said in the hotel where the two of us, with George Northcliffe, first met Paulo Tovarisch Korovin.

When those three people left, George off with his father to catch up on the forty-odd years they had never had together, with Judith off to her room after another disagreement we'd had, I was left alone. That condition of solitude is still the same today.

* * *

The night of the *superfluous* name-calling took place in the bar of the hotel in Switzerland, where there were couples in conversation enjoying the warm evening together. I sat alone with my glass and nothing else to give me comfort. The situation is more or less the same today as it was then, the only real difference being that now I have my two delightful sons, but even they are normally miles away from me. Both of them are extremely well-behaved, polite and respectful; none of those constitutions of life have come from me. All I can imagine is the schools they attend are working closely with their mothers to install those qualities.

* * *

The melancholy that engulfed me would not budge as I pushed Judith to a vacant space in my mind, replacing her with Katherine. Each page lodged inside my mind having one woman's name on it seemed to hold another. I decided that would stay as the status quo, until I found time to shuffle the pages around.

With a glass in one hand and a cigarette in the other, I settled in to relive the short passage of time I spent with her. That time was all too brief, I thought, as I tried to dismiss but failed in recalling the bitter memories of the other man in her life.

That other man is the same Alexi Vasilyev I've already introduced you to. It was he who had recruited Katherine into what was then called the FSB, the replacement for the old KGB, knowing full well her father was bitterly opposed to her being in the same business as him. In those days, Alexi cared for nobody.

I could not see anything in his past that would have altered his disposition in any way. He could not care less for Paulo. It was he who first suspected Katherine's father, Tovarisch Sergeyovitch Korovin, better known as simply Paulo, of being a double agent.

But Paulo sat in one of the elevated seats in the Politburo and in those days Alexi was a mere soldier in the system. And soldiers were people nobody would bother about if they were to suddenly disappear. As fearsome as Paulo's reputation was towards those he had reasons not to like, Alexi never stopped antagonising him by his inquiries.

Eventually, Paulo had enough. He arranged for an electrical fault to plague the apartment block at 173 Tangshaya Street in Moscow's Tagansky 18 District. For almost a week, the same blue van with the matching coloured pavement screen, was parked outside this block where Alexi Vasilyev lived in the penthouse suite. Then, on the final Thursday in the month of August of that year, the van and screen were gone when Vasilyev arrived home from his work, eager to find the bathtub and ready himself for a night of exciting bliss with Daphne, who worked at the *Izvestiya* newspaper.

No doubt Daphne would know what the editor of newspaper had in mind to run with when it was published in the morning. If she did not know what it was when Alexi arrived, he knew plenty of ways she might be tempted into telephoning the editor to find out. Then Alexi would know the news before it was news and he would find out in the most pleasurable way God had devised.

Alexi placed his key in the lock that night, turning the handle to open the door, but instead of unlocking the door the handle had become an electrical conductor that should have delivered one thousand volts of direct current through his body, killing him instantly. Obviously, it didn't work.

Something in the devious system had gone wrong, but when he was taken to hospital he didn't spend much time on the *why* it hadn't killed him. He wanted to know the *whereabouts* of the owners of the blue van.

Alexi left the hospital in the middle of November that same year, having delegated FSB agents to find the perpetrators who, when found, were beaten to within an inch of their lives to discover the name of the man behind the attempt on his life. One of the two gave in before the other. The payment for the job had come from a Russian Mafia boss, a Mikhail Artyomovich Sidorov. No one from the FSB volunteered to go asking 'Miki' who had paid him.

* * *

Alexi wasn't Russian by birth, he was Polish. Another thing Alexi was not by the time of leaving hospital was a low-ranking FSB agent. During the time of recuperation, he found a new expertise of digging into fellow FSB officers' official histories, finding deliberate lies or misleading information. His ability at *digging* brought dividends. After his discharge from hospital, he was propelled from being a mere soldier to becoming a director of a relatively new Home Security Unit.

With that position came prestige and power. The prestige allowed him to function in ways making him more valuable as the American agent with the stage name of Vagabond, and the power came when he was displaying his thespian talents on a worldwide stage.

When Alexi could not find any trace of Mikhail Artyomovich Sidorov in Russia, he asked his American control, who asked the CIA for help. They obviously wanted something in return. Shortly, Sidorov was traced and put in an aeroplane, then, after a pain filled period of time on a deep sea fishing trawler, he became a permanent resident of Jeannette Island, in the East Siberian Sea, where his intense punishment was delivered wilfully slow.

In return for the CIA favour, Alexi gave them Katherine Friedal, daughter of the, believed-to-be-dead, esteemed member of the Council of Ministers, the First Chief Directorate. Even Katherine did not know her father was alive. But Alexi knew, he could smell it.

That's round about the place I came in. As I told you, Katherine screamed her head off about Crows.

'*Tell Lord Harry, the name of Percy Crow.*' She hadn't spoken to her interrogators for days and hadn't seen me for years, but the next in line for the Mercers', number two, Howard James Fredrick Mercer II, better known to me as Jimmy, summoned me to the place of dear Katherine's incarceration, asking the British for help. I managed to uncover some uncomfortable truths for the nobility and the high-born of the United Kingdom that could have led to the downfall of the monarchy. I also managed to find a son I never knew I had, and the wife who later gave me a son.

* * *

Alexi Vasilyev was the only living source inside Russia who knew beyond doubt the Mafia had not successfully presided over Katherine's father's death, but he had no intention of ever letting that secret escape his solitary grasp. As soon as he was able, he set about finding a man with a name he could use in his hunt to achieve the distant objective he had set himself.

It was a difficult search, but it was an even harder scheme he was devising. It took him almost four years to find the man he needed—a captain, whose rank was unimportant. It was in his name where the value lay: Dimitri Georgievich Oborka, who found himself instantly promoted. Not only was he promoted to the rank of Colonel, Oborka was appointed to the position of Alexi's personal secretary as well as put in charge of his twenty-four-hour protection.

On a day of apparently no importance, Alexi called the Colonel into the inner sanctum of his utilitarian offices on Ulitsa Kuznetsky Most, a place that suited a high player such as Vasilyev, being situated in a fashionable area of Moscow. Once Oborka had settled in, and without the need of any nicety, Alexi dictated a medium-length communication of authority which he gave to Dimitri to carry next to his passport inside a shiny new black document case, with the distinctive polished smell of expensive leather. Alexi had the initials of D.G.O. embossed in gold leaf on an outside corner.

The case was a symbol, Alexi said, to remind Dimitri how important his mission was. With a lightweight suitcase carrying clothes for an overnight stay and his chest beating with pride, Colonel Oborka boarded the Finnair flight for New York, leaving Russia from Sheremetyevo International Airport.

He could not sleep on the flight. It was the adrenaline of excitement that kept him awake. This was a first-time experience of being on an aeroplane for Dimitri. His service in the Russian army had been in a pivotable position, one that can not be forgotten or ignored for, without his craft, armies will not move far, nor very quickly.

He was a logistical statistician, permanently

based in the city of Ryazan, not far from Moscow in Western Russia. Any travelling time he had undertaken was either spent in the back of a transport lorry, or now, because of his rank, on the back seat of the Zvezda staff car he had the pleasure of being chauffeured in.

On the morning following his arrival in New York, Dimitri waited for Katherine Friedal, her married name, to emerge from the apartment building on Riverside Drive, Manhattan. He took the next cab in the rank and after appeasing the driver's worries over him being a stalker of the beautiful woman who had just exited, by offering double the fare in his broken English, followed her cab to Nordstrom Department Store on West 57th Street, just south of Central Park.

He had to wait for over an hour before he had his chance to hand this lady Alexi Vasilyev's letter. When able, Dimitri followed his orders diligently. Even before she thought of asking him, he told Katherine the name of the man who sent him to deliver the typed message, as well as ordering him to hand her the separate piece of paper containing his fully typed name, that looked lost on it.

* * *

On his return to Moscow, Colonel Oborka wasted no time in passing on his account of America and the encounter with Katherine. He reported how he thought she had shown genuine surprise when he'd mentioned the name of the sender. Furthermore, with what seemed to be earnest concern to Dimitri, she inquired after his health and he told her how he had been confined to a wheelchair for almost a year before his spine miraculously recovered enough strength for him to walk with just a stick.

He told her Alexi had suffered burns to his right hand down to the bone, costing him three fingers. There were additional burns to his right arm, as well as burns to his upper torso. When he told her Alexi Vasilyev suffered an ischaemic stroke causing the problem to his back, she was close to tears.

Dimitri told her his back had recovered most of its strength and the doctor had said it should recover further, but, he told Alexi, she was still emotionally distressed.

When Katherine asked how it had happened, Dimitri repeated Alexi's message using his exact words: 'My Tovarisch General told me you must meet with him to know exactly what occurred.'

Before following the customary procedure of being dismissed from Alexi's inner office, he was asked to expand his opinion of Katherine's demeanour on hearing the list of injuries his General had to deal with.

Colonel Dimitri thought deeply for a while, paying the same amount of careful attentiveness to his answer that he would apply to an army logistical problem.

He structured his reply in such a precise way it left no confusion about the lady having no idea his boss had been injured at all. He then looked on in astonishment and pleasure as Alexi smiled widely, whilst making the sound of a slight giggle. From the small amount of gossip Dimitri heard when enquiring of the personality of Colonel General Alexi Vasilyev before leaving his post in Ryazan to travel to Moscow, Dimitri thought both functions were impossible for his General. Apparently, they were not.

He was grateful for the offer of his new position and rank, equally he was delighted he had accepted.

CHAPTER TWENTY-FIVE

ALLIANCES

The alliance that developed between Valery Agapov and Page Boucher proved to be of significant value. At first, it was more fruitful for the French than for the Russians, but that was not the way it was presented to Valery's superiors. He boldly told how Page opened the way forward for Russian influence in countries where their name and philosophy had not featured well. These previous countries, who would have turned their backs on any Russian advances, now had a door slightly open for them, courtesy of the French who had a foot firmly planted inside.

The countries he named were Israel, Lebanon, the Hatay Province of Turkey and Egypt, together with a place Valery's superior showed additional interest in: the two Sovereign Base Areas under British control on the island of Cyprus.

According to Valery Agapov, sympathetic Russian devotees were to be cultivated by monetary funding in each and every one of the places where the French would provide their local index of communist supporters. 'Yes,' he told Alexi Vasilyev. 'It may well take some time, but the prize of having influence in places previously beyond Russian reach was worth the wait.' Colonel General Alexi Vasilyev agreed.

* * *

The balance of exchanged intelligence swung decisively into Russia's favour when Valery was offered a gift-wrapped present from Kuwait. He was told he would able to meet with Sabah Al Salim in the Waxwing Hotel near the River Orontes in the city of Antakya, once known through the ages as Antioch, the cradle of Christianity, in the southernmost province of Turkey. The meeting conveniently coincided with an operation mounted by a small section of the mighty Russian military straddling both Turkish and Syrian territory It was one Valery developed an enthusiastic interest in.

The Russian leadership judged they needed a stronger alliance with Turkey in this matter, as it was to the motherland's benefit to pursue the war on the wandering Kurds that occupied land on the border between Turkey and Syria. By an act of deception,

Russia would lay the blame for the death of seven Turkish Army personnel at the door of the Kurds.

* * *

A company of five Russian special operation forces, the Spetsnaz, crossed the Turkey/Syrian border at a point near the Turkish hamlet of Kolcular. When they came upon the predetermined point, north of the Syrian village of Zurzūr, the officer in charge, a senior lieutenant, carefully chose a spot to set up the *killing zone*. When satisfied all met his perfectionist standards, he instructed the remaining four officers to conceal six magnetic mines on the borders of the tarmac road, underneath the spreading branches of olive trees mixed with the odd sycamore.

These custom-built mines were staggered three on each side of the road with grass scattered over any protruding edges. They were then primed. An extra mine, of regular issue, was buried a few yards from the road. It was not primed, its detonator was left lying near to it. The scene was intended to look as if both the mine and detonator had been discarded by undisciplined saboteurs in a hurry.

Near to that discarded mine, the senior lieutenant left an empty packet of cigarettes inside which was a short note of written instructions in Kurmanji, a language common to the Kurds found in that district. He kicked the packet under a small pile of broken branches.The discarded packet of cigarettes and spare mine with detonator would appear to have been left by clumsy terrorists, certainly not elite troops of the Russian military.

The five soldiers withdrew under cover and waited the eight minutes for the two cars to pass. The first staff car carried four Syrian army personnel, acting as protection officers for the two passengers behind travelling in the immaculately polished, black, second vehicle. Inside was the Chief of the General Staff of the Syrian Armed Forces with a representative from the People's Council of the Ba'ath Party, plus the driver.

No entire torso of any person was ever found, nor was most of the cars. The mines did what the Russians expected—completely obliterated the entire convoy. Satisfied all was correct, the Russians pulled back from the area, making for a point near Antakya, deeper into Turkish territory. Under cover of darkness, they were evacuated by an unmarked helicopter across the Black Sea to Odessa in southern Ukraine.

The following week, *revenge* for the killings was extracted by three Syrian air force MiG-29s that launched guided missiles into positions in northern Iraq, known locally as Kurdistan, where groups of Kurds were gathered. These groups included women and children. In all, thirty-seven Kurds were killed outright and another sixty-two were injured, but news of the attack was not covered by the mainline Western press.

* * *

When the words, *emissaries having more information can be found where the pastures are closed in the north,* were first said, I made inquiries, as I've told you, into the whereabouts of Judith Meadows. I had an idea she had been sent to a northern part of the British Isles, but I was unaware of her exact location. Through various contacts not afraid to bend a few rules, I traced her to a one-time home of a Scottish laird, Gardie House, on the island of Bressay in the beautiful but extremely cold Shetland Isles. I knew the cryptic message was meant to concentrate my mind on finding her. My real problem was with the—*why?*

If that was not enough, then the other message, passed to Katherine, the one containing the word *ruffled*, made it an indubitable certainty. Judith Meadows was the first person, of our company, to use the word 'ruffled'.

She was with George and me, at Paulo's hotel in Switzerland, when speaking of the others within his Russian organisation who, when told of his escapades in East Berlin, may have been nervous. Judith asked Paulo if he had any knowledge of his people being 'ruffled' by his behaviour. He made a point of remarking how he had never heard the word 'ruffled' before.

I considered his sizeable comprehension of the English language would tend to make the likelihood of his denial being more a lie than the truth. After all had finished and I was alone with time to think, it crossed my mind for the briefest of moments, that Judith's use of that word was a code for something that only she and Paulo knew. At the time of those thoughts, I was undecided if it was a harbinger of evil or good. Maybe I was wrong, I told myself, and it was simply a word she used in conversation. It didn't matter now, nor did it matter then. Perhaps it was an unusual word for Paulo, after all.

* * *

Time had moved along, leaving me with another question to answer. Was the use of the same word, this time by Katherine, a coded message that was intended for only me to find? My task would be to find something that must be kept from Katherine's Russian's watchers, who would be monitoring everything she and I did? Wow!

I recalled being with George and Sophie in Paulo's London apartment, when he used the word whilst relating a story about Jimmy Mercer's forthcoming quest to spread the good book America to the Middle and Far East. Did Paulo use it knowing that

Sophie's powerful memory would remember the time, if ever I came stumbling along looking as 'ruffled' as ever? Could it be another moment of Iraqi recognition, only this time it was me recognising Paulo's 'tradecraft'?

I spent hours looking at every anagram I could associate with the word 'ruffled,' then translating all of them into Russian before assessing if it could be a name of someone, or the name of a place or object. I found several possibilities, particularly with places, but alone, I had little or no chance of finding something compatible.

* * *

I needed to know if the political outrage that followed the uncovering of Judith Meadows was still making her name a taboo subject for the mandarins of British intelligence if I raised it? If I asked Jerry for help, it could set off alarm bells ringing in other offices where I would prefer them not to know. At least I had a good start by knowing where she was being kept. That was something not shrouded by the uppermost top secret classification. It was my first thought that she may have been included in the Special Access Program, but fortunately, that was not the case. My way in could be through Sir Leonard Miles. It might be he who could get me there and back without anyone else knowing. I would have to be careful.

* * *

I had to ask myself if I could involve someone who, at this stage, I could not completely rule out of the issue —but what was the issue I was supposed to find? Was it just the illegal agents? If it was, then I had sent those names to Section 9. But according to Alexi Vasilyev's cryptic message, the UK had 'illegals' operating in Pakistan and India who would be threatened by exposure.

In both those two countries, I would not be surprised to find they had retained capital punishment for treason, because that's what *illegals* would be charged with if caught. I knew nothing of them, having to leave their fate in the hands of Jerry Furley and his profusion of analysts.

Sir Leonard Miles asked me about my source, in regards to the information on the UK's illegals in Pakistan and India. But he did not ask about the South African illegals I was asked to find. What's happened to them? I wondered. I asked no questions. I just told him what he wanted to know without any embellishment, still undecided what to do about Gardie House, on the island of Bressay.

* * *

The message Katherine was handed in New York carried more than a cordial invitation, as well as more than one threat. The first threat was—*The Russian government will oppose their use in every and any way.* Here, I guessed, the message referred to the nuclear as well as the conventional weapons held in the South African arsenals. Although the second was not as threatening, it carried an ominous warning hidden in the composition of the last part of his message—*I had the impression that it would not be long until this person is a member of your highest level Security Council.*

However, he should not be allowed to ruffle people's feathers. On the other hand, he would be a veritable prize on your sleeve, if you needed another one, Harry!

'He would be a veritable prize on your sleeve, if you needed another one, Harry.' Who, or what, on earth could that refer to? I wondered, my eyes growing tired as I continued looking at it.

At least I knew I was looking for a male of the species, but I certainly had no need of prizes or trophies. I was being drawn closer to decide what I had to do with Judith. The decision was inevitable!

* * *

First, I did my research. Gardie House, in the Shetland isles, had passed into the hands of the Lord Lieutenant of Shetland sometime in the early 1900s. At the end of the First World War, it became something far more sinister than just a protected building of Scottish heritage. Thrust behind the thick, cold, grey granite stones of its outside walls, or locked behind its equally cold, uninspiring, locally sourced building blocks, were kept some of the most treacherous people ever to be found in the wider reaches of Great Britain.

On the island, successive governments had either interned, or continued the internment of, those who were never eligible for a verdict of guilt passed down on them in an open trial by their peers.

Another reason for the secrecy the island afforded was to shield the public from any stark, iniquitous headlines brandishing the names of those who spent time locked away for treason on this small island across the sheets of accusing Fleet Street newspapers.

Here, behind sturdy bars, under heavy keys turned in stout locks, were those who had been adjudged as untouchables, persons who posed the same infectious contagion as lepers of Biblical lessons. In fact, all of those who the general populace had been judged to have no wish, or need, to be reminded of their repellent betrayal.

In British justice, it is the Crown that bears the burden of establishing guilt beyond doubt. Innocence is guaranteed until guilt is proven beyond any reasonable doubt. Those principles do not apply to those who are confined to Bressay. Nowadays, there was not the need to keep more than the one internee.

The one prisoner Gardie House now held was, Ms. Judith Meadows, one-time Soviet spy handler, trained assassin and, what's more, murderer of my father and brother.

During the whole of her time in circulation, Meadows handled only one Russian asset. A priceless agent for the Soviets. One who was far from being an *illegal* in any sense of the word other than a strict definition within the world of espionage. A man who had enjoyed an education along the same lines as myself. The man was a professional in every sense. Able to evade capture until I came along, stumbling over an old photograph of him with Judith when both of them were very young.

* * *

This man was considered an especially valuable asset to the Russians who wanted to part-exchange him—to which, with our arm twisted up our back by our friends the Americans, we agreed. A month, rather than years after Judith was secretly sentenced to several lives in custody, the man in question was part of an *exchange* conducted by a few pallid-coloured, raincoat-clad, Russians for an American flier forced down over a part of the then Soviet Union called Ozero Nerangda.

On capture, the pilot denied his plane carried photographic machinery. However, his denial was quickly found to be the lie that it was, but even if he wanted to tell his interrogators another lie, about where those photographs were sent he couldn't, as he didn't know.

Very few people knew those photographs of highly-secret Russian restricted areas ended up on the desks of five analysts in a very special underground facility found within the Lincoln National Forest in Otero County, New Mexico.

* * *

A crucial element in this case came when one of the counter-terrorism desks on the seventh floor at Vauxhall Cross received a request from the FBI, asking them to recommend a British army officer above the rank of Captain who was competent in translating various Southern African languages, including: Bemba, Nyanja, Zulu, Xhosa, Ndebele, Venda, together with a good working knowledge of Swati, Sesotho, Sepedi, Tsonga and Tswana Shangani, Shona, Sotho, Tonga.

Most importantly, they said, he or she must be a fluent speaker of Afrikaans. They needed the person for an unspecified period to work with a communication officer from a photographic analyst station. It all sounded rather vague, Jerry thought, nevertheless he ploughed on.

The one officer who stood out with these all requirements was a person he was aware of, Viscount Bottomly, a communication officer who had experience of being used in counter-terrorism, when stationed in Iraqi.

There was one request Jerry Furley made before feeling able to recommend any serviceman or woman, and that was why put such emphasis on Southern African languages; in particular, why the Afrikaans?

The reply he had back from the FBI was ambiguous in the extreme. Apparently, what they wished for was —*a better understanding of that region of the world.*

* * *

The assignment began innocently, with Winston and an American female pilot, who was stationed at the Air Force base beside this complex I've mentioned in New Mexico, sharing a few cups of coffee with each other over a period of days. It started to blossom into perhaps something else when she suggested they go for a drink with some friends of hers.

The relationship progressed into another intensity until some uncomfortable choices had to be made. One of those choices fell to Rachel, the American airwoman, after Bots' curiosity extended into the IP addresses of the missile defence system where she worked.

The choice that Rachel, who was a senior administrator at the base, should have made was to report the episode of Winston's curiosity to one of her superiors, but she chose not to.

Instead, she asked him why he wanted to know and he 'came clean'. He told her he was working for the South African intelligence service and wanted to supply them with the coordination points for simple outward communications. She bought into it in a small way. Rather than have him court-martialled, she sent him back to London with a 'bad boy' note pinned to his shirt tails.

Jerry mentioned this sad episode of Bottomly's career in a derisory way, as if judging my relationship with him to be closer than it could ever be, but Jerry did not know all of what I knew at this stage, and I was undecided as to whether I would tell him everything—or nothing at all.

Before making that final decision, I asked Furley if there was any more to this story, and lo and behold, there was. It was dynamite! Perhaps a reason for Rachel's leniency lay with what had happened whilst Bottomly was getting to know her.

* * *

During that time, she had told Winston the story of how her family had originally come from a farm near Hartbeespoort, a South African town, north of Johannesburg. It was there, way back in time, they lost not only their farm, their cattle and their home in the second Boer War, fought between the mighty British Army and the badly equipped Boer settlers, but also the lives of members of her past family.

The mother and father in the family were both slaughtered by the British after they were rounded up with a party of twelve other farming settlers, that included four children. One was a daughter of the family with her younger brother. First, they were marched for seventy miles without a break of more than five minutes, until those who survived reached the concentration camp the British had built to house this type of prisoner.

Once in the camp, they were made examples of by the guards, because their daughter would not comply with the guards' wishes. She would not divulge the name of the source who was giving the Boers military secrets of British deployments, armaments and proposed strategies.

Her mother was thirty-eight, her father older by three years. Her brother was two years younger than her. He was ten. The guards had told the girl what would happen to her family if she would not obey. They would not ask anyone else. '*Oh, no!*' they said,

'*Their future rests with you, girl.*' All day they repeated their threats to her.

The twelve-year-old girl's name was Angel; yes,
believe it or not, that was how her parents saw her,
but not so these guards. It's doubtful she ever knew
the name of the source of the leaked information, but
if she did, she never divulged it.

To the British guards she was a nuisance, but a
useful one. She was raped all day by those guards, as
were the members of her family. Well, I'll leave you
to imagine the degradation and obscenities they suffered before the bored British guards shot them.

The girl managed to escape during the night, and
until the day she died she would say her escape was
possible because one of her torturers did see an angel
in her. He left a door open for her to escape and for
his conscience to return.

* * *

All those tragic events happened in or around the
year 1900. The girl named Angel turned into a
woman who lived until she was eighty-six. She had
two daughters and three sons to keep her company
throughout her early years. Later, she had seven
grandchildren to keep her on the move, always
smiling as she did so. She often thought of facing
death as a release from the memories that haunted
her life so strongly that sometimes she wished she

had the strength to take her own life, thereby depriving God of it. Thankfully that never happened.

Seven years on from her final breath, her first great-great-grandchild was born. That child was a girl, born in September 1981, by which time the girl's branch of the family had moved from South Africa to Paris in France. The girl's name was Colette.

CHAPTER TWENTY-SIX

SPIES IN THE PARK

Valery Agapov had not been hard to find; what was difficult was what to say. By the time I arrived at our meeting, I had forgotten which question I had mentally listed as my first. I hadn't forgotten to ask about the origin of the cryptic message that had Judith Meadows' name written all over it, but I'd gone through my rehearsal time after time and that question was not the first I'd prepared.

We met in St James's Park, a park I knew particularly well as the family's old bank of Annie's is situated around the corner. The location of Annie's meant, with my abhorrence of the disgusting reek of London's traffic, I would invariably walk through the park to either visit the bank, or to visit friends in government offices.

When I had cause to quietly wander through

this, what I considered to be the prettiest of all London's parks, I would often think of the park benches being taken up by foreign spies, as it is so near the seat of government along with the offices of the top civil servants.

My dislike of London is well known, so the opportunities to stroll through the open park at night were not that numerous. Be that as it may, my fanciful opinion of St James's Park being a perfect den of spies at night is neither here nor there, what is important is the fact the park is just too well-lit for spies to operate, unless of course, there was a power cut.

It was easy to arrange a meeting with Agapov without the assistance of either the Home Office or Bottomly, as one night when Bots was bragging about his nights in Crocketts, mentioning not only his prowess on the tables but also how well he did with some of the beautiful women who were there, I managed to get him to open up—*a bit*.

It was Winston himself who told me how he and Valery set about concealing their clandestine meetings. Agapov persuaded Gerald Neil to employ a female croupier on his recommendation. Gerald was hedonistic in much of his sexual pursuits, which for Valery made him an ideal match for one of his stable of courtesans, a young lady calling herself Jeanette. Jeanette was the channel through which the two-way messaging to meet with each other would pass.

With Gerald's death, Crocketts was ceded to

Phillip, his twenty-six-year-old son, who took over the licence and day-to-day running of the club. Both Valery and Winston were known to Phillip. How that came about I didn't know, nor was it, I thought, important.

I visited the club and to my great delight I found the delightful Jeanette to still be there. I left my written request to meet with Agapov with her. Three days later, I waited at the café in St James's Park, at the appointed time, not sure if my message had been received or not.

I'm not a patient man. That lacking quality had been mentioned by many, often by Serena during the few years we spent together. Her vocation taught her how to be more even-tempered than I was. By that remark I don't mean she was calmer, just more equally balanced in her approach to people. I kept my temper, whereas she did not.

If a delivery was late, resulting in manufacture being unnecessarily delayed, she would explode. But she would think nothing of spending hours teaching Breno how to measure the stride of his horse, or to set up the approach to difficult jumps. I would tell him once about something and expect perfection. She was right; I was wrong. I was a tremendously bad teacher. But it was my patience on trial here.

I found myself checking my watch for the fourth time, even though there was a whole minute to go before the allotted time of the meeting. My patience was fading away. I ordered another coffee, my second, just as he entered the open-air venue. I changed my order to include another cup and rose from where I sat to shake his hand, thanking him for coming.

"Either you were quite resourceful in contacting me, Lord Paterson, or our mutual friend the Viscount told you something I hoped he would not. Should a part of me regret a loss of trust, or should I be pleased I've widened my list of acquaintances? What would you like from me, your esteemed lordship?"

* * *

I thought about a quick punch into his heart for being needlessly sarcastic, but I could not guarantee his level of fitness, so a punch could kill him if I wasn't careful. The next thing that came to mind was to forget diplomacy and jump straight in. Which I did.

I asked him what it was like to be a close friend of the Russian Prime Minister as well as being the director of Directorate Q in the Russian Foreign Intelligence Service. I was thinking of asking if it would rain at the weekend, but thought better of it, leaving nature to surprise me.

He was quick to correct me in respect of Putin. Of course, he was not the Russian Prime Minister, he was the President of Russia. He added an apology in between sipping his coffee about being unable to give any details about the Directorate Q position he held, which was a shame but something I could learn to live with.

The misappropriated email with file was mentioned, but nothing regarding its contents. I tried to encourage Valery to give me at least an idea of how many names were included and what positions those names held. He merely smiled before commenting on the unseasonable chill in the air. His reticence was the same when I asked about Samantha. Was it he or Sabah Al Salim who made the ultimate decision to tell Bottomly to end her life? Or did Winston make the decision on his own to want her dead?

* * *

I can be misled. I'm only human, being confused by things I see, or sometimes by words I hear. I can read things that have on more than one occasion caused me to be mistaken. But to be intentionally deceived, that's altogether another matter. It was when I said the name of 'Winston,' in my question of 'did he want her dead' that I knew I was being cheated. As the deception settled inside my mind, I was able to see clearly once again.

When you ask a question you run the risk of exposing your lack of understanding of a situation, but by quantifying that question by the addition of a hint of a smile, or a change in the tone of your voice, it's possible to deceive the person you're asking into be-lieving you know more than you actually do.

I came away from asking more questions about Winston and guided the conversation onto the name of Yuri Bogdan and the Pegasus Mercantile Company. Was Howard James Fredrick Mercer II a name Valery could connect to Pegasus? Not directly, he an-swered, as Mercer was director of American National Intelligence.

Sure, he added, he must know of its existence. He could possibly know its aim and maybe know where it operated, but to work inside its perimeters, then no, he didn't think so.

Was it the Yuri Bogdan name, I asked, at the head of the email sent to Viscount Bottomly, suggesting Samantha Burns be killed? He screwed his lips up, shrugging his shoulders without making a sound. I told him the email was traced to the Russian embassy in Paris, but before I could continue he protested at the perceived interference.

I proposed advising the French to run a check over their buildings in London, looking for Russian implements that shouldn't be there. We considered that, as this was probably a daily operation, it would be best to leave the status quo as it was, without ei-ther party making any adjustments.

I continued from where I had been interrupted, asking if the email from Yuri Bogdan said, *SAS autho-rise extraction?* Did the email mean Sabah Al Salim instructed Bottomly to eliminate Samantha Burns? A Russian stone face greeted my assumption, but he was soon smiling after I asked the waiter if I could get two bacon rolls and he asked me what bacon rolls were! My turn to shrug.

All was going reasonably well, as though we had been friends for years, as the ten or twelve tables at the café began to fill with, no doubt, other spies or would-be traitors. I asked the question that could amount to my new friend's downfall; did Bottomly pass him any information about the Mujahideen inside Pakistani Intelligence as far back as 1989? My question seemed to make Agapov feel very insecure. He wanted to walk, no more coffee. Three cups a day was his limit. But he wasn't forthcoming on where he had taken the other two, nor if he, or someone else, measured the caffeine in each cup. I wondered if the measurement was important? Or perhaps my question was the reason for his agitation?

One's mind is a strange vessel in which to store information, is it not? Does its survival depend on quick turnover being the best possibility? For most people, short-term storage is best. Discarding that which is not needed makes room for the memories that we need room to keep. But that's not the answer for all.

The mastery of long-term memory storage is not, I think, for the ordinary. Not for those who have no need. Certainly not for the drinkers of more than three cups of coffee a day. I wondered if Valery's long-term memory as a meteorologist was good or bad? But I had no memories of the weather to test him with.

How was Sergei Ivanov nowadays? That's right, Valery. The same one that's listed as an assistant attaché here in the Russian Embassy in London? I asked him as we walked towards the lake. He laughed. It was the kind of loud, raucous laugh that makes the ducks fly away, as watching spies press the camera button on their phone. Only this time he could not give a fig for cameras or protocol.

"No doubt your next question will be about Alexi Vasilyev, will it not, my lord?"

Hmm, the man was good, was he not? I told him I thought Vasilyev was dead. He'd died in an electrical accident at his apartment block at 173 Tangshaya Street in Moscow's Tagansky, 18 district. Did he not? There was another laugh, this one was more circumspect, more modest in nature. A polite and mocking giggle would be a better description.

"My lord, was it not you who was in touch with one of Russia's principal liars, Tovarisch Sergeyovitch Korovin? Did Paulo not tell you he was a spy? Was it not you who relocated him here in London? You most likely visited him for about a week before he bored you with his ancient Cold War memories whilst playing you at his crooked game of chess.

"His illegitimate son, accompanied by his wife,

would have called for a while until they too were bored and stayed away. Incidentally, is George Northcliffe your stepbrother, or step-uncle? A complicated situation is it not, my lord?"

Successfully, I side-stepped the last question, leaving me to admit to knowing Alexi Vasilyev survived the blast at his apartment. I then asked the question I'd come to ask. Was it Alexi who sent the message—*emissaries having more information can be found where the pastures are closed in the north?*

We walked on for a minute, side by side, with Agapov silently considering his answer. As he did so, I thought I could hear the echo of the gears in his brain clicking over. For an easier question to answer, I asked if Alexi still held the position of Director of Home Affairs. The answer from Valery showed he was nervous.

"We are not separated on this, my lord. Vasilyev is my superior. He holds more than one role in our supreme government, who have eyes watching wherever he goes. With that in mind, he wishes to help us both. You mentioned the name Sergei Ivanov earlier and you are correct in your line of thinking I used your friend Winston Bottomly to get more than just the insight Ivanov provided of South African politics.

"Alexi Vasilyev is particularly keen on knowing more of this far-right AWB and its fascist followers. As you must have read his message, you will know we are aware of the extent of the weapons held in South

Africa that my government is genuinely worried about. My superior, Colonel General Alexi Vasilyev, has asked me to ensure you understand we can take action, if that's what's needed."

"In part of your superior's message he asks for an exchange. I'm not sure what that meant other than perhaps he is offering information on what the French know of our operational agents inside Pakistan and Afghanistan, along with operatives we may have inside other government offices.

"Is your Alexi Vasilyev suggesting you may have an agent working inside our own intelligence service? Perhaps you have someone working inside our government? And what's more, is he offering us a name? I believe the word *ruffled* was used in the longer message as a deliberate clue. I think Vasilyev wants me to contact a person you may know, a woman by the name of Judith Meadows. I'm not sure how she can help."

We were still walking along the outer edge of the Park, having crossed the bridge, making our way back towards the Foreign and Commonwealth Offices. I had decided a full-on assault was called for, including the name of Meadows in my strategy. I was surprised by the answer it induced.

"I am under strict orders as to what I can and can't tell you. I understand you know my superior was almost assassinated by the traitor you resettled here in London. Perhaps, you are not fully aware of the extent of his injuries. I am at liberty to say that he is only able to walk with extreme difficulty and with aid.

"Most things in life are now very difficult for him to manage. For example, as much as he wanted to, he could not travel himself to hand the message to the traitor's daughter. Instead, he carefully selected a man from his many secretaries to send in his place. This person was selected after great care was taken to find a suitable messenger.

"The name of the man who was sent is Dimitri Georgievich Oborka. Oborka wrote his name down, with English language spelling, and gave it to the lady he met in New York. I was told, repeatedly, to make sure you knew the actual name was important.

"My superior's envoy said the lady who he handed the folded message to asked him who had sent it. When she knew who the sender was, she asked him how Alexi Vasilyev was. Sadly, Oborka reported the lady cried when he finished telling her. I don't know the relationship Vasilyev and this lady shared, but I imagine it must have been very close." Before he continued, we stopped walking.

"Another reason why Vasilyev could not travel to London is he holds very senior roles in our security service. Travel from Russia to the West, for a person such as he, is still difficult. It is easier now the Cold War has ended, but not so for everyone. One thing for sure is he cannot travel too often, so he picks his destinations with, what can I say..." He stopped speaking for a second to think of the correct word he wanted to use.

"Great deliberation, yes, that is right," he smiled, somewhat haughtily.

"Where has he travelled, Valery?"

"I cannot tell you that. I would be shot if he knew I'd told you. I could tell you if you promised not to say anything to anyone else, my lord, but I must be sure."

There was a certain Dickens' *Fagin* quality about his character, with an unctuousness to every word he uttered. I told him he could rely on me to keep a secret, which seemed to be what he wanted me to say. He indicated one of the nearby bench seats where he suggested we sit. It crossed my mind that in measured distance we hadn't walked far, as I certainly wasn't tired.

It puzzled me how he could be, but it wasn't worth arguing about so I complied with his request. As we sat, I asked if the walk had been too taxing for him as he appeared awkward in sitting. Apparently it hadn't, but that was not the impression I got. I did not comment. I kept any thoughts I had to myself.

"My superior is a suspicious man, my lord, it is in his nature now more than ever. He and I share a secret, we both have a large interest in the politics of South Africa. The ruling party there, the African Nationalists, follow much of the communist doctrine. I would like to think we could be a guiding light for them, but not today.

"I know my superior does nothing to singularly amuse himself. Everything he does, he does it for a reason. I thank you for indulging me with my bad English. I try to practise as much as I'm able, but it's not always possible. Here, there is a chance where you could help me. This word 'ruffled'; I would like to know what it means, if that's okay with you?"

I gave him a rough outline of the meaning, trying hard all the time not to think of Judith. He was smiling when I finished. I wasn't sure why.

"That's one of the things I'm finding hard to come to terms with. Your desire to ingratiate yourself with us. There you are, head of Directorate Q of the Russian intelligence service, which some would say is a showcase to the world on counter-terrorism.

"That's if we had a more conspicuous world, of course. You obvious ly want something that's locked away in the Great British cellar and you're hoping that by helping us we'll give it over. You may find we haven't much left in the cellar nowadays, Valery. All sold off to pay the Americans for saving mankind from Adolf. Sorry, about that, old chap.

"But while we're on the subject of what you want, what's your interest in the two British bases on the island of Cyprus? I can tell you there's nothing of importance there. They are just two old RAF bases we have left on that side of the Med. They can't worry your lot in the Kremlin, surely?"

I tried my best to appear perplexed by Russia's interest, as well as being totally indifferent to anything Great Britain may have. He laughed again, only this time it was a more a controlled laugh which stayed in his voice whilst he spoke.

"I love the way the English understate the importance of their achievements. Those two bases are vital to the Americans, as well as the rest of NATO. We know spy planes use both bases, as do drones in the ongoing operation against our common enemy, ISIS, but it's not that side of operations we are interested in. It's the radar we would want, my lord. Perhaps, you might be open to offers of gold from the Russian treasury?"

CHAPTER TWENTY-SEVEN

THERE'S STILL TIME TO DIE

My feelings for Judith Meadows had drastically changed over the few days we had spent together at The Hall. My first reaction was, as I've testified, one of disbelief that an intelligent female would starve herself in order to be a size zero, simply to adhere to a sense of fashion. I started to wonder if it was a criminal offence to have sex with a skeleton, or, first of all, take one on a railway train. I'm not sure I didn't ask! If I did ask her, I'm sure I would still be carrying the scar.

She was a feisty woman, someone that eventually I came to first admire and secondly fall ever so slightly in love with. At least I thought I'd fallen in love.

When I first came across Ms. Meadows, she was conducting an inquiry, an in-house, by the rules set out in Standing Orders, written by self-righteous, civil service mandarins of Whitehall, kind of an inquiry. Hers was to discover who had murdered my father and then, later on in the same week, my younger brother just as he was to follow the family tradition of taking the *chair* at *Annie's*. By the time the inquiry was nearing its end, I found I had mellowed and grown very fond of her. I had also discovered a characteristic that could never be tolerated.

For months after she was taken from my company, I stupidly suffered from a malady inflicted more often on the young than those whose age should have precluded them from a lover's heartbreak. But the Paterson blood, coursing strongly through my veins, would not behave as it should.

Age had not stood as my protector.

* * *

It had been an arduous journey starting at The Box, or Legoland, or whatever vogue name you preferred for the Vauxhall Cross offices of MI6, and with the head of that organisation, Jerry Furley, who was understandably sceptical about the proposed visit.

He had naturally read the psychological reports composed on me as I sat and watched the qualified specialists write in full, or mark their scores between the omnipresent one to ten in the side panels of the medical journals they used to make notes. On his desk, to the left of the assorted coloured files, it lay unopened as if in arraignment, the last review from the experts.

In the smoky air that circled above the report, I thought I could make out something written in the cloud. *What could it be? Ah, yes. There it is—To whoever it concerns. The subject is cured now of all Meadows and her ilk.*

A sprinkling of fine Scottish whisky accompanied the amiable bisection, until at last the serious smile I'd worn had opened the door to what I'd come for—permission to travel to Bressay, to interview my nemesis. Once again, no allowance for private amenities allowed.

"You can pose as a third-class tourist and a scruffy one at that. No first-class travel for you, Paterson."

So, with top-floor permission, I went searching for the solution as known by—*the knowledgeable emissary in the pastures that are closed in the north.*

* * *

Gardie House, on Bressay, carried a 'Listed Building' status. As such, the house and gardens could legitimately be closed to visitors for a number of valid reasons, keeping its only resident far removed from any unwanted scrutiny would be one. The island was only accessible by boat, or ferry from the fishing port of Lerwick, where there were two boats patrolling the seas around the island, crewed by Royal Navy personnel, or legitimate 'Bird Wardens', who could act as the external, unpaid, prison wardens watching for an escape of the only detainee on the island.

The *onshore* naval base had been forewarned of my arrival; even so, there was no twenty-one-gun salute, nor any traditional boatswain's piping of *on-board* as I stepped onto dry land, having sampled the ferry ride from Lerwick.

As I stood there for a moment drinking in the smell and sounds of the sea, I hoped the cannons behind me on the battlements of Fort Charlotte would not be discharged at me, now, or at any time in the near future.

* * *

I had flown from the City of London airport, having taken a cab from my club. I caught the 08:40 flight, arriving at Edinburgh roughly three hours before the time of a connecting flight. However, I managed to combine some estate business before the first flight after lunch to Sumburgh Airport, on the southern tip of Shetland Isle, arriving just after three o'clock in the afternoon. The flight, carrying eleven passengers along with myself, was functional, if a little bumpy, but the views were a worthy spectacle, some, I thought to be matchless.

I took the only cab from the airport to the ferry

located at the other end of the island and the drive along the spine of Shetland was magical in itself. In every direction I looked, on the flat or on the hills, the surface was covered in a luscious green velvet down. The first part of the journey was strictly impersonal, which made the last part the more princely, yet try as I might to fully enjoy my cab ride where the taximeter ticked over quicker than the car travelled, I could not.

I hardly understood a word the driver spoke because of an accent his ancestors would be proud of. Try as I might to make him understand my hearing was bad due to the landing of the plane, he either could not or would not speak up, but there was no hiding the rolling of his eyes that I caught from the driver's mirror. No doubt, in his opinion I was another invading Englishman come to vandalise his beautiful home. If that was indeed his opinion, it did not stop him taking my money.

The drive took roughly half an hour, during which time I saw hundreds more sheep than cars and another hundred times more sheep than humans. Where I live in Yorkshire, it can be isolated in a harsh winter but the solitariness did not last for long. Not like here, where solitude could be a guarantee.

* * *

By the time the ferry I'd taken to the island of Bressay pulled away for its return journey, I had looked at everything and every person around me, but there was not a naval officer or rating in sight for a welcome. There was yet another sullen-looking Scotsman I noticed sitting on a bench, gazing aimlessly out to sea who, on being asked if he knew where I could find Gardie House, rose from the seat, stood with help from a sturdy, shepherd's crook and, in a voice I could easily understand, told me to tag along behind and he'd point it out. I've never been a forceful religious-minded person, but having said that, I was instantly reminded of the Biblical tale of the Good Samaritan.

Had I been more alert, observing my surroundings rather than losing myself in idle dreams, I would have seen the 18th-century house behind its granite walls, as it was the only nearby building.

This imposing, Scottish mansion, built in 1724 on the shores of the natural harbour of Bressay Sound, was now what's fondly known as a *Stone Frigate*, the informal term for a Royal Naval shore protectorate.

Behind those sturdy grey walls, the building housed a company strength of eighteen naval personnel, including two officers: the commanding officer of the base, Captain William Lloyd, with his adjutant, Lieutenant Murray who was waiting for me at the gatehouse.

After a courteous offer to carry my bags which I declined, he led me along the side of the house to where he said I would be able to look into a basement area, where the object of my visit, Judith Meadows, would be.

At the precise moment I looked down into what appeared to be the laundry room, she glanced up out of the window. I quickly turned away as I was sure she saw me!

I felt myself blushing as though I'd been caught scrumping apples and didn't know what to do. I fashioned a nod of my head in her direction as I walked away. *This isn't going to be easy*, I soundlessly reminded myself.

"You know our prisoner, sir?" the adjutant inquired of me.

"I did a long time ago, Lieutenant. I think she may have changed by now," I gravely replied.

The End

This Story Continues in Part Two of —-
My Truth Your Lies
Subtitled: Revelation

ABOUT THE AUTHOR

 Daniel Kemp is a prolific story-teller, and although it's true to say that he mainly concentrates on what he knows most about; murders laced by the intrigue involving spies, his diverse experience of life shows in the stories he writes both for adults and children.

* * *

To learn more about Daniel Kemp and discover more Next Chapter authors, visit our website at www.nextchapter.pub.

What Comes Before
ISBN: 978-4-82416-496-4
Large Print

Published by
Next Chapter
2-5-6 SANNO
SANNO BRIDGE
143-0023 Ota-Ku, Tokyo
+818035793528

5th January 2023